S0-BFB-983

Revenge

ALSO BY NIGEL MAY

Trinity
Addicted
Scandalous Lies
Deadly Obsession
Lovers and Liars

Revenge

Nigel May

Bookouture

Published by Bookouture
An imprint of StoryFire Ltd.
23 Sussex Road, Ickenham, UB10 8PN
United Kingdom
www.bookouture.com

Copyright © Nigel May, 2017

Nigel May has asserted his right to be identified
as the author of this work.

All rights reserved. No part of this publication may be reproduced,
stored in any retrieval system, or transmitted, in any form or by
any means, electronic, mechanical, photocopying, recording or
otherwise, without the prior written permission of the publishers.

ISBN: 978-1-78681-115-8
eBook ISBN: 978-1-78681-114-1

This book is a work of fiction. Names, characters, businesses,
organizations, places and events other than those clearly in the
public domain, are either the product of the author's imagination
or are used fictitiously. Any resemblance to actual persons, living or
dead, events or locales is entirely coincidental.

To Lottie Mayor, my perfect French Fancy, for sharing
St Tropez and the largest crème caramel in the world. *Je t'aime.*

PROLOGUE

Ripping her supersize false lashes away from the tender flesh just above her eyes, showgirl Cher Le Visage looked into the mirror in her makeshift dressing room, softly lit by an array of light bulbs. Not having used her favourite designer lash remover – she'd plumped for the best brand she could afford these days – she watched as her skin started to turn an angry shade of red. Cher felt her eyes sting and smart, a film of moisture blurring her vision as she experienced the force of her own fury now that her titillating moment on stage was over. She'd regret it in the morning, but right now Cher wanted to remove every trace of her performance outfit and not think about what her life had come to – even if that meant red raw eyelids. The skin would bruise, no doubt, but she'd become more than adept at covering up those telltale signs with clever shading and blending lately. Needs must when the devil strikes.

Throwing the lashes into the mesh bin, Cher cast her attention to the poster on the back of the door. It spelt out the name of the event she was appearing at: The Iguazu Falls Charity Blast. An event to raise awareness and as much moolah as possible for the ongoing conservation of the area and wildlife at Iguazu Falls, the magnificent collection of waterfalls cascading across the border between Brazil and Argentina. Cher hated charity gigs – no matter how beautiful the location – as they never paid well, but she was fully aware that she had only managed to blag her name onto the bill because one of the organisers was a lifelong fan of hers. She should think so, seeing as she'd once blown him rather expertly, backstage at a gig he'd organised back in New York. When was that? Oh yes, back when she almost had a career and almost had her name written in lights. These days her name was no more than half an inch tall on the lower reaches of a raggedy poster.

She read the other names listed, all above hers. Crazy Sour, the world's favourite girl band, were headlining. Oh, the shame of that. A woman skilled in the art of showgirl tease having to play underling to that frothy trio of pop tarts. That wasn't what Cher had gone to school for. Put in all the hours for. Not that the girls in Crazy Sour were as wholesome as the world seemed to think. Any fool could see that.

Cher bent down to loosen the straps on her dual platform cage boots and kicked them off as she walked over to the poster to study the other names: Madhen, the ultimate good-time party band; Jemma Louisiana, the country and western star; Ellie Sweetrose, the hot soul sensation every trendy young thing and their dog were currently making out to if the newsstands were to be believed. Names, names, names – blah, blah, blah. All hosted by LA reality star Nova Chevalier, Latina actress Rosita Velázquez and some third-rate comedian who'd managed to scrape in to finish in the top five on *America's Got Talent*.

There must have been about a dozen acts on the bill and yet her name seemed to be the smallest.

She'd come such a long way in her time, even if her career highs hadn't been as astronomically sky-high as she'd once hoped, but surely there had to be life in the not-so-old corsets, suspenders and basques yet? She was a burlesque queen. A performer skilled with feathers, frills and flirtation. A temptress of tease. She would not be a washed-up glamour puss at the age of twenty-eight. She would make sure of that. She had options. There were always options.

No, tonight may not have been lucrative when it came to being paid for her services on stage, but maybe it would be in other ways. There was enough potential from those she'd seen tonight. Even if the professional world had decided to place her at the bottom of the bill, she was more than aware that her shapely legs and ample breasts could still attract a lover when required. And not just the one. Not that any of her lovers seemed to be providing her with love in its most romantic form right now. Passion, excitement, sex, variety, kink and on occasion brutality seemed to be washing over her in abundance, but when it came to hearts and flowers and Cupid's heart-seeking arrow, her love life was emptier than her bank account. Others found their soulmates, why couldn't she? At least one that she truly wanted. Why was the grass always greener?

Cher sat herself back down in front of the mirror and tugged gently at the specialist burlesque pasties covering her nipples. After years of dancing in the spotlight, a place where thankfully the drama of her act could momentarily camouflage the heartache of her unsatisfactory love life, Cher was adept at removing the small, sequinned, decorative saucers that every showgirl wore without too much discomfort. She stared at herself in the mirror and contemplated her own misery.

People would say that she deserved to be unhappy. Years of bitching and playing the diva were bound to rub a few people up the wrong way, and when word spread that a star was difficult to work with, and maybe not as popular as she once was, then the writing was very much written on the wall – in sparkalicious, glittery letters you could see from another galaxy. Cher Le Visage was seeing her own star descend quicker than the waters of the nearby Iguazu Falls. And she knew that she only had herself to blame.

Cher had enjoyed spending a few days in Brazil, but it was obvious from the position of her dressing room – furthest from the stage, at the back of the huge marquee erected to house the 'talent' – that neither the celebrity crowd nor the event organisers saw her as a big draw. Crazy Sour's dressing room was no doubt all champagne, white lilies, scented candles and overhead fans to combat the stifling Brazilian heat. What did Cher receive? A six-pack of water and a desk fan that lacked the power to blow out the most pathetic of naked flames. But at least the money, meagre though it was, would be enough to keep the wolf from the door for another few weeks. And if it wasn't, she'd be on eBay, Twitter and Facebook selling her outfits to the highest bidder in double-quick time.

No, screw the lush Brazilian forest and the furry little coati critters that she'd been gushing to the press about over the last few days, charity needed to begin at home, and Cher was determined that tonight would be a turning point to move things in a beneficial direction for her. Things would be so much better from now on. She would make sure of that. She'd look after number one – at whatever cost and no matter who it hurt.

Lovers, haters, past, present… She'd seen them all tonight. Well, fuck them all.

Cher was interrupted from her thoughts by a gentle tapping at the door of her room. She'd been expecting a visit. She picked up her gossamer robe and slipped it around her, all that she could cope with given the intense heat backstage. Underneath the flimsy material she was naked apart from her underwear.

She answered the door. The person standing there let their eyes scan down Cher's body. Even with the robe on, there was little left to the imagination.

'What are you staring at?' snapped Cher. 'It's not like you haven't seen it all before. You'd better come in. We have to talk.'

'No expense spared, I see,' mocked the visitor, stepping in and looking round.

'Funny you should mention money, that's what I need to talk to you about,' said Cher. 'You owe me, or else…'

*

It was about an hour later that a whisper of news started to scuttle its way around the backstage area of The Iguazu Falls Charity Blast. Some people were shocked, a few cried, some stated their surprise that it hadn't happened before, many asked 'Who?' and one person just smiled, knowing that their work for the evening was done.

Cher Le Visage had been found on the floor of her dressing room wearing nothing but her underwear and the gossamer robe, strangled by a feather boa. Her eyes bulged from their sockets, a look of panic written across them for all to see. Her body was a map of bruises. The showgirl had teased for the very last time.

CHAPTER 1

St Tropez, France, five years later...

'So are you feeling like a Tropézien yet?' asked the petite blonde waitress as she placed an espresso martini on the table. 'How many weeks have you been here now?'

'Completely, darling. This is my seventh,' smiled Dexter Franklin, flashing a set of paid-for white teeth that were as bright as the lights reflected in the St Tropez harbour waters before him. 'And I still haven't banged you yet,' he added quietly, as the waitress wandered off to serve another table in the portside bar he had been frequenting nearly every night since arriving on the Côte d'Azur. 'I must be losing my touch. It wasn't that long ago I'd have had your knickers down before you had time to say *bonjour*.'

Despite what he'd said, Dexter wasn't feeling at all like a Tropézien, the name given to people from the famous French town situated south-west of Nice, the very definition of a jet-set playground. He suspected he never would, even if the opening of his brand-new deluxe eatery in the town was now only a matter of a few weeks away. As one of the top Michelin-starred celebrity chefs in the world, and a man who had managed to try every course on a menu of women around the globe, the Brit was contemplating the fact that he had definitely launched easier ventures in his time. The latest addition to his ever-expanding list of gourmet restaurants, Trésor, in the backstreets of St Tropez, was still in the process of being finished. The electrics weren't quite working, the plumbing in the bathrooms definitely left something to be desired and the furnishings he had chosen and paid for on a trip to Marrakesh weeks earlier had not yet left Morocco. It seemed the Moroccans had no sense of urgency when it came to shipping his choice of tables, chairs, brightly hued cushions and wall hangings to their new home in the South of France.

Dexter was not about to panic, though, about the fact that his treasure chest of a restaurant – the idea behind the name Trésor, the French word for treasure – was not suffused with a selection of exotic, romantic, dramatic colours. He had lived his life down to the wire and had built up a successful multimillion-pound business by doing so. As yet, there was no need to worry.

Dexter liked St Tropez. He liked the quirky mix of razzle-dazzle and old-world charm that it seemed to blend as perfectly as the coffee liqueur and vodka in his espresso martini. The waitress had done a good job, as ever. Maybe he should offer her employment. Easy on the eye and a dab hand at making drinks. Dexter cast an eye over to the bar where the young woman stood behind the marbled worktop, shaking another cocktail into life. He watched as her small and incredibly pert breasts jiggled in time to her shaking under the tightness of her work blouse. He only stopped himself when the waitress caught him watching and smiled suggestively. She was flirting. Something Dexter always liked.

Dexter was never short of female attention. His sizzling mix of floppy, jet-black hair, permanent five o'clock shadow and eyes as rich, inviting and dark as a ramekin of caviar were a hit wherever he went. Women were like a taster menu to Dexter. He had loved before, given his all, but most of the time he was satisfied with a mouth-watering nibble before moving onto another course, not allowing himself to become bogged down with one familiar flavour when there were so many more that his palate craved. And since he had added TV star to his impressive CV, after his turn as a judge on a celebrity cooking TV programme, Dexter's appetite was sated with increasing regularity.

Except in St Tropez. This must have been the longest Dexter had been without sex. And that was something that needed sorting. Perhaps that was why he wasn't quite feeling the Tropézien vibe yet. St Tropez seemed to ooze sex, glamour and celebrity from behind every shuttered window and from below deck on every fancy floating penis extension that lined the harbour. Maybe he needed to go a little deeper than his busy schedule had allowed so far. He cast another glance over to the waitress, who was now serving a cloudy mint and passion fruit concoction to the table alongside him. She once again threw a moment of flirtatious eye contact in his direction as she sashayed back to the bar area, glancing back over her shoulder as she pushed against the swing doors at the back of the bar and disappeared into the corridor beyond. As the door swung back open, Dexter could see that she was unlocking the door to the disabled toilet. He felt his cock rise to attention in his trousers as she pushed open the door and slipped inside.

Dexter stared down at the pile of invitations that he had stacked up on the table in front of him. He had come to the bar to write them out personally. To make sure that those names he had pre-selected in his mind to come to the opening of Trésor were given enough notice to guarantee their attendance. It would be a night to remember, Dexter was sure of that.

He picked up his pen, ready to write the name on the first invitation. His cock still pushed urgently against the material of his trousers.

He put the pen back down and turned to the elderly couple at the table next to him. Using his better-than-basic grasp of the French language, he asked them if they could keep an eye on his table for a few moments, pointing to the washrooms to demonstrate his meaning. They nodded politely.

Dexter stood up and moved as quickly as he could across the bar, trying not to draw attention to himself and the sizable and very noticeable erection displayed under his linen trousers. As he reached the disabled toilet door he tried the handle. The door opened revealing the waitress standing inside with her knickers in her hand. She definitely noticed the size of Dexter's trousered erection and let out an anticipatory gasp of pleasure. Within seconds it had been freed and Dexter had slid his length into her.

It was half an hour later that the Michelin-starred chef returned to his table, his St Tropez sex drought well and truly over. He nodded a polite '*merci*' to the elderly couple, who were still watching over his tower of invitations, their drinks very much drained. They left as soon as he returned.

'*Merci* indeed, *mes amis*,' whispered Dexter as he picked up the pen and began to write the first invitation.

CHAPTER 2

Dear Miss Stanton,

Celebrity chef Dexter Franklin cordially invites you to be his guest for an evening of the finest dining at his new restaurant, Trésor, situated amidst the glamour of the Côte d'Azur's St Tropez. A fusion of French cuisine with the spicy flair of Morocco is guaranteed to delight as you are invited to be an integral part of the first night of a brand new culinary adventure…

'So what the hell is he going to do? Serve me a plate of couscous in a velouté *sauce*? What kind of oddball fusion is that? It'll taste rotten,' blurted out Mew Stanton as she took her seat for her latest in-store book signing at the front of London Piccadilly's Waterstones. Her latest cookbook, *Cooking: As Easy As 1-Mew-3*, was already topping the culinary hardback charts, blocking both Nigella Lawson and Jamie Oliver from reaching the top spot, and a long line of people had already gathered to have their £20 copies personally signed by the star. They politely applauded as Mew took her place, the sound of clapping causing her to look up from her conversation with her publisher, Olivia Rhodes, about the invitation she had received that morning and wave, as sincerely as she could, at those gathered.

'You will go though, won't you, Mew? I can RSVP for you if you wish, and move your book tour schedule to make sure you're free. It's great press, seeing as we look after Dexter's books too. Yours are selling better than his though right now,' said Olivia, watching as her number-one author ran her fingers through her long blonde hair and slipped on a pair of funky glasses. Whether Mew needed them for reading or whether she merely wore them to be fashionable, Olivia neither knew nor cared. She looked great either way. As long as copies of *1-Mew-3* kept flying off the shelves at a quick-cook speed then she was happy to do whatever her top-selling author needed. And besides, Olivia loved spending time with Mew. She loved her full stop. Not that she had ever told her this. How unprofessional would that be? But Mew was the epitome of Olivia Rhodes's ideal woman, with her full-flowing mane of blonde hair cascading down her pink-tinged, girl-next-door skin, still blemish and wrinkle free at the age of twenty-nine. Her clothes were always that fashionable hybrid of vintage meets designer. Olivia thought she was beyond cool, and longed for even an ounce of Mew's style and flair. Not that Olivia's publishing salary didn't allow her to buy some of the finest names on the high street. It did. It was just that Olivia didn't seem to wear them very well. She could make Prada look like Primark.

'So does it clash?' asked Mew, beckoning the first of the fans over to the table to have her book signed. 'My schedule?'

'I don't think so, no. But I'll make sure it doesn't. I'll RSVP for you and arrange flights and rooms. Dexter has given the name of the hotel on the invitation. He's paying for everything. You leave it to me. Right, I'll leave you to sign your books, Mew. If you need me I'll be with the Waterstones people over there.' Olivia knew how happy Mew Stanton would be when she had arranged everything she needed for a few days in St Tro-

pez. She'd bag her the best suite in the hotel, the five-star Arlequin. She'd already googled it. It had a private beach for guests.
And beach meant beachwear, which hinted that Mew might be
showing off as much of her rosy-glow flesh as possible in the rays
of the Côte d'Azur sun, a thought that pleased Olivia greatly.
And seeing as the women of St Tropez were famed for being the
first to sample the freedom of topless sunbathing back in the
1960s, Olivia was hoping that the same exhibitionist ways still
abounded now. She made a mental note to buy herself a new
set of bikinis for the trip. Ones that she could slip off very easily
given the chance. Not that she had personally been invited to
the restaurant opening, but seeing as she was Dexter's publisher
too she was certain she could wangle that with the most fluid
of ease, add her costs to Dexter's next book launch budget and
be heading to the South of France with her favourite client in a
very excited heartbeat. Olivia could feel her own heart starting
to flutter as she began talking to the people from Waterstones.
Talk of author sales figures tumbled from her lips despite her
head being full of images of Mew Stanton's figure wearing the
teeniest of bikinis under the Mediterranean sun. To her it was a
portrait as hot and inviting as St Tropez itself.

*

Mew looked at the front cover of her latest cookbook, the photo
of her staring over the top of her funky framed specs whilst
browsing her own recipe book, one of her hands held to her
mouth in mock shock was a strong and fierce image. She liked
it. But then she had suggested it. Image was all to Mew Stanton, it always had been. And now that she was considered to
be one of the most influential and trendy celebrity chefs in the
country, it was more important than ever. A win on TV sensation *Someone's Cooking in the Kitchen*, where the latest stars tried

their hand at whipping up a menu of culinary delights, and a young fan base were the perfect ingredients for lucrative literary success.

She opened the book and stared up at the fan, a woman only a couple of years younger than she was. 'Who shall I dedicate it to?' asked Mew, professionalism now oozing from every pore.

'To your number-one Crazy Sour fan, Penny. I have all of your CDs and I used to dress just like you when you were in the group. I think I must have seen you at least a dozen times. You were so amazing,' enthused Penny, little flecks of spit flying excitedly from her mouth as she spoke.

Mew kept her smile painted on as she signed the book, but it was strained. She was thankful for her former life, but was desperate for people to forget she was ever in that bloody pop group.

To Mew, being in Crazy Sour seemed like a million years ago – it was another life. She closed the book and handed it back. Mew's doll-like fixed expression of gratitude covered any sign of her annoyance at having to think about days gone by. It hadn't always been herbs and spices that had brought Mew such fame. In fact she had once been a spice girl of a very different kind.

*

It was the day after her twenty first birthday that Mew Stanton saw the advert online asking for female singers to audition for a new girl band being put together by 'a showbiz insider'. Her first thought was that the 'insider' would doubtless be some dirty old man looking to parade a long line of impressionable young girls through some dark and dingy backroom in the arse end of London, offering them a Beyoncé-style lifestyle in exchange for a quick feel underneath their tight-fitting tops. She knew enough about the seedy world of showbiz to know exactly how these things worked. A great set of pitch-perfect lungs were secondary as long as the 'talent' was just as happy on her back as she was behind a microphone. She'd heard first-hand. In great detail.

But Mew had ambition, and her weekly karaoke sessions – blasting out the latest Rihanna or a classic slice of Whitney to an audience of beered-up lads in the pub who would rather be watching Arsenal play footie on the TV – were not fulfilling her desire to move centre stage on a big scale. But she had nothing to lose and everything to gain, so she responded to the ad, sending off an audition tape of her singing and saying why she wanted 'world fame' and why she believed she had 'that certain *je ne sais quoi*' as instructed. Much to her own surprise, she heard back within a fortnight, telling her where to go for the audition itself.

The audition was a great deal more professional than she had imagined. The insider was indeed a major name in the music industry, an American rapper with a track record of managing hip-jiggling, bottom-twerking girl band action. Mew had seen him on MTV, being interviewed at his LA crib. When she took her place in front of him in a W1 swanky hotel room, as far removed from a seedy London back-alley dive as it could possibly be, it was only then that she had suddenly started to realise just how important the next five minutes of her life might be. This was big shit and she needed to make sure that she nailed her song. All plans that she had of singing her first choice, Avril Lavigne's 'Girlfriend', a tune she had belted out with rocky gusto on many a night out, disappeared into thin air as she stared at the music mogul in front of her. He was wearing his trademark jet-black sunglasses, major bling decorated his neck and he had his arms outstretched as he sat on his makeshift throne. It was only a hotel chair, but to Mew it gave him an air of gravitas that she desperately needed to match with her singing.

'What's your name, sugar?' His voice was a rich baritone and he tilted his head to take in what Mew was wearing – a tight skull-emblazoned T-shirt, cheerleader skirt, knee-high socks combo. Mew couldn't see his eyes behind the shades but she hoped that his gaze was appraising.

'Mew Stanton.' Despite a sudden wash of nerves, there was no wobble in Mew's voice. She was determined to appear strong and confident. This was to be her time, she could feel it.

'What are you singing for me?' His words were clipped and direct without being nasty. He had doubtless sat through countless auditions already, and from the queue of girls that lined the corridor outside his hotel room it was clear that there were still a few more that he had to listen to. 'The CD player is there for your backing track.' He pointed to a sound system.

Mew made a decision. Despite her look being pure Avril and her backing track CD being firmly housed inside her mini backpack, she decided that a change of song was definitely wise and that the CD could stay there. It was a risk but one that she knew she could chance. If she'd learnt anything growing up, it was that sometimes a risk or two needed to be taken and that you had to make the most of every moment.

'I don't need that. I'm singing a cappella and clapping along to keep a perfect beat.'

The mogul raised an eyebrow behind the sunglasses. 'Sweet, name your tune.'

'"Fergalicious" by Fergie.'

'Double sweet.' He nodded. 'I'll be honest, I've listened to a sea of Britney, Christina, Whitney and Avril Lavigne today, so shaking it up with a little Fergie pleases me hugely. As long as you do it justice, of course – she and will.i.am are friends of mine. Now hit it.'

Silently thanking her lucky stars that she had ditched her Avril audition, Mew raised one of her hands in the air, clicked her fingers to gain a beat and then burst into a flawless rap of the worldwide hit. She bounced her hips and clapped along to the words as she sang, her movements sexy without straying into slutty. She had expected her attempts to be halted after twenty seconds or so, but after three minutes of flicking her blonde locks from side to side, body-rolling her chest to the words and retaining eye contact with Mr Sunglasses, she was finally silenced by a visual stop sign from the music man. He smiled.

'I'll be in touch.'

'Thank you.' Mew didn't say another word as she picked up her backpack and walked towards the hotel suite door. As she opened it, the next girl in the queue behind her pushed her way past and skipped into the room, nearly knocking Mew to the floor. Had she been anywhere else she would have given the girl a mouthful, but seeing as this was a chance-in-a-million audition she bit her tongue and remained silent as she heard the girl, a mass of Titian curls on her head and wearing a skirt that obviously doubled up as a belt it was so tiny, announce to the man that she was called Holly Lydon and that she would be singing 'Toxic' by Britney Spears.

'Good luck, sweetheart,' murmured Mew under her breath as she shut the door behind her. 'I think your man is all Britneyed out.' She smiled to herself, certain that Holly was one aspect of the competition she didn't have to worry about.

As it happened, Mew was wrong. Two weeks later she received a phone call from the record company behind the audition, saying that the LA rapper she had sung for wanted to see her again – alongside two other girls, to see if there was the right chemistry between them. An excited Mew, feeling that her moment of success could finally be imminent, hot-footed her way

to a dance studio in central London as instructed. The first of
the two girls waiting there, alongside a host of record company
execs and the LA rapper, was an ebony-skinned woman called
Leonie she remembered talking to before her audition. She was
nice, with a strong, athletic physique. She was incredibly quiet,
but Mew guessed she must have a killer voice if she'd been invited back. The other girl was Holly Lydon, already seated and
stretching out on the dance studio floor, her legs splayed left and
right into virtually different time zones in the tightest pair of
Lycra leggings ever sewn. Obviously her rendition of 'Toxic' had
been a tour de force. As Mew entered the studio, Holly spotted
her straight away, lifted herself up off the floor and bounded
over to where Mew was standing.

'How funny, I never guessed they'd pick you. You'd have been
last on my list, if I'm honest.' She didn't see fit to give a reason.
'Suppose it makes sense though, that they'd pick a blonde. You've
got me, the sexy redhead, and then the sultry black lass to give
it that urban street cool, so I guess a blonde like you completes
the picture. United colours of whatnot and all that. I'm Holly.'

'I know,' said Mew. 'I'm Mew.'

Mew had hoped that the three girls would have no chemistry. That maybe Leonie and she would gel but somehow Holly
would stick out like a sore thumb and become the initial member that never quite made the grade. Sadly it was not to be. Mew,
Leonie and Holly looked great together and more so their vocals
were perfectly matched. Mew had to admit that the threesome
had been well picked. Leonie was sweetness and light, yet with
dance moves that would shame JLo, and despite having an ego
that was already climbing skyscrapers, Holly had an amazing
voice and a distinct look that was once seen, never forgotten.

But Holly also had the ability to rub people up the wrong
way with every word that tumbled without thinking from her

mouth. A fact that Mew learnt as the three girls left the dance studio at the end of that day, having been told that it was looking pretty certain they would be the successful trio picked to be the 'next big thing'.

'Oh my God, can you imagine! We could be bigger than Destiny's Child. And I'll be the Beyoncé, up the front with the best voice and all the magazine features. Fucking London O2 here we come. Laters.'

As Holly flounced off, leaving an incredulous Mew and a smiling Leonie standing there, a dislike that had been brewing all day spilled over from Mew. 'If she stays in this band, I swear to God I will kill her. She's a total bitch. Don't you think?'

'She's quite something,' said Leonie, her answer far too vague and Switzerland for Mew's liking.

'Well I don't like her,' stated Mew.

It was a feeling that never left her. Not when the trio of young women signed the contract turning them from three unknowns into Crazy Sour, a new girl group. Not when they had to lie in magazine and website interviews, saying how pally they really were and how the three girls were like sisters. Not when they scored their first multi-national number one and embarked on their debut sell-out tour. Not when they filled London's O2 for the first time. Not when they broke America and saw their faces plastered over billboards and Greyhound buses in every state from Ohio to Oklahoma. The feeling lasted right the way throughout their entire Crazy Sour career until the moment that Holly Lydon managed to force the group to implode on itself and split up.

Mew Stanton had never liked Holly Lydon. In fact, she would go as far as to say that she hated her. She blamed her for a lot of things. A hell of a lot.

*

'It's such a pity your solo stuff didn't work out,' gushed the fan as Mew handed the copy of *1-Mew-3* back to her. 'I kinda liked your first single. What a shame you didn't release any more. It was quite a good tune.'

'I did. I released another two before being dropped,' remarked Mew through gritted teeth. Her post-Crazy Sour solo career had flopped quicker than a popped soufflé with her first single missing the Top 20 and her two follow-ups not even denting the lower reaches of the Top 40. A planned solo album, *The Sound Of Mew-Sic*, was shelved immediately.

'Good job the cooking worked out then, eh?' enthused Penny the fan, oblivious to her own lack of tact about something that Mew had once held so dear. 'So what are Leonie and Holly doing these days? Are you still in touch?'

'No. I believe Leonie has made some gospel albums in the States and been on *Dancing with the Stars*,' fudged Mew, not really knowing whether that was the truth or not. She deliberately made no mention of Holly, choosing not to.

'And Holly?' asked Penny, like a dog with a bone.

'No idea. Really, I have no idea. I haven't seen her since she walked out on the band.' Mew could feel herself tensing.

'Any chance of you guys getting back together then? Doing a big reunion and going all grown up ten years on?'

Mew was over Penny's inquisition and pointed to the queue behind her. 'I must really move on to the next person, Penny, they have all been waiting patiently.'

'Oh, okay,' said a deflated Penny. 'I'd love Crazy Sour back together. Back for good. Shame.'

As Penny shuffled off, the thought of a Crazy Sour reunion seemingly dashed, Mew's thoughts turned a deep shade of blood red.

Back together. Back for good, she thought. *No chance. From what I remember the only 'back' Holly would be interested in is the one she lies on with her legs in the air. Stupid bitch.*

Mew painted on her smile once more and beckoned for her next fan to come forward.

CHAPTER 3

Dear Miss Lydon,

Celebrity chef Dexter Franklin cordially invites you to be his guest for an evening of the finest dining at his new restaurant, Trésor...

Holly Lydon had been as surprised as anyone when she'd received the invitation from Dexter. There was no question that she'd accept it though – the thought of a trip to the South of France sounded fabulous and would maybe give her a taste of the high life again. It had been ages since she'd found herself in any kind of glamorous location. The thought of huge yachts alongside the harbour front and trying to spot the celebrity inhabitants of the area's ultra multimillion properties was just what she needed to add some spice to her post-Crazy Sour life.

In just a few years her world had changed from staring out at rows of adoring fans as she and the other two members of the world's favourite girl band shimmied their way across the stage at the Hollywood Bowl to staring at the overhead fans rotating ad infinitum on the ceiling of the latest hotel Holly happened to find herself 'working' in.

Holly's latest port of call was a motel just outside San Diego and about ten kilometres from the Gulf of Mexico. Chateau Marmont it was not, although Holly had to admit that it was a lot more hygienic than some of the fleapits she had found herself in recently. The walls, floors and surfaces were a lot cleaner than the bare-bones accommodation she had been expecting when the man currently busying himself between her legs as she lay naked on the surprisingly white sheets had called through to book her. He was one of Holly's regulars and had been for about the last eight months or so, and she had to admit that he was one of her few clients who still managed to ignite some of her nerve endings when he placed his lips, or whichever chosen body part, onto her erogenous zones. And for a woman who had experienced a lot of sex in her twenty-eight years on Planet Earth, that was saying something. The fact that he was a Tinseltown producer with a wife and three smiling kids back at home in Beverly Hills was neither here nor there. To Holly he was one of a dwindling list of stateside clients who still seemed to think that the ex-pop star was worth a pop in the bedroom department.

Holly Lydon was a high-class call girl, with a speciality for men – or women, if the dollar, pound or euro was right – of the kinkier variety. The producer she was presently entertaining was decidedly fond of having his backside spanked, humiliated and being called a 'very naughty boy' after he'd explored and worshipped every inch of Holly's body.

It was obviously a kink that he couldn't explore at home with his vanilla wife. So he had been coming to Holly, insisting that they drive to a location far from his 90210 ZIP code.

Holly had to admit that this type of motel, or 'sex hotel' as they were becoming more commonly known, was a cut above some of the others she had been in. Even the porn on the TV looked like it had been filmed with high production values. In some sex hotels the choice was limited to watching some hairy-bushed European frau make out with a man pretending to be her plumber, and looked like it was filmed so long ago that the 'actress', should she still be alive, would probably nowadays be living as a grandma on the outskirts of Baden-Baden. This hotel was gleaming and for a by-the-hour establishment was pretty glorious. Condoms, Viagra and lube nestled alongside body lotion and shampoo in the bathroom, and ceiling swings and Kama Sutra chairs could be ordered from room service alongside tacos and cervezas if need be.

There were no windows in the room, which was standard, as most people who went there were probably sneaking off behind their partner's back, and entry was via a garage where cars could be hidden and parked.

Holly let her mind wander as she heard a groan of delight from between her thighs. The producer was enjoying himself. That was all that mattered. He'd pay for more and that was what Holly needed. Her mind meandered to the days, not that long ago, when she was able to stay in the best hotels in the world to undertake her post-pop job. The Atlantis in Dubai, the Hiltons of the world, the Velvets, the Ritzes, all the six-star luxury establishments that she had loved. If she'd learnt one thing during her time in Crazy Sour it was that success brought riches of all kinds – financial, addictive and carnal. Holly lapped up sex. And when she suddenly found herself without a pop job it only seemed right for her to use what she had underneath her clothes to keep the funds flowing in.

Men seemed to love it, and without advertising what she was doing, Holly managed to bed clients in every continent. Men flocked to her as word began to spread: the Arabian sheikh with the penchant for bondage; the famed Chinese scientist who adored sex toys; the French torch singer with a desire to serve and adore his mistress Holly. Holly was fresh-faced, knew no boundaries when it came to sex and would make sure that a client always left with a smile on his face and a deep-seated satisfaction a little lower down.

For a while, life after Crazy Sour was a lucrative and hedonistic one for Holly. Money flowed, as did drugs and drink.

But then it had all gone wrong. After a drug-fucked kinky night of humiliating a seemingly poker-straight politician into licking her boots and lapping his servings of the finest champagne from a metal dog bowl, an overly confident Holly became loose lipped and spilled the beans about her famous client to someone she thought was a friend. Before she knew it, the shamed MP's face was all over the papers, a 'reliable source' detailing exactly what pleasures he liked to sample behind closed doors. Holly escaped mention but a no-smoke-without-a-fire mentality spread across her large client base and, before she knew it, her days of private jets to Muscat and penthouse stays at Shanghai hotels dried up. Almost overnight, yet another career choice in her life seemed to crumble before her very eyes, its destruction the result of her own careless stupidity.

Having bought a decent house on the outskirts of LA with the money she had made from Crazy Sour, Holly found herself locked away at her only bolthole for weeks on end, literally not knowing where her next payout would come from. The few clients that remained, maybe oblivious to her connection to the shamed UK MP, were based stateside, and Holly focussed on trying to keep them as sweet as possible. She was still keen to make cash as and when she could. But for somebody who had been pretty much allowed to spend without thinking for all of her adult life, money soon became tight and every dime began to count. The former pop star who had become a high-class call girl was now facing a future as a former high-class call girl who had become a low-rent kinky specialist.

How had Holly managed to fall so spectacularly? She knew she only had her propensity to brag to blame. But it pained her that all of her famous clients would now be getting their kinks satisfied by somebody else. Why should she be the one paying the price? She'd show them, somehow she would. She'd have the upper hand.

As another groan of pleasure emanated from the heat between her legs, Holly grabbed the producer's head and lifted his face away from her sex. 'Somebody's been a naughty boy, haven't they? Somebody needs to be punished. Come here.'

Holly sat up and watched as the producer obediently placed his naked body face down across her lap, the feeling of his evident desire pressing against her flesh. She raised her hand and brought it down against his ass, causing the skin to redden. A whimper of delight escaped from the producer's lips. Holly continued to slap him, stroke after stroke after stroke. She was angry with herself for letting life go so wrong and was more than happy to take it out on her client's butt cheeks. And besides, he'd paid good money for it. Maybe if she slapped him harder he'd pay some more. She needed to fund some spends in St Tropez after all. Dexter would be expecting to see her. Why else had he sent her the invitation?

Dexter Franklin. Now there was one definitely kinky man.

The man across Holly's lap let out another squeal as she let her palm connect with his buttock a little harder than before.

'Oh, shut up. You love it,' stated Holly, continuing with her punishment. He did, they all did. Holly always had the upper hand, if she thought about it. Perhaps it was time for her to play her trump card.

CHAPTER 4

Dear Mr Riding,

Celebrity chef Dexter Franklin cordially invites you to be his guest for an evening of the finest dining at his new restaurant, Trésor…

'I consider gastronomy to be today's art, young man, and what you and your equally juvenile colleague have served me today has been nothing short of a Jackson Pollock. And that isn't a compliment, just in case your grasp of English and the art world is as poorly seasoned as your take on flavours. I've always considered Pollock's paintings to be a bit of a car crash – as was that meal, and it's a car crash I'm amazed I've managed to survive. The meat contained more fat than a weekly batch of porky specimens at Slimming World; the vegetables, which should be crisp to the fork and explosive to the taste buds, were as lacklustre as your poorly executed attempt at a beard; and the drizzle of sauce that tried to bring both meat and vegetables together in flavoursome harmony was as tasteless as the late Joan Rivers, may she rest in peace. My critique will not be glowing, as you can imagine.'

Restaurant critic DC Riding tipped the peak of his wide-brimmed straw skimmer hat and adjusted it so that his eyes were shielded from the sun that was beating down against his forty-three-year-old skin. Not that the broken veins on his nose and the drooping bags of loose flesh under his eyes gave the impression of a man who really cared about the beauty regime his skin could totally benefit from. His eyebrows were bushy and shot vertically upwards from their follicles, giving him a permanent look of surprise – or sneering incredulity. His chins, for there were many, rested in folded layers on the fabric of his rollneck sweater, underneath a checked tweed jacket, an odd choice given the intensity of the sun and his perspiration-slicked skin.

But then DC Riding had never been a man who dressed for the heat of a glorious spring in Stockholm, which is where he currently was. His precise location was on a boat in the middle of the Swedish capital's archipelago, the collection of 30,000 islands, rocks and skerries spreading eastwards from the city out into the Baltic Sea. He was there as the honoured guest of two trendy young Swedish chefs who had decided to take their lives in their hands by inviting the most acid-mouthed of restaurant critics to sample a taster menu for their new restaurant on one of the islands. DC had already taken an instant dislike to the two young chefs when he'd read online that they believed that they could 'challenge the kitchen greats of the world with decades of experience behind them', even though neither of them had experience that would equate to a decade between them. 'Bum-fluffed upstarts' was how he branded them before he'd even boarded a plane from his home in London to the Swedish capital. When DC was in a scathing mood, nothing was off limits – even the beard-growing abilities of the two trendy cooks.

The two chefs now seemed mightily crestfallen as they faced the fusillade of insults, potentially torpedoing their dreams, as they sailed with and escorted the critic back to Stockholm. DC had eaten food that, had he paid for it, would have cost him enough krona to keep a Swedish family of four in shopping for a good few months. Stockholm was expensive at the best of times, but the prices that the two young men were charging just because they were seen as the hot young kitcheneers in town was another point that DC was more than happy to discuss.

'You two seem to think that just because you're all trendy of face and tattooed of sleeve you can charge the earth for your food. I looked at your prices. They make The Ivy look like Burger King. Ridiculous. But if you are going to charge such extortionate prices then the food needs to match up. Today's food felt like it had been prepared by two kitchen workers who should have peaked at dishwasher and busboy, not two of this glorious nation's supposed new finds. I don't know what the Swedish word for shambolic is but I'll be sure to include it in my review.'

DC pulled a hanky from his pocket and dabbed his cheeks and the back of his neck where sweat had begun to gather. The two chefs stared firstly at each other, a look of horror volleying between them, and then directly at DC.

As DC descended from the boat he felt his phone vibrate, signalling the arrival of an email. He clicked it and read the attachment. 'Well, well, well…' He smiled. 'An invitation to Dexter Franklin's new St Tropez restaurant. How marvellous. I've not seen him since that debacle at his New York restaurant. What a strange night that was. Well, what I can remember of it… Hopefully the food will be better at this one.'

DC opened the rear door of a waiting Mercedes and waved to the two chefs still standing on the deck of the boat, staring at him. He never walked anywhere if he could help it.

'Toodle-pip, lads.'

CHAPTER 5

Dear Miss Velázquez,

Celebrity chef Dexter Franklin cordially invites you to be his guest for an evening of the finest dining at his new restaurant, Trésor…

'So this is the scene where the mummy corners you in the tomb of the pyramid and you are so hypnotised by his eyes underneath the bandages that you succumb to his beauty and let him kiss you and push you up against the sarcophagus. His hands explore your body and then you see his body crumble away to dust, leaving you terrified. I want lots of heaving chest and deep breaths in this shot, Rosita. Ramp up the sexiness.'

It was the producer of actress Rosita Velázquez's latest flick, the low-budget *Mummified*, who was giving direction. Not that Rosita felt she needed it. If there were two things in life she was sure that she could do, it was act and play sexy. And no extra in a badly made mummy's costume was going to change that.

'Consider it done,' she said, adjusting the shoulder-length wig and the gold, bejewelled bikini she was sporting to give herself maximum cleavage and curves come the call of 'action'. She'd already made fifteen films since her first youthful appearance at the age of fourteen, and even though her latest was the lowest budget to date, she still had hopes that it could make her the 'Hollywood royalty' she had always dreamt of being.

The only trouble with wanting to be Hollywood royalty was that you had to be known in Hollywood, and despite being one of the biggest stars in her home country of Brazil, Rosita was as famous in La La Land as every other jobbing actress who spent her days serving salade niçoise or power smoothies in some celeb-filled restaurant while waiting for her big break. The fact that she was a household name in Brazil yet couldn't even seem to get arrested once she crossed the border was a constant source of annoyance and inner disappointment to her.

She'd nearly made it on countless occasions in the past, almost securing bit parts opposite the DiCaprios and the Pitts of this world, but never quite. Always an understudy for the hardiest of leading ladies or a 'you're not quite right' due to accent, skin tone, height, age… The list seemed endless at times.

How could the likes of Alicia Vikander swan out of her native Sweden and suddenly be clutching an Oscar when Rosita wasn't even being considered for daytime soaps and the latest slice of the *Sharknado* franchise? 'Early thirties' and 'past her sell-by date' were not words that the fiery Latino was allowing into her vocabulary anymore. Her age was going downwards, twenty-nine next birthday – despite her passport showing quite clearly that she was in fact thirty-four – and she would not stop striving for worldwide recognition for her craft until the day she had secured her own star on the Hollywood Walk of Fame.

That's what kept her inner fires burning. Recognition. Not money, she had enough of that. Beautiful homes in São Paulo, Paraty and Rio were paid for with a constant supply of lucrative sponsorship deals, and now that she had a rich, globally known boyfriend on her arm, there was branding to be done. But while the rest of the globe said *nao* to what Brazil had been saying *sim* to for years, Rosita was not happy to be anybody's plus one. And playing second fiddle to somebody else's tune was never her instrument of choice. She needed main billing. Her ego demanded it.

Which was why the invitation she had received that morning before coming to the set had intrigued every fibre of her being.

Dexter Franklin. Now there was someone she hadn't been expecting to receive an invitation from. She wasn't normally on the Christmas card or invitation lists of her exes, especially ones where the relationship had ended so badly. Actually, make that catastrophically. And add to that the fact they were now 10,000 kilometres away from each other. Rosita, as ever, was filming on some São Paulo backlot, barking orders at anyone within hearing distance, and Dexter would doubtless be serving up suggestions for something magnificent to do with steak tartare or snails on the Côte d'Azur.

To be frank, if it was just a case of seeing the admittedly strikingly handsome Dexter open up his latest restaurant then she would have probably passed on the 20,000-kilometre round trip, but location- and date-wise, the offer of a jaunt to St Tropez was perfect. She'd checked her diary, the dates fitted beautifully. As for location, it couldn't be more perfect. She would ask her assistant to make the five-star arrangements, especially as it seemed that Dexter was paying for it all. She'd also have to have a word with her make-up artist of choice. She'd need to look her best for the South of France.

Though she couldn't for the life of her work out why Dexter had chosen to invite her after their last encounter. Where had it been? It must have been South Africa. Why was she doubting herself? She knew it was. How could she forget?

No, Dexter could serve what he liked to her on opening night, but Rosita was sure that the invitation was serving something much more delicious than any haute cuisine: the chance to spread her wings and branch out on her own. No matter how awkward the experience may be.

Rosita's thought snapped back to the mummified actor in front of her as the producer yelled 'action'. Before she knew it she was pushed backwards onto the sarcophagus and the roughness of the bandage fabric rubbed against the softness of her olive skin. A frisson of fear swept across her at the apparent harshness of his act. Normally her ego would have cried for the extra to stop, calling for a make-up artist to rush on set to cover any colouration of her skin. But the diva let it pass as she kissed the unknown lips beneath the wrappings. Her mind was elsewhere. On a red carpet in the South of France to be exact.

CHAPTER 6

Dear Mr Franklin,

Celebrity chef Dexter Franklin cordially invites you to be his guest for an evening of the finest dining at his new restaurant, Trésor…

Leland Franklin was just about to launch himself on a zip wire into the wilderness. That wilderness being the sweat-soaked air three hundred feet above the lush deep green of the forest of the Sierra Madre Occidental near Mexico's Puerta Vallarta. His latest daredevil televisual treat, filmed from every angle for his globally syndicated show *Frankly Extreme*, would be to show the group of C- to Z-list celebrities following him across the stunning Mexican backdrop how to dangle perilously from the thin wire that had been erected just for the show. Their aim was to reach their next overnight camp where they would doubtless be forced to swim naked in leech-riddled waters, fend off a violent iguana or drink their own body fluids through desperation. All of this while TV's number-one action man, Leland, made his way back to the nearest five-star hotel to prop up the bar all night with a pint of beer in one hand and one of his many female fans in the other. Despite being seen as a rough and ready true survivor of the al fresco life, Leland Franklin had enough money in the bank to make sure that he never slept under the stars again.

The current star he was sleeping under was that of Rosita Velázquez, his girlfriend of eighteen months and someone who, despite possessing beauty on an epic scale, had already begun to bore Leland. She was hot, but somehow the uncharted territories of countless tender-fleshed telly runners, buxom TV directors and glamour-girl contestants on his show seemed to fan Leland's sexual flame to a much greater degree these days. As executive producer on his own show, he had the final say on who worked with him, and more often than not under him.

Looping his hands through the circles of rope attached to the bracket on the zip wire, Leland flexed his muscles, ready for take-off. The reason for the action was three-fold. One was to stretch out his arms, preparing his limbs for the strain they were about to undergo. The second was to make sure the cameras could capture every inch of his masculinity. His rugged blond looks and sculpted body were both trademarks of the Leland Franklin brand and no episode of *Frankly Extreme* would be complete without the obligatory topless shot of a hairy-chested Leland hacking his way through the dense vegetation with a survival knife in his hand and a smug grin plastered across his stubbled face.

The third reason – and, to Leland, the most important, now that *Frankly Extreme* was into its fifth season and had established itself as a show that was pretty much incapable of being pulled, with multimillion viewing figures from Johannesburg to Jaipur – was to show off his body bulges to the lady standing behind him as he prepared to take to the zip line.

'So my brother is opening another of his blessed restaurants,' whispered Leland, referencing the invitation that had been passed on to him via his management that morning. 'I'm surprised I'm being asked, given our feelings for each other, but hey, this season will be wrapped in a few days' time so maybe a few sun-soaked days hobnobbing in St Tropez will be just what I need. I'm sure I could swing it for you to come with me if you fancy a little relaxation after you win this show. Bro's paying, more fool him.'

The lady in question, who was now positively purring with delight at the thought of heading across to Europe with Leland, was Missy Terranova, one of the show's 'celeb' contestants who, despite having only been in the public eye a matter of months, was gaining column inches across the world due to a rather notorious affair. The former Canadian hotel receptionist had made a splash into the seedy world of celebrity after revealing in explicit detail the finer nerve-tingling details of a sexual four-week adventure she had immersed herself in with a hotel guest. Not exactly a scandalous tale until she revealed that the man in question was in fact a European prince who had been visiting Canada on a charity tour with his pregnant girlfriend. The subsequent fallout had resulted in an embarrassing royal separation for the shamed prince and his girlfriend and a coast-to-coast US tour for a fame-hungry Missy. TV shows and celeb magazines from Maine to Miami screamed out with yet another juicy titbit from the starlet the newspapers called the 'Woman Who Put the Ho in Ho-Tel' or featured a borderline pornographic shot of Missy wearing not much more than a tiara and a wink. Leland had spotted her womanly charms on a chat show and insisted she be auditioned for his latest series. She passed the audition by saying she'd turn up.

'Are you kidding me?' cooed Missy, jiggling what she housed in her khaki vest top with excitement. 'Are you sure I can come?'

'I don't see why not. It doesn't say plus one on the invitation but I'm sure I can wangle it.'

'But what about your girlfriend?' Missy raised her eyebrows.

'Like I say, it didn't say plus one, so there's my excuse to Rosita. Plus, she's working on some Egyptian-themed horror flick right now so she's probably up to her nipples in plastic scarab beetles or something equally naff. That'll keep her busy while we nip across to Europe.'

'Right, we're rolling, Leland.' The voice came from the cameraman positioned alongside the TV adventurer. 'We have been for a while.'

'Then I suggest you make sure that last conversation never sees the light of day if you want to be back here working on series six,' remarked Leland, raising his voice from the whisper he'd been speaking to Missy in.

The cameraman nodded his head. Like every other member of the *Frankly Extreme* crew, he knew what could be – and more to the point what couldn't be – considered for airing.

'Right, you lot,' shouted Leland, aiming his voice at Missy and the line-up of faded pop stars, *Next Model* flops and what-was-your-name-again daytime telly actors ready to follow his instructions. 'We're ready to zip wire. Hold on tight and I'll see you on the other side of this ravine. Just do as I show you and you'll be fine.'

A sea of nervous and mostly unrecognisable faces stared on as Leland shot one of his killer smiles into the lens of the camera. He flexed his arms again.

'So, you really think I can win?' whispered Missy again.

Leland turned to face her and whispered back. 'Honey, if you suck my cock and let me ride you again like you did last night then it's a dead cert.'

Leland turned back to the cameraman and flashed him a 'who's the boss' glare. 'You didn't hear that either, okay?'

Missy was beaming as Leland launched himself out into the yonder, a machismo cry of strength and power escaping from his lips as he did so.

CHAPTER 7

It was midnight and Dexter Franklin stared at his new St Tropez restaurant's dining area. He had to admit it was his finest yet; now that the Moroccan décor and furnishings had finally arrived and been installed, his initial vision had become a reality. Today had been the day, a long one, but the one where everything had finally come together. Trésor, his St Tropez culinary masterpiece, was everything he wanted it to be. It looked chic, designer, with a palette of bright, luxurious hues, possessing exactly the kind of vibrant electricity that he required. And with opening night only a few days away he knew that its combination of explosive firework-coloured interior design and the artisan-cool terrace would be a hit with the jet set who flocked to the French town with euro-splurging regularity.

How apt that the interior should be clashing in colour and remind him of fireworks, thought Dexter, as he scanned the list of those attending on his laptop. Clashes and fireworks were definitely on the menu. Nearly everyone who had been sent an invitation had accepted. The normal list of restaurant hangers-on would be making an appearance no doubt. Reality stars desperate for another five minutes in the spotlight or talent show judges not exactly overrun with work between seasons. Let them come. Let them attempt to shine in their own vulnerable self-importance. Dexter would smile sweetly and serve them willingly. But the fireworks would come from a small list that he had been determined to invite. There were five names that really mattered, and to Dexter it was that fivesome he would be particularly attentive to. He knew they'd come. The offer of paying for them to be his guest for a few days was too great for the likes of them to resist. Whether they could afford it or not was not a consideration. They were all that shallow. Dexter just needed them there.

His daredevil brother, Leland, his ex, Rosita, the snidey critic, DC, TV's current cooking goddess, Mew, and the washed-up has-been, Holly.

'Let the fireworks commence,' smiled Dexter, slamming the laptop shut.

As he locked the door behind him and walked out into the cool night air, he could see the lights of the portside bars and restaurants twinkling in the harbour waters in the distance. A hubbub of chatter and noise, the chink of glasses and the banter of many different languages seemed to fill the air. A cloud of richness and contentment washed over him. Dexter felt happier than he had in weeks. His plan was coming together.

CHAPTER 8

'I have to admit, these views are breathtaking,' cooed Mew, as the helicopter transporting her from Nice airport to the coastal delights of St Tropez swooped to the right, allowing her and her fellow passengers a clear panorama of the brilliant blue waters of the Mediterranean Sea below them and the frothy peaks of the waves gently breaking onto the beaches and inlets of the Côte d'Azur coastline. 'When I was with the band, all I saw of the world was through taxi windows and the inside of hotel lobbies. At least this trip is starting in glorious style.'

As Mew marvelled and stared out of the window of the privately chauffeured helicopter that had been laid on by Dexter to transport them from the airport, she may as well have been talking to herself, as none of the other passengers paid her any attention.

There were three people in the helicopter with her. One was their pilot, Giuseppe, who Mew had clocked with much relish as he greeted his guests at the airport. With hair as black as charcoal and as lustrous as the rainforests of Brazil, his obviously toned core fitted neatly inside his epauletted pilot's shirt. He was pure sex appeal. As Mew felt the coarseness of his stubble graze her cheeks when he greeted her with a double kiss – one of her favourite parts of being on the continent, so much nicer than a poker-stiff handshake – she felt herself blush. Giuseppe's beauty had been the first sight to take her breath away, long before the majesty and the grandeur of the landscape had even come into consideration.

Mew could still feel the heat on her face as Giuseppe turned to Olivia Rhodes, who had been glued to her side ever since they had taken off from London. Quite why her publisher had insisted on being on this trip was beyond Mew. She may also represent Dexter's books, but as far as Mew was concerned she was as welcome on the French outing as rat droppings in a restaurant kitchen. She was such an awkward woman and Mew had visibly cringed as Giuseppe attempted to land a kiss on her cheeks, Olivia swerving around clumsily in an attempt to avoid his welcome.

It was Olivia who was sitting across from Mew in the helicopter as they sped along the coastline. It was clear that Olivia was not a seasoned flyer, as she had spent most of the journey with her face deep in a sick bag.

As Olivia retched yet again, Giuseppe tilted his head back towards Mew and unleashed a killer smile. He held his fingers aloft in a circle and asked 'Is she okay?' sufficiently loud enough for Mew to pick up his rich accent once more. Italian, she would imagine. They weren't far from the Italian border, Mew knew that, and his tones were definitely not French. She would have to probe him further on their arrival in St Tropez. He was definitely an attraction that had been added to her 'things to do' list.

Mew replied, 'She's fine. She finds the flight a little rocky.' Mew swayed her hands back and forth to signify her meaning and returned an equally radiant smile. She added a slight giggle to show both interest in the pilot and also that she didn't really give two hoots about Olivia's dislike of any sudden motion in the air.

As Giuseppe winked at Mew and tilted the aircraft into another slight angle, it appeared that neither did he. He was obviously not that big a fan of Olivia either. Even over the sound of the helicopter's engine, the noise of Olivia trying to empty the contents of her stomach into the small paper bag could quite easily be heard.

Nice one, Giuseppe, thought Mew, as she looked out of the window and down at the terracotta roofs and Lego-like villas rushing by below her.

The other person in the helicopter, along with Mew, Olivia and Giuseppe, was DC Riding. Mercifully, the other person booked on the flight hadn't turned up at the airport as planned – quite frankly, where they would have sat themselves was a mystery worthy of Hercule Poirot. In the back row of the craft, spreading himself rather grotesquely over two seats, was the food critic. Despite his love of all things gastronomic he was far from keen to see any recent edible offerings returning to say hello from the lips of Olivia Rhodes. A point he was being more than vocal about.

'Oh, for Christ's sake, woman, can you please stop that infernal chundering?' he snapped, swiping his handkerchief across his brow to mop up the slick of perspiration that coated his skin. He was hardly dressed for the French Riviera climate: his oversized cotton patchwork jacket and full-length linen trouser combo was definitely more flamboyance than function. His only nod to the summer weather was a pair of sandals on his feet, which would have been rather more visually appealing had DC bothered to cut his toenails or moisturise his feet. Pedicure was not a word in DC's somewhat colourful vocabulary. Which, when it came to expletives, seemed to be rather sizable.

'I did not bloody well come all the way here to see you throwing up your stomach lining into a paper sodding bag, missy. St Tropez is supposed to be all jet set and couture, glamour and glitz, millionaires and oligarchs. It's all about style, you silly lady! Not about watching some bad flyer throwing up her airport Krispy Kreme doughnut or whatever it is you've bloody well downed before boarding your flight. Where's your fucking class, woman? You wouldn't see Anna Wintour landing in St Tropez with a woman with bits of sick in her hair, would you?'

*

As the helicopter landed and the trio of passengers descended from the craft, all three of them were glad to have their feet back on terra firma. Even before the blades of the sleek black chopper had stopped rotating, they were each plotting what their next plan of action would be and looking forward to a few free days as the guest of famed celebrity chef Dexter Franklin.

DC Riding lurched his way across the tarmac and stared up into the clear blue sky as he did so. The sun was directly overhead and harsh against his skin. But his famed critiques were often harsher than any midday sun could ever be. Dexter Franklin had learnt that the hard way when he'd invited DC to the opening of his New York restaurant. DC had hated the food. In all fairness, he'd not really been able to taste it properly as he'd had somewhat of a shocking head cold on the night itself. He probably should have erred on the side of caution and gone back another night, when he was feeling better, for a truer taste. Nothing houses any taste or flavour whatsoever when you're totally blocked up, but he had a deadline to meet. Even though it was highly unfortunate that DC's rushed and not at all fair review of Dexter's Big Apple venture had caused major ripples in the celeb world and severely dented Dexter's reputation, well, it was hardly DC's fault if the celebrity world hung onto his every word and trusted his critique implicitly, was it? Critic trumps chef. And that was how it should always be, in DC's opinion.

So Dexter's New York restaurant was an epic fail. Whoops. Shit happens. Jog on.

As DC wiped his brow again, the intensity of sun irking him somewhat, he just hoped that the celebrity chef had something spectacular up his sleeve as far as Trésor was concerned. Otherwise DC would just have to air his opinion to the world, no matter the consequences. Hopefully Dexter had learnt from his New York mistake. The next few days would prove whether he had or not.

While DC contemplated Dexter Franklin, the two women walking behind him were thinking about very different things. Mew, tossing her long blonde hair from side to side as casually and yet as flirtily as she possibly could, was trying to work out just how she could keep Giuseppe in her life for another few hours now that his job as their pilot was over.

'Do you know St Tropez well then, Giuseppe?'

'I do. Like the back of my hand.' He held up his right hand and laughed. Mew flushed as he spread out his fingers. His hands were enormous and she immediately imagined them wrapped around her body and cupping her face as he kissed her. There would be no resistance. She just needed to make it happen.

'It's my first time here. I know nobody and could do with somebody to show me around. I'm sure there are some fabulous sights worth seeing.' Mew let her eyes scan slowly down his frame as she made the suggestion.

As she spoke, one of the workers from the airfield was trying to extract her huge suitcase from the helicopter. Even though Mew would only be in St Tropez for a few days she had packed as if she were undertaking a round-the-world cruise. Her motto was that it is always wise to have options when it comes to looking beyond fashionable.

She watched the man struggle.

'Oh my, how on earth a girl like me is supposed to move that into my suite at our five-star hotel is beyond me. I hope the workers there are as big and strong as you, Giuseppe.' She squeezed his arm as she spoke. Solid muscle, just as she had suspected.

'Well, I'm not flying back to Nice until later tonight, so if you'd like me to come and help you, I can maybe tell you some of the sights to see like Eden Plage or Le Club 55. I could always take you up the *citadelle* too.'

'That would be wonderful. You can be my guide and show me the sights.' Not that Mew had any intention of checking out the Plage place or whatever the club was called. Not yet anyway. The only sight she intended to explore was the map of beauty ready to be discovered underneath Giuseppe's uniform.

Watching Mew, Giuseppe and DC in front of her, a still queasy Olivia felt a streak of jealousy rush through her as she watched the object of her affection with the pilot. What did he have that she didn't? She knew the answer.

She looked at DC's rotund figure swaying into the shade. What an odious man. She'd heard his every word in the helicopter. Had he not been such an influential critic she would have launched back at him. Behind her spectacles, Olivia Rhodes was not as meek and mild as some might think. What a pity she needed to keep him sweet, really. Dexter was still her client and, who knew, one day DC could be critiquing Mew's very own restaurant should she ever care to open one. Olivia was sure it would be a success. She'd make it so.

CHAPTER 9

The blast of the Porsche 911's horn and the celebratory look-at-me tone of Missy Terranova's exuberant screams of delight sounded together as Leland Franklin shot through yet another set of *feux rouges* on the coastal road leading from Sainte-Maxime to St Tropez. The fact that the adventurer had narrowly managed to avoid killing an elderly French lady and her toy poodle by the wispiest of margins seemed to be of no concern to either Leland, driving the turbocharged car, or to Missy, in the passenger seat of the convertible with her hands in the air, waving her Louise Coleman silk scarf in the breeze as the couple sped through yet another set of traffic lights. So far they had scared the life out of at least three groups of schoolchildren, some British tourists and about half a dozen old age pensioners.

'Another twenty minutes and we'll be there, sweet cheeks,' stated Leland, one hand on the steering wheel and the other working the under-the-hemline delights of what Missy was airing to perfection beneath her mini-skirt. Namely her hairless pussy. Her cries of exultation were not just from the speed they were travelling at along the French streets.

'I think I'm going to be there in twenty seconds, baby,' smouldered Missy, spreading her legs as far apart as her skirt would allow in order to give Leland as much access to the folds of her sex as possible. Her orgasm was rising and on the verge of being beyond the point of no return. 'Don't you dare stop now.'

Never one to do as he was told, Leland immediately withdrew his fingers from within her and watched her, keeping one eye rather unsafely on the road as he contemplated her need for him. He could feel his erection rising within his trousers. He had no doubt that he'd be banging Missy as soon as they arrived at the hotel, but there was something about seeing her there, surrendering herself to his desire and looking almost helpless in her want for him that made him know he wouldn't be able to wait another twenty minutes.

Placing his fingers to his mouth and licking Missy's juices from them, Leland felt his cock grow harder. Missy watched as he did so and purred her delight. There was longing in her eyes.

Making his mind up, Leland yanked the Porsche steering wheel to one side and veered off the main road and onto a dirt track. The terrain, slightly bumpy after the smoothness of the road, caused the car to bounce a touch and Missy let out a squeal, accidentally letting go of the scarf and releasing it into the air. She slipped her head around to watch it looping in the breeze before finally coming to rest on the verge of the track. It had been a gift from Leland, but as one of the richest men on TV she knew there would be many more. Hell, they were heading towards one of the biggest collections of designer names in France. St Tropez housed Dior, Roberto Cavalli and Diane von Furstenberg to name but three. And Leland would be treating her no doubt.

'Oh, baby, I've lost my scarf,' cooed Missy as Leland brought the Porsche to a halt behind a shabby-chic villa set back from the road. It was away from prying eyes and exactly what Leland needed.

'Out,' he barked.

'What?' Missy wasn't sure that she wasn't already being given her marching orders so soon into the trip.

'Get out of the car and bend over the bonnet. If you think I'm waiting another twenty minutes to sample some more of that then you're sorely mistaken.' He pointed to the area between her legs. In a matter of seconds Missy had unbuckled her seat belt, hopped out of the car and bent herself forwards over the front of the Porsche, spreading her legs as she did so, exposing her willing flesh. The paintwork was hot against her skin but she didn't care. She knew what prize was to come.

'I'm sorry I dropped your gift to…' Missy was about to add the word 'me' when she stopped, unable to speak as Leland dropped his trousers and rammed his cock into her from behind. He went deep, causing her vision to blur momentarily with the sublime joy of it all and the extra heat that burned inside her.

Leland's strokes were hard and fast, a sense of urgency and danger coming from the fact that they could be discovered any moment. Leland clenched his buttocks with every thrust of his cock, slamming his length into Missy as she squirmed with delight across the bonnet. One side of her face and her arms rested against the paintwork, her hair spread out across the red of the car's exterior. Its heat, married with the force of Leland's plunges as he placed his hands either side of her tiny waist and pulled her onto him, making sure that every millimetre of his impressive weapon was within her, caused her to wince slightly.

For a while she lost herself in euphoria as he ploughed into her. Then the tone of Leland's breathing changed and became more frenzied. His crescendo was obviously imminent, as was Missy's.

'I'm about to explode, baby, fucking take it…' panted Leland as he released his seed into her, Missy's orgasm bursting into action at the same time. Leland grabbed Missy's hair as he felt the last few drops of his ejaculation drain from his cock, pulling her towards him so his lips could find hers as he climaxed. Their teeth clashed and their tongues swirled together angrily as they both peaked, jubilant in their sexual fever. Leland bit down on Missy's lip, his nirvana rolling into force, and again she winced slightly. But again, as her own explosion subsided, all she could think about was the joy she had experienced.

'That was incredible, Leland,' said Missy, standing back up and shifting her skirt back into position. 'I'll see if I can find that scarf on the way back. It was pretty expensive. And a gift from you.'

This time Leland did reply. 'There will be plenty more of that, don't you worry. You keep flashing the gash, I'll keep flashing the cash, got it? I told you that when I let you win *Frankly Extreme*.' He placed his hand back under her skirt and patted her pussy, in the same way an owner would pat an obedient animal. 'Now, let's get back on the road to St Tropez. My brother will be wondering where I am. I can't wait to see his face when I turn up.'

They climbed back into the car and sped off, leaving a trail of dust as the wheels of the Porsche spun across the ground.

CHAPTER 10

As Leland floored the accelerator of the Porsche and drove back along the dirt track to the open road, neither he nor Missy noticed a bus that had parked on the very place where the scarf had come to rest. If they had looked, they would have seen about a dozen or so people sitting in the vehicle, waiting patiently for the driver to finish his cigarette on the edge of the road and for one of the passengers to finish relieving herself, the strain of sitting on her second bus of the day, and being on that one for nearly ninety minutes, proving too much for her bladder to bear. Hence why she was squatting down behind the back end of the bus, as far out of sight of her fellow passengers as possible.

Holly Lydon had been in more glamorous situations, that was for sure. One moment in your life you're being wined and dined by an exotic millionaire and then the next you're squatting behind a French bus. And she only had herself to blame. If she hadn't been running late for her trans-Atlantic flight from LAX, dithering with her packing, then she wouldn't have missed it. If she hadn't missed it, she could have taken the helicopter into St Tropez like a real member of the jet set, as scheduled. But as it was, she'd had to pay for her own flight on the next available airline and then once she arrived at Nice Airport she realised that her only way of reaching St Tropez, a seemingly harder place to find than the Lost Ark, according to the tourist office, was to take two buses. The first went to St Raphael, where she'd then waited in the rather basic station for a connecting bus to take her to St Tropez. It was the few bottles of wine on her flight over and the extra can of energy drink she'd had at the bus station that had made her bladder start to pound. So when the driver had stopped with a screw-you arrogance in order to feed his nicotine habit, Holly grabbed the opportunity to relieve herself.

And it had been worth it. And not just for avoiding the humiliation of wetting yourself in public. Holly had found herself a rather fabulous Louise Coleman scarf lying in the dirt. It was virtually spotless and one of the latest range. And they didn't come cheap – Holly knew the brand. Some Mademoiselle was doubtless kicking herself at having lost it. But her loss was definitely Holly's gain.

Making her way down the central aisle of the bus, Holly passed the sea of faces looking up at her: a mixed-race lady with a baby perched on each of her arms; the Eastern European couple she'd heard chatting away in some spitty language that could have come from anywhere between Dubrovnik to Dusseldorf; and the sour-faced wannabe glamour puss who had indulged in one too many shots of lip filler and now resembled a badly tanned snapper fish. They all seemed to look at her as she shuffled past. Doubtless they recognised her from her Crazy Sour days. They'd had a few hits in France in the past. Maybe a number one, she wasn't sure. She could remember getting off her head backstage at a gig in Paris, but that was about all France said to her.

As Holly took her seat and unravelled the scarf to look at the daisy print, a tap on her shoulder came from the seat behind.

'Excuse me,' said a squeaky French accent behind her. It belonged to a small blonde woman, mid-twenties maybe, just a few years younger than Holly herself.

'It is you, isn't it?' said the woman expectantly.

'If you mean am I Sharon who works in a toothpaste factory called Minty Mouth in Halifax then yes, it is me.' It had always been her stock answer from her days in Crazy Sour when she didn't want to be bothered or couldn't be bothered to be bothered. The answer obviously came as a curt and somewhat disappointing answer to the woman.

'Oh. I thought you were Holly from Crazy Sour. I loved them.'

'I get that a lot,' said Holly, trying to shift her position away from the girl to end the conversation. 'Sorry to disappoint you.'

'You do look like her.'

'She's way prettier than me,' said Holly.

'Not at all,' replied the woman. 'Although I will say that I did always prefer Leonie and Mew. Everyone always said Holly was a bit of a wild child and loved the high life. Especially if you believe all of the papers.'

Holly's lips curled into a sneer at the thought of Mew. 'I wouldn't know. But if she were like that, then she definitely wouldn't be sitting on a stifling bus in the middle of nowhere, glad she's just had a piss but praying that the air con on here kicks in soon before she disappears into a puddle of exhaustion.' She paused before finishing with 'Would she?'

'I guess not. Sorry. I just had to ask.'

'No worries.'

'Well, have a good time in… wherever you're going to.'

'St Tropez,' answered Holly, now looking back down the bus as it pulled off the dirt track and back onto the road. 'I'm going to St Tropez.'

Holly was lost in thought about her destination. And the man she had come to see, Dexter Franklin. When had she last seen him? About the time that she tied him up for one of his much-loved bondage sessions. With a scarf not that dissimilar to the one she had just found on the road. There had been four scarves, all silk, and he'd loved the feel of them against his flesh as he writhed under her orders. What he doubtless wouldn't like now were the photos Holly had in her suitcase of Dexter all tied up and wearing nothing more than an expression of pleasure meets pain during one of their kinky sessions together. He'd paid her good money back then, and now he could start paying again.

Holly smiled as the bus sped past a sign for St Tropez. It was the first one she'd seen. The destination of her potential happy ending.

She'd wouldn't have been smiling had she seen the woman sitting behind her and the photos she had on her iPhone. It was amazing what you could snap if you hung out the back window of a bus in order to capture an image of a once world-famous pop star pissing in the dirt. She'd known it was Holly Lydon. That mass of red curls was instantly recognisable, and besides, she'd googled images of Holly coming through airports and her luggage, even down to the address label on it, was identical. Plus, she'd sneaked a peak at the name on it when she was placing her case in the luggage compartment underneath the bus. It was Holly Lydon. It said so.

And the woman couldn't wait to send the photo to her journalist friend who worked for one of France's biggest celebrity websites. She scrolled through the images of Holly with her knickers around her ankles, highlighted them and hit send. That'd teach Holly a lesson for lying to her. Sharon from the toothpaste factory indeed.

CHAPTER 11

'Well, this is highly impressive, I must say,' said Mew. 'I'll say one thing for Dexter, his taste in hotels is a lot better than some of the food he's served up in the past. Let's hope Trésor can deliver on this kind of scale.'

Mew, her arm still linked through pilot Giuseppe's, strolled into the reception of the five-star splendour of their St Tropez accommodation, alongside DC and Olivia. Mew smiled as she removed the large-brimmed sun hat she had been wearing and allowed her long blonde hair to come tumbling down around her shoulders. It felt good to be in the cool, pine-scented atmosphere of the air-conditioned hotel.

Giuseppe, who was pulling Mew's mammoth suitcase alongside him, let his arm unloop from hers and allowed his hand to travel down to the curve of her peachy posterior, skimming the fabric of her trousers with his fingers just enough to make his intentions clear.

Mew shot him a glance of approval. She was pleased that she and the pilot were definitely speaking the same language when it came to their intentions once they were alone.

'They do say the Arlequin is the finest hotel in the area,' he added, taking in the magnificent opulence of the lobby. 'It has its own private beach and excellent restaurants, with more Michelin stars than most places can dream of. I've never eaten here.'

'Oh, you will. In more ways than one,' smirked Mew, allow-ing her own hand to now move down Giuseppe's body and rest on the granite hardness of his buttocks.

Buttocks that DC had been staring at with great pleasure. Those were buns that he would have happily sunk his teeth into for the perfect amuse-bouche.

'At least I'll be guaranteed some decent food while I'm here then,' huffed the critic. 'As you say, Miss Stanton, Dexter Frank-lin is not always famed for serving the best food.'

'Why do you all keep slagging off Dexter's food?' Olivia said crossly, her face damp with sweat and crumpled from the travel-ling. 'Dexter is Michelin starred too and he has made some of the best dishes I've ever eaten. His cookbooks sell like crazy.'

Olivia spotted Mew shooting her a look that was sharper than a drawer full of steak knives and realised that perhaps up-setting her top client was not the best of ideas at such an early stage of their trip. 'Although your book of course is leading the way right now, Mew. Nobody seems to be shifting numbers like you at the moment in the publishing world. Nobody. We make a good team,' added Olivia, eager to appease her.

The smile that spread across Mew's rosy cheeks said that she had. But only for a second.

Mew continued, 'I think we all know that Dexter Franklin is more than capable of finding his way around a kitchen and plating up delights that the masses will like, but as you are well aware, the one thing that he managed to dish up in my direction with full gusto and more than a side serving of heartache was a huge slice of You're Dumped Pie in a We're Through Sauce.'

'Oh yes, I'd forgotten about that, darling girl,' interrupted DC, a knowing grin suddenly spreading across his face. 'Christ knows how, God knows you were pretty vocal about it. Of course, you and he were once very much an item, weren't you?

Until it all went so very sadly wrong.' A thought ricocheted around DC's head that even if the opening night of Trésor was not exactly top notch when it came to cuisine, then seeing the venom between Mew and Dexter after their much-publicised fall out would be entertainment enough to perk up any party. And if that didn't suffice, he was sure there had to be enough bubble-butted rent boys in the jet-set capital to keep an aging homosexual more than happy. St Tropez was not exactly famed for its twin-set-and-pearls brigade. It thrived on sin, sex and, DC hoped, satisfaction.

'Let's not go there, shall we? Now, don't you think it's time to check in? I'm dying to see our sea-view suites, aren't you?' said Mew.

'Agreed,' remarked Olivia. 'It's not very often I manage to find myself staying in fabulous places like this.'

'Then you should hang out with me more often,' offered Mew.

Olivia heard her brain screaming out 'if only' as she once again took in Mew's beauty. The publisher's edit button in her head somehow managing to successfully crop Giuseppe out of the picture.

He sadly slotted back into her vision as he and Mew moved towards the marble-topped reception desk at the far side of the grandiose entrance hall. DC, his eyes once again returning to the mounds hidden within Giuseppe's trousers, clicked his fingers with more than a modicum of arrogance at the hotel worker carrying his suitcase and followed the former pop star and the pilot to check in.

Olivia, still feeling a little queasy if she was being honest, brought up the rear as she joined them at reception. The pallor of her skin didn't go unnoticed by Mew.

'Are you still not right, Olivia? You're looking a little pale.'

'You won't be eating with me then?' stated DC, also noting the off colouring of Olivia's face.

'I just need to lie down for a while, that's all,' said Olivia. 'No, not yet, DC, I can't quite face anything just yet. Maybe I'll eat with you later instead, Mew? We can discuss a few things.' Olivia had no idea what she needed to discuss. If anything, she was very much surplus to requirements on this trip.

'Not for me, thanks,' said Mew. 'I've brought my very own takeout… Italian. Totally delicious.' Mew shot Giuseppe a side-long glance and a wink to make her meaning crystal clear. She then turned to the man behind reception, who had been patiently waiting for the new arrivals to finish their conversation. 'Hello there, reservation in the name of Stanton, please. All paid for and I suspect one of the best suites you have.'

Having checked in, Mew and a grinning Giuseppe sauntered away from reception, Mew looking back before they both headed into the elevator to deliver a wave to Olivia. She mouthed the word 'laters' and disappeared from view, the elevator door closing behind her.

Olivia felt her foolish heart sink. Giuseppe, all dark and swarthy. Dexter, all dark and swarthy too. Mew Stanton obviously had a certain taste in men. It wasn't the taste Olivia objected to, it was simply the fact that it was men in the first place.

CHAPTER 12

Two and a half years earlier...

The tension and excited air of expectation on the set of *Someone's Cooking in the Kitchen* was palpable and could have been easily sliced, diced and served julienne with one of the kitchen utensils Mew had been using earlier in the day to prepare her three-course extravaganza for judging on the show's finale.

Mew stood in line with the two other remaining celebrity contestants on the show and contemplated her chances. She was standing in the middle of the trio. Was that a good sign? An easier camera angle for the celebratory shot of the victor? She wasn't sure. She hoped, but nothing was certain in telly, she knew that from years in the media world and from soaking up advice, both much needed and often ill advised, from those around her. All she knew was that she had done everything she could to try and secure the title of this year's winner and that given that her pop career was flatter than a lonely pancake on Shrove Tuesday she needed to hear her name announced as the victor. This could be her big break. Round two of fame and a guaranteed way of finding herself back on the wannabe guest list for every TV show and party in celebsville.

She looked at her two rivals. On her left was Grace Laszlo, reality TV junkie and, like Mew, an ex-girl-band member. American Grace had tried and pretty much failed at every TV show she had found herself on since her career dive from glory after a class-A-fuelled, X-rated, caught-on-camera romp with a fan of her scantily clad band and US sensations Sexalicious a good few years earlier. Sexalicious had been major rivals to Mew's own band, Crazy Sour, back in the day, and even though the two woman had met on occasion and respected each other's talent, the cooking show they now found themselves on had definitely brought out more rivalry than ever before. Mew was determined that Grace would not win and hoped that the American's three-course offering of quail with port dressing, venison in huckleberry sauce and rich chocolate mousse with a walnut praline would pale into tasteless insignificance alongside her own gastronomic attempts.

Mew's other competition in the final of the top-rated show was standing on her right: Bollywood star and soap actor Deepak Mann, a dashingly handsome twenty-five-year-old, massively successful in his home country of India but adored in Britain for his role in one of the UK's most popular soap operas. His flavoursome trio of Indian-style mussels, duck breasts with orange, ginger and cinnamon and a dessert of mango brûlée was a definite challenger to her own menu.

But Mew definitely had a secret weapon that went above and beyond the very skilful and modern spin she had put on her own taste-bud-tingling delights of roulade of stuffed partridge, oven-roasted brill with pepper crust and a goat's cheese and vanilla ravioli with a red berry broth. Because she knew one of the three judges incredibly well – intimately, in fact.

She had fancied Dexter Franklin from the very first moment she laid eyes on him across the shiny pans and apron-strewed counters of the *Something's Cooking* kitchen. She'd seen his face in magazines and online and had even eaten at one of his UK restaurants in the past, but she had never quite realised just how hypnotising his eyes were, or how deliciously devilish the curling of his fulsome lips was, until she spied him in the flesh. There was a roguish quality about him, the look of a maverick who had obviously found his talent and made good. Dexter Franklin was the top dish on a high-end menu of manhood. And with the other two judges on the show being a camp Asian chef who looked about twelve and an Aussie pursed-lipped bruiser and total bitch of a food expert who wore her tattoos as if she'd come fresh from Wentworth Prison, Mew's interest in Dexter shot through the roof faster than a speeding Nutribullet.

He had won her over at his first 'hello'. On a scale of successful 'hellos' it was up there with Lionel Richie and Adele. Mew's heart had suddenly started beating in double time as her body began to glow with a heat to rival the most efficient of ovens. Desperately trying to contain her blushes, Mew had smiled as coolly as she could and stared straight into Dexter's devilishly dark eyes as she replied with a simple 'hi'. Something seemed to instantly connect between the chef and the ex-pop star and its delivery came layered with lashings of sexual seasoning and flirtatious flavouring. Mew knew in an instant that the two of them would become lovers.

It had happened after they wrapped on the first episode of the show. Dexter invited Mew to stay behind, insistent that he had a few suggestions that could improve her culinary techniques. As Mew knocked on the door of Dexter's dressing room after her fellow competitors and all but a few stragglers from the production crew had gone home, she knew full well that she wasn't there to discuss condiments and cooking times.

She had hardly closed the door behind her before their lips met, their obvious desire for each other spilling over at long last. Dexter's kisses were urgent and frenzied, his tongue snaking between her teeth and exploring her mouth with a passion that immediately sent a frisson of electricity bursting forth from her core. As his hands pulled her towards him and he cupped his palms across her buttocks, Mew heard herself sigh with pleasure, surrendering to the inevitable act that was to follow. As her body pressed against his, she could feel the excitement between his legs. Strong and ready for action, a beast caged. But not for long.

Mew attempted to undo Dexter's belt and unleash his weapon, her need for him inside her greater than she had ever experienced. But Dexter had other ideas. He pushed her hands away from his groin and placed his own palms back on her buttocks. Dexter was a strong man and in one swift movement he lifted Mew up and sat her on the countertop, her back against the row of mirrors that covered one wall of the room. He sank to his knees in front of her and began to unbutton her jeans as he did so. Mew lifted herself slightly off the counter, allowing the chef to manoeuvre her jeans down her legs. She kicked off her shoes, letting them fall to the floor. Her jeans followed suit, as did the pair of silk knickers she was wearing. Mew sat on the counter, totally naked from the waist down as the dark eyes of Dexter Franklin stared up at her from between her legs. There was something totally hypnotising about his gaze, a hundred words being said without uttering a single one. Dexter knew that Mew would surrender to his desires in any way possible. Not that this was about control, or domination of one partner over another. Far from it. Mew was more than ready to give herself up to the pleasures that she knew were coming her way.

As if reading her mind, Dexter spread Mew's legs as wide as he could and allowed his mouth to find the soft, wet folds of her hairless pussy. Mew gave a sharp intake of breath as the coarseness of Dexter's permanent five o'clock shadow grazed against her tender flesh. The sensation took her to heaven as he moved his tongue back and forth across her sex, dipping it as far as he could inside her and then flicking it across the prize above. She grabbed his head with both hands and pushed his face as deep into her as she could, relishing the waves of ecstasy that emanated from her vagina. The dressing room blurred slightly as her eyes lost focus, immersed in the nirvana of the moment.

It was only when her orgasm was over that Dexter removed his face from her folds. He stood up. This time his weapon was free of its confines, pointing towards her, a glistening of precum already dotting the tip. Mew only had a moment to take in the beauty of its size and shape before Dexter guided it into her. Again, the action took her breath away. Their bodies rocked together until Mew reached a second orgasm. It was only then that Dexter allowed himself to finally give in to his own desire.

After that first bout of lovemaking, the couple met most days for sex, sometimes during a lunch break from filming or more often than not in the evening when they were virtually alone at the studio. Any hopes that they had of keeping their affair secret were dashed when a runner on the crew informed the press of what was happening between judge and contestant. At first Dexter was angry, believing that it was nobody's business, but viewing figures on the show proved otherwise. The fact that Mew and Dexter were together made the show essential viewing. Would Dexter give preferential treatment to Mew, or would the other judges critique her with extra severity in order to overcompensate for the union between the two?

Viewing figures were through the roof and over six million people tuned in to see the final moment when a new star celebrity chef would be named. Would it be Deepak, Grace or Mew?

'And the winner is…'

Mew could feel her heart in her mouth as Dexter uttered the words she longed to hear. 'Mew Stanton.'

Dexter winked at her as he said her name. She had been the runaway champion, appealing to the majority of the viewers. Even if he could have fixed it for her to win, the show could not have had a better ending – not that either Grace or Deepak thought so. But the press, social media and fans of the show grabbed the result with both hands. Within a week nearly every magazine cover, blog and gossip column featured the new telly 'it couple', Dexter and Mew.

For Mew, life was suddenly more delicious than ever before. Life with Dexter was a delectable treat. It tasted good. The girl from Crazy Sour was back on top. Flying high at number one.

But just like any flavour, it was a palate pleaser that wasn't set to last. Before too long, the only taste that Mew was left with in her mouth was a nasty one. Out of nowhere, Dexter dumped her like a plate of end-of-service leftovers, giving her no explanation. That was when the trouble really began.

CHAPTER 13

At least the flowing white floor-length dress Rosita Velázquez was wearing was a little more comfortable than the rest of her outfit, given the fact that the temperature of the Côte d'Azur skies overhead was already heading into the mid-thirties.

'How Nefertiti managed to flounce around Egypt all day trying to rule people or whatever she did wearing a bloody headdress, enough jewellery to sink every yacht in St Tropez and cope with these bloody snake arm cuffs is beyond me,' moaned the actress, scratching at the metallic cuff wrapped around her left arm to prove the point. 'But I do look fabulous, even if I say so myself.'

Rosita gazed at herself in the full-length mirror positioned in front of her. Head to toe perfection.

'And I must say you have done a wonderful job on my eyes, Tinks. I am royal fierceness, darling.'

'I told you I would,' replied Tinks, Rosita's long-standing make-up artist of choice. After a lifetime of turning even the saggiest of eye bags and blotchiest of complexions into a red-carpet masterpiece, Tinks McVeigh knew that she was indeed the best in the business. Rosita knew it too and so did all of Tinks's A-list clients around the world. Whenever Rosita could, she would always see if Tinks was available before letting anybody else touch her precious skin. Tinks was always happy to oblige if she was free. There was something about Rosita that continually amused her – probably her pompous, never-waning belief in her own grandeur – and Tinks would often juggle much bigger and more internationally known stars around in order to cater for the Brazilian's needs. Plus, she paid big money. Megabucks. When Rosita had called to inform her about her impromptu visit to St Tropez, Tinks had jumped at the chance to accompany her. She was heading to the area soon anyway for one of her busy seasons at the Cannes Film Festival, as many of her clients would be in town and doubtless need touching up on a constant basis. A few extra days being amused – and paid – by Rosita and her fiery ways beforehand would be the perfect prelude to the madness of the festival.

'You know that nobody can finesse a smoky eye and an elongated liner like me, Rosita,' smiled Tinks, admiring her handiwork as Rosita continued to pout at her own reflection. 'Now, do you want to explain all of this madness to me one more time?'

Tinks circled one of her hands at the hive of activity that was going on around them, using the make-up brush she was holding to point at certain things as she did so. 'How exactly is this all working? I'm seeing a team of at least a dozen half-naked men, plastic wolf and cat heads everywhere and the biggest bank of speakers I've witnessed since I last worked a Beyoncé gig. And all of this on the deck of a yacht with more rooms than most hotels I've been in.'

'It's all about making a splash, dear girl. Arrival is all. And if making the ultimate entrance is a crime, then I plead guilty.'

'So how is this going to work?'

'Well, if I am in the area for the opening of my dear friend Dexter's restaurant…' Rosita paused for just a few seconds to consider the fact that she and Dexter were far from friends, but chose to gloss over that for the sake of her story to Tinks. 'And the film festival in darling Cannes is just around the corner, then I was thinking that combining the two would be the perfect way to bring people's attention to my new film.'

'This would be the mummy one, right?' asked Tinks.

'Yes, doll. Just wrapped. Crock of shit, as ever, but if CGI sharks rampaging through Las Vegas or out in space can get cinema-goers excited then I am sure I can fool people into believing that a few flesh-eating scarab beetles and a horny mummy can be worth watching. And I am superb in it, of course.'

'Of course,' agreed Tinks, smiling to herself at Rosita's self-confidence.

'Well, I may have tipped the press off that something rather fabulous might be happening in St Tropez harbour today in about…' Rosita took Tinks's arm and twisted it towards her so that she could read the make-up artist's Apple Watch. 'Oh, I think about an hour from now would be good, given that we'll need time to dock this yacht. It's fabulous by the way, isn't it? A mega-yacht, they call it. It's 230 feet long. Belongs to an oligarch friend of mine – huge fan, actually. He couldn't wait to lend it to me for the day. He's docking here for the entire festival. I'm his favourite actress. He thinks I knock spots off the likes of Jennifer Lopez and Eva Longoria. They were his old favourites. You can see he has exquisite taste.'

Tinks didn't know whether Rosita meant the oligarch's choice in yachts or Latino actresses.

'So, yes, we sail into St Tropez port in about an hour to be greeted by press galore and then the show begins.'

'And the show is what, exactly?'

'Nothing short of incredible, dear girl. St Tropez will have seen nothing like it. When Rosita Velázquez is in town then everybody needs to know about it. This will be my prelude to Cannes. A spicy warm-up if you will. Make a major ripple here and the organisers of Cannes will be requesting me to make the biggest of splashes at every celebrity party under the Côte d'Azur sun. I've always said that to arrive in style, then a person is definitely required to arrive big. Fanfare big. Unmissably big. You see?'

Tinks did. She had no real idea what to expect, but she knew one thing: with Rosita in charge, there would definitely be something big and worth watching happening in about sixty minutes.

*

'Shouldn't we have checked in at the hotel before anything else?' asked Missy Terranova, pushing her Prada sunglasses further up her nose to protect herself from the St Tropez sunshine.

'I figured a drink was in order first and this place is always said to be full of the movers and shakers of St Tropez, so what better way to start the holiday?' smiled Leland, moving his own Tom Ford aviators from where they had been resting in his thick mane of blond floppy hair and placing them over his blue eyes. 'That's why I had one of the waiters here drive the car back to the hotel. We'll cab it up there later. And besides, is this not the best view ever?'

Missy let her eyes scan across the scene. They were sitting front and centre on a pair of red wooden chairs at Sénéquier, one of the most famous bars in St Tropez and one that was placed at the very forefront of the port and had been since it was founded in 1930. She'd googled the bar before leaving her home in America to join Leland and had seen that it had been a hotbed of celebrity activity over the years. Stars from the arenas of politics, stage, screen and the fashionable catwalk world had been seen sunning themselves in Sénéquier, and even though Missy didn't know half of the names mentioned, she was now smugly adding her own star to that list. And their position right at the front of the famous bar gave them the best view of the row upon row of boats and yachts that were lined up along the Côte d'Azur port. It was indeed the best of views and epitomised wealth and decadence. A playground for the rich and famous. And now one for Missy and Leland. Was that Heidi Klum she could see walking on to one of the yachts? And Ivana Trump ordering champagne three tables up? She thought it might be. Missy smiled to herself. *Look at me.*

Missy drained the last drops of her cocktail, something red and fruity with a rather lethal dose of alcohol in it given the late afternoon temperature of the sun overhead, and placed her hand under the table to give Leland's leg a playful squeeze.

'What was that for?' he asked, signalling to a passing waiter for another round of drinks. A murmur of excitement rippled from some of the tables around the couple as other customers obviously recognised Leland, but this being uber-cool St Tropez, nobody said anything and all avoided direct eye contact. Leland noticed and felt a wave of ill ease at being recognised. Automatically he reached for a baseball hat on the table and slipped it on.

'For bringing me here. This is freaking glorious,' cooed Missy, gesturing towards the harbour. 'I love it. I could get used to this.'

'You're welcome, Missy.' Leland's tone was cold. He hadn't brought the starlet to St Tropez for her to get off on the views of the watery abodes of the mega-rich. She was merely there to please him as and when required. And as for getting used to it, well, there was no chance of that. Leland would be sailing off, just like the yachts, to his next sexual destination of choice as soon as he deemed his time with Missy to be through. Her fellatio skills were certainly to Leland's liking, but no amount of clever tongue-work would guarantee anything longer lasting than the next round of cocktails.

His mind wandered to his girlfriend, Rosita. She hadn't texted him for a few days. No surprise. He hardly replied to them these days. The bubble was definitely bursting. His pairing with her was beginning to bore him senseless. Eighteen months in and while Leland's star was bigger than ever, Rosita's was definitely beginning to dwindle. Being big in Brazil was one thing, but Leland was worldwide syndication these days and nothing less than that would satisfy him anymore.

Missy noticed that the adventurer was suddenly lost in thought, blankly staring out across the harbour, where a crowd had begun to gather.

'You admiring the view too?' she asked.

He didn't reply.

Missy carried on, oblivious. 'Ooh look, something's happening. Look, there's quite a mass of people now. Do you think somebody famous is in town?'

Leland stared out into the waters beyond the gathering crowd. A huge yacht was approaching the harbour. The closer it came, the more the sound of music could be heard in the air. A heavy bass beat pounded out, but it wasn't overlaid onto the usual accompaniment of expletive-laden rap music that Leland would normally expect. The music that ran under the beat was almost hypnotic in sound. Was it Indian? Leland listened as the music became louder. No, it was Egyptian.

'What the hell is going on? Shall we go see?'

'Yes,' squealed Missy excitedly. 'That yacht is incredible. Do you think it's a Kardashian or some royal family?' She stood up, linked her hand into Leland's and the two of them walked across to join the crowd.

'What's going on?' Missy asked a frizzy-haired girl with a microphone in one hand. She must have been in her late twenties and looked as non-St Tropez as you could be. In a world of bikini bodies, where every curve and physical attribute mattered to every shallow passer-by, she was dressed in a simple, loose-fitting white T-shirt and a pair of jeans. Classic – but as basic and non-showy as could be. Missy looked down at a name badge that was pinned to her shirt: *Fabienne Delacroix*. The writing underneath her name said *La Riviera News*. She was obviously press.

'Some silly actress wants to mark her arrival in St Tropez with another ridiculous display,' stated Fabienne, obviously not thrilled to be there.

'Oh, who is it?' squealed Missy, tightening her grip on Leland's hand.

Fabienne didn't reply as the yacht docked and the two gangplanks at the back of the boat were connected to the quayside by the staff on board the vessel. The music, now loud enough for the whole of the harbour of St Tropez to hear, filled the air.

Leland turned to Missy. 'Who did she say it is?' His words were barely audible above the Egyptian music.

'She didn't. It's just some actress apparently.'

Leland smiled, thinking of Rosita. An actress arriving in very loud style in St Tropez to an Egyptian backbeat – she would have loved this. Perfect for her latest film. He'd have to tell her if he rang her later, if he had time in between enjoying Missy. It was always an *if* lately.

*

'This has always been my dream, to arrive like this,' said a giddy Rosita to Tinks. The two women were standing on the upper deck of the yacht. 'How does my make-up look?'

'You look gorgeous,' said Tinks. 'Now go – get ready – it's your big arrival!'

Rosita clapped her hands together excitedly. Her big moment was finally here and she hoped that she could pull it off. She leant across to Tinks and kissed her on the cheek. 'Thank you.'

Rosita disappeared below deck, the fabric of her white dress wafting behind her.

Tinks moved to the front of the upper deck and stared down across the port. There was quite a crowd gathered. That would please Rosita.

'Right then, let the show commence,' said Tinks. 'Let's see you arrive, Rosita. Let's see you arrive…'

*

A bemused Leland and a beaming Missy stared on as the spectacle unfolded. As the heady intoxication of the music pumped from the yacht, two men appeared, one a deep shade of chestnut brown and the other as dark as charcoal. They were recognisable as men only from the neck down, their muscular chests bare and evidently oiled from the way they were glistening in the sunshine. They wore the tightest gold shorts, both of them filling them amply, a fact not missed by Missy and many of the ladies gathered.

'Jesus wept, what are they packing down there? A couple of pyramids?' yelped Missy, grabbing Fabienne's arm without thinking. Fabienne looked suitably underwhelmed.

Each man's face was covered with an oversized wolf head. A male voice boomed from the speakers on the deck of the yacht as the two men moved down the gangplanks and onto the walkway in front of the crowd.

'Welcome. I am Wepwawet, God of Ancient Egypt, a man with the head of a jackal. I guard the gates of the underworld.'

He writhed suggestively and a holler of appreciation went up from the crowd as he did so.

'Today, you enter our world,' he continued. 'A place of magic, of mystery, of deceit and betrayal. A place to be entertained and a place full of the most incredible characters.'

'He's just described my brother's opening night' laughed Leland in Missy's ear. She was too busy watching the jackal-men to reply.

'So let us entertain.' He thrust his hand in the air and the music stopped as if on command. For a second a hush fell across the marina and the crowd remained silent, transfixed by what was to come.

After what seemed like a good fifteen seconds, the music started again. The two men, now synchronised in their rhythm, began to move their bodies to the flow of the tune. The crowd erupted into cheers again.

The glass doors at the back of the boat, just above the gangplanks, opened and a head appeared around it. It was as comical and cartoon-like as the jackals had been scary. And just as plastic. The head was of a white cat with the largest curved ears sticking up into the air. As the doors opened to their full width, four other cats' heads, all identical, appeared in a line. All of them were perched on the bodies of chiselled men dressed in nothing more than gold hot pants.

Applause and rhythmic claps erupted from the crowd as the cats strutted their stuff. Even the downbeat Fabienne cracked a smile as the cats all faced to their right in a line, bent forward and slapped each other playfully on the backside.

'It's like a pussy version of *Magic Mike*,' said Missy, whooping along to the action. 'This is just fantastic.'

'I don't remember a lot of pussy in that film, to be honest,' said Leland, unable to tear his eyes away from what he was watching. For a man who had swum with stingrays in Tahiti and braved the iciest waters of Antarctica alongside whales, he was finding it hard to remember when he had seen anything quite so spectacularly weird.

As the cats continued with their dance, the two jackals also writhed to the sounds, spinning, dipping and thrusting as much as their plastic heads would allow.

'What is this all about?' shouted Missy, trying to make herself heard above the music. The music stopped just as she said the last word, the spectators boiling over into excited applause once again as the dancers hit their final pose.

For a second there was another moment of silence and then the male voice spoke once more. 'Welcome to our world. But every world needs a queen and here is ours. A woman of many talents. A woman of beauty and enchantment. A woman who beguiles and bewitches. The ultimate woman of strength. Please meet our queen.'

A chant quietly began to sound from the seven men gathered. The two on the quayside raised their hands above their jackalled heads and began to clap, coaxing the crowd to join in.

The cat-men on the boat split into two groups, two going one way and three the other as they moved down the gangplanks to join the jackals on firm ground. They too began to clap.

The chants became slightly louder.

'Ro-si-ta.' Each syllable was pronounced and lengthened to add emphasis. It was repeated over and over, becoming quicker with each repetition.

'Ro-si-ta.' Again and again. The crowd joined in with the chants.

Well, nearly all of them. Two people didn't.

One was Fabienne, who had no intention of joining in with the crowd's revelry. If she had wanted to be coaxed into clapping at the right moment and barking to order then she would have been born a performing seal.

The other was Leland Franklin. As he watched two huge jets of dry ice burst forth from either side of the open window of the yacht, and listened to the crowd chanting the name, it was as if a chain of lights suddenly connected in his brain. The Egyptian theme, the total ridiculousness of the show they had just witnessed, the introduction and build-up to a beautiful queen of talent and of course, the Cannes Film Festival just around the corner. He'd seen adverts for it on their journey to St Tropez. And the very name itself. Everything suddenly connected.

Through the dry ice, her hands raised in salutation, walked the deific form of Rosita Velázquez. She looked incredible and the crowd, regardless of whether they knew her or not, exploded into cheers.

'Hello, my people. Queen Rosita arrives!' Her voice was loud and triumphant.

Rosita scanned the crowd, her arms outstretched, as wide as her smile. The smile that stopped dead in its tracks when her eyes came to rest on Leland and Missy. They were still holding hands, Leland somehow forgetting in the mind-slap of seeing Rosita face to face in the most unlikely of situations.

He slipped his hand away from Missy's as he realised what was happening.

'Isn't that…?' Missy turned to Leland to ask. She didn't need to complete the sentence.

'Yes. It. Is.' The words were spread out and delivered with equal angst. All colour had drained from Leland's face.

'What the fuck are you doing here, Leland Franklin?' exploded Rosita.

At the mention of his name, a whispered excitement swept across the crowd.

'Not *the* Leland Franklin?'

'The daredevil one?'

'The one from the TV show?'

Fabienne recognised him. And she knew that he was with Rosita Velázquez. She grabbed her phone from her pocket and clicked a couple of photos. One of Leland and Missy, and one of Rosita in her Nefertiti outfit, looking far from happy. Fabienne had only been sent to the port to gain an interview with Rosita for a possible mention in *La Riviera News* but now she had a whole different story to report back. A short piece about the arrival of a two-bit actress is one thing, but a story of betrayal involving TV's top adventurer is quite another.

Rosita stared at Leland. 'I asked you what you're doing here, Leland.' Then suddenly, as if her emotions had got the better of her, she seemed unable to wait for an answer and turned to run back into the boat where Tinks was waiting for her. Leland pushed his way past the jackals and the cats and ran up one of the gangplanks to follow her inside, leaving Missy alone and awkward on the quayside.

Fabienne clicked another photo of Missy and then slinked off to return to her office, a semblance of a smile splashed across her features. It was the most she'd smiled all afternoon.

*

Dexter Franklin was smiling too as he walked away from the people gathered, a baseball cap pulled down over his face so that he wasn't recognised. He'd heard that Rosita was arriving in style and was determined to see it for himself. But brother Leland's involvement was a total bonus. He couldn't have planned it better.

CHAPTER 14

Whereas Rosita Velázquez's arrival into the jet-set capital of Europe couldn't have been more action-packed, the arrival of Holly Lydon was the total opposite. In fact, if it wasn't for the fact that she tripped over her own suitcase as she stumbled into the reception of the five-star hotel Dexter had booked her into, her arrival would have gone completely unnoticed.

'May I help you with that, Mademoiselle?' asked one of the hotel porters as Holly tried to struggle back up from the floor.

'Thank you,' smiled Holly, a little embarrassed by her own clumsiness. 'Where were you when I was dragging my case up the driveway from the bus stop?' She paused to take in the glitzy interior of the hotel. 'This is a posh place. And please ditch the Mademoiselle. It reminds me of when I was at school reading about families in my French textbooks. My name's Holly. Use that.'

'My name is Christophe. Please allow me to take your case to your room for you after you've checked in. I assume you are staying here and not just sightseeing.'

'Cheeky Christophe, and yes I am, all paid for at the cost of Dexter Franklin. I'm here for the opening of his new restaurant, Trésor. He's paid for everything. Although you are forgiven for assuming that might not be the case.' Holly looked down at her dishevelled travelling clothes.

'Oh, I've heard about that restaurant. It's the major talk of the town, in fact. The rumour is that it's going to be a real jewel in St

Tropez's crown. Lucky you. I'd love to go there. Far too expensive for the likes of me, I suspect. He's paid for everything? Even the bus?' There was a teasing tone to Christophe's banter. Holly had to admit that she rather liked him. And even though he was probably a decade younger than she was, nineteen perhaps, his almost white blond hair and deep blue eyes were an attractive combo.

'Are you this cheeky to all of your guests?' she asked.

'Only the ones I like,' he replied.

The two of them reached the reservations desk and, scanning the name on her luggage label, Christophe burst into French conversation with the man behind the desk.

Holly looked on, somewhat confused.

'I've asked for your room key and explained it's all paid for. But then surely you understood that if you studied French at school?' He raised one eyebrow.

'Well, Monsieur Smooth, I merely said I studied it at school, not that I actually learnt anything. I was always more of a creative type than a languages kind of girl.'

The man behind the front desk handed a key over to Christophe and smiled at Holly. 'We hope you enjoy your stay, Miss Lydon, and welcome to St Tropez. And I was a huge fan of your singing.'

'Ah… And there was me thinking that nobody would recognise me in my…' Holly glanced at Christophe before adding 'travel gear.' She grinned at the man behind the desk, muttered '*merci*' and waited to follow Christophe to wherever it was that they were going next.

Christophe looked at the room key and nodded his head. 'You have one of the best suites, overlooking the private beach. I'll show you the way. The lifts are over here, please follow me.' The porter wheeled the case towards the lift, Holly right behind him. He turned to her as he pressed the button and waited for the door to open. 'Should I know you, then? Are you famous?'

'I actually find it highly refreshing that you don't. If you did I'd be telling you that really I'm Sharon from the toothpaste factory.'

A sweep of confusion covered Christophe's face as they entered the lift and it began to ascend.

'Never mind,' smirked Holly. 'I used to be in a band called Crazy Sour. We had a few hits and then it all went a bit pear shaped.'

'Pear shaped?' Another look of confusion from Christophe.

'It went wrong. We split up. Disbanded. Decided enough is enough. Let's just say there were a few differences that we couldn't get over.'

'Crazy Sour. I don't know them.'

'That's because you were probably about five at the time,' smirked Holly. 'You didn't miss much, fear not. There's a whole lot of history since then and it's not a place I'd like to revisit. Even if the cash came in handy at the time. But let's just say I wasn't really cut out to be a squeaky-clean pop star.'

The lift door opened and Christophe wheeled Holly's case out to a nearby room. 'This is yours, Miss Holly Not So *Squeaky* Clean.' He emphasised the word 'squeaky'. What does that even mean? It's not a word I know.'

'It doesn't matter,' laughed Holly.

Christophe opened the door and led Holly into the room. It was much larger than Holly had been expecting and incredibly inviting, containing a huge bathroom, enormous bedroom and a living area that housed both a fully stocked bar and a massive wooden writing desk as well as a plush leather sofa.

'You can write some songs over there,' remarked Christophe, pointing towards the writing desk.

'Or I can ask you to mix me some cocktails over there,' replied Holly, signalling towards the bar. 'That's much more my style.'

'And this,' said Christophe, 'is your very own balcony. It overlooks the private beach. I think nearly all of the group here for the Trésor opening have been booked into the suites on this level. They're the best rooms in the hotel.' Christophe pulled back the curtains that decorated the window and slid open the doors leading out to the balcony. The sunshine immediately shone through, bringing even more of a warmth to the room.

'Well, I guess that is everything for the moment, Holly. If you need anything else then please feel free to ring through to reception and ask for me.'

Holly knew that she would be seeing a lot more of Christophe during her stay in St Tropez. He was cheeky and made her smile, and not a tremendous amount of things did these days.

'*Au revoir*,' he said as he went to close the door behind him.

'À bientôt,' replied Holly. It was one of the few things she actually remembered from her schooldays.

Alone in her room, Holly made her way out to the balcony. Just like the room itself, it was deceptively spacious. The sun felt good against her skin. She ran her hand through her mass of red curls, secured them with a hair tie at the back of her head and stared up at the sky. There was hardly a cloud to be seen.

Holly gazed down across the sea and onto the private beach below her balcony. The yellow sands seemed to stretch right out of view and around the corner. Her suite seemed to be on the end of a row of suites that looked directly onto the *plage privée* and she counted four that she could see before they continued around the bend of the sands. As she looked, a woman in the room next to hers stepped out onto her balcony. She spotted Holly as she ventured outside.

'*Bonjour*,' said the bespectacled woman, somewhat timidly. The accent was far from French.

Holly nodded and weighed up what to say in reply. The woman was more than likely part of the Trésor crowd. But before she'd had a chance to speak, the woman briefly checked the balcony on her other side and then disappeared back inside without saying another word.

'Weirdo,' muttered Holly as the woman vanished.

Holly was just about to head back inside herself to unpack and hit the shower when male laughter sounded from the balcony the strange woman had been staring at, two along from Holly. She could now see a man on the balcony who was dark haired, well muscled and apparently naked other than a towel wrapped around his waist. He carried a glass of red wine in his hand, which was no doubt as full bodied as he was.

'*Ciao.*' He nodded in Holly's direction.

'Hi.' Holly was about to launch in flirt force ten when she suddenly realised that she wasn't exactly looking her best or St Tropez chic. The travel leggings and hair-tied-back-severely-off-face combo were probably not her finest selling points and could in no way compete with his washboard abs and Abercrombie pearly white smile.

With a casual wave to show her interest before departing, she ducked back through the window and ran straight to the mirror. She untied her hair again and shaped it as swiftly as she could around her face, desperately trying to avoid a look that screamed 'I've just spent three hours on a bus in the summer heat'. She stripped off the leggings she was wearing and grabbed a sarong from her case and slipped it around her. The look was already ten times better and much more befitting of her location.

Giving herself the final once over, Holly ventured back out onto the balcony, hoping that the man was still there. He was, but sadly he was no longer alone.

Seeing that there was somebody else wrapped around the man on the balcony, Holly fell to her knees and hid as carefully as she could so as not to be seen. She did it for no other reason than not wanting to seem either desperate or indeed a gooseberry to their obviously romantic moment.

She stared over the stonework on one side of the balcony and attempted to see just who the lucky woman draped across the hottie was. It only took one glance in her direction from the woman in question for Holly to recognise her as ex-band member and definitely not ex-enemy Mew Stanton.

Holly felt a ball of jealousy and rage fall into the pit of her stomach. Of course, now that Mew was cooking up a storm in the kitchen with her new career, maybe it made sense for her to be at the opening of Trésor. But why did she have to be wrapped around somebody quite so delicious while Holly definitely wasn't?

Holly crawled back inside her room on her hands and knees to make sure she wasn't seen. She sat on the sofa and contemplated her feelings.

A few days in the company of Mew Stanton looked like a dead cert. And as she'd explained to Christophe, the Crazy Sour days were a whole lot of history that she definitely didn't want to revisit.

CHAPTER 15

Backstage, Wiener Stadthalle, Vienna, four years earlier...

Mew stared down at the photo she always kept at the back of her purse. It was a little dog-eared now, but it was still one of her favourites. Heaven knew how many times it must have been around the world over the last few years. It was the smile on her own face that she loved the most. That and the connection between the people on either side of her. It was an image filled with happiness, innocence and a wide-eyed excitement about the future. It was taken back in the days when she could only dream about being the singing success that she was now. She had always had aspirations to take the spotlight, even back then. Dancing around in front of the mirror in her bedroom pretending to be Baby Spice, tying her blonde locks into pigtails and smiling sweetly as she swayed her young body around to 'Wannabe' or 'Spice Up Your Life'. Never in her wildest dreams had she imagined, as she lip synced into a hairbrush or a Barbie doll, that one day she would be doing it for real as part of the biggest girl group around. Zig-a-zig that, Baby, Scary, Posh and co!

But that was what Crazy Sour had become. Multimillion-selling pop puppets who could fill stadiums with their wholesome, bouncy pop tunes and synchronised dance steps and whose faces stared down from teenage girls' bedroom walls in every city from Vancouver to Vienna.

They were in Vienna now. Another maximum capacity crowd. Apparently the tickets had completely sold out within five minutes of going on sale in Austria. So said the management. At least that was one thing they didn't have to worry about. There was no doubting the band's popularity. In an ocean of scantily clad, tongue-poking, multi-pierced, mega-tattooed, anarchic female pop stars that seemed to be filling the chart slots around Crazy Sour with increasing regularity, at least the band's fresh-faced angelic approach and butter-wouldn't-melt image seemed to constantly put them a cut above the rest when it came to shifting CDs and downloads. Kids loved them, mums loved them as good role models and doubtless wondered just how three girls in their mid-twenties could still pass themselves off as late teens – the women had highly skilled make-up artists and stylists to thank for that – and there were bound to be a few men and teenage boys out there jacking off to Crazy Sour photos with lascivious thoughts of bending the female trio into positions they'd never managed in their dance routines on stage. Right now, the wholesome trio of Mew Stanton, Holly Lydon and Leonie Conran were experiencing popularity on a mammoth scale.

But unbeknown to the fans, Crazy Sour were hanging on by a thread. A frayed one that Mew feared could be unravelled and destroyed at any moment. And the thought sent shivers to her very core. She loved being in Crazy Sour. It was all she had ever dreamt of and more. The odd con but mostly pros. Money was rolling in, the girls had been offered lucrative sponsorship deals from countries worldwide, firms desperate to use their Crazy name to their own advantage, and there was even talk of the girls starring in their first-ever film. In short, life should be sweet. As sweet as their image. But it wasn't.

Whereas as Mew craved the spotlight night after night, relishing the wave of excited adulation that came at her as she stared out into the faces of another sea of fans, realising how lucky and precious their success was, Holly Lydon was the antithesis of everything that Mew believed in. Holly had the looks, she had the talent, but sadly for Mew and Leonie, Holly also had a deep-seated wild streak in her that meant that she was hard to control. Mew would always do what was required to keep the band's uncontaminated image locked down. She always had. Even if it meant compromising what she really believed in, she would do it. Crazy Sour and their legion of idolising fans came first. Leonie was on a similar wavelength to Mew in the fact that she would do whatever was required to keep management happy, but Leonie was one of life's 'away-with-the-fairies' kind of women. She could sing, she could dance and she could perform to perfection, but if you asked her to achieve anything more complicated than how to plug her own hair straighteners in then she was vague beyond belief. Mew liked Leonie, she was good for the band's performances, but in life away from the stage she was worse than ineffectual. Interviews with her could be embarrassing in the extreme. After faux pas upon faux pas to the world's press about everything – from how she didn't understand how 'cheese plants made cheese' through to 'do cold wars only take place in countries where there's not a lot of sunshine then?' – it was deemed that she should be the one who sat enigmatically in interviews, looking great and smiling sweetly at the back but hardly saying a word. That way there was no risk of Leonie redefining the word 'stupid' a sentence at a time. Besides, Mew and Holly could talk for England.

But it was Holly who was the major problem in Crazy Sour these days. She had been becoming more and more of a headache over the last eighteen months. She'd always been brash, she'd always been loud, she'd always been opinionated, but as the Crazy Sour cash rolled in and each of the young women finally found themselves able to buy things they had only ever read about in swanky magazines before, the difference between the three pop princesses became glaringly apparent. Leonie treated herself to a turreted fairy-tale castle in the middle of rural England – remote, in need of renovation and ready to be turned into a palace of privacy where she could lose herself in between Crazy Sour duties. While improvements were being made, she lived in a hippy-style 1970s camper van that she also bought, a place where she could sit with flowers in her hair and hardly anything floating through her mind. Mew, forever the sensible one, made sure her future was looked after, paid off mortgages if required for friends and loved ones and bought a designer pad for herself in London's Chiswick. As for Holly, well, there was the designer bolthole on the outskirts of LA. That was her long-term plan, to be part of the Hollywood elite. Wasn't that where the best parties were held, after all? But apart from that, all of Holly's money seemed to be spent on the trappings of a pop-star lifestyle – the excesses of drink and drugs. But whereas they might have been expected and de rigueur to the patchouli-soaked rock bands that devil-horned their way across the globe, the narcotics weren't quite so befitting of the women who were supposed to be the purest-of-pure bunch of goody-two-shoes ladies since Charlie's Angels.

What had started with the odd thin line of cocaine here and there and the occasional drunken foray into a bottle of prosecco had become a spiralling addiction into wrap after wrap of any drug she could find and a compulsion to demand that male members of the Crazy Sour entourage, such as security guards, backing dancers and roadies, supplied her with both powder and fizz in return for pleasures of the flesh with increasing regularity. Word soon got around and management did their best to quash any excess talk and curb her habit, but Holly was a feral creature with no wish to be tamed.

Mew hated the fact that Holly could potentially ruin what Crazy Sour had built up. She had tried to reason with her, to tell her to calm it, that the image of the band could be put in jeopardy if she carried on being such a hothead but Holly was not for listening. She was having way too much fun to hear any words of sense and reason.

Mew hated the fact that she would now wake up every morning and her first thought would be whether this would be the day that headlines about Holly's wild ways would be splashed across the front pages of the tabloids or all over some gossip-mongering website. It was bound to happen. Success and a celebrity's star could fade so fast. She'd seen it happen. Extinguished way before its time.

It was only clever management and out-of-court payoffs and settlements that had kept stories and photos of Holly falling out of clubs with a white ring of shame around her nostrils, or a drunken quote given to reporters about the size of her latest conquest's trouser department, from being publicised everywhere. There was nothing wholesome about a girl whose love of the high life, of sex, drink and drugs, was rapidly becoming much more important than performing gig after gig and keeping the fans happy. Satisfying her own carnal and narcotic needs was obviously way more important to Holly than satisfying the fresh-faced wants of the Crazy Sour army of fans.

A few concerts had already been cancelled or postponed on their latest world tour because of Holly's antics. Just how many times would the press believe that one of the girls had succumbed to food poisoning once more or sprained yet another ankle? After five binned gigs already in as many weeks due to

Holly's inability to perform they were running out of potential ankles to sprain.

Mew stared at her reflection in the dressing room mirror and checked her watch. They were due on stage in thirty minutes. The support act, a young Austrian singer called Zoe, had already finished her set and the fans were chanting for Crazy Sour. The countdown was on to what Mew hoped would be another successful concert. It was what she lived for. She was a lucky woman. She knew that. If only Holly could feel the same.

Mew returned to look at the photo in her hand, smiling at what she saw there. A blanket of sadness for days gone by enveloped her and for a moment she thought she could feel the beginnings of a tear pricking at her eye. But any further thoughts were stemmed as the door to her dressing room flew open and an obviously drunk and grinning Holly stumbled into the room. A man Mew didn't recognise, equally inebriated, was holding Holly's hand and smiling like a deranged clown. It was clear that it wasn't just alcohol that was in their systems.

As the couple entered, Mew jammed the photo back into her purse and pushed it across the table in front of the mirror. She spun round to face Holly and the man.

'Holly, what the hell are you doing? This is my dressing room, not yours. And we're onstage in thirty minutes. Look at you, what the fuck have you taken?'

'Oh, come here, poor little lovely Mew…' Holly held out her arms, one still holding a bottle, and zigzagged her way across the room in an attempt to hug Mew. She ducked and swerved out of the way to avoid any contact but couldn't miss the pungent smell of alcohol and cigarettes that came from Holly. 'What's the matter, honey?' grinned Holly. 'Your dressing room. Yeah, that's right, we don't share them anymore. One each…' she slurred, giggling throughout and still stumbling in all directions. 'We can't even be in the same room as each other these days, picky bitch.'

Holly's last sentence was directed at the man holding her hand. Mew didn't need to be told. It had been a long time since the girls had shared a dressing room. Part of their rider these days was that each of the Crazy Sour girls required their own dressing room. Mew would happily have carried on sharing, but between Leonie's airy-fairy vagueness about everything and Holly's increasingly inappropriate behaviour she was grateful for a space of her own. Despite wanting the band to continue ad infinitum, Mew was well aware that she was spending less and less time with her bandmates away from the stage.

Not that she was certain the band were going to make it on-stage tonight, judging from the state of Holly.

'You need to sober up,' barked Mew. 'And what on earth else have you been taking? And who is this jerk?' she asked, pointing to the man.

'Stop being so fucking pious and holier than freaking thou. Chill out, Mew. You need to relax…' A swaying Holly held out the bottle again and offered it to Mew.

Mew snatched it from her and marched to a sink in the corner of the room to pour the remains of the bottle away. It was an action that incensed Holly.

'You stupid bitch, that was mine and Klaus's,' roared Holly.

'Who the fuck is Klaus anyway, Holly?'

'I met him when I went outside for a cigarette. He's working on one of those snack places being set up in the main entrance. We've been having some fun. It was easy to give security the slip and sneak off to *my* dressing room for a few hours. They're idiots. I think it was my dressing room, not sure really. Wherever it was, it did the trick.' Holly turned to smile lopsidedly at Klaus and winked, suggesting that whatever she had been doing with him, it had not been rehearsing her dance moves.

'Get him out of here. You need to get ready. You need to change into your first outfit.'

Holly, who was still wearing a pair of jeans and a T-shirt, shrugged and wobbled on her feet. 'We can go on late. There's more fun to be had. A few Austrians won't mind. They're *very* easy to please.' Holly winked at Klaus again.

'Fucking go and get ready now, Holly.' Mew was becoming more and more angry. Surely management should have checked that Holly was ready by now. Hair and make-up too. How had Holly managed to avoid all of that? Mew could feel her frustration rising.

'Screw you,' smirked Holly, not moving, her words slurred.

'Right, I'm fetching Mason, he'll sort you out and take him back to his pretzels or wherever he came from.' She pointed at Klaus. Mason was Crazy Sour's security and road manager, and the man who should have been making sure that the three members of the band were exactly where they were supposed to be. Which, in less than thirty minutes, was on stage.

As Mew, already dressed in her stage gear of neon-bright vest top and cargo pants, pushed past both Holly and Klaus to run out of the room in search of Mason, she could feel her fury bubbling. A tiny part of her wanted to turn around and punch Holly squarely in the face. To make her realise that she couldn't keep doing this. That she couldn't keep fucking up and putting the future of the band at risk. But Mew never would. Violence was something that she couldn't bear. She knew it would do much more harm than good. And besides, it wasn't up to her to sort out Holly – that was part of Mason's job description.

Mew could still hear Holly giggling away happily to herself as she left the room and ran down the corridor. She banged on Leonie's door. Maybe Mason was there? He wasn't. Just Leonie in a cloud of scented incense, her normal pre-show ritual. Where the hell was he?

She eventually found him outside a stage door, flirtatiously chatting with a beautiful blonde woman who Mew recognised as one of the support act's backing band. He was more than surprised to see Mew, as she always stayed in her dressing room until the last minute before the show.

'Hey, Mew, what are you doing here?'

'You need to come now, Mason, it's Holly. She's wasted.'

'Again? For fuck's sake. What is it this time?'

It was MDMA. They found it in Holly's jeans. Plus a lot of alcohol. By the time Mew and Mason made it back to her dressing room, they found a virtually unconscious Holly lying on the floor, a pool of vomit alongside her where nausea had suddenly slapped her hard. Klaus was nowhere to be seen.

Mason did his best to bring Holly round, knowing that his own job was obviously on the line for letting Holly get herself into this state yet again. Mew knew as she stared at her bandmate that the show was not going to happen. Yet again they would have to disappoint. Tears stabbed at her eyes as she thought of yet another international fan base's misery at their favourite group doing a no-show. What would the excuse be this time? Mew had chipped a nail, Leonie had developed a verruca? It was all becoming so pathetic.

'I need to get her out of here and into some kind of medical care. I think she's taken way too much for her own good.'

'For fuck's sake,' said Mew. It was anger, not sympathy.

'You stay here and I'll sort everything else out,' barked Mason, determined to take control. 'Stay in the dressing room and don't move. Tell Leonie to do the same.'

It was three hours before anyone came back to collect Leonie and Mew. They were two of the biggest pop stars in the world, yet for those three hours the two of them merely sat and waited, unsure what was happening in their own lives.

What was happening was that Mason, who was indeed later fired by Crazy Sour top brass for letting Holly find drugs and alcohol yet again on his watch, informed management that the show would need to be cancelled. When he told them why, a decision was made to can the rest of the tour. Holly was becoming too much of a liability. A replacement was considered but never actioned. Too many bands had failed with new members, the fans not taking to them. By the time another member of the security team came to fetch Mew and Leonie, the 16,000-strong crowd of Crazy Sour fans had been told that the concert had been cancelled and trooped disgruntledly into the Viennese streets, and Holly was already on a private jet back to the UK where she was to be admitted into The Abbey rehabilitation centre, a place for addicts to try and embark on the path to recovery. It was famed as a celebrity haunt for famous faces who were being forced to face their demons. Mew and Leonie were told that, for the moment, the band would be on hiatus and that all future engagements would be cancelled. Neither of them were to talk to the press and it was suggested that they keep as low a profile as possible until a decision about Holly's future and the reformation of the band had been made. Management told the press that the band had cancelled the remaining dates on the world tour due to one of the girls injuring her voice and that medical investigations needed to be made. They were searching for sympathy.

When Mew woke up the next day at her Chiswick home, she knew that the band was over. Even though nothing was yet confirmed, she knew that Holly's admittance into The Abbey was the death knell for Crazy Sour. Rehab didn't happen to wholesome girl bands.

Mew reached across her bed and grabbed her purse from the table alongside her. She opened it and picked out the photo, staring at the three faces there. Celebrity could be taken away at any time. Fame smashed into a million irreplaceable pieces. She knew that. Hated the thought. It was too hard to bear. Now, it seemed, it was her turn. And she hated Holly Lydon for it.

Mew put the photo down, pulled the duvet over her head and waited for the axe to fall.

CHAPTER 16

It was 11 a.m. and already the private beach at the Arlequin hotel was fizzing with activity. Christophe, on an extra shift to top up his salary, his blond hair positively glowing with vitality under the sun's rays, busied himself distributing drinks to those sun worshippers already gathered on the sands or around the tables of the bar that connected the main body of the hotel to the beach.

DC Riding, wearing an extra-large kaftan, wallowed in his poolside chair, snapping his fingers at Christophe for refills. DC was of the opinion that staff were there to serve and certainly not to be fraternised with.

'Morning. I trust you slept well'?' A voice interrupted DC's reading of his Angela Marsons thriller. It belonged to Olivia Rhodes, who placed an oversized beach bag on the table along-side him.

'I did, thank you. I see you're looking mildly better than you did last night,' replied DC. 'Did you manage to eat anything? I saw my way through the most exquisite *assiette de saumon fumé* last night. Totally divine. Dexter Franklin will certainly have a lot of competition to deal with if he is to make Trésor a Michelin-starred magnificence. The salmon was simply outstanding.'

'Well, I had room service. Dry toast. It was all I could eat. But I do feel better this morning.' She squeezed out a blob of sunscreen onto her arm and began to rub it in.

For a moment the pair sat in silence, both looking out across the sands. Half a dozen or so bodies were already lying there, some shading themselves under brightly coloured parasols while others seemed intent on frying themselves in direct sunlight. A couple of women had chosen to go topless, a fact that Olivia couldn't help but notice.

'So what are your plans for the day, DC? The opening night is not for a few days yet. It's very generous of Dexter to put us all up so far in advance. Normally with these kind of events I assume it's a fly-in, fly-out kind of situation.' Olivia couldn't help but let her mind wander to the fact that she hadn't strictly been invited and that her budget to be there would be coming from Dexter's next book. At least when he chose to write it. It was a fact DC didn't need to know. But for those truly invited, Dexter had definitely pulled out all of the stops. The hotel was paradise on a five-star scale.

DC took a lace-edged fan from the table and began to waft his already damp face with it. Olivia stifled a giggle as she stared at it. *Tres camp*, she thought.

'I was thinking of taking a massage here at the hotel,' said DC, the wafting doing nothing to prevent the beads of sweat grouping at his hairline. 'Apparently there are some very good masseurs in the area and one does become so stressed when travelling that maybe a little *me time* to relieve aching muscles might be good for my soul.' DC had already logged on to his favourite gay apps, Grindr and Scruff, to check out the abundance of willing masseurs in the areas. Much to his delight, there didn't seem to be any shortage.

'How lovely,' agreed Olivia. 'I was think of asking Mew if she'd like to take the free shuttle service into St Tropez with me. I'd love to see all of the fancy yachts in the harbour and maybe take a trek up to the citadel as well. The views from up there are said to be amazing.'

'Yes, that sounds, er, fascinating,' fluffed DC, his concentration not on the delights of the citadel and its views as he watched the much more delightful view of Giuseppe, wearing a buttock-hugging pair of black bathing trunks, sauntering onto the beach, a cocktail in his hand. As Giuseppe lay himself rather gloriously across a lounger near the water's edge, DC was already thinking that the pilot's ass was a view that should be given top billing on TripAdvisor for 'things to see in St Tropez'.

'I think Miss Stanton may have other things she'd like to see today rather than some dusty old castle, don't you?' said DC, nodding towards the Italian.

'Oh, is he still here?' said Olivia, her annoyance at his presence far from hidden. 'Hasn't he got helicopters to fly?'

'It would appear not. But he definitely appears to have his eye on that lady alongside him. The one…' DC searched for the appropriate words. 'The one flaunting it, dare I say.' He made the shape of two rather ginormous breasts with his hands as he did so, the effect overly comical and exaggerated given the fact that the woman in question's breasts were mid-sized, perky and standing almost erect. The woman they belonged to was lying flat on her back with nothing but a pair of bikini bottoms on and a large-brimmed hat covering her hair and face.

'Oh, you mean Miss Lydon?' said Christophe, arriving at the table with DC's cocktail. 'Isn't she fabulous? I met her last night and, I have to say, she seems a huge amount of fun. She's certainly taking the sense of St Tropez to her heart straight away,' he continued, referring to her topless attire.

'Enjoy your drink, sir. Would you care for one, Mademoiselle?' asked Christophe.

'Just an iced water, please,' she said. Her words were slow and disjointed, as if she wasn't really concentrating.

'Certainly, Mademoiselle,' replied Christophe, before moving off to the bar.

'You don't think he means Holly Lydon, do you? The girl who was in the pop group with Mew?' asked Olivia, as much to herself as to DC.

'I have no idea,' remarked the critic, slurping from the straw of his cocktail.

Olivia didn't need to wait very long to find out the answer, as the bare-chested woman removed the large hat from her face and sat up in order to grab her own drink from beneath her lounger. A mass of bright orange curls fell around her face as she sat up. She was instantly recognisable as ex-Crazy Sour member Holly Lydon.

'Oh my God, Mew is going to hate the fact that Holly's here. The two of them never got on, from what I can gather. I hope she's not here for the opening of Trésor.'

'So do I, what on earth is that bitch doing here?'

The voice was Mew's, who had heard Olivia's remarks as she was passing their table on the way to the beach to join Giuseppe. She stopped alongside DC and Olivia to stare at the spectacle of a near-naked Holly on the beach. 'And she can take her filthy eyes off him for a start.'

'Good morning, Mew,' simpered Olivia, scanning her eyes down Mew's combination of mesh vest top over sunflower-patterned bikini and a pair of Havaianas. Olivia could feel her nipples harden as she took in every curve.

'There is nothing good about it,' snapped Mew, and she stomped away from their table over to where Holly and Giuseppe, now engaged in conversation, were sitting. Both of them were smiling and as far as an irate Mew could work out, blatantly flirting.

'I thought you were residing in some LA backstreet these days, trying to work out how to revive the career you killed off,' spat Mew. 'What the hell are you doing here?'

Holly was ready for her encounter with Mew. She had known it was coming ever since seeing her on the balcony the night before. But even she had to admit the added bonus of Mew catching her flirting with Giuseppe was the *cerise* on the icing on the cake of awkward introductions.

'I'm here for the opening of Dexter Franklin's restaurant. I assume you are too, seeing as you've made a career out of shagging him into letting you win that stupid telly show.' Holly had to admit that she had watched Mew become victorious on the show with a very envious eye. Not that she would ever tell Mew. Suddenly her ex-bandmate was becoming known for something with way more longevity than the madcap days of Crazy Sour.

'I won that fair and square,' stated Mew.

'Tell that to the banging headboard in his bedroom, Mew. The other two didn't stand a chance. You could have served up steak and kidney pudding with oven chips and you would have won. He was thinking with his cock, not his culinary skills.'

'Er… Maybe I should leave you two alone,' stuttered Giuseppe, feeling very much caught in the crossfire between the two women. He had no idea how they knew each other or why they didn't like each other but it was clear there was huge animosity between them both. He stood up to leave.

'Now that's not fair,' said Holly. 'I was just having a lovely chat with your boyfriend here. He has been very welcoming.' Was that the telltale bulge of a sizable erection in Giuseppe's trunks? Holly thought it was, and deliberately let her eyes linger on it as she stressed the word 'welcoming'.

'I'll see you in the room. I'll come back up when I've finished with *this*,' sneered Mew as Giuseppe wandered off, somewhat perplexed. She turned to Holly. 'You leave him alone. He's nothing to do with you. Haven't you worked your way through enough men in your time?'

Holly was determined not to let Mew dictate the conversation. 'Only the ones with taste, Mew. Not just the ones that I can blow into giving me a career. That's kind of tragic.'

'From what I've heard you will get down on your knees and suck anyone dry for a handful of cash and a one-way ticket to Slag Town. You are the queen there, after all.'

'And you will always be a lady-in-waiting. Second best at everything. You might be top of the heap now with your cooking skills, but it's only a matter of time until another celebrity manages to slip between the sheets with Dexter and win the next series. If he's a judge then perhaps I should audition. I could have him slavering over these in no time.' Holly shook her boobs to demonstrate her meaning. 'He loved them before, after all.'

It was the first time that Mew couldn't volley back a suitably cutting retort straight away, suddenly feeling wrong-footed. 'You wish. The man has more taste than to go with a skank like you.'

'I think you'll find it's not just a singing career we've shared.'

The thought of Dexter being with Holly hit Mew like a bad case of indigestion.

'Fuck right off.'

Holly grinned from ear to ear as she watched the anger wash over Mew's face.

Christophe appeared alongside the two young women.

'Could you ladies please keep your voices down a little? This is not really the kind of conversation our other paying guests are keen on hearing,' he ventured, slightly embarrassed at having to ask.

Mew didn't reply and looked around to see everyone staring in their direction. Without saying another word she turned on her Havaianas and marched back towards the hotel.

'Do give your boyfriend my love,' shouted Holly as she watched Mew leave.

'He's not my boyfriend,' yelled Mew without turning back.

'Then that, my friend, is a green light for me,' said Holly, her voice now lowered so that Mew couldn't hear.

Holly kept smiling as Mew disappeared out of view. Her first encounter with her ex-bandmate had been a lot more pleasurable than she had ever imagined.

Christophe smiled at Holly and raised an eyebrow. 'Would you care for another drink?' he asked.

'Yes, I'll have the same again, please,' beamed Holly. 'Although really I'd like to say, "I'll have whatever she was having,"' she added, fully aware that Mew hadn't ordered any refreshment. 'Because that is exactly what I intend to do.'

Christophe took Holly's glass and walked back towards the bar, passing both Olivia and DC on the way.

'Spoilsport,' said DC. 'Did you have to stop that? We were having a marvellous time listening in.' He beamed widely, still fanning himself.

DC may have been happy, but Olivia certainly wasn't. She'd seen the rage on Mew's face as she stomped back from the beach and wanted to help calm her down. Maybe now wasn't the time to suggest a trip to the citadel together, but she would see if she could be of help anyway.

DC ordered another drink as a hopeful Olivia scurried off after her client.

CHAPTER 17

Fabienne Delacroix hated celebrities, so working on a newspaper like *La Riviera News* was not exactly the perfect job for her. As a rule, the daily newspaper and its accompanying website was full of vapid, self-obsessed, fame-hungry celebrities who had as much talent in their entire bodies as Fabienne had in her left big toenail. As least that was how she saw it.

There were days when the reporter still wondered exactly how she had ended up on a rag like *La Riviera News*. She would much rather be reporting about women's rights or immigration problems between the French–Italian border, but somehow the serious-headed school of journalism seemed to have passed her by. When she had been at college she had dreamt of reporting on the really important issues of the day. Of murder investigations and bank robberies. Things that mattered. Things that would make a difference. But somehow, through bad luck, lack of opportunities and ill-fated career moves, she had ended up working as part of the team dealing with the jet-set world of St Tropez. And every goddamned fibre of every goddamned designer frock seemed to mentally bring her out in hives of despair and disappointment about the colourless world that she lived in. There must have been thousands of other journalists who would have loved to report on the latest 'who's been seen with who' tittle-tattle from St Tropez's famous Le Club 55 and Bagatelle Beach, but to Fabienne every report lacked depth, intrigue and, more than anything, any kind of long-lasting importance. For her, the clear blues waters of St Tropez were as shallow as they could be.

But occasionally the thirty-one-year-old would manage to salvage a crumb of satisfaction from the things she was called upon to write. Rarely, just once in a blue moon, she would return home to her small apartment in Gassin, the peaceful and picturesque French village located on a steep hill not far from St Tropez, and think *job well done*.

Today was one of those days.

As she pushed open the door to her third-floor apartment and found herself greeted by her loyal purring housecat, Gisele, Fabienne was feeling good about her work. For a change, she hadn't been writing simpering words about the extraordinary beauty of some two-bit glamour model who had obviously achieved her success through blowing the macho head of a modelling agency, or trying to translate the expletive-riddled interview of a foul-mouthed hip-hop star breezing into St Tropez on a boat the size of his own ego. No, today she had been able to take one of those vacuous, insipid celebrities and report that things had gone wrong for them. Ended in disaster. And nothing pleased her more.

Having made herself a mint tea, Fabienne sat herself down on her fabric sofa and unfurled the latest issue of *La Riviera News*, excited to read her article.

Gisele leapt up and joined her mistress on the sofa, curling herself up into a contented fluffy ball as Fabienne began to read.

The headline said it all: '*FRANKLY CHEATING!*' The subheading underneath continued, '*TV SUPERSTAR CAUGHT RED-HANDED WITH AMERICA'S MOST INFAMOUS WOMAN AS GIRLFRIEND ACTRESS'S RIDICULOUS CINEMATIC LANDING BACKFIRES.*' What should have been another glossy, dull-witted foray into the land of celebrity, a simple and soul-destroying piece about an unknown actress trying to impress the crowds of St Tropez in the run-up to the Cannes Film Festival, had become a feature of the most tantalising and damning delights. The ridiculousness of the Egyptian-themed landing at the harbour, all cat heads and wolves and cartoon-like muscular men, to promote Rosita Velázquez's latest film — she'd forgotten to mention its title, though to be honest she wasn't sure she could remember it — had been eclipsed by the scandal of discovering Rosita's boyfriend, the world-famous TV adventurer Leland Franklin, wrapped around Missy Terranova. Fabienne hadn't recognised her, though she had guessed she may have been 'somebody', and some of the others in her team at the *Riviera* office recognised her straight away. When they had explained to Fabienne who it was, she was glad that she hadn't known. She was incredibly beautiful, Fabienne could appreciate that, but the thought of being famous for having sex with somebody else made her feel dirty.

But the combination of desperate actress, red-blooded reality TV gold and America's latest slut on the block were a great cocktail, and Fabienne had delighted in every word she wrote of the misery that Rosita had obviously felt on spying her beau lip-locking with another. How she would have loved to have been a fly on the wall at the encounter between the two on the boat, but she had copy to file and now that copy was out there in black and white, with some fabulous colour photographs, for the whole world to see.

Fabienne put down the paper and began to open her post as Gisele stretched out over her lap and curled herself into a ball once more.

The first envelope she opened was an invitation to the celebrity opening night of new St Tropez eatery, Trésor. One of the

Riviera News team would be expected to go. Normally Fabienne would have handed the invitation over to someone else, but something told her that maybe the actress, the TV adventurer or the bit on the side might be in town to go to the event. Hopefully all three of them.

Fabienne put the invitation down and began to stroke Gisele, the thought of watching the three people she'd written about pinging through her mind. She'd accept the invitation, and hopefully so would they. She really wanted to see them squirm in each other's company. And she could be there to report on it all and rub some more salt into their self-obsessed wounds.

The opening of Trésor would hopefully be a celebrity event that Fabienne Delacroix would genuinely look forward to. One that may be more about red faces than red carpets. And that very much appealed.

CHAPTER 18

Leland, Missy and Rosita weren't the only ones making news headlines for all the wrong reasons, as Holly found out the moment she googled herself on her iPad Pro. Still smiling from her encounter with Mew on the private beach, Holly had managed another twenty minutes of baking herself in the St Tropez sunshine before a distinct feeling that she may be turning herself a deep shade of poppy made her quit the sands for the shade and refreshment of the hotel bar.

Christophe was just serving her a glass of something bright orange steeped in gin when she found her latest appearance online.

'Oh, you are shitting me!' cried Holly. 'What the hell is that?'

'More pretty words I see,' said Christophe sarcastically, arching his eyebrow.

'Well, look at this.'

Holly turned the iPad to face Christophe. He immediately blushed. The image on the screen showed Holly crouched down on the edge of the road, relieving herself, the photo taken the day before on her journey to the hotel. She didn't know who had taken it, but her mind immediately went to the girl who had talked to her on the bus. She had obviously recognised Holly. Thankfully there was nothing too revealing on show but the image was still far from elegant. And neither was the headline that accompanied it on the red-top website Holly had found it on: '*WEE-WEE MADAME! EX-POP STAR HOLLY'S BUS-TING FOR IT IN ST TROPEZ!*' The article went on to crack jokes about how Holly used to '*be famous for being piddled not piddling*' and how she had gone from '*having number ones on iTunes*' to '*having them behind buses on French dirt tracks*'.

A further quick search revealed that countless websites had used the photo, which had indeed first appeared on a French celebrity gossip site before being syndicated worldwide. Whoever had taken it had profited well from Holly being caught short.

'I don't know what I'm more upset about,' said Holly. 'The fact that a photo of me taking a wee is all over the internet or whether the headline decided to call me a Madame. Surely at my age I can still count as a Mademoiselle. I'm only twenty-eight, for God's sake. I shall need to stop sunbathing if it's aging me.'

'You look fine,' said Christophe. 'I've seen much worse photos.'

'Oh, believe you me, doll, so have I. There have been much worse,' said Holly thinking of all the X-rated photos she'd happily posed for. 'I just can't believe that I hardly ever find myself in the papers these days, but the moment I do make a splash it's because I'm literally making a splash.'

'I see what you mean,' grinned Christophe 'But surely, you are a famous person. We have lots of them here in St Tropez. They flock here and all of them pose in every direction because they want to be in the papers. Look at that actress who arrived in the harbour yesterday with all of that ceremony. She only did it because she wanted everybody to notice her. Even if it did end up that she was in the news for the wrong reasons because she caught her adventurer boyfriend with another woman. Isn't that what you all want? To be seen. Maybe not quite like that,' he said, pointing at the iPad, 'but if I did that nobody would care. You do it, and because you are famous, people want to see it. You must like it deep down, non?'

He smiled and placed a small bowl of pistachios on the table alongside her drink. 'You are one of the famous ones, enjoy it,' he smiled, before walking off.

*

Holly Lydon had been described as many things – a wild child, a tearaway, a bitch – and she had lived up to each and every one of those tags. But underneath it all, that was not who she was. Playing Holly Lydon, being the over-the-top pop star, the gobby one, the one with all of the answers – even if they weren't necessarily the right ones – was an easy role for her to play. Because it helped her mask what was really going on inside.

Holly had been an only child. Her mum, Shirley, worked as a barmaid in a pub in one of the rougher areas of Birmingham and it had been a huge surprise to her when at the age of twenty-one she had discovered she was pregnant. A one-night stand with a lorry driver who was just passing through had resulted in a beautiful six-pound, four-ounce baby girl nine months later with a shock of red hair and the most heart-melting of grins. She was called Holly, as she was born on Christmas Eve.

Life was hard for Shirley, and even though she did everything she could to make sure that Holly was clothed, fed and watered, money was always tight. There were no grandparents to speak of as Shirley's dad was dead and her mother, a deeply religious lady, could not allow herself to see past the fact that Holly was born out of wedlock. A bastard child, as she called her. All contact between Shirley and her mother was broken, the mother-daughter bond far greater between her and Holly.

Holly grew up in the tiny flat above the pub where her mother continued to work. There were a few men in Shirley's life but none of them seemed to stick around long enough for Holly to consider them a potential dad. It was a rarity if a man stuck around for longer than a month. Holly remembered a handful of them as being pleasant, buying her the odd gift, a My Little Pony or a doll to keep her amused while her mother worked, but somehow none of the relationships lasted. Until Uncle Warren.

Warren was a construction worker from a local building firm. He had come to the pub to undertake some work on the outside structure. Shirley had served him and his workmates tea, their eyes had met and they had fallen for each other. It was less than six weeks before Warren, a handsome vision of muscles and football tattoos supporting his beloved Birmingham City FC, moved into the flat with Shirley and an eleven-year-old Holly.

At first everything was as it should be. Warren was attentive, caring and a good boyfriend to Shirley. But the ease and temptation of being under the same roof as so much alcohol became too much. Warren would spend his evenings propping up the bar, watching his girlfriend in action. She was popular with the punters and Warren, fuelled by the beer after demanding that Shirley freely serve him, would often become jealous as he saw her professionally flirting with other customers. Often, he would start a fight and Shirley and her fellow bar-workers would have to break it up and then Shirley would end up putting a completely hammered Warren to bed. Holly would hear the rows as she tried to sleep in her bedroom, sometimes blocking out their arguments with her headphones and singing along to her favourite tunes. If there was one thing that Holly could do, it was sing. Her schoolwork was poor, but the words that erupted from her soul as she sang along to Robbie Williams and All Saints were beyond A-plus. Singing was her escape from what was happening on the other side of her bedroom door.

But then came the night when her bedroom door was opened.

Warren had been drinking again. This time in the flat. Shirley was out for the night, having a few well-deserved hours away from the grind of working behind the bar. Holly had spent the night in her room pretending to be Janet Jackson in front of her mirror and playing with toys. By 10 p.m. she had put herself to bed.

She woke up to the feeling of a hand over her mouth. It was rough and big. Warren. She could see his face in the half-light that shone into the room from the ajar bedroom door. She could feel her heart beating loudly inside her as she tried to understand what was happening. The smell of beer and ciga-rettes was strong on his breath and Holly tried to scream as she realised that his grip was hurting her. The scream was silenced by his hand.

Warren yanked back the duvet, revealing Holly's body. She wore pyjamas but still the air felt cold against her.

The next five minutes were the most frightening that Holly had ever experienced. Warren pulled her pyjama bottoms down and let his calloused hand roam freely across her body, the other one still stifling any noise that she attempted to make. He was rough and his hands travelled to sacred places that even her own had never been. She could feel the tears running from her eyes as he finished his exploration. She could feel the hurt coming from her lower body. A pain that she suspected would never go away. Any feelings of love or respect that she had once felt for Warren vanished into thin air as he bent his face close to hers and whispered menacingly, 'If you tell your mother about this, then I will kill you both.'

She never did tell Shirley. She couldn't. She was scared that Warren would be true to his word and silence them both. The abuse happened on a few occasions, every time as painful as the last. But Holly's love for her mother somehow gave her the strength to deal with it. It was horrendous, but the thought of Warren killing, or even harming her mother, was incomprehen-sible.

Holly was fourteen when she came home from school to hear from her mother that Warren had died of a sudden heart attack at work. She wasn't sorry. Shirley, however, was beyond destroyed, and even though a piece of Holly wanted to share with her mother what an abusive and vile man Warren had been, hearing her mother's tears of misery night after night meant that she never could. Holly needed to be strong, to not be the scared little girl she was when she was trapped in the bedroom with Warren. She needed to be there for her mother, to help her through everything, her most reliable crutch. Just like she had always been for Holly. Holly dug deep to find the strength. She burrowed into her core to find another Holly, one who would never let herself be scared and vulnerable and meek again.

It was her singing that gave Holly the force and the confidence to be as strong as she needed to be. When Crazy Sour came along and Holly the pop star was born, it was exactly what she had been looking for. Now she was somebody as far removed from the scared little girl in the bedroom as she could possibly be.

She loved playing the pop star, being the typical firecracker that people expected her to be. Bland was boring. Indifference insignificant. Which is why she immersed herself in a world of drugs and drink. That was what worldwide stars did. They went off the rails. Wasn't it the late Prince who said 'Let's Go Crazy'? Well, Prince had it right – that's what Holly was going to do.

Drugs, drink and men helped her forget. She would never have to be vulnerable for a man again. With money came power, and with power came the ability to be on top, and not just in the bedroom. Men were her playthings. They loved her. And she loved them loving her. It made her feel that her body was a thing of beauty, not a place for abuse.

Then Crazy Sour imploded, a conclusion that was forced upon her. Did she cause it? But wasn't that what the badass one was supposed to do? And then it was on to her next role. The controlling of men as a call girl. Sex had become something glorious to Holly, not something dirty and to be feared. It worked for her, not her for it. But even though her life had been a whirlwind of orgiastic, hedonistic action, Holly had somehow managed to keep a fairly low profile as far as the press were concerned post-Crazy Sour. Secrecy was paramount in all areas. After nearly having her fingers burned with the story about the boot-licking MP and the dog bowl full of champagne, Holly was careful to keep her life as private as possible. It was almost as if call girl Holly was another part of her that she didn't want to admit to. She wasn't ashamed of anything she had done in her life, and her high-class activities around the globe had certainly brought in the cash in multi-zeros for a while, but Holly the pop star, Holly the call girl and Holly the loving daughter were three different people.

Clients may have seen her spreading her legs and enticing them to sample the pleasures of her sex, fans may have seen her giving it her all on stage and gyrating with a slick confidence to the Crazy Sour songs, but what none of them saw was the scared little girl still deep inside her. The girl who had faced fear full on, in that bedroom with Uncle Warren. The one underneath the act. The one who, despite her role in Crazy Sour and the sordid nature of her post-pop activities, was not the column-inch-seeking missile of a bitch that people portrayed her as.

She sometimes questioned her life choices. Why carry on being a prostitute? That was what she was, after all. But she couldn't stop herself. Sex was easy money. And being in control of her own body and making it work for her was still the best way to drown out the fears of the abuse she had suffered from Warren.

And she needed the money. Now more than ever. So yet again Holly Lydon would have to play an act. To be the super-bitch and extort the money she needed to see herself right. And not just her. Shirley too. Another secret. Another thing hidden from the press. Another moment of privacy. Holly could never let her down.

*

'Another drink? Hey, are you okay?' It was Christophe's voice that brought Holly out of her thoughts about her mother and what she needed to do. A tear was rolling down her cheek.

Holly wiped the tear away and painted on a smile. 'Never give me gin,' she bluffed. 'Always makes me sad. Yeah, I'll have a drink, please. Just a cranberry juice, I think.'

'Sure.' Christophe headed back to the bar.

Holly tried to gather her thoughts. What had Christophe said before, about the actress arriving at the harbour in St Tropez and finding her adventurer boyfriend with another woman? Adventurer? It couldn't be, could it? She googled a few key words and sure enough up popped the *La Riviera News* story about Rosita, Missy and the man she had thought it might be. Leland.

Holly read it with relish. Leland Franklin – now there was a flashback she hadn't planned on. She cast her mind back to their first encounter. It must have been Brazil. Yes, of course, the charity event at the Iguazu Falls. Once a rogue, always a rogue, it seemed. Another woman gets her fingers burned. When would the female of the species learn?

'Well, if there isn't a familiar face at every turn in this town this week,' said a voice from in front of her. 'Are you in town for my blessed brother as well?'

Holly looked up from her iPad to find the man himself standing there. A vision of thick blond hair and those blue eyes.

'Hello, Leland,' she said, suddenly a little flustered. Her skin prickled. It was the way he had always made her feel.

CHAPTER 19

Dexter Franklin had deliberately kept his distance from his special guests. Even though he was paying for their stay in St Tropez and was positively revelling in the fact that Rosita, Holly, Mew, DC and *dear brother* Leland were all within pebble-tossing distance of his new venture, he didn't really want to see any of them until the big opening night itself. And that was a mere forty-eight hours away. Trésor was ready to be launched and not a gemstone from the Moroccan-themed interior was an inch out of place.

'It's looking good, very glamorous in an *Aladdin* sort of way,' remarked the waitress coming from the kitchen into the main area of the restaurant. 'You should be very proud of yourself. St Tropez has nothing like this. You have Kyoto for sushi and Thai, Le Grand Café for Asiatic and Le Byblos for light bites, but this, Mr Franklin, is definitely going to rock this town into a whole new gastronomic vibe. I think you should fly in on a magic carpet for the opening night and wear nothing but harem pants and a waistcoat. Show off that six pack and hairy chest of yours.'

'Oh, you think so, do you, Toni? Well, I think that would be a little crass given the prices we're charging in this town. People want haute cuisine, not high jinks, and please drop the Mr Franklin. It's not like we haven't, er… *met* before.'

Indeed they had done so much more than just meeting. Toni was the petite blonde that Dexter had slept with in the bar a few weeks earlier. Her sexual skills were as polished as her waitressing and when Dexter had offered her the chance to come and work at Trésor as one of his launch team she had jumped at the chance. Toni had also jumped into bed with the celebrity chef on numerous occasions, hence her detailed knowledge of Dexter Franklin's six-pack and hairy chest. It was a job that she was very much enjoying – in more ways than one.

'And I'm so glad we did,' she smiled. 'This restaurant will be amazing. I have no doubt. The food will be just incredible, the company will be wonderful and the host will be the talk of the town.'

'I hope so,' remarked Dexter, taking Toni in his arms and allowing his lips to find hers, feeling himself rise to attention inside his chef's uniform pants. Dexter was a stickler for always wearing his whites at work, even when he wasn't cooking, and it would be those that he'd be sporting for his opening night, not some dodgy harem pants, even if his latest conquest did think it would be a cute idea.

The waitress pulled away from Dexter, more through necessity than want. She was enjoying the feeling of his tongue inside her mouth, his lips against hers and the hardness of his erection pressing into her, but there was work to do and top restaurants did not miraculously open by themselves without a great deal of planning. 'Hold on, Dexter. I have things I need to do.'

'Can't you include *me* in that list?' he smiled.

'Not for now, *non*. I want to work out who is sitting where. I trust you have a seating chart?'

Dexter begrudgingly let her loose from his arms. She was right, there were still things that needed to be arranged. And a seating plan was definitely one of them.

Dexter considered his options. The opening night would be busy. The press would be there and also some of the major play-

ers of the St Tropez world. But they were merely supporting
cast to the main 'stars' themselves. There were only a few who
would be invited to the top table, annexed in a small offshoot
of the restaurant, away from the prying eyes of others in a space
cocooned with the finest Moroccan silks. They were here for a
reason and that was for Dexter to have his say. Whether they
liked it or not. Dinner was to be served with an extra serving
of enjoyment as far as Dexter was concerned. His enjoyment. It
was time for payback.

He took the waitress by the hand and led her to the private
room where his special guests would be seated. He counted the
places at the table. Five. Perfect. Plus a place for himself. That
was very important. And maybe room for one more too, if need
be. That would be just as important. Perfect in fact.

He read the guest list of the five names to the waitress and
stated where they were to be seated. She wrote the names down
in the order specified by Dexter. The last name on the list was
Holly Lydon.

'Are you okay with all of that, then?' asked Dexter. 'I'll have
to leave you to it for a while as I'm being interviewed by the local press about the opening night. They've been invited, so it's
the least I can do. I'm popping down to Sénéquier for the interview. You can reach me on my mobile if you need anything else.'

'No problem,' said Toni. 'I'll busy myself here. I'm thrilled
you're trusting me with your special guests' room. Will I be serving them on the night? You have a huge team of waiters ready
to go, after all.'

'Yes, but none as sexy as you. But I'll make sure you have
help,' said Dexter, before leaving her alone.

The waitress started walking around the oval table that filled
the centre of the room. She ran her hand along the silk curtains
that covered the walls as she did so. As she passed from chair to

chair she spoke the names of those who would be sitting there. 'So Mew Stanton is here, then Leland Franklin next to her, then DC Riding at the end of the table. Rosita Velázquez will be seated here and finally Holly Lydon will find herself here.'

Toni clapped her hands excitedly and reached into her apron pocket to pull out her phone. She clicked on the Photos icon and scrolled through a few of the pictures. They were all of Holly Lydon squatting behind the bus. The very photos that had now been blitzed all over the net. 'Oh, I'm glad you're coming. I shall look forward to seeing you again, Miss Lydon. Or should I call you Sharon, from the toothpaste factory?' She clicked the phone off and dropped it back into her pocket.

CHAPTER 20

DC Riding was wandering through the reception at Arlequin, contemplating booking his much-wanted massage, when he first spotted him. Six foot three, perhaps, very muscular and possessing a close-cropped skinhead. He was carrying a holdall with him, yet somehow he didn't look as if he was checking into the hotel. He wore a tight T-shirt to show every sinewy part of his body in full mouth-watering glory. His trousers, a shiny pair of black jeans, unusual given the glorious weather, were also incredibly well packed and DC couldn't help but stare at the impressive bulge at the centre of them. Was it his imagination or was the man actually staring right back at him and openly smiling? If DC didn't know any different, he would say that he was giving him the come-on.

Suddenly the penny dropped. Of course, the man was a rent boy.

DC smiled back, a little awkwardly. He needn't have worried, as the man returned a huge grin and winked at DC.

The critic looked at his watch. It was early afternoon. He had told Olivia, Mew and Giuseppe that he might join them on an afternoon jaunt to Ramatuelle, one of the local villages, but quite frankly the history and quaint Gallic charm of a mountain village could shove itself into oblivion. His afternoon was suddenly planning itself out nicely. And seeing as he had the money to pay for it, which hadn't always been the case, DC could see that the only steps he'd be taking this afternoon would not be through the windy streets of Ramatuelle, but to the delights of his hotel suite, accompanied by his new beau.

With a swish of his kaftan, DC flashed his best come-hither smile and sashayed his way to the lift. As the door opened and he stepped inside he turned to see the man standing right behind him.

'Hello,' smirked DC.

'Bonjour,' said the man.

DC had barely had a chance to say '*vive la France*' before their lips met and the man pulled DC roughly towards him. The critic swooned as the elevator door closed and whirred into action.

*

Dexter Franklin had been grilled by sweeter journalists than Fabienne Delacroix in his time. She was a little brusque and seemed totally against everything that St Tropez represented. Her sensible knee-length skirt and grey blouse, complete with a smattering of cat hair, hardly screamed couture. And as for the riches, Fabienne looked like she didn't have enough for even a decent hairstyle and make-up. And what about the celebrity? It was clear that the famous playboys and glitterati of St Tropez were not top of Fabienne's '*joyeux Noël*' list. He allowed the sour Fabienne to question him as to why he was opening another overpriced restaurant that only the elite could afford, about whether he intended to stay in St Tropez or just pocket the rewards that the restaurant would doubtless make and then run off somewhere else, and why he had chosen the celebrities he had to attend the opening night and whether they were the only ones available. Dexter, who had been grilled by everyone from Piers Morgan through to Ellen DeGeneres in his time, couldn't wait to answer.

'Trésor will be competitively priced and offers a style of food that I saw lacking in St Tropez. I will be hands-on with my restaurant for the foreseeable future, but naturally I will be looking to carry on with my chain of restaurants by opening others in different places. The celebrities coming are all here for different reasons but they all mean something special to me and I am so pleased that they will be there to share the evening.'

Fabienne noted everything down in a pad as he spoke, as well as recording it on a machine placed between them on the table at Sénéquier. A bottle of rose wine, now half empty, mostly drunk by Dexter, stood alongside it.

'I trust you will be there too,' said Dexter. 'I'd like you to try the food.'

Her answer surprised him. 'I can't wait to come. I'll be honest, I'm not a fan of celebrities, but I do like beautifully cooked food and even though I have no love of so-called "celebrity chefs" I have read enough about you to know that you have studied hard and probably deserve the respect you have. Even though I am sure I will find the likes of Rosita Velázquez and Leland Franklin totally mind-numbing, I shall be pleased to come along and sample what is on offer. And, I have to admit, I took great delight in writing about them in today's paper. Did you see Rosita's arrival on the yacht yesterday?'

'No, I didn't have the pleasure,' lied Dexter.

A sudden thought occurred to the reporter. 'I guess I shouldn't be talking about your brother like that. Sorry. I am sure he is a very nice person.' It was now Fabienne's turn to lie.

'No worries. Leland and I have had a few differences over the years. What siblings don't?' He sighed, keen to change the subject. 'So I guess I'll see you at the opening night.'

He watched as Fabienne snapped shut her pad, clicked off the recorder and placed them both in her bag. She held out her hand for Dexter to shake.

'Thank you for your time, Mr Franklin. I shall see you in a few days. This interview will be in the paper and online tomorrow,' said Fabienne, before heading off along the walkway at the front of the port.

Dexter watched her go as he continued with his wine. He liked the bizarre Fabienne Delacroix. She was very opinionated, totally abrupt and spoke before thinking. She also obviously hated anyone who was famous and in her opinion not in possession of a modicum of talent. Plus, she liked good food – and that he could guarantee.

He thought she was perfect. The perfect addition to his plan for the opening night. He'd considered she might be when he'd spotted her at Rosita's landing the day before.

*

The contents of the holdall Mr Muscle Man had been carrying had come as a surprise to someone of even DC's broad mind. The clunk as it hit the lift floor should have been a good indicator that there was definitely something quite extraordinarily heavy and made of metal inside it. It was one of the hugest butt plugs that DC had ever seen. And he had been privy to a fair few during his forty-three years on earth.

'My word, dear boy, was that a traffic cone in a former life?' remarked a now naked DC as the equally naked rent boy – Henri – reached into his holdall and pulled out the sex toy. A pile of bank notes sat on the bedside table, DC's payment in advance for Henri's time.

'I like to play, what can I say?' answered Henri, his cock bouncing upwards towards his chiselled abs.

'Oh, so do I,' slavered DC.

Henri continued to pull out an array of items from his holdall. Long lengths of blue rope, bondage tape, nipple clamps.

The bag appeared to be bottomless, a Mary Poppins bag for the sexually depraved, able to store much more than at first seemed feasible.

DC's eyes widened with every reveal. 'Oh, Henri, how delectable. I'll just go and freshen up and I'll be right back.'

DC moved from the bed and headed to the bathroom. When he returned a few minutes later, Henri had laid everything out on the floor and was wearing nothing except two leather wrist cuffs and a bondage mask over the top half of his face. In one of his hands he carried a paddle, which he slapped with considerable force against his other hand. There were two white tablets on the bedside table alongside the cash.

'Ready to play? There's some E there if you want it. My treat.'

DC didn't need asking twice, especially when everything sounded even more gloriously filthy and sexual when said in a rich French accent. Jumping gleefully and a little more vigorously than maybe a man of his size should really dare to, DC popped the pill in his mouth, swallowed it and fell onto the bed face down, placing his hands behind his back, ready to give himself up to the pleasures of the flesh. Both the bed and his buttocks were still wobbling as Henri began to tie him up.

*

It was three hours later when Henri left, having pocketed the money and shown DC a rather fabulous time with his holdall of tricks. DC, who was very much still out of his head from the drug, waved the rent boy goodbye as he vacated his suite.

'Now that was so much better than a trip to some peasant-laden mountain village,' he said before crashing out, his body a mixture of sore and satisfied.

Just like Dexter, he too had experienced the perfect meeting.

CHAPTER 21

Rosita Velázquez was far from happy.

'Read my lips and they will tell you. I will not have that man flaunt his latest slutty *conchita* in front of everybody. Have you seen the papers? And it will be all over the websites and blogs too. Him and some woman who is already famous for sleeping her trampy ass across the States – and now she manages to grab the headlines instead of me. So much for my perfect pre-Cannes arrival. Enough is enough.'

The actress tossed the newspaper across the table to Tinks as the two women sipped on multi-coloured cocktails on the top deck of Rosita's fan's superyacht. Despite only having asked her fan if she and her team could 'borrow' the yacht for her big entrance into St Tropez the day before, she had not yet seen fit to disembark the vessel for good. She had other things on her mind.

Tinks picked up the paper and scanned the headline. She winced as she read the words. 'Yep, this Fabienne Delacroix is certainly not your biggest fan, is she?' she said, reading the article's byline.

'I am third billing, for fuck's sake,' snapped Rosita, hating the fact that in such a damning article she didn't even warrant the gold or silver medal. 'Leland is called a TV superstar, that piece of skank he was with is called infamous and what do I end up with? I am "ridiculous". If I ever meet the stupid journalist behind that article I swear to God I will hold her down and force-feed her a bucket of escargot. Shells and everything. I will make the woman choke and never forget the day that she wronged Rosita Velázquez.'

'You tell her,' replied Tinks, slightly amused by Rosita's rant. 'She doesn't know who she's messing with. Now, if you've finished that cocktail, let's reapply your lipstick and you can head out into St Tropez and turn some heads. Even if your entrance yesterday didn't go quite to plan, you can still play on the fact that Leland is here and you are still his girlfriend. Work the brand. Do a vintage Brangelina, despite how that particular star pairing ended. My advice is to keep holding up that beautiful face of yours and don't let anyone know that this stupid article has gotten under your skin.'

Rosita knew that Tinks was right. When she had confronted Leland the day before as to why he was actually in St Tropez, she knew that his being there could only be to her advantage, even if the landing was supposed to have been her special moment and hers alone. They would both be at the opening of Dexter's restaurant together, and in the run-up to Cannes, being seen on the arm of her multi-syndicated man was the perfect solution. She just needed to make him, and the rest of St Tropez, forget about Missy fucking Terranova. Which was why she was heading out into the town. She had booked herself an appointment with Dior to make sure that she looked not a cent short of a million euros for the rest of her stay. A stay that would see her decamp to the Arlequin hotel booked by Dexter for her. It had already occurred to her that he had invited both her and Leland separately, which was an odd thing to do. Maybe he had correctly guessed that neither of them would actually bother telling the other – hardly surprising, given what had occurred between them all in the past. A thought of Dexter flitted across her mind. It made her smile.

Rosita leant forward to allow Tinks to reapply her Mac lipstick. The shade was a pretty plum called Rebel, the perfect complement to her olive skin tones and her rich, jet-black hair.

Tinks's words were running through her head as the lipstick was applied. Tinks was right: Fabienne Delacroix didn't know who she was messing with. Neither did Missy Terranova. That would have to change. As would the fact that the world outside of her native Brazil didn't seem to know who Rosita was at all. Maybe the next few days in the company of the Franklin brothers could change that.

As Rosita left the yacht a few minutes later and headed across the port in the direction of Dior, she was determined that everything was about to change. She looked immaculate – her hair tied back, her make-up polished. A floaty halter maxi dress, a pair of Gianvito Rossi strappy sandals and an oversized pair of Tom Ford sunglasses completed the look. No, despite a shaky start Rosita was determined that St Tropez and the run-up to the Cannes Film Festival would work for her. What was the saying? *Start where you are, use what you have, do what you can.* Well, Rosita was in the jet-set capital of Europe, she had the looks, ambition and ruthless drive to not let anything or anyone stand in her way and she was determined to do exactly what was required to make sure that she wouldn't be anything less than gold-medal position from now on. Her days of being nearly there but not quite would have to end soon.

As Rosita arrived at Dior, her credit card ready for a serious workout, thoughts of both Leland and Dexter kept flip-flopping in her mind. The thought made her happier than she had been all day.

CHAPTER 22

Iguazu Falls, Brazil, five years earlier...

Holly needed to take her mind off things. She'd had yet another row with Mew and Leonie and they hadn't even been on stage yet. Mew had been in a bad mood ever since Crazy Sour had arrived in Brazil for the charity event they were singing at. She was biting everyone's heads off, which was odd, seeing as their location, the impressive Iguazu Falls, was said to be one of the most natural and peaceful wonders of the world. Even Holly had been impressed when she'd seen them. Leonie had loved them too, literally trying to tell anyone and everyone about the legends and spirits behind the falls on repeat. That was why she and Holly had argued. Despite being steeped in mystery and spirit, the only mystery Holly had been interested in solving was where she could find a decent drink backstage in the specially built marquee. She was bored and needed a livener. That was the only spirit she needed, despite Leonie's storytelling.

That was the trouble with headlining. You had to wait until the end of the night to actually go on stage and perform. And Holly was becoming impatient. She wanted a drink and perhaps a little pick-me-up to revive her flagging spirit. Maybe something powdery, white and ready to snort. That would be perfection. But backstage at a charity event all about the glory of nature and the preservation of lush forestation and wildlife was not exactly the best place to try and track down a bag of an illegal class-A substance. The entire backstage bar area at the event was all about drinks infused with guarana, and virgin cocktails with more leaves and healthy greenery spilling out of them than there was actual drink. Holly was not impressed.

She'd be glad to get out of this godforsaken country. This event was certainly becoming a real mind-fuck. Too much pain at every turn. Holly's brain was frazzled. And the lack of excitement of any kind backstage was not helping.

She checked her watch. Another ninety minutes until she and the girls were due to perform. She needed to find something to occupy her time, to keep her busy, otherwise she'd be raiding the nearest medicine cabinet and chopping up paracetamol in an attempt to gain some kind of high.

Was there anybody here she could try and score from? She looked at the people gathered around the wooden benches and tables in the bar area. One of the show's hosts, reality star Nova Chevalier, was holding court with three of the stars from the event line-up. Holly loved Nova's massive TV show *Champagne Supernova*, and knew that somebody of her huge and instantly recognisable fame would not be dealing in bags of nose candy. What about the people with her? One was some Brazilian actress Holly didn't know but the crowd had gone wild for. Then there was the devilishly handsome male singer, Matthew, from Madhen, the band that had performed earlier in the evening. Holly had watched him strutting his funky, feisty stuff on the charity stage and liked what she saw. His performance was wild and electric. She had spoken to him and the pair had posed for selfies after the band had finished their set. He'd been telling her about his attempt to represent his home country, the UK, in the Eurovision Song Contest. It hadn't quite happened, his song not having been picked by the public. Holly shared her own tale of how Crazy Sour had been asked to do the same early in their career but thankfully, as far as she was concerned, the *nul points* idea never got past mere suggestion. She liked Matthew a lot and found him hugely entertaining but she couldn't consider him for her current needs. And besides, he seemed to be fawning all over Nova – obviously a big fan of her show too.

The other person in the group was Jemma Louisiana, the country and western sensation who'd already performed. She was sugary sweet and Holly doubted if she housed anything more exciting in her moleskin trouser pockets than the plectrum she used to pluck her guitar.

On the drink and drugs front Holly was drawing a blank. There were a few event workers and backing dancers milling around the bar area but none of them looked like the words 'blitzed', 'trashed' or 'nose candy' would ever be in their vocabulary. It was seriously looking like her desire for something stronger than a mocktail caipirinha would have to wait until she'd passed border patrol and quit the country. For a nation so close to Colombia, Brazil was becoming a major drag.

Defeated, Holly turned to leave the bar area and return to her dressing room. Maybe a quick snooze before the show would stem her want for narcotics. As she turned she collided with a man who was just entering the bar. He was considerably taller than her and his body was solid as she ran into him, but all thoughts of his obviously well-muscled physique went out of the window as she took in the rather garish design of his shirt, a green and pink mass of what appeared to be swordfish and some kind of flower. They looked like the ones she had given to her mum, Shirley, in a large bouquet once when she had gone to visit her. If she remembered rightly they were called hibiscus. Her mother loved them. Said they were her favourite. The shirt was loud, proud and as far as Holly was concerned, shouldn't have been allowed. It was retina-burning in its colour.

Not afraid to open her mouth, Holly was about to let the wearer know in no uncertain terms that his taste was beyond dodgy, but stopped herself as her eyes drifted to the face above the shirt. It was as beautiful as his choice in clothing was ugly. His eyes were the bluest she had ever encountered and his thick blond hair flopped in a swirl of delight across his forehead as he looked down at Holly. A spark of something in his eyes as he smiled at her, scanned her ample chest and said sorry hinted that it was more than mere apology.

For a second or two there was silence, neither of them saying a word, both of them taking in what they were looking at. It was Holly who crumbled first.

'I know you… You were on stage earlier, weren't you? You're that adventurer guy, I've watched your stuff online. You're totally mental.' The words poured from her mouth as she realised who she was speaking to.

'Thanks… I think,' laughed the man towering over her. 'And yes, I am. I'm Leland Franklin. I'm here to talk about Brazilian forestation. And as for mental… I'll let you decide on that one.'

Holly couldn't stop looking deep into his baby blues as he spoke. They were hypnotic.

'I knew it. I watch you online. I'm Holly. I even subscribe to your YouTube channel,' said Holly.

'You and about three million others,' said Leland dryly. 'So you like what I do then?'

'Like, yeah!' exclaimed Holly, unable to hide the smile that was painted across her face. 'I was watching a video of you wing-suiting in Florida yesterday. It was incredible.'

Leland was loving the fact that the red-haired beauty in front of him was already a fan. He had been feeling pretty stressed since arriving in Brazil and the adulation from the young woman in front of him was much needed.

'That's where I've just come from. That's the latest video. I'm pleased you liked it. I was stoked to be doing it. I'm going to try and abseil down the Iguazu canyon while I'm here. You should try it with me. I'd love to have a pop star on board – especially such an attractive one.'

It dawned on Holly that obviously Leland recognised her too. The fact pleased her. The thought of abseiling down some of the most dangerous waterfalls in the world didn't. 'So, you're a Crazy Sour fan, eh? I never knew our tunes were so popular with your macho, intrepid explorer types. Although I think I'll pass on the abseiling, cheers. That said, me and the girls did take a boat ride out into the spray of the waters today to do some interviews, which was great fun. We were soaked but I loved it. But I couldn't suspend myself on a rope halfway up a cliff. That would freak me out.'

'Scared of heights, eh?' enquired Leland. Even though the two of them were now fully engaged in conversation, the close proximity between them from when they had bumped into each other had hardly widened at all. They were evidently enjoying being within breathing distance of each other.

'I prefer highs of another kind,' said Holly, the words laced with rebellion. She was determined to let Leland know that she was not as pure as the band's image and pop music might suggest. 'But I would love to do something with you.'

'Oh really?' He raised an eyebrow as she asked, understanding her meaning. 'Well, maybe you'd like to discuss joining me on one of my videos and we can make sure that you keep your feet firmly on the ground – or at least not too far into the air. It's good to get a little high, isn't it?'

As first meetings went, Leland Franklin was rapidly becoming her perfect man. He was as suggestive and flirtatious as she was. She knew that she'd made some bad partner choices in her time, but something told her that going with the flow with the adventurer would definitely be worthwhile.

'I'd like that. Do you have time now?' she asked. 'I'm not due on stage for a bit and we could bang out some details in my dressing room. I have one to myself.' Holly felt a frisson of sexual electricity radiate from between her legs at the thought of Leland joining her.

Would he agree?

As they entered her dressing room less than a minute later she had her answer. They were no sooner inside than Leland reached into his pocket and pulled out a small, clear bag of cocaine. Holly's eyes lit up.

'And there was me thinking that a man like you would be all healthy, surviving in the wilderness on a diet of rainwater and witchetty grubs.'

'I like to live and play hard. In all areas of life. And when it comes to danger, I like experiencing it in as many different ways as possible. Whether I'm halfway up Everest or alone with a very attractive woman in her dressing room.'

He stepped towards her, and before she had a chance to refuse, Holly felt his lips find hers.

For a second they lost themselves in the heat of the moment, allowing their hands and mouths to explore each other. They only parted to let Leland move to the counter and tip out the contents of the bag. There was enough powder to form two fat lines. As she watched the adventurer chop them into straight rows, Holly pulled her T-shirt over her head and revealed the balconette bra she was wearing underneath. Leland showed his approval, his eyes widening in delight as he caught sight of her in the mirror. He rolled a note, leant over to snort the powder and handed the money to Holly. She savoured the sensation as the powder shot up her nostril and hit the back of her throat.

Her lips found Leland's again and she moved her hands down to his belt buckle to free what was evidently a large and thick erection that had grown to a full, impressive length within his trousers.

Holly sunk to her knees as she undid the zip and freed his member. She took Leland's cock in one hand and guided it towards her mouth. She let her tongue explore its full length as he slid it as far into her throat as he could. Given its size, Holly's expert ability to deep throat was much needed. Lost in rapture at what was going on between his legs, Leland reached out to steady himself against the wall. His hand landed on one of the posters detailing the event and in his ecstasy at the fellatio he was receiving he pulled it from the wall. It fell to the ground alongside Holly.

As she continued to enjoy his rod, Leland pulled his shirt over his head and also dropped it to the floor. It fell alongside the poster. The sight of the two things lying there momentarily distracted Holly from the sexual performance she was giving and she stopped sucking his cock.

'Don't stop. That was blissful,' said Leland. He placed his hands either side of Holly's head and attempted to guide her mouth back to his aching member, eager for her to continue. He could feel his desire rising rapidly. This woman could definitely suck cock.

Holly let out a giggle.

It didn't go unnoticed.

'What's so funny,' said Leland, a little put off.

'At least your taste in women and music is a lot better than your taste in fashion. That shirt is hideous!'

Leland looked at the shirt and the poster alongside it. The garment had fallen across the guest list of those attending. His own name, a late addition, was nowhere to be seen.

'Well, forgive me if we don't have Armani up Mount Kilimanjaro or Prada in the Gobi Desert. And my taste in women isn't always so fabulous either. And as for my taste in music, I think it was you who said I was a Crazy Sour fan, not me. I'm more of a Coldplay kind of man. Now suck.'

He guided Holly's mouth back to his member as swiftly as he could. A few minutes later he was spent.

CHAPTER 23

The village of Ramatuelle might have only been a twenty-minute car journey from the melting pot of glamour that was St Tropez, but it may as well have been a thousand galaxies away. The difference between the heaving celeb-soaked lifestyle and continual bumper-to-bumper traffic of St Tropez and the picturesque serenity of the medieval village nestled in the mountains above the millionaire's playground was extreme. And a very welcome find for Olivia Rhodes. It brought with it an inner peace and tranquillity that the jet-set madness of Tropez could never deliver.

The only thing that wasn't welcome for the publisher was the fact that her cab ride there had been shared by both Mew Stanton and her latest friend, Giuseppe. And it was Giuseppe who was rapidly becoming the annoying wasp in the honeypot of adventure and potential that Olivia had envisaged when she had first offered herself up to join Mew in the South of France.

As the three of them descended from their cab at the parking area just outside the tiny village, Olivia heaved a sigh of relief. The last twenty minutes had seen her, Mew and the Italian pilot all squashed into the back seat of their transportation. By the time the three of them had reached their destination at the village, 130 metres above the glorious Bay of Pampelonne, Olivia was fit to burst.

Her annoyance was due to the fact that both Mew and Giuseppe seemed to be oblivious to her, as Mew adjusted her shorts back into position and Giuseppe lit up a cigarette on vacating the cab.

'Well, that was a fabulous ride,' grinned Mew. 'Good job I'm not wearing a skirt.'

Giuseppe grinned back. He had spent the entire journey running his hands along Mew's legs and attempting to guide his fingers underneath the hemline of Mew's shorts. His titillation had only been stopped by firstly the tightness of the fabric and secondly by the constant tutting of Olivia as she spied what he was trying to do to the object of her own affections. He and Mew had spent most of the journey noisily locking lips as well, every action seeming to rub salt into Olivia's ever-growing wound as she realised that her fantasy of being with Mew was never going to happen. A fact that she was both brutally and sadly aware of.

As the sun beat down overhead and the three of them walked up an incline leading them into the main village itself, Olivia knew that it wasn't just the increasing temperature of the day that was causing her to become hot under the collar. It was the fact that the woman that she found herself fantasising about more and more didn't seem to even notice that she existed, unless she was informing her about book sales and royalty cheques. And to watch her being slavered all over by the machismo-packed Giuseppe was beginning to irk Olivia deeply.

'So when are you going back to your day job then, Giuseppe? Surely celebrities can't fly into St Tropez all by themselves, can they?'

Giuseppe gave a wry smile. He could see that Olivia had more than just a passing crush on Mew, and it amused him. The woman positively panted with desire each time Mew so much as tapped a fingernail.

'The owner of the helicopter company knows that I work hard and I am due some time off, so I asked if I could have a few days now. It does seem the ideal time to show you ladies the attractions of the area and to make sure you have a good time.'

'You are certainly doing that,' grinned Mew, squeezing Giuseppe's backside as they walked.

Olivia watched Mew do it. The action incensed her more than she dared show. How could Mew be so stupid? All Giuseppe wanted was sex and a free hotel room in five-star St Tropez luxury, for God's sake. A quick fling with a woman who was more than happy to pay for his services by allowing him to share her Arlequin room. Olivia bet he did it all the time. Mew was probably the latest of a long line of women. Young, silly, vulnerable women who experienced one flash of the Italian pilot's dazzling smile and crumbled into his arms and into his bed in a heartbeat. The very thought of it incensed Olivia. How dare he take advantage? Mew deserved better.

'Have you not got a wife or girlfriend to go back to?' snapped Olivia. 'Won't she be missing you?'

Mew stepped in, annoyed by what she was hearing.

'Do you see a wedding ring on his left hand, Olivia? I don't. And even if there was, does it really matter? I'm having some fun and that's all that counts. It's been a while since I had somebody sexy to play with.' She winked at Giuseppe as she spoke. The thought crossed her mind that the last man she had fallen for was Dexter Franklin. She pushed it to one side. 'So lay off Giuseppe, why don't you. It's my choice to have him here and nobody else's. He's making me happy. That okay?'

Giuseppe expelled a cloud of smoke from his cigarette and flicked the butt into the gutter at the side of the road. He leant in to kiss Mew full on the lips. The cloud of cigarette smoke passed behind the couple and directly into Olivia's face. She let out a cough as she watched them kiss. She wasn't sure what made her feel sicker: the dark, horrid smell of the Gauloises, or seeing Mew being such a pushover. Kissing that man's ashtray couldn't have been the most pleasurable thing in the world, but then she suspected that his breath wasn't top of Mew's list of the Italian's attractions.

Olivia was annoyed with herself. She'd been chastised. Told off. Put in her place. And by the woman she idolised. She walked two paces behind the couple as the three of them reached one of the main areas of Ramatuelle, the Place de l'Ormeau. It was a pretty scene, and still fairly quiet given that it was relatively early in the holiday season. Olivia took in the beautiful church with ornate bell tower, narrow streets paved with flowers, a tiled fountain and the obligatory portly old lady sitting on a bench. It was idyllic. Typically French. Shutters on every window. A scene of old world charm.

But Mew was the most beautiful thing of all in Olivia's eyes. Even if that parasite of a man was fawning all over her. It wouldn't last. It never did. Look at Mew's last relationship with Dexter. That had ended so badly. Mew never seemed to learn.

Olivia sat down outside the church and reached into her bag to pull out a bottle of water. It was a hot day and refreshment was needed. She tipped her head back and tried to relax as she felt the coolness of the liquid hit her throat.

Giuseppe would only hurt Mew. Just like Dexter had. Olivia couldn't let that happen. Nothing should upset poor Mew, nothing. Mew deserved better. Mew deserved Olivia.

*

Olivia Rhodes had always been a person who fixated on things. It was why she had always done so well in life. It had started at an early age. When she was about six at school she had decided that her show-and-tell would be the best. To secure this she had secretly and underhandedly managed to lose, damage or ruin all of her challengers' brings. She was clever. Nobody suspected what she was capable of. How Jennifer Greenwood's prize bible had ended up down the toilet nobody knew. The same with Ryan Jackson's collection of stick insects. Who had left the glass lid off their tank? It was a mystery. But Olivia had been behind it all, at the epicentre of destruction but as blameless as could be. Olivia's show-and-tell was the best. Just how it should be.

The same had happened when she had taken up ballroom dancing in her early teens. She was skilled and loved dancing with her friend Jacqui. There was something joyous about dancing with Jacqui and feeling their bodies close to each other that she didn't experience when she danced with one of the few males in their dance group. As boys were few and far between, the teacher was happy for many of the girls to dance with each other. Jacqui and Olivia excelled, and when the group held a competition to find the top partnership, everyone knew it would be between the two young girls and one other couple – Anna and Craig. It would be neck and neck. Olivia couldn't let Anna and Craig win.

On the way to the dance competition a fourteen-year-old Olivia hid behind a dense clump of bushes situated on a busy road outside the dance hall. As Anna wandered past, all smiles and a vision in layers of candyfloss-coloured petticoats, Olivia ran from behind the bush to join Anna and engage her in conversation. As she did so, she allowed her own foot to somehow find itself in front of Anna's leg, accidentally tripping her up. At least, as accidental as a deliberate action can be. Anna never made the competition and returned home, her twisted ankle in bandages, unable to compete. With her main competition out of the way, Olivia and an oblivious Jacqui were awarded the top prize.

Olivia's working life had been just as sneaky, but with the seemingly harmless Olivia never held to account for her own actions. Her first job in a publishing house was as a very junior assistant. Her boss was no more than two years older than her, but she waved her seniority around like a baton twirler and seemed determined to put lowly Olivia in her place as often as she could, sending her on needless errands with increasing regularity. While potential blockbusters were being discussed in boardrooms and foreign deals being made, Olivia would find herself doing cake and coffee runs, being asked to shred pointless documents or, at worst, organising hair and nail appointments for her boss. Over time this began to wear Olivia's patience down and grate at her soul. As had happened many times before, it was at that moment that all sense of reason would desert her and all she could see was the need to erase the object of annoyance.

She seized her opportunity when a work experience student came to work alongside her and her boss. A meeting was arranged to discuss a book that Olivia herself had noticed in the slush pile – the scripts and books that flooded in from unknown writers, often falling by the wayside but occasionally containing a hidden gem. Olivia had read one of them and immediately spotted its promise. On mentioning so to her boss, her thoughts were poo-pooed and pushed to one side. Within forty-eight hours, her boss had called a meeting to talk over 'her latest discovery'. It was the book that Olivia had found. Olivia was not even invited to the meeting and she and the work experience girl were sent to fetch cakes for those attending. Olivia told the work experience girl to pick anything and everything with nuts in it, as her boss was allergic.

As the cakes were served and her boss tucked in, not questioning for one minute that her demands of no nuts would not have been listened to, the offending foodstuff took its effect and within minutes Olivia was arranging an ambulance to take her boss to the nearest hospital. The meeting was put on hiatus for a short while, Olivia offering to chair it as soon as her boss was safely dispatched to accident and emergency. Olivia knew the book inside out and impressed those around with her insightful knowledge of it. She was instrumental in turning the debut author's novel into a multimillion-selling international sensation. It was the book that saw Olivia headhunted to another publishing house, leaving her boss behind.

When an investigation was made as to how the nutty cakes had been served, it was the poor work experience girl who took the blame. Olivia wouldn't let anyone mess with her chances. It was the same in all areas of life. The word no was not a word Olivia liked to have crop up in her vocabulary. Nothing and no one would stand in her way.

*

Mew, Giuseppe and Olivia looked down from their viewpoint at the highest point of Ramatuelle's famous cemetery. After enjoying a crepe and a glass of wine together in one of the village's quaint restaurants, the trio had made their way back to the taxi rank to pick up their ride back to St Tropez. Seeing as they had some time to spare before their transport arrived, it was Olivia, a lover of any kind of place steeped in history, who suggested the short walk to the cemetery. Giuseppe and Mew could not have looked less interested, but seeing as their cab was still a good ten to fifteen minutes away, they had nothing else to do.

'The most visited grave here is the one of Gérard Philipe, a famous actor who died in 1959. His grave is covered in ivy and shaded by a laurel tree. How marvellous,' enthused Olivia, scanning her guide map as the others stared down at the vineyards and fields that stretched out for kilometre after kilometre in front of them. The only thing that separated them from a fairly severe drop into the lush greenery below was a wire fence at waist height.

'Never heard of him,' said Mew. 'Any other famous people here?'

Giuseppe mindlessly flicked yet another cigarette butt into the air and over the edge of the fence. An annoyed Olivia watched it arc through the air and then disappear from view. She felt her jaw tighten.

'No, Mew, not that I can see. Although I did hear from somebody at the hotel that apparently Jackie Collins used to come here, as she adored the serenity.'

'To the cemetery?' asked Mew, not overly enthused.

'No, to Ramatuelle in general. I was told she loved it here. I can't imagine any of that racy action she has in her books happening here though, can you?'

'I could, with me and Giuseppe in residence. There are a few chapels and hidden gateways where we could indulge ourselves in all sorts of mischief.'

Giuseppe pulled Mew towards him to show his agreement, his lips finding hers again. Olivia felt her jaw tighten once more.

'Not in a church please,' added Olivia somewhat stiffly. 'You'd be arrested and placed in the ancient prison here. It has an Arabian style and looks like a Turkish bath, but it was actually a jail built under Napoleon III.' Olivia had her nose back in the guide map. She pushed her glasses up her nose as she spoke, stopping their descent down the slope of perspiration.

'I know who I'd rather be under,' laughed Mew, half-heartedly trying to twist away from Giuseppe.

'Is there any need for that?' seethed Olivia under her breath.

'Let's head back to the hotel and sort that out,' said Giuseppe, leering somewhat. 'The taxi should be here in…' He checked his watch. 'Three minutes.'

'Just enough time for me to nip to the toilet,' said Mew. 'There's a public loo over there. I'm not risking doing a Holly and squatting down behind some bush. She's all over the internet.' Mew laughed before letting the smile fall from her face as she pulled Giuseppe close. 'As long as she's not all over you.'

'I have no interest in your friend, believe me.'

'But she does in you, that was clear from her behaviour on the beach earlier. And she is *not* my friend. Never will be. Now, if you'll excuse me, I'll head to the toilet.'

Mew left, leaving the awkward pairing of Olivia and Giuseppe alongside each other at the fence. Silence hung in the air for a few moments before a horn sounded from just outside of the cemetery.

'The cab is here,' said Olivia in relief.

Giuseppe lit another Gauloise. 'Mew is still in the toilet and I am not ready. I'll just finish this.' He held up the cigarette.

Olivia walked away in the direction of the cab. After a couple of steps she turned back around to look at Giuseppe. The pilot had his back to her and was staring out across the vineyards.

No one would see her do it. One push and Giuseppe could just fall to his doom. She could say that he fell flicking his cigarette butt into the air. Maybe stumbled on a loose bit of gravel. That sounded reasonable. It wouldn't come back on her, even if she had been the one to push him. Five seconds and it could all be over. And she would be there to console Mew.

She took two steps towards Giuseppe and held out her hands in front of her. She looked over her shoulder to see if there was any sign of Mew. There wasn't.

All sense of reason deserted her again.

She was within touching distance of the Italian when a voice sounded behind her.

'Cab is here,' said Mew. 'Come on, you two. Let's split this joint.'

Olivia lowered her arms and headed off to the awaiting taxi. Giuseppe was safe for now. It would have been so easy to watch him fall. To take him out of the equation.

But the time wasn't right. Not now. The moment of anger-stained madness had passed.

The three of them climbed into the cab, this time Olivia taking the front passenger seat, and sped off, back towards St Tropez.

CHAPTER 24

The sun was beginning to set over the private beach at the back of the guests' St Tropez hotel as DC Riding shuffled his way into the piano bar that opened out onto the golden sands. He was still slightly sore from his earlier encounter with Henri and gingerly placed himself on a bar stool and ordered a margarita from Christophe, who was behind the bar.

'Don't you ever stop working? You've been on shift all day and seem to have about a hundred different jobs in this place,' asked DC, shifting in his seat to try and achieve some semblance of comfort.

'I enjoy my job and if a double shift is offered I take it. I need all of the money I can find,' said Christophe, reaching for a cocktail shaker. 'When you live in a place surrounded by rich people you begin to realise how poor you are in comparison. And luckily I am good at many different things.'

Obviously angling for a tip, thought DC. He looked around the bar. It was empty apart from a man seated at the piano that dominated the middle of the space and a pretty, dark-haired lady of about twenty-five, sitting alone in the far corner. She was well dressed but the look on her face was far from fashionably happy given the splendour of her surroundings.

DC scanned his watch. Nearly half past seven. He was a few minutes early. A note had been pushed under his hotel suite door an hour or so earlier, saying that Dexter Franklin requested his company in the piano bar. Apparently the chef was keen to speak to the critic before the opening of Trésor and DC, as free as a bird, had leapt at the offer, thinking that a few drinks would be an acceptable way to spend the evening.

His cocktail mixed, DC placed the glass to his lips and tasted it. It was to his liking. He nodded towards the barman, showing his approval, and moved to a table alongside the piano. The man seated there began to play as if on command. A spot of Gershwin, if DC wasn't mistaken. 'Summertime'. One of his favourites from *Porgy And Bess*. The tinkling of the jazzy piano music filled the bar, bringing a smile to DC's face. Theatre was one of his great loves, away from food, and the song brought back some happy memories of nights out from his past. It obviously didn't have the same effect on the lady sitting across the bar, as her face was still stony and seemingly impatient.

DC lifted his glass in her direction and nodded. She gave a curt smile, which faded as quickly as it had arrived.

'Suit your sour self, dear,' muttered the critic under his breath.

Next to arrive in the bar was Olivia Rhodes, her face sunburned behind the ever-present spectacles. She moved to DC's table and spoke to him without seating herself.

'Evening, Mr Riding. I trust you've had a good day. Such a shame you couldn't join us in Ramatuelle. I'm in a bit of a hurry but I've had a message to say that Dexter wants to meet me here to discuss the restaurant opening, and I'd like to talk to him about a future book, so I guess I'll see you after my meeting.'

'You too, eh? I had a note under my door saying that Dexter wants to meet me here too. Maybe he'd like me to be involved. He knows how much my words can count. Maybe I should write the foreword for him.'

'Oh. I see. My note was under my door too. And yes, that is certainly an idea.' But an idea that Olivia had no urge to take DC up on.

'Well, you might as well wait with me and then he can decide who to see first when he arrives, can't he?'

A little put out at obviously not being Dexter's number-one priority for the night, Olivia sat herself down next to DC and beckoned to Christophe to bring her a tonic water.

Five minutes later there was still no sign of Dexter, but Holly walked into the bar, followed thirty seconds later by Mew and Giuseppe. Despite spending as little time in the sun as Olivia during their trip to Ramatuelle, Mew's fair skin was already turning a deeply attractive shade of chestnut. It also possessed the glow of a woman who had just been partaking in something totally desirable. Namely sex with the pilot holding her hand.

Both Olivia and Holly shot Mew a look of disapproval, but both for completely different reasons: for Olivia, the sight of Mew holding hands with the pilot scratched at her inner emotions; and Holly didn't like to be in the same time zone as her former bandmate let alone in the same bar. Holly gave her best flirtatious smile to Giuseppe as he spotted her, causing a glare of dislike to volley back in Holly's direction from Mew.

Mew and Giuseppe moved towards Olivia and DC while Holly, feeling a little lonesome, went to sit alongside the dark-haired woman who was on her own. She had seen her before somewhere, but she wasn't quite sure where.

'Hi there. I'm Holly,' she said, holding out her hand to the woman.

'Missy,' she replied.

Of course, the penny dropped. She was Missy Terranova. Holly recognised her as the woman in the online article she had been reading about Rosita's arrival into St Tropez and how she had caught Leland red-handed.

'Pleased to meet you,' she offered, quietly considering the fact that she and Missy had a lot more in common than the fact that they were in the same bar.

While the two of them exchanged pleasantries, Holly doing virtually all of the talking, Mew conversed with Olivia and DC while Giuseppe headed to the bar.

'We're heading out for a meal. Giuseppe has been telling me about Coquillages et Crustacés, a speciality seafood restaurant here in St Tropez that's been listed in the Michelin Guide. Apparently the food is served up on a huge seafront terrace. It even has its own fish shop and is a total must-go. Giuseppe has never been there and says it's supposed to be incredibly romantic. He insists we're to go. Who am I to say otherwise?' cooed Mew

'I dare say he'll insist you pay as well,' said Olivia. 'I've read about that place and it's not going to be cheap, is it?'

'Drop the attitude, Olivia, please. With the royalties coming in from my latest book you know damned well I can afford to eat at any restaurant I choose. And pay for whoever I like. The way my books are flying off the shelves right now, I could spend a week eating at the finest Michelin-starred restaurants in five different time zones and the food and flight bills would hardly dent the money rolling in.' Mew painted a smirk across her face at the smug thought of just how successful her culinary career was right now. 'And if I choose to spend it with Giuseppe then nobody, especially the publisher reaping the rewards of my success, is going to tell me otherwise, you hear me?'

'I just meant that he might be taking advantage of you, that's all,' replied Olivia, her skin turning an even darker shade of scarlet at the thought of upsetting Mew once more. Somehow she was unable to stop the words tumbling from her lips before putting her brain fully into action. 'I know how much you were hurt by Dexter.'

Mew placed her hands on her hips and looked Olivia straight in the eyes. 'Do you have to mention that man? Isn't it bad enough that I'll have to suffer his fucking opening in two nights' time? And he wants to meet me here tonight as well for a pre-opening chat. Fuck knows what that's about, I had a summoning note underneath my door. He's probably desperate to grill me about some decent recipes. Run out of ideas of his own is my guess. I'll spare him ten minutes and then we're out of here.'

Mew checked her watch and realised that Dexter was already late. 'Mind you, he should have been here ten minutes ago.'

'To see me as well. I had a similar note,' said DC.

'Me too,' added Olivia.

'Me three,' shouted Holly from where she was sitting. 'Forgive me for butting in, but I had exactly the same note saying that I should be here at half seven.'

'Do you have to eavesdrop on other people's conversations?' asked Mew with a disparaging look.

'You're hardly being quiet,' returned Holly.

'What about you?' asked Mew, looking in the direction of Missy Terranova. 'Seeing as you're the only other person here, I'm guessing that you might be waiting for Dexter too.'

'You guess wrong, she's waiting for the much more handsome brother – me.'

The voice, deep and resonant, came from Leland Franklin as he entered the piano bar. His appearance caused three of the women in the room to momentarily lose their train of thought. Leland was pure sex appeal.

Missy's face, which had hardly cracked into anything more than a grimace since her arrival in the bar, gave out a stare that could only be described as a strange mixture of both fury and relief that Leland had arrived. Holly had to catch her breath for many reasons as she stared at the man before her. So many memories came flooding back yet again. Leland was hard to shake from your system, however much you might want to.

As for Mew, all she saw was the man who had helped to finish off Crazy Sour once and for all. And that was why she hated him. Without him, all of those times that she spent feeling washed up after the split of the band, and before the rise of her cooking career, might not have happened. She blamed him. She blamed Holly. She blamed them both.

For once, Mew was unable to speak.

The only other woman in the room, Olivia, saw nothing more than some man she recognised from the TV, from the press and as being the brother of one of her clients. He was one of those adventurer types. He was big news – that she did know. One of her friends published his books. But she'd never seen his show.

'Good evening, everybody. Anybody seen my brother? I'm supposed to meet him here but I'm a little late. Has he been and gone?' said Leland, strolling into the bar.

'You too. Fancy that. Dexter's a rather popular man, isn't he?' said DC, rising to his feet and extending his hand in Leland's direction. 'I'm DC Riding, food critic.'

'Pleasure.' Leland shook his hand. 'I'm Leland Franklin.'

'And this is Mew Stanton and Holly Lydon, they used to be in a band together. This is publisher Olivia... er, Rhodes, was it? And the lady over there, I'm afraid I don't know her name.' DC's attempts at introductions were poor to pitiful. 'Oh, and that man at the bar was our pilot from Nice to here.'

'I think I know most people here. Some more than others, as you may have read. The lady over there as you say, PC, is Miss Missy Terranova, and she came to St Tropez with me.'

'Oh, hello,' said the critic, attempting to recognise the vaguely familiar name. 'And it's DC, not PC. It's short for Daniel Craig, believe it or not.'

'Christ, I'd hate to see you coming out of the surf in tight James Bond bathers.' Holly had said it, rather louder than planned, before she had time to stop herself. A giggle erupted from all parties in the room, apart from Missy and Giuseppe, who had now rejoined Mew near the piano.

'Don't listen to them, PC,' laughed Leland. 'I'd knock that body of yours into shape in the wild. I'd find some muscles in there for you.'

DC was not pleased. 'I'm perfectly happy as I am, thank you. And like I said, it's DC, not PC.'

His words fell on deaf ears as Leland moved over to where Missy and Holly were sitting. Both shifted awkwardly in their seats as he sat down.

Missy stood up to greet him. She was clearly fuming.

'Where the hell have you been? I haven't seen you for the best part of twenty-four hours.'

'That, *darling*, is because he's been with me, his beloved *girlfriend*.' The emphasis on the last word and the richness of the accent meant that it could only have come from one mouth – that of Rosita Velázquez, who had arrived in a flurry of sequins and shimmer at the main door of the bar, wearing a silver floor-length gown that was much more suited to the red carpets of Hollywood than it was a piano bar in the early season in St Tropez. But the gown, if slightly ill-suited, was nothing short of drop-dead dazzling.

She continued, 'And that, my dear, is how it will remain. Good evening, everyone. Rosita's here. But you can see that, of course. How are we all?' Rosita spoke as if all of those gathered in the piano bar automatically knew her. The sea of mixed expressions that greeted her proved that they didn't. Holly and Mew had both seen her before, Holly recognising the final piece of the jigsaw from the article she'd read earlier and also recollecting that she'd seen her in Iguazu some years earlier, as had Mew. Olivia had maybe read something about her in a magazine back in the UK. Was she an actress? She wasn't quite sure. As for DC, well, he knew exactly who she was. They had met on many an occasion. And occasionally he had enjoyed it. Giuseppe just saw a fantastically beautiful woman, but knew neither her name nor her connection to anybody else.

'Nice outfit,' said Holly, unafraid to speak. 'Very.'

'*Obrigado, meu docinho*,' purred Rosita. 'Those personal shoppers at Dior are worth their weight in gold, aren't they?' She scanned Holly's outfit, a David Bowie 'Starman' T-shirt and faded denim jeans. 'You should try it.' There was a tone to Rosita's voice indicating that her words were more than mere polite suggestion, and maybe a tip that Holly should take on board.

'Now I am here to see Dexter. I have been requested. A card was left in my suite. Is he here at all?'

'Your suite?' asked DC. 'Aren't you here with Leland, if he's your boyfriend?'

'Let's just say there was a mix-up with the reservations, so we have two suites right now, but that will be changing as soon as Missy, as you Brits say, *slings her hook*.' Rosita pointed a perfectly manicured fingernail at Missy as she spoke. Missy remained silent, inwardly fuming that she was quite rightly being turfed out of the suite she had been able to share with Leland. She had no intention of going any further than the suite that Rosita would be vacating. Rosita read her mind.

'And if you think you're having my suite, then think again. My make-up artist, Tinks, will be staying there to give this,' she said, swirling her hand around her own face, 'her expert attention. No, Missy, if you are considering staying in St Tropez, then I suggest you head to the backstreets, where the other *prostitutas* hang out.'

Missy looked to Leland to defend her. No defence came. As tears began to sting her eyes, Missy stood up and fled through the door of the piano bar. Giuseppe watched her go, bemused by what was happening. For a few moments, silence filled the room. Other than the sound of the piano, which was now playing 'The Lady Is a Tramp', which seemed more than apt. Nobody said a word.

It was Mew who broke the silence. 'Do you mean Tinks McVeigh? She used to sometimes do our make-up when we were in the band.'

'That's the one. She works with all sorts, not just stars like me.'

'Even stars who have never been heard of before?' snipped in Holly, determined that Rosita would not be throwing her shade. 'I read about your arrival in St Tropez online. You'd never see Jennifer Lawrence or Kristen Stewart arriving in such a… unique style, would you? I suspect they'll arrive for the real festival, when it begins, probably on a red carpet, like most well-known actresses.'

Rosita decided to ignore Holly's jibe. 'Now, seeing as Dexter is not here yet, maybe I should entertain you all with a song.' This was clearly something not open to negotiation.

Rosita flicked her hand through her dark hair and pulled it to one side of her face. She seated herself alongside the rather puzzled man at the piano, forcing him to shift position. 'Do you know "Feeling Good" by Nina Simone? Some say I sing it better than her. I prefer an old-time classic and not one of these stupid pop songs that little girls sing.' Was she aiming her dig at Mew and Holly? She was fully aware of who they both were.

The pianist nodded and began to play. On cue, Rosita began to sing. Her acting may be slated, but there was no way that anybody was going to say anything about her singing. She was pitch perfect and delivered the song with a sultry sexiness that most singers could only dream of.

As she finished the last note, her arms outstretched in the air, all eyes were on Rosita. DC, Leland, Mew, Holly, Olivia, Giuseppe and Christophe all applauded. For a few moments everyone gathered there had actually forgotten why they were there in the first place. To meet Dexter Franklin.

Which begged the question.

Where the hell was he?

CHAPTER 25

Dexter Franklin was also *feeling good*, but it had nothing to do with the spot-on rendition of the Nina Simone number Rosita had just performed. Not that he had missed a note of it. Neither had he missed a juicy morsel of the action that had just taken place in the Arlequin piano bar. He'd seen it all. And heard every last word. And not even stepped foot inside the room.

Dexter leant back into the comfort of the leather sofa in the front room of the apartment he'd been renting in St Tropez ever since he had arrived weeks earlier. The soft leather gave a tiny squeak as he shifted position. It made him smile. It was a squeak that he'd noticed from day one. The leather was soft and wrapped itself around his naked back as he relaxed into it. A pair of earphones hung around his neck; the ones that had allowed him to hear every bitchy moment of the conversation between those gathered in the piano bar. It was amazing what a few small bugging devices dotted around the room could do when required. And a couple of well-placed micro-cameras filming everything and feeding it back to Dexter's laptop. It was hardly *Mission Impossible* but it had certainly achieved exactly what Dexter needed. To sit back and tune into what was being said by his chosen guests. To see whether any of them had worked out why they were there. To see just exactly how they would react when they were finally all in the same room together. To be able to watch from afar and yet know that his presence was strong in the room nevertheless. To make them think about who they were. And what they had done.

Dexter watched on the screen of his laptop as Rosita flounced away from the bar, obviously bored of waiting for him. She was quickly followed by DC. Dexter had seen enough to know that the group was stirring itself nicely into a frenzied recipe of emotions. He closed the lid of his laptop and poured himself a glass of quality red from the wine bottle alongside the laptop. His reward for a good night's work.

He walked towards the windows of the apartment, which opened up onto the small but charming balcony that looked down onto one of the narrow backstreets of the town. As he opened the doors a face smiled up at him. Seated at a round table, an empty wine glass in front of her, was Toni from Trésor. She was scrolling through photos on her iPhone. She stopped as Dexter stepped out onto the balcony and refilled her glass.

'A successful night, then? Did the bugging devices work?'

'Very well indeed. It was quite some show.'

'So they were placed well, then, right where you needed them to be?'

'They were perfect.'

'I told you they would be. It's always good to have a helping hand, don't you think?'

Dexter nodded without saying a word. Whether it was the strength of the full-bodied red or the liquid tone of the girl's accent, he wasn't sure, but he suddenly felt a little light-headed. In a good way. As if a rush of satisfied excitement was bursting within him.

Images of what Dexter had seen on the laptop went through his mind: Rosita's arrogant beauty; Leland's brutish inability to stop his cock from straying; Mew and Holly's loathing of each other; the squirming and fawning nature of DC Riding. It was all falling into place. It was all as planned. Not that any of them knew it yet. They had no idea.

Dexter's house speciality was to be a dish called payback and he would enjoy serving each and every one of them his very own delightful version. Now that was *feeling good*.

CHAPTER 26

Rosita waited for no one, not even Dexter bloody Franklin. How dare he keep her waiting? How dare he make her feel that they were to have a little one-on-one time? Isn't that what his invitation had suggested? It certainly hadn't mentioned that a whole room of reprobates would be there too – including Leland's new bit of skirt.

Why did she put up with Leland? That man couldn't commit to one woman if his life depended upon it. And given just what kind of man Leland could be, she wondered sometimes if being part of the Leland Franklin worldwide brand bandwagon was worth it. Did she really need to put her own blind ambition before all of the things that a relationship with Leland Franklin, intrepid TV action man, entailed? How ironic that it was more often Rosita who found herself in a somewhat perilous place than the man she was joined to. A man who thought nothing of swimming with the most vicious of sharks.

Rosita was determined that Leland's latest bout of infidelity would not scratch at her soul. She couldn't let it. She needed to remain positive and upbeat about the upcoming Cannes Film Festival. If she was to shine like a star there and make sure that it was her name on everybody's lips, then she needed to be bringing her A game to the table. She could ask Leland to accompany her to the red carpets of the movie world, but seeing as he'd already managed to fill the newspapers with his own infidelity, tarnishing her perfectly planned and original arrival into St Tropez, she couldn't risk him removing her from the spotlight again. This would be something that she would need to do herself. Unless, of course, she could persuade somebody else to accompany her. Somebody who wouldn't extinguish the flame of her own burning ambition with their already explosive global popularity. God, sometimes being the other half of a worldwide success really sucked. And doused a person in envy. But that was playing the fame game. Would people talk about David if it wasn't for Elton, Ayda if it wasn't for Robbie, Scott if it hadn't been for Kourtney? Rosita doubted it. But she knew that outside of her own country she was little more than Leland's plus one. And after reports of her arrival in St Tropez, she wasn't just a plus one but also a number-one laughing stock.

No, she would have to show Leland that she could do this on her own. Or at least with more of an equal by her side. Somebody who wouldn't automatically outshine and somebody who would definitely gain her column inches.

Dexter Franklin may have been a no-show tonight, but it was his face that was filling Rosita's mind as she reached the lift in the hotel reception to take her up to her suite. If the world thought that poor, hapless Rosita Velázquez was putting up with Leland's cheating ways, then they had to be convinced otherwise – and what better way to do it than with his brother on her arm.

As Rosita entered the lift she let the image of the two brothers fill her mind. Two different looks, one dark, one light. So different in so many ways. Yet both equally as enticing to Rosita for very different reasons.

She watched the door shut as she cast her mind back to her first meeting with Dexter. It was a time she could never forget. She never wanted to.

*

Chefchaouen, Morocco, just over two years earlier...

Chefchaouen. A tiny town in Morocco's Rif Mountains. A place hidden away from the madness of the celebrity world. A town containing a beautiful medina with a dizzying array of narrow blue houses in its equally narrow streets. Every shade of blue, from pale to bright, a relentless yet mesmerising assault on the eyes and a colourful backdrop to the people living there, shuffling along the streets in their djellabas, the traditional Moroccan garb for everyday life. Every corner was a fusion of colour and texture and every doorway a hidden delight of design. A world of wonder and a place where the unexpected delights of Planet Earth revealed themselves around every bend.

Rosita Velázquez wasn't wearing a djellaba. That would never do for the pages of *Vogue Brasil*. And after all, that was why she was in Chefchaouen. It was the only reason she had endured the rather turbulent and excruciatingly long flight from Rio to Dubai and then the subsequent connecting flight to Casablanca. As if that hadn't been enough, she had then been required to take a six-hour bus journey to the mountainous isolation of Chefchaouen. As she arched back against the vibrant blue of one of the town's famous buildings, her hands above her head as her diaphanous Carlos Miele multi-blued silk gown skimmed idyllically against the curves of her flesh, Rosita knew that the journey had been worth it. She was looking a million dollars, or perhaps she should say about three and half million Brazilian reals. She might have converted it into the local currency of Morocco, had she actually bothered to find out just what it was the locals managed to spend. Not a lot, she guessed, as she placed her hands on her waist and bent her upper body forward, turning her head to one side to add yet another designer shape to the portfolio of photos being snapped by the *Vogue Brasil* photographer.

The heat of the streets was stifling, caused both by the sun overhead and the sets of lights erected by the *Vogue* team and pointing in her direction. Despite the heat making her slightly lightheaded, her skin starting to glow with the first traces of perspiration, Rosita was determined that her latest foray onto the cover of the prestigious magazine – her fourth, if she remembered correctly – would be her best yet.

Her thoughts were interrupted by Tinks McVeigh as she rushed onto the set, brushes and powder in hand.

'That forehead is starting to glow. And I am not surprised, in this heat,' said Tinks, her brushes snapping ninja-like into action as they swept across Rosita's hairline, crushing any potential shine. Rosita allowed herself to relax for a moment as Tinks went about her business and another of Rosita's *Vogue* team handed her a bottle of water.

'Dinner tonight then, just you and I?' asked Tinks as she added another fine layer of powder to Rosita's face. 'And we'll try and find something that isn't just a plate full of mutton.'

'That's a plan,' replied Rosita. 'As beautiful as this place is – if you like your food served by a gap-toothed man within spitting distance of a severed goat's head – I could murder a lobster from Antiquarius or any of the seafood at the Albamar.' The reference was a nod to two of Rosita's favourite and very expensive restaurants back in Rio, a million light years and a million lifestyles away from the food she, Tinks and the others had been experiencing in the blue town.

'We'll find somewhere with a decent menu, Rosita, I swear to God. I am a little over the lack of choice in this place, strikingly beautiful though it is. It could do with a Starbucks on a few of these street corners too.'

'Mint-infused tea or a nous-nous made of half coffee, half milk is all they have in this town, darling,' countered Rosita. 'Although you're right. What I wouldn't give for an iced caramelised honey latte right now.'

'I second that. So, I'll find somewhere decent for us tonight and the others can fill themselves up on some local flock again, yes? I can see that you are over spending night after night with them.'

'You got it,' Rosita replied. It was true. Even though they had only been in Morocco three days, she was already over the fawning of the crew on their nights out, even if she loved being the centre of attention deep down. A night with just Tinks for company would be a welcome one.

As Tinks moved away from the actress, Rosita herself was distracted. She couldn't take her eyes off a man who had just come into view around the corner of the street. He had jet-black hair and eyes that appeared to hypnotise even from their distance across the narrow street. He was unshaven and all man, and even though he was obviously not a local he somehow looked very much at ease amidst the slightly ramshackle surroundings of the town.

She had no sooner spotted him than he had her, the dark discs of his eyes staring straight into her soul. Rosita felt her heart give a slight flutter underneath her designer outfit and heard the photographer call for her attention as she continued to stare at the man. Even though turning her attention away from the vision of masculinity across the street was the last thing she wanted to do, she knew that she had to finish the shoot and please the people from *Vogue*. As she began to pose again and the camera clicked away she could still feel the eyes of the stranger upon her. She didn't mind at all. If anything, knowing that she had his attention was the spark she needed to take her poses to the next level. A fact that the photographer seemed to appreciate as he aired his praise.

Within ten minutes the shoot was complete. Much to Rosita's delight, the man was still watching her, his appreciation clear, judging from the smile painted across his face. As the photographer, assistant and stylist for the shoot moved towards her, their arms all raised in sycophantic praise, Rosita brushed past them all as politely as she could.

She headed towards the man, fully aware that the floaty folds of her Carlos Miele would look nothing short of sensational as they wafted behind her. He was even more handsome up close, almost taking Rosita's breath away as she stared into his eyes. It was as if he invented the word *sexy*, the line between macho and beautifully inviting a wafer-thin one indeed.

'Hello.' He spoke first. 'Having fun?'

Rosita caught her breath and replied. 'Photo shoot for *Vogue*.' She tried to play it down as much as possible but the mere words caused a perfectly shaped black eyebrow to rise on the man's face.

'Impressive,' he answered. 'Should I know you? This isn't the kind of place you see a lot of famous faces. Although you do seem somewhat familiar.'

'Thank you. I haven't seen many men like you around here either. You seem quite the…' Rosita searched for the word she needed, before settling on '…exception.'

'My name is Dexter Franklin. Pleased to meet you.' He leant over and kissed her on both cheeks, his stubble rubbing lightly against her flesh. And you are?'

'Rosita Velázquez. I'm an actress from Brazil.'

For a second a flash of concern shot across Dexter's face at the mention of the actress's homeland. He let it pass.

'I'm Dexter Franklin, and I'm a chef. You might have seen me on TV?'

'Oh, thank God. Maybe you know a decent place to eat around here that isn't bathed in the blood of a severed piece of livestock,' said Rosita in relief.

Dexter smiled. 'The food here is amazing, even if the preparation methods are hardly the kind you'd see back home. And the spice shops are incredible. Some of the best I've visited in the world. The bread, too, is out of this world, as is the meat, if you give it a chance. Why don't I take you to dinner tonight? Or even better, how about I make you something. I'll prove to you that Moroccan food, especially in a town like this, is a beautiful thing.'

Rosita's lips curled into a deep smile. Was Dexter flirting or merely attempting to prove her wrong? She assumed both. But whatever the meaning, she was not refusing his offer.

'I would like that. Which restaurant will you be taking me to? Shall we say seven thirty?'

Dexter laughed. 'I said I'm a chef. I'll be cooking. I've hired a riad here for a few days in the centre of the medina. It sleeps eight but I'm there on my own at the minute. I've been here buying things and gathering ideas for my next cookbook and also for a future venture.'

'Cookbook? Then I am in good hands, aren't I?'

'The best, in my opinion,' said Dexter. 'Six million viewers and thousands of readers can't be wrong.'

Rosita continued to smile. She was becoming very keen on Dexter Franklin.

'Six million viewers? That's a lot of people watching you in action. Lucky them. So are you on TV at the moment?'

'Yep, just finished the latest series. I'm the judge on a TV show. Famous people come on and cook up culinary delights and I tell them whether they fly or die.' He let the words linger before adding, 'You should take part, you know.'

It was an invitation that Rosita relished – appearing on something like that would definitely raise her profile beyond the borders of Brazil. She didn't even consider the fact that cooking was not exactly top of her skill set. She needed to become more acquainted with Dexter Franklin and his hypnotic gaze told her that she would have no trouble doing so. 'I'd love to,' she purred.

'So I will see you later then, Rosita. How do I contact you?'

'I'll give you one of my cards,' said Rosita. 'My make-up lady has some in her vanity case.'

Rosita walked back over to where the photo shoot had been taking place. Tinks, the photographer and the stylist had all been watching Rosita talking to Dexter. Tinks smiled as Rosita reached her, Dexter just behind her. She'd instantly recognised him. She'd never done his make-up but he had one of those faces that nobody who had ever seen him on TV or in the flesh would forget in a hurry.

'Tinks, this is Dexter Franklin, chef. Dexter this is Tinks McVeigh, my make-up artist of choice. You should let her loose on that handsome face of yours.'

'I'll remember that,' smiled Dexter.

'Now, Tinks, would you kindly give Dexter one of my business cards?'

She watched as Tinks did so.

'My cell number is on it. And I'll write the name of the place we're staying on the back. You can come and collect me at seven fifteen from there, yes?'

She jotted down the name of their hotel and passed the card to Dexter. He knew the place and agreed. For now, Rosita's work was done.

'If you'll excuse me then, Mr Franklin, I must finish my work here. I'll see you later.' Rosita turned away from him, her actions provocative, coquettish and a little dismissive.

Dexter could read her like a book. He knew Rosita was teasing him and that she would be his later tonight. He had met many women like Rosita Velázquez before and he knew exactly how to work her. He'd win her over in the bedroom after he'd won her over in the kitchen. As he walked away from Rosita and Tinks, compiling a shopping list in his mind, Dexter knew that he was very impressed with Rosita. More impressed than he had been by a woman since… Well, he knew exactly when.

'He's cuter in the flesh than he is on TV,' said Tinks to Rosita. 'You know who he is, right?'

'I do now,' smiled Rosita. 'And by the way, in case you hadn't guessed, our dinner's off tonight. I'll be dining with Dexter.'

The next morning, Rosita woke up in Dexter Franklin's muscled arms, having spent her first ever night in a Moroccan riad. It was beyond basic, but the actress normally only satisfied with five-star accommodation didn't care. She had woken up with both a new-found respect for Moroccan food and a new-found desire to discover more about the joyous lovemaking techniques of a certain British chef.

CHAPTER 27

Missy was nowhere to be found and Leland wasn't really sure that he gave a shit. She was hot, had breasts that defied gravity and blowjob skills that could suck an orange through a straw, but so did countless other women that he'd managed to bed over the years. If she was choosing to go AWOL in the sun-baked streets of St Tropez then Leland had no intention of worrying about it, especially now that Rosita was on the scene. Despite his growing boredom with the actress and her temperamental ways, if they were at least in the same time zone then maybe he owed it to her to try and at least play the doting boyfriend and willing lover whilst they were together. At least until the launch night of Trésor was out of the way at any rate.

Missy had run from the piano bar and not returned. She was upset, that was clear even to a player like Leland, but if she thought that he was going to run after her then she was sorely mistaken. Leland never chased women. Even hot ones.

Having ordered a beer from Christophe at the bar, he added the cost to his tab and took the drink out to the private beach at the back of the hotel. The evening air was still warm and the frosty nature of the beer was just what he needed after the frosty reception he had received during the rendezvous at the piano bar. How dare his fucking brother not turn up? What was he playing at? Again, Leland wasn't sure he cared. For a second he contemplated phoning his sibling. Why not? Might as well hear it from the horse's mouth. He pulled his phone from his pocket and was about to dial Dexter when it rang.

The name of his London agent, the ball-breaking Rachel Jerome, appeared on the screen, and for the next five minutes Leland sat deep in conversation with her. It was only when he hung up that he spied Holly Lydon staring at him from a sun lounger no more than a few feet away.

'That seemed like a pretty positive conversation,' said Holly idly.

'My star continues to grow,' replied Leland triumphantly. 'That was my agent. She's booked me my first-ever live arena spectacle tour. Bear Grylls did it recently and it was hugely successful and made major bucks for him so now it's my turn. It'll be interactive and I'll take the audience on a virtual tour of some of the daredevil things I've done around the world. I'll see if I can blag you a pair of tickets. I dare say it's the first time in a long while you've been inside an arena, eh, love? Isn't that what you used to do back in the day?'

'Screw you, Leland. I've played at more arenas than you and your Boy Scout routine ever will,' snapped Holly.

'Oh, Crazy Sour Grapes! How delicious.'

'Not really. I don't miss the lifestyle. I hated the fame, as you well know. That's why I went off the rails.'

'Now those were good times,' Leland said slyly. 'You certainly knew how to party, didn't you?'

'As did you. But I did it to block things out. You did it because you loved the danger, the sense of power and control, and you couldn't give a fuck what anybody thought about you, including me. You still don't, I see.'

'Which is why we ended up in the same place, isn't it?' remarked Leland. 'Seems like yesterday you and I were breaking the rules at The Abbey.'

Holly's face went white for a moment as she thought about her time at the UK's famed rehabilitation clinic. It was there that her pop career had finally been smashed into an endless symphony of irreparable pieces. And it was Leland who had delivered the final blow.

*

The Abbey, nearly four years earlier...

'When I was told I was coming here to get clean, this isn't exactly what I'd expected, but it's so much better than I thought it might be,' laughed Holly as the jets of hot water showered down against her tender flesh. She pushed her mass of red curls back against her head, flattening them down as much as she could, and stared up into the eyes of the man sharing the shower with her. The same blue eyes that she had stared into on countless occasions over the last few weeks. Ever since she had been admitted into The Abbey by the Crazy Sour management, directly after her meltdown in Vienna. The eyes of Leland Franklin.

'Yes, I didn't imagine for one second that a spell in here would be quite so much fun. But then I didn't know that I was going to bump into you again, did I?' smirked Leland, pulling Holly's naked body towards him underneath the spray of the shower. His lips met hers and as he kissed her he let his hands drift down her back to the curves of her backside. He placed a hand on each cheek and squeezed firmly. The action caused Holly to wince slightly.

'Hey soldier, calm it, I don't want another telltale bruise. I'm like a peach and trying to explain the dark marks on my arm last week to the nurses was not easy. *Mean Girls* ain't got nothing on the bitches in here.'

Leland didn't apologise and merely grinned. Their sex together – half a dozen times so far, in just under a fortnight since Leland had admitted himself – had indeed been rough and forceful. Holly didn't mind it, happy to lose herself in the ferocious and passionate heat of the moment, but trying to explain herself to the nurses and experts giving her the treatment the Crazy Sour management team said she needed was not easy. Leland was definitely a slap and tickle man – with the emphasis on the slap. There was only so many times you could say you'd bumped into a wall or fallen out of bed.

Holly had been more surprised than anyone when she ran into Leland in rehab. She hadn't seen him since their explosive encounter in Brazil, and despite the frenzy of their first hedonistic session together, everything that had happened to them since meant that they had never had a chance to reunite. Leland's career was shooting through the roof whereas Holly seemed to be hell-bent on trying to shoot her pop career up her own nose. But it seemed that Leland's love of nose candy had also seen him admitted into the UK's most famous rehab for the rich, famous and unstoppable.

'When do you leave?' asked Leland, allowing his hands to loop around Holly's body to cup her breasts.

'I have a meeting with the main man here after this and then they're going to discuss what happens next. I want to get out. I miss my mum. She needs me. And I need her to be honest. If this place has taught me anything it's that I don't need all of that shit I was putting up my nose. I was only doing it to take my mind off being in the group. The constant scrutiny from everybody. From Mew and Leonie and everyone around me. And the press.'

'But from what you've told me, your management have succeeded in keeping things pretty under wraps. You're supposed to be sweet and wholesome.'

'And you know I'm not,' grinned Holly, rubbing her hands across the hard flesh of his pectoral muscles. 'Far from it. But I was heading into a dangerous place and I wasn't prepared to stop. I was doing it to forget what was going on around me. To forget about everything. To run away. It was only going to be a matter of time before stories got out there. This place has saved my bacon.'

'What does a young woman like you have to forget about? You're rich, hot and part of a band that every teenage girl in the world would love to be part of.' Leland scoffed slightly, unable to comprehend exactly what a girl like Holly would want to run away from.

Holly bit her bottom lip, wondering whether to reply. She had shared drugs and her body with this man, could she share her soul? For a moment she thought about telling Leland about the abuse she had suffered at the hands of her Uncle Warren. How being rebellious and losing herself in drink, drugs and experimental sex was her way of pushing the fear she had experienced to the back of her mind. She had shared it with the experts at The Abbey. Could she share it with Leland? She decided not.

'The press. The lifestyle. The bitching. Some people in the spotlight turn into recluses to get away from it all, some have meltdowns in public and others, like me, choose to unleash their dangerous inner wild child.' That was another thing that she had discussed with the staff at The Abbey. She had been there nearly a month and was determined, hard though it had been, that she would stick to the straight and narrow. It was a miracle that the press hadn't latched onto her being in rehab in the first place, and even though the constant glare of fame was something she didn't want to return to, she knew that she might have to. She was contractually obliged. Certainly having a clear set of nostrils was making her head feel a lot clearer about how important Crazy Sour actually were. And the money spoke for itself.

'So when do you leave?' repeated Leland.

'Tomorrow, hopefully.'

'So no more secret liaisons with me then? I'll have to find myself some other little hot body,' smiled Leland. He wasn't joking.

'How we've gotten away with it so far is beyond me,' said Holly. Their meet-ups had been organised with skilful military precision in order to gain some stolen sexual moments together. The Abbey was not a fan of inter-inmate unions and sex was added to the list of no-can-do's while under the watchful eyes of The Abbey staff. Thankfully they weren't always as watchful as they thought.

'I shall miss this,' said Leland, positioning one of his hands between her legs and placing two fingers inside her.

'Well, how about one for the road, as they say. The road of the straight and narrow.' Holly's words were breathy and anticipatory as Leland removed his fingers and guided his now fully erect cock into her. She was about to ask him if he too had managed to quell his need for narcotics, but the tingling nerve endings between her legs as he moved his length inside her stopped her from saying anything.

Holly lifted her legs up, one on either side of his body, and allowed Leland to carry her in his strong arms as she moved up and down on his thick shaft. The water from the shower bounced off her skin as she gave herself up to pleasure. Leland's hands were on her buttocks again and she could feel the pressure he was applying there as he moved her young body up and down the hardness of his flesh. His grip tightened as he felt his own release of excitement rising, as did Holly. As the two of them came together, their bodies united in momentary euphoria, Holly let out a scream of delight as her body juddered into completion, riding his cock. Leland slapped her butt cheeks as his own release swept joyously through his body and he let his teeth and stubble graze across the exposed flesh of her neck.

Holly knew she would have marks on her skin. But at that moment, she didn't care. Sex with Leland Franklin was worth it.

Holly was clean, and in her mind felt better than she had done in years. Even though the thought of hitting the stage with Mew and Leonie and returning to the treadmill of fame scared her, she was ready to give it a go. She had managed not to be annihilated in the press and had gotten away with all of the things that no good-girl pop poppet should ever do. The management knew her secrets, as did the girls in the band – she had even shared a few of her sordid tales during pillow talk with Leland – but at least the press and, more importantly, the impressionable league of Crazy Sour fans out there didn't know.

As Holly left The Abbey she was ready to face whatever was to come next. To return to the bosom of the band.

It never happened. A week later virtually every newspaper, blog and website in the land ran the same news shocker: Leland Franklin's tell-all story of his stint in The Abbey and how he had found sexual solace, albeit briefly, in the arms of Crazy Sour band member Holly Lydon. Not even the clever management behind the girl band could quash the story. Leland's star was deemed to shine brighter. Details of their first tryst in Iguazu, the night of the murder of Cher Le Visage, and the tales that Holly had shared with him were paraded on the pages of every tabloid going. For a red-blooded TV star like Leland, the press was fine, giving him a macho edge that allowed his career to ascend even higher, but for Holly it was the death knoll.

Cutesy girl band members do not snort coke, shag countless men and drink themselves into oblivion. Well, not according to their young fans and their mothers they don't. The Crazy Sour world tour that was due to be rescheduled was shelved for good and their record sales dropped through the floor. As Mew had feared, Holly had inadvertently caused the destruction of the band.

*

'So why did you do it?' asked Holly, as Leland drained the last few drops from his beer glass.

'Do what?' Leland knew full well what Holly was talking about. His words were wrapped with smugness. He'd been expecting the inquisition at some point.

'Stitch me up at The Abbey. Tell the world that I was some kind of crazed junkie.'

'Well, you were.'

'But it still wasn't your place to tell the world. I was off the drugs and booze, at least for a while. You know how hard it was to do that. You know how strict that place tried to be, even if we did manage to bend a few of the rules.' For a second Holly flashed back to their secret sexual meetings at The Abbey, to the times in the shower, or against a tree in the tranquillity of the gardens. Even though she had waited a long time to confront Leland about what he had done to her, he was still one of the most attractive men that she had ever met and the mere sight of him still sent unwanted yet unstoppable chills through her core. He was as enticing and as dangerous as the coke she'd managed to temporarily kick at The Abbey.

'You told me how much you hated the fame of the band, so don't tell me that your poxy group going up in smoke wasn't welcome. I did you a favour.'

Holly could feel her anger rising but was determined not to explode. 'I had issues with being in the band, yes, but it wasn't your choice to bring it to an end. You had no fucking right to do that.'

'You took the drugs. I didn't force you to.'

'Yes, and I got away with it. Somehow. I've made mistakes. We all have. Done things I regret and things I'm ashamed of. But I did manage to kick the drugs at The Abbey. All of that good work and good faith that people put in me was ruined by you. By your need for a story to boost your career. You used me.'

'People know that you're not sweetness and light, Holly. So don't pretend otherwise.'

Holly knew he was right. What was she, after all? A whore. A harlot. A prozzie. She used to be a high-class one, but she'd scuppered that herself by returning to the drugs and blabbing to the wrong person. She could only blame herself for losing the moneymaking potential she had had when she was working flat out around the world on her back. But maybe she wouldn't have been in that position if the band had continued. Maybe her current money woes would never have happened had she been able to continue with Crazy Sour. Even though a piece of her mind told her that she would have gone off the rails again had she gone back into the group, shouldn't she have been allowed to discover that for herself? Instead of having the chance taken away from her by Leland Franklin. That was the reason she disliked him. But then, that was the reason she disliked herself. She could see that she and Leland were very similar. And the thought scared her. But in his macho world, he'd survived the story of life at The Abbey. As a role-model pop star, she hadn't.

'You disgust me. I trusted you and you betrayed that.'

'Oh, come on, darling. It was a drug-fucked shag in Brazil and a few bunk-ups behind the drugs police at The Abbey. Nothing more.'

'But it cost me my career.'

'And it helped make mine. Funny that, eh? You win some, you lose some.'

Leland laughed as he stood up. His words were callous and uncaring. 'Fancy another drink? For old time's sake.'

Holly could feel her skin turning the colour of her hair. An anger gripped her but she was determined not to let it boil over. She merely shook her head.

'Suit yourself. I suppose I had better go and see Rosita anyway. Shame, we could have made a night of it. Tried out the shower in your suite.'

He winked as he walked off.

Holly knew that she had herself to blame for a lot of things that had happened in her short life, but as she watched Leland strut off to the bar, she hated the feeling that he caused inside her. Such an attractive man on the outside, yet oh so ugly on the inside. He made her feel vulnerable, scared and weak. A frightened little girl. And that was something that she had never wanted to feel from a man again. Not after Uncle Warren.

CHAPTER 28

The slight breeze that blew across the seafront terrace at Coquillages et Crustacés was a welcome one for Mew as she waited for Giuseppe to return from choosing his lobster at the restaurant's in-house pool, where the delicious offerings were lined up ready to meet their maker.

She reached down into her bag and pulled out her purse. She flipped through a wad of euros to the photo at the back and pulled it out, looking at it in the fading light of the Côte d'Azur evening. A smile spread across her face as she took in the three faces there. A mother and two children. For a moment a shell of sadness encased her as she thought about all that had passed.

'You okay?' asked Giuseppe, returning to the table having condemned a rather juicy-looking beast to its demise. 'What are you looking at?'

'Oh, nothing,' fudged Mew, shoving the dog-eared photo back into her purse, determined to change the subject. 'Have you picked then?'

'Oh yes, he's mine,' said Giuseppe, signalling to the restaurant staff member pulling an enormous lobster from the pool.

'I assume you mean the lobster, not the man,' said Mew.

'Yes, I'll leave the man-on-man stuff to DC. He's a funny thing, isn't he?' Giuseppe's accent made it hard to tell whether he meant funny ha-ha or funny weird. It was left for Mew to decide.

'But he's harmless,' she said. 'I thought he might have wanted to join us tonight. If this place is supposed to be as amazing as everyone says then I thought he might have liked it. I'm glad he didn't though. And besides, he scuttled off after Rosita as soon as she had finished singing her song. That was quite something. He is obviously a fan. Silly man.'

'He may not be here but have you seen who is?' said Giuseppe. 'I saw her on the way to pick my dinner. She can't leave you alone, can she?'

'Who?' said Mew, though she didn't really need to ask. She knew exactly who the pilot was talking about, and a quick glance to her right confirmed it. Sitting at a table on her own was Olivia Rhodes. As soon as she caught sight of Mew staring across at her she stood up and moved over to where her favourite client and her new beau were sitting.

'Isn't this place adorable?' enthused Olivia. 'When you mentioned it, I googled it and thought that I simply must come. I did ask DC but he ran off after that actress woman. I won't sit with you two though, if you're having a meal. A romantic one, I mean.'

Mew didn't say a word, staring coolly up at Olivia. She was beginning to think that maybe Olivia was a lot madder and a little more dangerous than she had ever thought. Why was she on this trip, after all? She couldn't seem to turn a corner without her being there, and their visit to Ramatuelle had been borderline awkward to say the least.

'Well, enjoy your meal,' said Giuseppe, ready for Olivia to depart. He wasn't keen on her. Firstly because she looked like a librarian and secondly because she freaked him out.

'Have you read about this place?' asked Olivia, seemingly in no hurry to return to her table for one. 'The name of it is taken from the song "La Madrague" by Brigitte Bardot, the sex symbol from the 1960s, who lives just around the corner from here. She's the darling of St Tropez. She was so beautiful and loves animals, so I adore her. The song talks about abandoned beaches and the most exquisite seashells and shellfish – and something about the loss of summer. Well, the French for seashells and shellfish is coquillages et crustacés, and that's what this place is called. How fabulous.'

'Indeed,' deadpanned Mew.

'And while I was googling, I was reading all about Saint Tropez himself. It's a fascinating story. Do you know it?'

'Yes,' said an uninterested Giuseppe at exactly the same moment as Mew said 'No'. Olivia only heard one voice and it wasn't the pilot's. Giuseppe picked up his phone from the table and started to tap out a message to someone, obviously unimpressed.

Olivia continued with her speech at a huge rate of kilometres per hour. 'Well, St Tropez is named after this martyr called Saint Torpes and apparently he was in Pisa at the time of Nero and was beheaded for something or other. How ghastly is that? And his rotting body was placed in a boat with a dog and a rooster and set sail. A dog and a rooster, for heaven's sake. And as it landed here in St Tropez, the town was named after him. Fascinating. There's a big bust of him at the Église de Saint-Tropez. I am thinking of maybe going down there tomorrow. You can come if you want, Mew.'

There was no mention of Giuseppe, who was still face down in his phone.

'I'll leave you to check out the big bust yourself. I think busts are much more your thing than mine.' Mew's meaning was clear.

'Oh yes, you mean I like… That I am into… Yes, you do know me so well. That I'm a…' Either the cocktail she had drunk at the piano bar was a little stronger than Olivia normally encountered or her brain was fizzing into overdrive as her unfinished words were spat out at breakneck speed.

Nobody said a word, a cloud of awkwardness hanging in the air.

'Well, history lesson over,' Olivia said eventually. 'I'll leave you to it. Have a good night.'

'Freaky-deaky,' said Mew, as Olivia walked off. 'I think I need to bag me a publisher that loves my books more than she actually loves me. That was pretty awkward. She can't even seem to say the word *lesbian* in front of me. It's not a problem, but she does seem to have a bit of a crush, eh?'

'I find her weird. She is always staring at me like some kind of serial killer. Like she wants to chop me up and do away with me. She hates me being with you.'

'Well, I like it, so if Olivia wants me to go all bisexy Lindsay Lohan or Cara Delevingne on her publishing ass then it's just not going to happen. It's not my thing. What floats my boat is what you have in your pants. Good luck to her though.'

Any further talk of Olivia was stopped by the arrival of their food.

*

As Mew and Giuseppe picked up their lobster scissors and cracked into their dinner, back at his apartment on the other side of St Tropez, Dexter Franklin felt an air of sadness wash over him. Even though the evening had been just as he had planned, watching his invited guests squirming in each other's company, all soaked in confusion by his no-show, Dexter could feel a niggle of grey spread itself across his brain as he thought about what he'd seen. And there was one person who was causing it. The man who always had done. His brother, Leland.

Having left Toni alone on the balcony of his apartment, Dexter retired to his room as soon as the funk he was feeling started to take hold. He poured himself another glass of wine and lay on his bed, his flesh heating slightly as he let his head flood with images of Leland. It was a sensation that he was used to. It had occurred many times throughout his life and always when he began to overanalyse his brother.

Leland Franklin, two years younger than Dexter, was somehow the man who had always managed to make Dexter question himself, doubt himself and second-guess everything that he did in life. He wasn't so much his brother as his rival. Even though both of them had excelled in their own fields of expertise, why was it that Dexter still felt his skin start to prickle and the bubbles of sweat start to form on his neckline when he found himself in the company of his brother? Or even when he was watching him from afar. Blood was supposed to be thicker than water, but as far as Dexter was concerned the blood between them was toxic. It always had been.

Dexter drained his wine glass, placed it on the bedside table, closed his eyes and lay back against the sheets. They felt icy against the electricity of his skin, cold against the slick of perspiration that suddenly seemed to coat him. The sensation, in no way pleasant, immediately transported him back...

*

Thirty years earlier...

Eight-year-old Dexter Franklin could feel the rivulets of sweat running down his neck, across his shoulders and onto the sheets of his bed. Despite pushing his duvet, decorated in his favourite *Danger Mouse* cover, down to the bottom of his bed, he still felt unbearably hot. But his temperature had nothing to do with the air in his bedroom, the one he shared with his younger brother, six-year-old

Leland; this was a heat caused by fear. Of torment and anguish. Nerves about the unknown. Of what the hours of darkness between his mother putting him to bed and the much-welcomed daylight would hold. Hours that seemed like an eternity.

Leland Franklin may have been two years younger than his brother, but he possessed the confident air of a bully. He did what he wanted, when he wanted, and most definitely to whomever he wanted. And already standing an inch taller than Dexter and possessing a body that seemed to be somehow stronger than his elder brother's, Leland had no problem in asserting his authority. He may have been the younger brother, but as far as looking up to Dexter was concerned, that wasn't an option. Being stronger meant being mightier. And being taller meant that the only way to look at Dexter was to look down at him. Which suited Leland perfectly.

'Scaredy-cat, scaredy-cat, lying there all wet and fat,' taunted Leland, leaning over his brother and jabbing at him with his fingers, one jab after another, then raising his hands above his head, balling them into fists and bringing them down hard, drumbeating rapidly against the rippling flesh of Dexter's belly.

Dexter was one of those children who somehow, despite being sporty and loving the physical pursuits that life afforded him – tree-climbing, dog-walking, brook-jumping – still found his body wrapped in a rippling mass of wobbly flesh that Leland loved to tease him about. Dexter wasn't fat, by any stretch of the imagination, but alongside his younger brother, whose body was taut and lean, his skin pulled expertly around his naturally athletic frame, he always felt out of shape and ugly. It was a vulnerable point that a cruel Leland was quick to pounce upon, night after night, when the two brothers were alone.

'Dough ball boy!' Leland's fists pounded against Dexter's stomach. Dexter wanted to move, to scream, to fight back, but something always stopped him. He knew that Leland was stronger and bigger than he was, despite his age. He knew that his parents wouldn't believe him if he cried to them. Who gets picked on and beaten up by their younger brother? Only a wimp, a wuss, a girl. They'd never listen to him. They never did. Was Leland their favourite? They would never say so, but that's how it felt to Dexter.

So Dexter let his brother do it, time and time again. And it wasn't just confined to their bedroom at home. When they were sent to boarding school, Leland would grab any opportunity to play dirty. Even when Dexter finally lost his puppy fat and saw his body develop into a thing of strength, an always stronger Leland would still pick on him, always away from the authoritative eyes of the teachers, but instead, the cruellest of all, in front of the mocking sneers and jeers of his classmates and school friends. Dexter would find himself ambushed in a lonely corridor, his head shoved under the brutal flush of the school toilets. Or his bag emptied and tipped out of the window, watching his schoolwork semicircle in the breeze as it fell to the floor. Or the humiliation of having his blazer torn from his body and thrown into the out-of-reach branches of a nearby tree. Small, insignificant actions that stacked up, turning Dexter into a boy who was always looking over his shoulder and afraid of what he might bump into around the next corner. Leland, popular with many of the lads who shared his lessons, was always ready to show off, to make sure that he was top dog. Never caught, always smart with his actions, creating maximum harm with minimal risk of comeback.

The bullying only stopped, turning instead into bitter rivalry, when Dexter reached his sixteenth birthday. His parents organised a party and presented Dexter with a top-of-the-range bicycle as a gift. It was sleek, smart, shiny and bright. They also presented him with a cake in the shape of a rugby pitch, Dexter's favourite sport at school and one he excelled at. Leland had also hoped to be on the team, but for once his skill was nowhere as good as Dexter's and he had failed to make it. It was a fact he abhorred.

At Dexter's birthday party, when the eyes of their parents were busy elsewhere, Leland pushed the cake to the floor and scratched the paintwork on the bike, spoiling its newness.

When Dexter ran to his parents to snitch on Leland, neither of them believed him. Leland was the younger brother; he wouldn't do that. Why would he? He didn't need the things that Dexter had. He had his own. But he wanted to make sure that his were better. And that meant ruining those belonging to others. A doe-eyed statement of innocence from the fourteen-year-old was all that Leland needed to escape blame. From that moment on, Dexter knew that he would never trust his brother. And soon that mistrust became hatred.

It was a feeling that had never gone away for Dexter. As he opened his eyes again and stared at the ceiling of his St Tropez apartment, he lifted his head off the sheets. A circle of dampness remained from where his sweat had soaked onto the material, just like it had all those years before, night after night, when he was scared of what his brother would do next. He pounded his fists into the sheets, just as Leland had to Dexter's tender flesh all those years before. Violent and unpredictable. Some things would never change.

CHAPTER 29

Anything more than a brisk walk seemed to stray into the realms of difficulty for DC Riding. After a lifetime of eating the finest gastronomic treats and the most full-bodied of wines, he was definitely beginning to feel that he was looking and feeling way beyond his forty-three years. His waistline was the biggest it had ever been, and whereas a fast-paced walk a few months ago would have resulted in nothing more bothersome than a fine film of perspiration across his forehead and cheeks, he was now finding that after merely a few steps he was dripping head to toe in sweat.

It was a fact he was fully aware of as he made his way as quickly as his body would allow across the reception at the guests' St Tropez hotel. His eyes were on the prize ahead of him, namely the woman who had glided out of the piano bar a few minutes' earlier, Rosita Velázquez. He dabbed his face with his handkerchief, monogrammed as ever with the initials DC, as he finally arrived alongside her while she waited for the lift.

The look on her face told her that she had been expecting him, and she curled her lips into a knowing grin.

'You need to cut down on your carbs, you big monster. I should put you in touch with my nutritionist, Ricardo. He would soon shift that wobbly mass of stomach.' She patted DC's belly as she spoke.

DC wasn't in the mood for a critique of his BMI. 'I'm a food critic, darling. It comes with the territory. Would you trust a blind chauffeur or a deaf soundman? I think not. So why would you trust a stick-thin food critic? And besides, some people find it highly attractive.'

'Don't be so touchy, big boy. You know I like to tease you. I always have.'

DC couldn't disagree. Rosita treated DC like she did all men, with an air of condescension and a serving of flirtation as thick as dulce de leche.

Trying to catch his breath from the excesses of his jog across the reception, he started to question Rosita about why she was in St Tropez.

'You know full well why I'm here. For the opening of Dexter's restaurant and to try and make my mark on the Cannes Film Festival. I'm surprised you're here though. Dexter's hardly your number-one fan, is he? Not after all that nasty business in New York. You nearly crippled him with your cruel words. Not that I made things any better, I suppose.' Rosita paused for a moment of recollection, lost in thought as she considered the past.

'No, doing the dirty with his brother is not exactly the best way to keep your man idolising you, is it? Anyway, don't they say that feeling hurt and lonely after a break-up is totally natural and that you should spend time with your family to get over it? You sure knocked that one on the head, doll, didn't you? Maybe you should have sung "Tell Me It's Not True" from *Blood Brothers* around the piano. It would have been more befitting, don't you think?' It was now DC's turn to curl his lips into a grin.

Rosita wasn't amused. 'You and your bloody musicals. You gay men are all the same. You only have to be in the same fucking time zone as a *Les Misérables* overture or a *Gypsy* poster and you start gaining an erection,' she scoffed, before adding, with what was more than a hint of sarcasm, 'What a shame your attempt at one didn't work out.'

'Do you have to remind me of that? I've been trying to erase that from my brain ever since all that hideous business in Brazil. You talk about me nearly crippling Dexter, Jesus, that show nearly crippled me financially. I'm sure it would have done had it not been for...' His words were left hanging as he concentrated on the images in his head. 'Well, you know...'

Indeed she did, and for just a millisecond Rosita could see a real moment of hurt and heartache written across DC's features. Was it matched by a brief instant of fear in his eyes as well? Rosita thought it may have been.

'Horrid times,' said Rosita. 'Best we forget.'

But DC couldn't.

*

Iguazu Falls, Brazil, five years earlier...

DC was sitting in the catering area at The Iguazu Falls Charity Blast and, to be honest, he wasn't really enjoying his day. He was only here for the money. It was far too hot for the Brit, and the show he had seen so far had not exactly been his favoured flavour. If it had featured the delights of some of his Broadway favourites then he would have been more than happy to endure the Brazilian sunshine and ridiculous heat. He'd have happily sweated his way through a selection of numbers from Patti LuPone, Chita Rivera or Idina Menzel but no, all he'd had to feast on entertainment-wise was some country and western puppet, a few cover versions and the threat of some dreadful girl band who were topping the bill.

He had to admit he had enjoyed Cher Le Visage's burlesque display. Strange, given what had passed between them. He'd always been a fan of hers, even if her turn on stage had been very short and the audience's response somewhat lacklustre. What a comedown. She'd say it was his fault, no doubt. And in his view, burlesque didn't really have a place on a large cavernous stage. It needed to be in an intimate environment so that every sequin could be admired and pored over and every jiggly moment could be savoured. DC found it strange how gay men, including himself, seemed to love burlesque so much. As far as he could make out, it was about the pomp, grace and femme-fabulous side of it all, nothing to do with slavering over the hint of a woman's nipples or a delicious expanse of flesh. That didn't interest him in the slightest. But as a craft and skill, he adored the flamboyance of it all.

That was why he had attempted to fund his own flamboyant off-Broadway show twelve months earlier. *Muse Magnificent* had been touted by the pre-production press as the next big thing to potentially transfer to Broadway. It was the tale of a lowly woman, genius in the skills of song, dance and theatrics, who would manage to become the goddess of her art. Her phoenix-like rise to fame, and the dangers that accompanied it, was a tale that audiences around the world would flock to. A *Xanadu* without the roller skates, a *Cabaret* with more feathers and frippery. It had been DC's dream since the first time he had seen a West End show at the tender age of nine, back in London. Years later, with the money that he had made from his job as a critic around the world, he was finally ready to realise his dream. He hired a top writer, director and producer, the best choreographers and found the perfect venue – it had to be New York, the home of the best theatre, in his opinion – and now he was ready to turn his vision of *Muse Magnificent* into glorious technicolour reality.

All he needed now was a star in the making. Someone with the requisite razzle-dazzle to turn the show into a sensation. After extensive auditions he'd hired Cher Le Visage. He'd seen her many times in UK venues and he loved her work, even if he knew that she had a reputation for being difficult – 'bitch' was the word that most employers used. But when she had sung and acted for him she'd won him over with her believability. She was dynamite, and showed a side that her burlesque act had never showcased before. There was more to her than just feathers and tassels and DC became instantly star-struck all over again. He needed her. He wanted her. And Cher, searching for a job that would send her US profile into the stratosphere, signed on the dotted line for a small fortune, blowing the show's budget. Rehearsals began, chorus and understudies were hired and for a brief while all was harmonious. It was only when tickets went on sale that it became clear to DC that *Muse Magnificent* looked like it might not be as *magnificent* as planned. Spiralling costs, rewrites insisted upon by diva Cher and a lack of experience from DC plunged the show into chaos, and with an American audience who only saw Cher Le Visage as a UK burlesque clothes horse, ticket sales were abysmal. After consulting a few people around him, some of whom he listened to, some of whom he didn't, DC decided to pull the show and declare himself bankrupt. *Muse Magnificent* never even made it to opening night. The critic had failed to live out his theatrical dreams, his savings swept away in a sequinned flourish.

Realising his failure, DC cut his losses and escaped, ruthlessly falling through loopholes and legalities to avoid paying anyone for their time and effort. Cher was one of the casualties and failed to see most of the fortune she had been promised. And word spread that it was Cher who had caused the production to collapse. Nobody wanted to work with her for fear of a repeat performance. Just like DC, she found herself virtually penniless.

Which was why, twelve months later, both of them were appearing at a charity event in Brazil – Cher to make any money she could to recoup her losses and DC as one of a bank of critics asked along to promote the joys of Brazilian food.

Cher, still sporting her stage outfit, approached an unsuspecting DC, who was immersed in a plate of *churrasco* meats cooked on the Brazilian-style barbecue set up in the catering area.

'So you can afford to eat now? Not so bankrupt anymore, are we?' DC jumped and nearly choked on the sausage he was tasting. He had been expecting to run into Cher at some point – it was bound to happen given their close proximity – but he was still unprepared for their encounter.

'Oh, hello, Cher.' His words were hesitant.

'So we're both working this shithole, then?' Cher said coolly.

'Well, this is for a damned good charity and the scenery out here is absolutely amazing.' DC felt compelled to defend his attendance.

'You're only here for the money and you know it. You don't give a shit about greenery and forestation unless you're cruising around Hampstead Heath looking for a cock to suck.'

Cher's words were harsh but true.

'Well you don't seem to have lost any of your charm since *Muse Magnificent*,' sniped DC. If Cher was going to be aggressive then he was not going to roll over and surrender.

'That's about the only thing I haven't lost, thanks to you bad-mouthing me to all and sundry about that show. I've hardly found any work because of you over the past year. I'm reduced to bottom of the bill at gigs like this. I don't have any money, I don't have any credibility and my employment chances are about as slim as Stephen Hawking's if he went up for the lead in *Starlight Express*.'

'I had to pull the show. It made financial sense.'

'For you, maybe. But not for me. And going bankrupt – very smart move. Left me high and dry without a leg to stand on.'

'You know I'm a fan of yours. I always will be.' DC could hear how pathetic his words sounded, even if what he said was true.

'Tell that to my overdraft, you prick.'

'I *am* sorry.'

'Then show me. I want money and I want compensation. I need you to put my career back on the straight and narrow and that means a whole heap of cash. It's been a year from hell and you owe me.'

'But I'm bankrupt. There's no money.'

'So you're doing this for a free plate of chorizo are you?' Cher flicked the edge of DC's bowl with her manicured finger, causing one of the pieces of meat to spill out onto the table. 'It's been a year, rules change. I've spoken to my lawyer. You're earning money and you owe me.'

'I need any money I earn myself. The show wiped me out.' DC mopped his brow.

'I don't give a shit. I want my money and I want it soon. The law is on my side. Or else…'

Cher's words were threatening and DC's skin prickled.

'Or else what?'

'Or else I tell the world that you fiddled with half the male members of the chorus line, or I tell them that you groped me and threatened me with violence, or that you keep underage sexual images on your computer.'

'But I didn't, I wouldn't and I don't.' DC was baffled by her accusations.

'You'd have to prove it. It would be your word against mine. I can win over some of the crew that you didn't pay. I still speak to some of them on Facebook and Twitter. They'd be all for making a fast buck from the man who cheated them out of their salary. And I'm sure some of the more tech-savvy ones could hack your PC to fill it with all sorts of disgusting stuff. You'd be ruined.'

'That's low. Hellishly low.' But DC could picture it happening. Cher was not a woman to be messed with – as many had found out over the years.

'So think on and cough up the cash you owe me. You've got until I vanish out of here, which will thankfully be later today, to come and find me. If I've not heard from you by the time I board the plane back to the UK then you can expect a few meaty accusations coming your way.'

With that Cher smiled at him and marched off.

DC didn't know that Cher was bluffing. She'd not spoken to a lawyer and had no clue whether the law was now on her side or not, but she was determined to try and make the critic give her what she was owed. She was fed up of men trying to dominate her. Why should she roll over yet again?

As DC watched her strut from the catering area, a flurry of glistening sequins and feathers, he felt rage stain his soul. He needed to make sure that Cher didn't try and ruin him. He had no doubt she would try. Cher Le Visage was a woman who would be more than happy to spill some scandalous lies to aid her cause.

DC just couldn't allow himself to take that chance.

*

Back in the reception of their St Tropez hotel, the lift doors opened and Rosita swept inside, leaving DC still dabbing himself with his hanky.

'It was a horrid time, DC. But I still think you should forget all about it,' she said, pressing the elevator button for her floor. 'Cher Le Visage was a nasty piece of work and deserved everything that came her way. I hated playing understudy to her in *Muse Magnificent* and was thrilled that the show was canned. That production should have been mine, as you well know, and if I couldn't shine in it, then I'm bloody well sure that no one else should have. Especially somebody as nasty as her.'

As the elevator doors closed, DC was silent, his mind filled with thoughts of the showgirl. He had to admit that Cher was a vile woman and that her dying was really the best thing that could have happened to him. It saved any possible career-ruining destruction of his character and had stemmed her vicious threats once and for all.

CHAPTER 30

Back at her table at Coquillages et Crustacés, Olivia was contemplating what to order from the extensive menu when her attention was caught by a woman on the far side of the restaurant. Maybe a few years younger than Olivia, she was dressed simply in a pair of jeans and a smart-casual, loose-fitting blouse. Her hair was tied back away from her face. A face that was staring directly at Olivia.

Olivia felt her cheeks colour as she stared back at the woman. As she did so, the woman, who was also dining alone, began to smile.

The smile was the spark that lit the fuse of something special within Olivia. It was as if a million tiny explosions detonated within her chest, all of them suddenly making her feel more attractive and more available than she'd ever done before. Automatically, she smiled back, trying to hear her own heartbeat above the cacophony of fireworks sounding within her.

What was happening? Everything else in the room seemed to fade out of focus as she looked directly into the woman's eyes. She was reasonably pretty. She had a friendly face. Really friendly. She appeared interested. As was Olivia. This hadn't been on the menu for the evening.

It was the other woman who made the first move, a fact that Olivia was hugely grateful for. There was no way she could even look down and nonchalantly browse the menu let alone stand up and walk over to the woman. She could sense her cheeks burning as the woman approached her table.

'Bonjour.'

'Bonjour. Er… my French is really bad.' Olivia giggled nervously.

'Then I will speak English. I hope you don't mind me speaking to you. But something told me I could. I am dining alone. I have to review the new menu for my work and I was wondering if you would care to join me – unless you're waiting for somebody, of course. The meal will be on me. My treat. It's not nice to be alone, is it?'

Olivia held out her hand to the woman. 'I'm Olivia Rhodes, pleased to meet you. I work for a publishing company.'

'How fabulous. I am a writer for a local paper. My name is Fabienne Delacroix. Pleased to meet you.' Fabienne leant in and kissed the publisher twice on the cheeks. It felt fabulous to Olivia. The signs were definitely looking good. It was only a few more minutes of conversation before she found herself seated at her new friend's table. As the French woman had said, there was no joy in being alone, was there?

'Please choose something you like the look of from the menu, Olivia, and we can talk about what you are doing here in St Tropez,' said Fabienne. There was a direct tone in Fabienne's voice that Olivia had to admit she was really rather enjoying. Fabienne seemed a little stern yet somehow incredibly sexy to Olivia.

'Now, what do I like the look of?' asked Olivia, trying to concentrate on the words on the menu. But she already knew. It was the woman across the table.

When their food arrived fifteen minutes later, Olivia was in full flow, telling Fabienne about how she was in St Tropez with her client Mew Stanton, the pop-star-turned-chef. She didn't even look in Mew's direction when she mentioned her. In fact, she didn't think of Mew or indeed the odious Giuseppe all night long. She only had eyes for one person. And what's more, Olivia didn't even seem to be aware that every dark thought that had been in her head earlier in the evening had now turned a healthy shade of tricolour red, white and blue.

Vive la France indeed.

CHAPTER 31

'Good morning, everybody. The captain and the crew are happy to welcome you on board *La Pouncho*. For your own safety we ask you to remain seated during the trip, on which you will discover the beauty of the peninsula of St Tropez.'

Holly thought the usage of the word 'everybody' was a little liberal, seeing as there were only three tourists other than herself seated upon the wooden benches at the front of the small vessel as it set sail from St Tropez harbour. Two of them were a young couple, seemingly intent on necking each other with great ferocity and totally oblivious to the voice coming from the electronic equipment. The other was a lady of around fifty, with round glasses perched on her nose and her hair scraped back into a small but perfectly formed bun.

None of them were looking at Holly, or indeed appeared to recognise her, which pleased Holly immensely as she wanted to be alone with her thoughts. She needed to switch off and escape the madness of what her day-to-day existence was dealing her. Which was why she had retired to bed pretty soon after her altercation with Leland on the private beach, slept for a good nine hours and risen early to take a boat trip showcasing the homes of many of the rich and famous who owned properties in the jewel of the Côte d'Azur crown. It hadn't been top of her list of things to do in St Tropez, but when she had read a flyer for it in the hotel reception she knew it would be the perfect way to lose herself for a few hours and not think about how dirty, cheap, and frightened Leland had managed to make her feel the previous evening.

'On our right we glance at the Portalet Tower and the Tour Vieille, built in the fifteenth century. The house against the Tour Vieille, with the four storeys and the green pastel shutters, is where the great French singer Charles Aznavour used to live.' As the voice sounded, Holly turned her head and stared at the house. It reminded her of Lego brick houses she used to construct alone in her bedroom above the pub when her mum had been working. At first they were makeshift and basic, but as she became older the designs she came up with would be more complex and imaginative. She had been playing with one of them earlier that night. The night that Uncle Warren had first entered her room. She could remember it lying on the floor the morning after, alongside the deodorant can she had been using as a makeshift microphone to pretend to be Janet Jackson in the mirror. Both things so innocent, yet still to the present day they sent shudders of dread down her spine.

'Now we enter a small bay in the Gulf of St Tropez called Baie des Canoubiers. It takes its name from hemp, a plant that used to grow here and was used for making ropes and clothes. We now come to Granier Beach, famous for the first nude scenes in Roger Vadim's 1956 film *And God Created Woman*, starring Brigitte Bardot.'

Holly tried to push all thoughts of Uncle Warren and her encounter with Leland out of her head as she watched the abodes of the mega-rich pass by the boat. There was a time when she could have thought about buying a house somewhere swanky like St Tropez, using the loose change from just a few Crazy Sour appearances. She could have lived alongside George Michael with his chimney-stacked house, been given a golden key like the residents of the luxurious Chateau Borelli at the top of the hill – a snip at ten million francs each – and paddled near the sumptuous boathouse owned by Mohamed Al-Fayed. But that was before it had all gone wrong. Before Leland Franklin had made sure that a post-rehab reunion for Crazy Sour was out of the question.

'Near the water, near the huge central steps, is the former house of The King, Elvis Presley. He never lived in that house, which was bought by Hollywood Studios for him.'

Holly stared across the calm waters at Elvis's Florentine style house. It seemed incredibly grandiose. What a waste, to think that Elvis had never lived in such a beautiful house. Never been able to appreciate its decoration. Never wandered around the grounds. The thought made Holly sad. Elvis had died before he could benefit from it. Tears needled her eyes as she considered the idea, but she wasn't sad for the King of Rock 'n' Roll – far from it. She was sad for somebody much closer to her heart. Somebody else who had not been able to appreciate all of the niceties of life that she'd finally been able to have, and had always deserved. Somebody whose life had suddenly become pretty much a waste too.

*

Los Angeles, three years earlier...

Holly had not had the best day. In fact, she had not had the best couple of months. For the second time in her life, the 'trade' that was bringing in the big bucks had suddenly been cut off. Extinguished like a firework that had sparkled brightly for so long but had suddenly become no more than a tiny spark, fizzling away into the finality of nothingness. First it had been

Crazy Sour and now this. The only saving grace in her demise as a high-class call girl was that at least her mum, Shirley, and anyone of importance to her, had not found out that she was the mystery woman at the centre of the boot-licking, drug-fucked politician sex scandal that was currently splashing its way across papers, mags and websites in every country around the world. But even if her name had escaped the column inches, it had not escaped the gossip, and Holly's lucrative river of money had gone from free flowing to beyond parched overnight.

And with her mother currently staying with her at her LA home, the rumour mill tittle-tattle couldn't have come at a worse time for Holly. She dreaded waking up in the morning and having to explain to her mother just why there was a battalion of reporters and photographers outside her front door. Luckily, so far, this hadn't happened. And Holly prayed that it wouldn't.

'That'll be forty-five dollars please,' said the girl behind the counter, handing Holly the biggest bouquet of hibiscus flowers that she had been able to find in the whole of LA. They were her mother's favourites and always had been. The name meant 'delicate beauty' and it was a nickname that Shirley had given to Holly early on in her life. Wherever Holly was in the world, the mere sight of a hibiscus would always remind her of her wonderful mother. She'd even had one tattooed on her left foot while on tour with Crazy Sour.

Holly handed over the money, suddenly aware that she seemed to be counting every dime in the aftermath of the politician scandal, and walked out of the florists onto the street in order to hail a cab to take her back home.

Holly stared out of the cab window as she instructed the driver where to take her: Mar Vista, West Hollywood. The place she had called home for the last few years, ever since buying her impressive but decidedly un-showbiz house there. Holly loved it. Even though it was close to the glitz and glamour of Tinsel Town, it was still far enough away to escape the madness that had been her life in Crazy Sour and provide her with a backdrop of some kind of normality. Mar Vista was a melting pot of Asians, African-Americans, Latinos and whites and she felt she fitted in there. There was a cool vibe about it that she liked, yet the greenery and freshness of the area somehow reminded her of her life growing up back in the UK. The only time she headed back to the UK these days was either for a client or to see her mother.

But at least four or five times a year, Holly would pay for Shirley to fly across the Atlantic and visit her at her Mar Vista home. It felt good to have her mother around – the one person who had always been there for her and never let her down. It was satisfying for Holly to be able to give her some kind of payback. She would never tire of seeing her mother's face light up as she wandered around her home, staring at the gold and platinum discs that adorned the walls, noting the million-plus sales in Japan, the music industry recognition in Australia. The rewards of Holly's success were clear to see. As clear as the proud smile on Shirley's face every time she came to stay.

The two women would spend all of their time together during their visits – almost like sisters, as opposed to mother and daughter – ordering in takeaway and sitting in their PJs, working their way through their tower of DVD favourites, which constantly sat alongside Holly's television. It would be the same every visit. If Shirley was staying with her daughter for a week, Holly could have bet her last dollar with complete confidence that they would watch, laugh, sing along if need be and repeat every line of *Grease* (both the original and the shocking follow-up, *Grease 2*), *Dirty Dancing*, *Strictly Ballroom*, *Moulin Rouge*, *Pretty Woman*, *A Chorus Line*, *Chitty Chitty Bang Bang* and *Clue-*

less. It was what they did. And for Holly it was those magical moments that meant everything.

As the cab pulled up outside the house, Holly was sure that Shirley would be lining up another classic for them to giggle over together. She was in the mood for *Grease 2*. Retro boy-meets-girl nonsense with the eye-twinkling delights of Maxwell Caulfield – her mother's ultimate man back in the day – and the gum-smacking coolness of Michelle Pfeiffer. Yes, that would fill the next few hours quite nicely.

Holly balanced the hibiscus bouquet in her hands as she inserted her key into the back door of the house and pushed it open. She called out to her mum as she did so. There was no reply.

She tried again. Still nothing.

Walking into the kitchen she placed the bouquet down on one of the stone countertops and yelled out again. It concerned her slightly that there was no reply. Holly had only been gone a couple of hours, desperate to scan newsstands to see if she was mentioned in any mags, and Shirley hadn't said she was going anywhere. Maybe she was in the loft, or the toilet, or was having a snooze. Holly tried to not let it worry her. But a ripple of concern spread across her as walked into the front room.

The ripple exploded within her as she took in what was before her. Shirley was lying face down on the floor, in front of the television, her body somehow twisted into a mass of angles. Immediately Holly knew that her mother wasn't sleeping. Her position looked far from comfortable. The DVDs were spread out in front of her, a jumble of cases and discs spilling across the floor. Had Shirley fallen into them? It looked that way. The thought vanished as Holly ran towards the body, her worst fears curdling inside her mind. Was her mother still alive? Had Shirley been attacked by intruders? Why wasn't she moving? Lightning strikes of panic flashed across her brain.

Holly's tears were already flowing freely as she knelt down alongside her mother and angled herself to look at her mother's face. *Please let her be breathing.* She couldn't tell. Her face seemed somehow twisted and contorted. Holly screamed, louder than she ever had before. Louder than any scream she had ever heard. Louder even than the Crazy Sour fans who had virtually deafened her over the years. But their hysterical screams had been of joy, of adulation, of fever-pitch delight. Holly's was of utter fear. A fear that her world had just come to an end.

*

A chill caused by the thoughts of such a horrid, life-shattering moment snapped Holly back from her recollections and into the present. The nightmare of that day three years ago was a moment that she tried not to visit, but it was one that often crept like a thief into her mind, ready to steal away any happiness that lurked there.

Trying unsuccessfully to push the thought aside, Holly stared out across the bay at the houses of the St Tropez glitterati. Not that any of them really seemed to live there, according to the boat's commentary. Houses were constantly shuttered, visited maybe once or twice a year, the riches inside dusted off for an odd fleeting visit from some fly-by-night celebrity. She couldn't ever imagine laughter ringing out in these places like she and her mother had experienced during Shirley's visits to LA. Like she and her mother had always experienced, even in the money-pinching days of life in the poky flat above the pub in Birmingham. There had always been laughter. Moments of joy and togetherness. The sound of the mirth from a family tie that was bound with the strongest of knots. Until that day three years ago when Holly had found her mother's body in her West LA front room. Then the laughter had stopped.

Shirley was still breathing. The paramedics who arrived said that Shirley had suffered a massive stroke – violently strong for a woman of just forty-seven years of age. She was lucky to be alive, but the damage to her brain would be irreparable. The cause was unknown. According to the experts it was something that 'could have happened at any time'.

Shirley would never recover, but over the next few months Holly made sure that her mother was in the best place possible. Shirley was all the family Holly had and she arranged for her mum to stay in America. At first Holly was keen to have her living under her own roof but the constant care that Shirley would need could not come from one so young or inexperienced. Holly would have to play speech therapist, psychologist, physiotherapist, occupational therapist and specialist nurse. All she wanted to play was the role of doting daughter. With the help of those in the know, Holly found a recuperative home not far from her Mar Vista house. Shirley would be provided with the care she needed 24/7 and given a life as comfortable as she could hope for. Not that there was much hope. She was existing, no more than that. Living had ceased the moment the stroke hit. There were days that Holly thought perhaps her mother would have been better off dying. But on the rare occasions when there almost seemed to be a glimmer of recognition, of fight, in her mother's eyes, a faint gratitude that Holly was still in her life, then all thoughts like that vanished. At those moments Holly knew that having Shirley still in her life was the most precious thing of all.

The home was expensive. Care didn't come cheap. Holly sold her mother's house back in the UK, and then sold as many of her possessions as she could and a lot of her own to fund the mounting bills she was experiencing. Her life as a call girl was not paying what it once had, and as time went on, Holly's ability to make money from the fame game treadmill of appearances and endorsements faded too. Opportunities didn't seem to come knocking with the regularity they once had.

Now all that she really had left was her home. That and the Crazy Sour awards that decorated its walls. The ones her mother had loved. In the house that her mother had loved. She couldn't sell that. Not now. Not until she had exhausted every possible avenue. Even if that meant doing something that didn't sit easily with her, the frightened, vulnerable version of Holly Lydon who was scared she wouldn't be able to support her mother. She would have to play the role of superbitch and make sure that Dexter Franklin paid her handsomely for the incriminating photos that she had stashed within her St Tropez hotel suite safe. Shirley deserved nothing less than the best, and Holly would do everything she could to make sure she had it.

Shirley Lydon had had her life all but taken away from her when she'd suffered that terrible and tragic stroke, her own vitality wasted away to nothing. Life was so cruel. What a waste of such a wonderful woman.

As Holly jumped down from the boat and walked back across the portside in the direction of her St Tropez hotel, she was determined not to waste the opportunity that the photos gave her. To provide for Shirley. That was all that mattered. Despite any doubts she might have, Dexter would have to pay. And he would have to pay big.

CHAPTER 32

Morocco, over two years earlier...

'Your jet awaits, if you'd care to step aboard.' Dexter's voice was smooth and borderline smug as he watched the reaction on Rosita Velázquez's face. She had to be impressed by his actions. Her knowing smile told him that she was.

'So, just where are we going and why would I be getting onto a flight with you when I have none of my own luggage, my passport, a change of clothes and more importantly not a scrap of make-up on – which believe you me is not a common occurrence in my life? I like to be red-carpet ready at every opportunity.'

'I think this will sort all of that out.'

Dexter pointed to the far side of the airfield just as a car pulled up. The back door opened and out stepped Tinks McVeigh. She was carrying her trusty make-up case in one hand and as she spotted Dexter and Rosita she lifted up her other hand to wave something. Rosita could see that it was her Brazilian passport.

'And my luggage?'

As if on cue, another car pulled up behind the vehicle in which Rosita's make-up artist had arrived. It was much larger and the driver hurried to open the hatchback of the car. It was filled with Rosita's cases.

'Son of a bitch…' purred Rosita in disbelief. She was lost for words.

'So, you have no more excuses. Climb aboard and we can be in Dubai for supper. You said you wanted to sample The Palm as soon as possible, did you not?'

Rosita had known many men in her life, but never before had she been as poleaxed as she had been by meeting Dexter Franklin. The man was quite something. It had been less than twenty-four hours since their first meeting in the backstreets of Chefchaouen, yet already she was totally smitten. As smooth operators went, he was one hundred per cent silk.

As she climbed up the steps to the aircraft and into the coolness of the interior, she had to admit that it had been quite a morning and unlike anything she had ever experienced before. She settled herself into the comfort of one of the soft leather chairs and didn't say a word as Dexter sat himself in the chair next to her. He was smiling from ear to ear, obviously pleased with himself. Rosita couldn't stop grinning either. The celebrity chef had played a blinder and had definitely won her admiration.

He leant in to kiss her, but she placed her fingers to his lips and pushed him away. Dexter gave her the look of a scolded puppy. 'I don't think so. Not until *this* is back to its visionary best,' she said, circling her face with her fingers.

A smiling Rosita beckoned to Tinks, who was just boarding the flight. 'Darling, can you sort this please?'

'At your service,' said Tinks, before emitting a whistle of appreciation. 'Now this is one fancy private jet. How on earth did you manage to arrange all of this in the middle of nowhere?' Her question was aimed at Dexter.

Dexter winked at Tinks in response. Truth be told, it hadn't been easy to organise. But as soon as he had woken up alongside Rosita that morning he knew that he wanted to please the beauty lying in his arms.

Rosita had been dozing as Dexter climbed out of the riad bed they had shared for the night. He had not expected her to stay over, but her attentions towards him once they had eaten and sampled the delights of a bottle or two of red wine were clearly amorous. Attentions that Dexter had no intention of rebuffing. Rosita was red-hot to look at and as their night of lovemaking had proven, she was red-hot in the sack as well. The serene sleeping beauty that occupied his bed now was a thousand lifetimes away from the energetic lover who had given him a sexual workout unlike any he could remember for the longest time. She was fierce and feisty and fabulous to look at. Which was why, knowing that Rosita was due to leave Morocco in just a few hours, potentially never to be seen again, he had to spring into action.

Dexter was booked to leave Morocco and head back to the UK in a few days' time, but there was nothing stopping him from going right now. From going anywhere, in fact. He had finished what he needed to do in the blue town and meeting Rosita had given him the urge to turn any plans he had been making upside down.

Dexter had made a couple of phone calls, arranged exactly what was needed and climbed back into bed alongside a dozing Rosita by the time she had started to emerge from her slumber.

It was nearly an hour later that a reluctant Rosita was dressed and ready to leave, aware that the start of her long journey home was imminent. She went to kiss him goodbye, unsure what to say or how to carry on what had started so blissfully well between them. An unexpected joy from nowhere.

'I must head back to my hotel. Tinks will be wondering where I am. I need to go. Even if I don't really...' She left the words suspended in mid-air.

'I've arranged a car to take you there. It's picking us up just around the corner.'

'Us?'

'I thought I'd accompany you back to yours. I guess I just wanted to spend a little more time with you, if that's okay.'

Staring into the enticing blackness of Dexter's eyes, Rosita couldn't imagine why it wouldn't be.

She kissed him, letting her tongue explore inside his lips, no words necessary to convey her meaning.

It was only when they were in the car that Rosita realised that maybe something was afoot. Instead of the car driving back to her hotel to meet the others, the vehicle headed out of town and into the arid countryside. Despite her feeble protestations as to where exactly they were heading, Rosita was intrigued by the uncertainty of her new adventure.

'Trust me,' said Dexter. 'I rearranged a few things.' She knew she did trust him. It was only when they pulled up in front of the private jet that she realised just how much trouble her new friend had seemingly gone to with his rearranging.

And when Tinks appeared with her requirements for the flight, Rosita knew that Dexter had thought of everything. The thought made her smile.

She was still smiling as Tinks finished off her make-up and the engines of the private jet revved into action. Her cases had all been loaded and, as far as Rosita could work out, it appeared that Dexter had done everything possible to make her journey to Dubai as incredible as possible.

'So, how on earth did you find a private jet in the middle of nowhere?' asked Rosita.

'I have travelled on them before you know,' Dexter laughed, reaching out for Rosita's hand. 'I just had to ring a few places, but money talks, wherever you are. And it was easy to phone Tinks and arrange the rest as you gave me her number yesterday, when you suggested I use her in the future. Her work does speak for itself.'

•

Dexter cupped his palm under Rosita's chin and admired her face.

'Thank you,' said Tinks with a nod of her head. 'I did my best.'

'What about the crew from the shoot?' asked Rosita. Not that she really cared.

'They're travelling back as planned. But I figured you'd want Tinks here. Especially if we're going to spend a few days in Dubai.'

'A few days? And since when do you organise my social calendar?' laughed Rosita. 'I may have films to shoot back in Brazil for all you know.'

'You told me last night that you didn't.'

'Did I?' It was true, she didn't. But a girl always liked to have an air of mystery. Damn that wine making her loose-lipped. What else had she said?

'Staying where?'

'At The Ritz Carlton, I trust you approve.'

Rosita did. The hotel was one of her favourites.

'How many rooms did you book?'

'Three. I didn't like to assume.' Dexter placed his hand on Rosita's knee and squeezed her leg to emphasise his meaning.

'Very wise. One for each of us,' said Rosita, not that she had any intention of the third room being used at all. But she didn't want to appear too keen.

The three of them strapped their seat belts into position and within a few minutes their flight was heading skywards. Dexter had his hand in Rosita's.

It was ten minutes into their journey before any of them spoke again.

'I'm just going to freshen up,' said Rosita. 'I assume there's a room at the back of the plane. I really should change my outfit from last night.' As she hadn't planned on stopping over, Rosita was still in the same clothes as the night before. She'd showered at the riad but had not had an opportunity to change.

'There's a whole suite,' said Dexter, his suggestion clear. 'Shall I come with you?'

'I'd love you to. It is going to be a few hours before we land in Dubai, after all.'

Tinks chose to ignore the brewing sexual tension and buried her head in a fashion magazine.

'You go ahead, I just need to send a couple of texts. I'll see you through there in five.' He pointed to the back of the plane and winked.

Rosita twisted on her heels and sashayed her way down the plane. Dexter watched her ass jiggling a little as she moved. The thought stirred his loins into movement.

Dexter reached into a pocket and pulled out his iPhone. His day was going perfectly, but something was niggling at the back of his mind. He knew what he had to do. He typed the words into his phone and pressed send. The action made him smile.

Standing up, he made to follow Rosita.

'See you in Dubai…' smirked Tinks.

'That's another six and a half hours away,' said Dexter.

'I know. As I said, see you in Dubai.'

The chef moved to the back of the plane and opened the door to the separate room there. He was greeted by a naked and enticing Rosita lying on the bed, her clothes from the night before strewn across the floor. Dexter's erection grew to full length as he looked at her. She was an exotic beauty. Just his type. Tinks was right. He would need every minute of the next six and a half hours to enjoy the pleasures of Rosita's flesh. He closed the door and began to undress.

As a totally bewitched Dexter was positioning himself between Rosita's willing legs, the text message that he had sent moments earlier arrived at its destination. The recipient read the words: '*We both know this isn't working. I'm done. Thanks for being a great contestant but I'm seeing somebody else.*'

'Contestant? Contestant? What the fuck does he mean by that? Surely I was more than that, for fuck's sake?'

It appeared not. And in one message their relationship was over. Used and abused. Humped and dumped. Shagged and bagged. Fucked and chucked. And for somebody else. And to a raging and totally distraught Mew Stanton, that was inexcusable.

CHAPTER 33

It wasn't just Olivia Rhodes's appetite for exquisite shellfish that had been satisfied on her night out at Coquillages et Crustacés. For a woman who normally didn't have enough confidence in her personal appearance to try a new hairstyle or even be so bold as to change her brand of mouthwash, when she woke up the next day she was grinning from ear to ear with inner confidence. She basked in the delicious afterglow of waking up in the arms of a woman who appeared to hit all of the right buttons. She'd certainly been hitting a few during the night after the two women had cabbed their way back from the restaurant to Fabienne Delacroix's small apartment in Gassin to spend the night.

Olivia wasn't normally a woman to give herself so easily. In fact, when it came to relationships and affairs of the heart she was nigh on car crash. But there was something about Fabienne that seemed to erase any hesitation she would usually have about leaping into bed with a partner. Fabienne was deeply intelligent, attractive enough to make Olivia's heart flutter, yet not so drop-dead that Olivia found herself thinking she was punching above her weight, and to the publisher that was a great reassurance. Plus, half a bottle of wine in, Olivia literally found herself hanging off her every word. She was fascinating to talk to and the complete opposite to all of the trite bitchery, simpering glances and fawning admiration that had become her staple conversation with those gathered for Dexter's opening over the past few days. And that included Mew.

It was Dexter that the two women were discussing as they lay in bed, *chez* Fabienne, enjoying a breakfast of croissants, jam and strong black coffee. The early morning light of Gassin streamed through the windows where the shutters had been pulled back and the sounds of the street from outside hung in the air. Fabienne's cat, Gisele, lay at the women's feet as they ate, her eyes closed and curled up in complete soporific bliss. It was a scene that Olivia was loving. As she spooned another heap of jam onto a croissant and placed it in her mouth, she couldn't remember the last time she had felt quite so comfortable and at ease. And also very excited about the possibilities of what potentially could be around the corner. Neither woman had appeared to wake up with any awkwardness about their actions the night before. *As the French say*, mused Olivia, listening to Fabienne talking about Dexter, *je ne regrette rien...*

And, it would seem, neither did the reporter.

'I interviewed Mr Franklin the day before yesterday. I actually quite liked him. Considering he has become one of those TV chefs back in your country I thought he might be somewhat of an idiot, all so-called good looks and charm but with no gravitas, just hoping to make a quick euro by opening a substandard restaurant here in my country.'

Olivia laughed. 'My country? Your country? That's all very Brexit, very "them and us".' Olivia reached out and took Fabienne's hand in hers.

Fabienne didn't laugh but she did keep hold of Olivia's hand, a fact Olivia enjoyed deeply as a shot of warmth passed through her. She did, however, ignore all mention of Brexit and continued to discuss Dexter.

'But no, I liked him, and I look forward to the opening of his restaurant. Even if the puerile ramblings of the celebrities there will turn my brain to the consistency of soft crab.'

'Dexter is a lovely man. Very kind and incredibly handsome. Not that he's my type, of course,' fluffed Olivia, stating the obvious. 'But as his publisher, I can say that he has always been a delight to work for.'

'You said so last night,' said Fabienne. Her words were brusque but not rude.

'Did I?' questioned Olivia. Maybe she'd downed more wine than she remembered.

'I am pleased you are going to the opening night as well. You seem like such a normal person to have found in a place like St Tropez. As a rule it's full of crazy young girls from the world of show business wearing the most ridiculous of micro-bikinis and sipping Moët at Bora Bora, or its aging playboys with skin the colour of Doritos trying to find some kind of hard-on for those crazy young girls at Bora Bora. That's a beach bar here, by the way. I would offer to take you, but you're worth better.'

'I have heard of it. One of the girls at my hotel has mentioned it, I think.' Olivia was sure Mew had namedropped it to Giuseppe when they were in Ramatuelle. It was the first time she had thought of Mew that morning, and it suddenly struck her that normally Mew would be the first face she imagined upon awakening. The thought that she now had someone else to think about pleased Olivia. 'So, you think I'm normal? That's a good thing, right?'

'Oh, very. It's so hard to find in this town. I just hope we are sitting together at the opening. I may have to insist.'

Olivia felt another ripple of cosiness pass through her.

'Who knows?' she said, making a mental note to contact Dexter immediately on leaving Fabienne's to make sure that this happened.

Normal. Olivia liked that. Normal as in good, decent and dependable. Not as in boring, drab and uninteresting. That was what Fabienne meant, wasn't it? She'd said so, hadn't she? God, she would hate it if Fabienne already found her boring.

'Anyway,' said Fabienne, a smile filling her face as she put her breakfast plate down. 'I don't have to be at work until a little later because of working late last night, reviewing the new menu, so I am thinking that we should make the most of our time, don't you?' She reached over and kissed Olivia fully on the lips and allowed one of her hands to roam downwards to Olivia's breasts. Her nipple hardened immediately at the touch.

Olivia immersed herself in the pleasure wrapping itself around her, her kisses becoming more and more urgent as her arousal heightened.

Fabienne let her hand travel down across Olivia's stomach and disappear under the edge of the duvet to find its destination. The eager wetness between Olivia's legs beckoned Fabienne's touch and she closed her eyes in ecstasy as Fabienne inserted her fingers into her.

Olivia widened her legs to allow deeper access, causing a now disgruntled Gisele to leap off the bed and head towards the open window to sit on the sill there. Olivia didn't care. It was now her who was purring with joy.

*

Mew Stanton was partaking in breakfast too. But unlike Olivia, she didn't have anyone sexually exciting to share it with. And that was a fact that was pissing her off hugely as she nibbled on her third slice of toast and allowed Christophe to top up her coffee cup.

Sitting opposite her was DC Riding, who was not so much nibbling as taking humongous bites into what he thought might be his fifth piece of toast. He'd lost count, lost in the delight of piling flavoured *confiture* high upon each and every slice.

'You're working *again*, I see,' he quipped at Christophe as he turned to fill DC's cup too.

'I told you, I'm from a family who never say no to a few extra euros if the offer is there. My sister is the same. Our mother and father taught us to be like that. Now, can I fetch you anything else?'

'That'll be all.' It was Mew who answered, her words very dismissive, cutting off any further conversation even if DC had possessed an urge for something else. Christophe moved off to serve another table.

'Are you having a slice of total cow on that piece of bread?' asked DC. 'Because that's what you're being this morning. What the hell is the matter with you?'

'Nothing.'

'Liar. I know I'm not your man of choice for early morning entertainment. Where is your Italian stallion this morning? Has he finally had to go back to work, fly one of his machines and stop sponging off you?'

Mew merely smirked, but her annoyance at DC's words was clear. Giuseppe was indeed the reason she was in a serious funk. She was beginning to wonder whether the Italian had been using her after all. Their meal out at the seafood restaurant the night before had been more or less good, despite the annoyance she felt at his continual texting throughout the meal. But when it came to paying, Giuseppe and his iPhone had conveniently disappeared when the bill arrived. He tended to do that a lot. Had he paid for anything since their arrival? No. Not that Mew minded. It was the fact that he hadn't even offered to do so that irked her.

And this morning he had refused sex before breakfast. Actually said no. To her. Mew Stanton. And then dropped the bombshell that he was indeed heading back to work for the day as he had flights to pilot. Not even Mew's best bedroom moves to try and keep him entertained had stopped him showering, dressing and exiting their suite with a cursory '*ciao*', leaving Mew rather frustrated. Was Giuseppe taking her for granted? She hoped not. Otherwise he would be another one to add to her long list of man failures. And that happening in front of the likes of Holly Lydon was a total no-no.

She'd been dumped before and it hurt like hell. Dexter Franklin. That's why she had to serve up a slice of revenge. Especially after that fucking text he'd sent her calling her a 'good contestant' and telling her that he was 'done'…

*

After the text, two years earlier...

Reporter Nush Silvers was the person to go to when one had an axe to grind, and Mew had been sharpening hers with spiteful relish ever since she had received the text from Dexter knocking her unceremoniously into touch.

She had left it a week or so after his text, hoping that some kind of further explanation would follow. She had made half a dozen attempts to contact him but his ringtone signalled that he was still abroad. Mew had simmered her anger for about ten days before she decided on a plan of action. She would hit Dexter where it hurt, and seeing as she was unable to do that emotionally she chose to do it professionally. Which is why she had instructed her agent to set up an interview with Nush Silvers – hard-hitting, no messing. Because Nush didn't fill up the news columns every day with her 'stories', any celebrity splash with a Nush Silvers byline immediately drew attention and commanded respect.

As the two women sat down opposite each other at London's Groucho Club, Nush could see straight away that Mew was a woman with a story to tell. If Nush wasn't wrong, the reality TV show winner was looking after number one. And that meant that her other half, Dexter, was more than likely in the doghouse. As a coupling they had made for one hundred per cent news gold. Was Mew about to say that their recipe for making the perfect partnership had suddenly gone sour? Crazy sour? As Mew unfolded her story, she was proved right.

Two hours and two bottles of prosecco later, Mew had let loose her poison about life with Dexter Franklin. About how he had dumped her by text, called her no more than a 'contestant' and now wouldn't return her calls. How she was hurting after giving so much to the relationship and about how he had doctored the programme's editing so that Mew's menus and airtime somehow seemed favourable over that of her fellow contestants.

She had originally planned to leave it there, more or less the true facts, but whether it was the bubbles from the prosecco hitting her head or the need to make sure that Dexter really understood how much she was hurting, she couldn't help but add a few extra ingredients of her own to the Nush Silvers exclusive.

By the time the two women were air-kissing goodbye to each other, Mew had told Nush that Dexter had admitted to her in private conversations that his restaurants were not always at the top of their gastronomic game when it came to hygiene and cleanliness. How he often resorted to cheap cuts of meat and passed them off as the highest quality and how rats had become a major problem at some of his flagship restaurants around the world. None of it was true, but as the words tumbled from her lips, somehow Mew didn't seem to care. She hoped her waterfall of lies would drown Dexter Franklin.

It almost did. The damning front-page story from Mew seemed to simultaneously spread to every blog, magazine and TV show across the land, managing to eclipse any kudos that Dexter had built up throughout his career. Even though he disputed the facts and threatened to sue Mew for defamation of character, he was informed by his lawyers not to. It would merely be his word against hers. Even if it could be proven that his restaurants had never experienced a problem with rats, how could he ever prove that every cut of meat was of the best quality. They'd all been eaten by now. Or indeed that every venue in his chain had always been sparkly clean. No amount of food hygiene certificates could ever begin to obliterate the damage done by a few moments of spiteful, idle gossip from a vengeful ex.

Dexter maintained as much of a dignified silence about it all as he could, hoping that Mew's words would soon become history, reduced to the next day's fish'n'chips wrapper the day after publication. Smothered in grease and fat seemed a fitting ending for such low-rent lies, in his opinion.

His lack of reaction had shocked Mew. She had assumed that he would try to crucify her too. But he hadn't. He almost went underground. It never really gave her closure on their relationship. Why had he dumped her, what were his reasons? Who for? Maybe that was why she had been so keen – surprised, but keen – to accept his invitation to St Tropez for the opening of Trésor. They still had unfinished business and at least if they were in the same room Mew might be able to get some answers.

*

Mew stood up to leave the table she was sharing with DC and merely said 'Laters' as she left the critic contemplating his sixth slice of toast. Dexter was doing it now, wasn't he? Going underground. He'd not turned up to meet any of them in the piano bar the night before. None of them had seen him yet.

But tomorrow night she would see him, at Trésor. After such a long time of not understanding why Dexter had dumped her, she was, in a masochistic way, looking forward to hearing his answers. Even if they might not be exactly what she wanted to hear.

DC waved after her as Mew disappeared out of sight. 'Moody piece,' he said, mid-chew, tiny pieces of breadcrumbs spitting across the table.

*

Olivia had a spring in her step that could have sent her stratospheric. As she kissed goodbye to Fabienne, the two women having arranged to meet later that night, and made her way out onto the warm, jasmine-scented streets of Gassin, she knew that something monumental had happened over the last few hours. She had just met someone who was literally blotting out every other thought in her head.

Fabienne Delacroix may not have been perfect to most of the world – and certainly not to the fashion-obsessed folks of St Tropez – but to Olivia Rhodes she seemed totally perfect, everything she needed in a woman. She had opened her mind with talk of theatre, politics and female rights, opened her eyes with her viewpoint on the shallow values of celebrities and the trite world that Olivia often found herself immersed in, and she had certainly opened the floodgates of Olivia's own sexuality, stimulating the blooming of her own personal rose.

Olivia had never doubted where her sexual tastes lay, but the gentle, tender and yet somehow thrillingly piquant flavour of her lovemaking that morning had been unlike anything the publisher had experienced. Why had she never come across a woman like Fabienne before? Why on earth had Olivia been wasting her time thinking for one second that Mew Stanton, beautiful though she was, would ever be able to fulfil her dreams? She wasn't even into women. Olivia winced at her naivety over Mew as she wandered down the narrow streets of Gassin towards the taxi rank that Fabienne had advised her to head to. Mew was stunning, but she was no more than a poster girl, a fantasy that Olivia would never be able to be part of. She wasn't real like Fabienne – deep and caring, not afraid to say what she felt and possessing a confidence that allowed her to do so. Olivia would never diss Mew, but somehow all of her thoughts, desires and lusting for her client had vanished in a French heartbeat.

Olivia raised her head to the skies, enjoying the feel of the sun on her face as she entered a medieval terrace known as Promenade Dei Barri. She caught her breath as she took in the spectacular panoramic view that people seated in the restaurants on the terrace were able to look down on. It was magnificent, and for a second, Olivia felt a wave of happiness wash over her that she hadn't experienced since way back when. The cocktail of the sun kissing her skin, the smell of the jasmine that hung in the air and the lush view that she looked out upon were a heady mix. Fused with the glow she was still feeling from meeting Fabienne, Olivia couldn't help but smile, and decided that she would stay in the village a while and savour the moment with a coffee. She was in no rush to head back to Arlequin. She picked a restaurant, found a table and sat down.

A few minutes later, as a petite waitress served her coffee, Olivia began to look around the terrace. It truly was beautiful. Gallic to the extreme. The canopied eateries were alive with the sound of cutlery and vibrant chatter. A few tourists had gathered, the cameras flashing in admiration as they walked across the stonework streets. Olivia felt a lifetime away from her usual coffee haunts on the sidewalks of London's Pimlico or Kensington.

Olivia was just placing some euros on the table to pay for her coffee when her attention was grabbed by the sound of brash female laughter coming from the restaurant next door. It was at odds with the serenity of the terrace and she immediately looked in the direction it came from. She wasn't alone, as every other person seated nearby seemed to do the same, as if hoping that a silent yet deadly stare would stop the sound from spoiling the calm that caressed the air.

The person laughing riotously was just out of sight to Olivia and she craned her neck to see where it had come from. As she did, the sound of a man's laughter erupted forth as well, adding to the disharmony of the scene as a plume of cigarette smoke rose into the air. Something told her that she recognised the laughter. For a second she was unable to place it. A sixth sense told her to try and keep herself as hidden as possible as she moved her position to gain a clearer view.

It was a good job she'd listened to her inner voice. Olivia's eyebrows raised upwards in surprise as she caught sight of the two people sitting there. Obviously very much together were Missy Terranova and Giuseppe. A bottle of wine, somewhat premature given the early hour of the day, sat on the table.

Olivia watched as Giuseppe's hand travelled up the soft skin of Missy's leg and then he leant forward to find her lips with his. The kiss between them was urgent and not one normally shared by two people just meeting for a morning catch-up. Missy wrapped her hands around the back of Giuseppe's head, clearly relishing the closeness of their touch.

Olivia could feel her senses boiling. She didn't give a shit about Missy. In fact, she didn't blame the girl for doing what she was doing. She'd obviously been screwed over by Leland

Franklin with the arrival of Rosita. She was a free agent and didn't seem to have any trouble flitting from one man to another like a bee choosing which flower to land on next. That was her prerogative. But as for Giuseppe... Unless something dreadful had happened since last night, the pilot was supposedly still meant to be sharing a suite with Mew, liberally using her interest in him to gain as much as he possibly could while in St Tropez. And although the bill was all being charged to Dexter, Olivia couldn't help but feel that Giuseppe was definitely taking advantage of Mew.

Even though Olivia had found a new object of desire in Fabienne, and rightly realised that she and Mew were never to be, she still liked Mew a lot. Why wouldn't she? And Mew deserved the truth. And the truth was that her so-called 'man friend' was currently giving lip service and possibly a whole lot more to another woman.

There was no way that Mew knew about it. But as Olivia sneaked across the terrace in search of a taxi, careful not to be seen, she was certain that she would do soon. Just to seal the deal, she grabbed her phone from her pocket and snapped a clear but long-distance shot of the two of them, Missy and Giuseppe, deep in... Well, it wasn't conversation. But it was evidence.

CHAPTER 34

Dexter could feel the butterflies in his stomach. He'd experienced it many times over the years and it still didn't become any easier. In just over a day's time, his latest venture, the restaurant that he hoped would be his most successful yet, Trésor of St Tropez, would open its doors to his gathered invitees. Over a matter of hours, his months of hard toil and stress would be evaluated and splashed across newspapers and blogs across the globe. And if those reports were unfavourable, then he could say *au revoir* to Trésor, and the seemingly endless pile of cash he had sunk into it, faster than the serving of an entrée.

He dreaded this moment, right before an opening, when the pendulum of fate could swing beautifully in his favour or act as a wrecking ball to destroy his latest hopes and dreams. And there was nothing he could do about it. That was what made the calm before the storm such a gut-wrenching one. The end result was out of his control. He could prepare the finest food in the world, kit his restaurants out with the finest décor, make sure that all of his guests were fed and watered on time and to perfection. But it would only take only bad review or one whisper of a pathetic critique to bring all of his hard labour crashing down like a house of cards. And Dexter would be the joker of the pack. He'd had it happen before. New York. DC Riding. So much loss and all down to one man's opinion. Twat.

Dexter blew a cloud of cigarette smoke into the air and watched as a smoke ring formed in front of his face and twisted its way upwards into the air. He tried to push any thoughts of DC out of his mind as he watched the ring dissipate into nothing. He hadn't seen him yet. Not in the flesh anyway. And there was a lot of flesh to see. He'd seen him on the screen when he'd watched them all in the piano bar. All of them thinking that he was going to turn up. Let them think what they wanted, Dexter was in control. He would see them as and when he chose – and that would be tomorrow night.

Except for one. He thought this might happen, that he'd have to see one of his chosen few beforehand. It did fit his plan – and theirs, he suspected. That was why he was sitting in Sénéquier, the St Tropez bar along the harbour side. He'd been told to be there. He checked his watch. He was right on time.

He stubbed his cigarette out in the ashtray and waited. The butterflies still fluttered.

*

Holly gave a final flick of her eyelashes as she applied a last layer of mascara and checked her appearance in the mirror of her hotel suite. Her sun-kissed skin was a soft shade of caramel and her eyes were accentuated with a deep smudge of coppery gold eye shadow. Holly was looking as naturally beautiful as was possible while wearing a full face of cosmetics.

She really didn't need it, but to Holly it felt like protection – her warpaint as she headed into battle. She knew that she looked good on the outside, even if she felt far from peachy on the inside. She'd read a quote once from a famous actress: 'Make-up can only make you look pretty on the outside but it doesn't help if you're ugly on the inside. Unless you eat the make-up.' It was a quote Holly loved. The thought of somebody chomping down a bag full of MAC to make themselves feel better brought a smile to her face.

But as she quit her suite, took the elevator to reception and walked out into the warm St Tropez air, it was a quote that had never rung more true for Holly. Despite looking *Next Top Model* gorgeous, she did feel ugly on the inside. And that was down to what she needed to do. There were times when being a bitch really sucked. And as Holly checked the contents of her bag and walked off down the street in the direction of the harbour, she thought that this was definitely one of them.

*

Dexter spotted her in the distance right away. The flaming colour of her russet curls, the bounce of her walk, the confidence in her stride as she paced towards Sénéquier, that winning smile – all were unmistakable. He could see why anyone would fall for her charms. There was definitely something beguiling and bewitching about Holly Lydon. There always had been. He had enjoyed his time in her company. But as she approached his table at the bar and smiled, he knew that she was not there for a jaunt down memory lane. Her smile was no more than a veneer of politesse to disguise what was really going on beneath the surface. The thought made Dexter a little sad as he remembered back to the first time he'd seen that beautiful smile up close.

*

Saudi Arabia, three and a half years earlier...

Dexter Franklin had been the guest of Saudi billionaire Zayn Malouf for about three weeks and frankly he was becoming bored. There were only so many times you could swim in the private health spa, meander around the horribly faux Japanese garden, tee off on the specially built golf course or take one of the countless quad bikes owned by Zayn out for a test drive on the Saudi sands. And being waited on hand, foot and finger by a team of obedient but seemingly mute servants was severely beginning to grate. Dexter could have coped with it had he been staying in a place that had some kind of life around it, but Zayn's ridiculously huge, yet utterly tasteless property in the middle of one of Saudi's many deserts was as remote and as guarded as possible, and that meant that visitors, guests and in fact any kind of interesting conversation were as unlikely as finding a Caffè Nero or a 7-Eleven in the middle of the arid desert.

But how do you tell a billionaire that you're bored? Especially one who has brought you to his home to discuss the possibility of financing a new restaurant for you in Abu Dhabi, in the neighbouring United Arab Emirates. The young billionaire, an international playboy of notorious reputation, had dined at one of Dexter's restaurants and loved it so much that he now wanted to discuss opening a swanky eatery in one of the richest cities on earth. Something that Dexter himself would never be able to do on his own, given the costs involved, despite his already huge success. Dexter had leapt at the chance and less than a month after Zayn had eaten at one of his restaurants Dexter was being privately helicoptered into the hidden sanctuary of the billionaire's world.

At first it was highly entertaining and the two men would talk until the early hours about the riches that Zayn possessed and the boys' toys inside the mansion. The finest whiskey, a box of Stradivarius cigars and a home cinema offering everything from *Harry Potter* through to hard-core porn were all at Dexter's disposal. Zayn was a likable man, no more than late twenties in age, and his good looks were obviously a hit with the ladies. A fact he was keen to share with Dexter, telling him all about his conquests around the world. Models, singers, actresses, sports stars. He had bedded them all and seemed proud, when fuelled by an abundance of drink, to share details in pornographic glory. Dexter, himself no angel when it came to women, was happy to share his own ripe tales of women he had known.

But then Zayn was called away on business, leaving Dexter on his own at the Saudi mansion. The billionaire had said he would be away for less than forty-eight hours and that Dexter was to treat his mansion as his own until his return. It was on his second evening alone that a knock sounded on Dexter's suite door.

He opened it to be greeted by a smile that instantly won him over. Standing there was a woman who had the face of an angel but a glint in her eye that told him there was definitely a devilish streak bubbling away under the surface.

'Can I help you?' asked Dexter, his cock immediately stirring at the vision in front of him. There was a familiarity about the woman but he couldn't place it.

'Hello,' she said. 'My name's Molly. Zayn sent me.'

'To do what?' Dexter didn't really need to ask. He knew exactly why the woman was here.

'I'm a friend of his. He thought you might like to meet me. His business will keep him away for another few days and he didn't want you to become bored.' She opened her eyes wide and gave a flirtatious lick of her top lip as she finished the sentence.

'Where have you been hiding?' he asked. Her colouring proved that she wasn't local to their surroundings. Her hair was pulled away from her face and fastened with a clip at the back. Her outfit, a loose-fitting one-piece jumpsuit in black, was fastened at the waist with a belt.

'I was just a private jet away, that's all you need to know.'

'Oh, I see…' Dexter let the words hang. 'So how do you suggest you stop me from becoming bored?'

Dexter didn't resist as Molly pushed him into his suite, wrapped her arms around him and began to kiss him urgently. Dexter had no intention of protesting as his dick sprang to attention inside his trousers.

Within seconds their clothes were discarded and their two naked bodies were entwined on the bed. Obviously his stories to Zayn about women he had been with in the past had not fallen upon deaf ears. Molly was a gratefully received gift from his new billionaire acquaintance, and one that Dexter was more than happy to unwrap. Her appetising curves and the skilful way that she swooped down to take the full thickness of his shaft in her mouth were definitely a more attractive way to spend the time than another venture out on the quad bikes.

Feeling his seed mounting as she expertly worked his cock, Dexter placed his hand at the back of her head and pulled the clip from her hair, watching with delight as her head of terracotta curls unfurled around his cock. A primal urge within him told him that he didn't want his climax to arrive just yet. He moved Molly's mouth away from his member and manoeuvred himself around the bed until he was behind her. She was on all fours, her round, inviting ass cheeks facing his erect member. Total lust gripped him as he took in the beauty of her body, the dipping of her spine as she readied her body for his cock and the small heart tattoo at the base of her back. There was another one on her left foot. The whole vista was a sexual invitation that no red-blooded man could resist.

Tilting her body at an angle where he could see the wetness of her sex between her legs, Dexter dipped his fingers and then ploughed his cock into her, burying his full length within the folds of her pussy. He rode her hard, enjoying the feel of her tight around his solid shaft. It wasn't long before the two of them came together, Dexter managing to hold off on his own release until it was clear that Molly too was on the verge of sexual euphoria.

The two of them lay together on the bed, their bodies fused together in the afterglow. For a moment there was a little awkwardness between them, neither sure of what to do next. It was Molly who broke the silence.

'So Zayn reckons he won't be back for at least another three days as work commitments have cropped up, but he has paid for me to be here until his return.' She had no worry in letting Dexter know that she was on the meter for her services and she could see from the grin that spread across his face that he wasn't averse to the idea. She needed to make sure though, and added, 'If you'd like me to.'

'Just how are we going to fill three days?' asked Dexter, his words peppered with suggestion.

'I'm sure we'll manage to find something to occupy us,' smirked Molly, raising herself off the bed and walking naked to the far side of the suite where she had dropped her bag. She picked it up and walked back towards Dexter. His eyes were immediately drawn to the small triangle of hair between her legs and the fullness of her breasts. She was ticking every box. Young, toned and eager to please. Just how he liked his women.

'I thought you might like some of this.' She pulled out a bag of white powder from her bag and waved it in his direction.

'Coke?'

'Of course. It's Zayn's favourite drug for… you know. And he told me that you'd probably like some too.'

Dexter nodded his approval. Drugs were another thing he had spoken about with Zayn during their late-night chats. The billionaire had evidently taken it all on board. Dexter didn't use it very often but he had to admit that he loved the rush it gave him.

'Where the hell did you manage to find that in this country? I was amazed Zayn even had alcohol in the house.'

'When you're a billionaire, Mr Franklin, I think you'll find there's a black market for everything, no matter where you are. Even in the middle of nowhere.'

'You know my name?'

'Zayn told me. Is that a problem?'

'No. And yours was Sally, right?' He couldn't remember what she had said as way of introduction.

'Holly.' She immediately went to correct herself, inwardly cursing that she had let her real name slip out. When she was 'employed' then she was always Molly. It just seemed easier, a way of distancing herself from her former life. But the damage was done now and it seemed silly to try and correct herself. Plus, something told her that she was going to enjoy herself with Dexter Franklin, and that she could trust him.

'Well, come here then, Holly, and let's sample a little piece of what you're offering.'

Holly sat herself back down next to Dexter and went to open the bag. As she did so, Dexter reached over to the bedside table and grabbed a note from the open drawer. He pushed it shut and began to roll the paper into a tube.

When he looked back at Holly he could see that she was tipping out a fat line of powder across the top of her left breast. Her chest was young enough to still sit firm and proud, and the powder rested where she placed it.

'You're a chef. Well, here you are, dinner is served. Welcome to your starters,' Holly giggled.

In an instant Dexter placed the rolled note to his nostril and snorted the line of powder clean off Holly's breast.

Once he was done, she reached for the bag again. 'Now, where am I going to snort mine from?' She was staring directly at his cock.

'Well, it sure beats one of the gold tabletops in this place,' said Dexter with a grin.

'Pretty gaudy, eh?' said Holly, busying herself with the coke as she attempted to arrange a line across Dexter's dick. 'I've always said that about Zayn. He may have the money but his taste in décor leaves a lot to be desired. Now lie still, no twitching, and hand me that note.'

Dexter tried not to move as he watched her kneel between his legs and suck up the coke that was perched precariously across the length of his penis.

'I'm impressed,' said Dexter. 'You didn't waste a grain of it.'

'Practice makes perfect. And anyway, it doesn't matter if I do,' replied Holly, sniffing the powder into her system. 'I've got enough in my bag to satisfy the riders of a million rock bands. I am going to be here for days, after all.'

'Too fucking right you are,' said Dexter, the feel of the coke fizzing through him. 'Now, come here. You and I are going to have a lot of fun.'

Indeed they did. Over the next seventy-two hours, Dexter and Holly hardly put their clothes back on. And their naked fun was incredibly adventurous. It was clear that Holly was a girl who could cater for all, and that Zayn had a darker, kinkier side than even Dexter had realised from their conversations. As a result of Holly's numerous visits to the billionaire's home, she knew exactly where to find his collection of sex toys, ropes, cuffs, masks and carnal accessories to make sure that any thoughts of boredom were beaten, whipped, pummelled and spanked out of him. And Dexter was loving every minute, allowing Holly to push him into sexual situations that he had only ever seen on screen before. He'd always thought of himself as having a considerable interest in kink when it came to affairs of the bedroom, but Holly took things to a whole new level.

By the time Zayn returned from his business a few days later, Dexter was slightly battered and bruised, ached in places he didn't even know he had and possessed a mind that was still jumping-bean active from endless days of cocaine, even though his body was barely more than a husk. He was also totally one hundred per cent sexually satisfied. Whether it was the luxury of their Saudi surroundings, the heat of their solitude or the mind-bending, limit-shattering effect of the drugs, there was something about Holly that made Dexter Franklin roll over and surrender. She was in control and he was more than happy to serve her. But after seventy-two hours, he was definitely glad of a rest. There comes a time when even the sexiest of scorch marks from having your wrists bound by ropes and silk scarves strays dramatically from pleasure to pain.

*

The ropes and scarves were in clear view on the photos Holly dropped onto the Sénéquier table in front of Dexter. As were a host of sex toys liberally scattered around the chef on the bed in his suite at Zayn's mansion. His eyes, wide and crazed, betrayed the drugs he had obviously taken.

'So, it is true,' he remarked.

'What?'

'That you took photos. And I assume you're not showing me them simply to remind me what a fantastic time we had.'

'I need money.'

'So I heard. Word gets around, Holly. Or should I say Molly. I know a lot of people who have used your services over the years. A lot. And a lot of them are running scared, saying that you have all sorts of photographic evidence you could use should you choose to. And now I see that it's true. I had a feeling you'd taken some pics, but I was too blitzed to remember.'

Holly had taken photos of many of her clients: Premier League footballers, movie actors, politicians. She had snapped them all *in flagrante*. She had never really intended to use the evidence, but now that cash was running out, then perhaps the time had come. She was reluctant to send them to the tabloids, as perhaps then her own name would be implicated, and that was not something that Holly could deal with. She was hardly proud of herself for stooping to blackmail, especially when such intimate photos were involved. Fame was not a badge that she had ever worn with ease and notoriety and infamy were two she didn't even want to consider. But if people did pay up, then so be it. And that the money was being used to pay for the best care for her mother certainly appeased any doubts in Holly's conscience.

Holly knew that she had to try and make Dexter pay for her silence, even if she didn't really like the idea deep down. She was about to say so but Dexter beat her to the subject of cash.

'So how much are you asking me for? This is no surprise to me. I knew you'd come. I wanted you to. Why do you think I invited you to St Tropez? You're hardly major news these days, are you? The Crazy Sour days are long gone. You turning up to the open-ing of my latest restaurant isn't the biggest coup for the press, eh?'

'When did you realise it was me?' asked Holly, ignoring his dig at her lack of A-list kudos.

'I didn't recognise you in Saudi Arabia, if that's what you mean. I hardly recognised myself. But I knew I had seen you before. Something rang a bell. I asked Zayn and he filled me in. From chart to tart. And a great one at that, I'll give you that. And now you want me to give you money.'

'I do.' Holly attempted to keep her steely cool, even though she could feel her heart pounding within her ribcage. 'And I'd like it while I'm here in St Tropez. Pay up and the photos are buried for good. It's what you want, surely. It's what anybody would want.'

'You tell me,' said Dexter enigmatically. 'And if I don't pay up?' For someone who was being blackmailed by something that could potentially ruin his career, there was a still a cocky swagger to Dexter's words.

'You'll see…' Holly was unsure what to say. She hadn't even considered the possibility of a negative answer from the chef.

Dexter stood up from the table and grabbed the photos. 'I assume you have other copies of these. You're a shrewd piece. How much do you want?'

Holly nodded. 'I want half a million. You can afford that ten times over but I think that's a fair price.' Her words wobbled somewhat as she made her demands. 'But I need it while I'm here in France. I'm not leaving till I have it.'

'I'll see.' Much to Holly's surprise, Dexter moved away from the table, the photos rolled into the palm of his hand. 'I'll give you my answer at Trésor tomorrow night. I assume you're still coming?'

A twinge of vexation shot through Holly. Wasn't she supposed to be the one in control here?

How had Dexter Franklin read her so well? He knew that she was only in St Tropez to blackmail him and extort money. She didn't really give a toss about his Moroccan-themed restaurant. He knew that. He seemed to know everything.

And as she watched Dexter walk away from Sénéquier, she also knew that she had no choice but to go to the opening of the restaurant the next night. Especially if she wanted to get her hands on the money.

CHAPTER 35

'You are fucking kidding me. The rotten, lying little bastard. I bet that was who the fuckwit was texting all the time last night.'

Mew was not exactly pleased to see the evidence on Olivia's phone of Giuseppe and Missy together.

The two women were sitting on the private beach at the back of Arlequin. Mew, for once, had been pleased by Olivia's arrival, finding herself bored with her own company. Giuseppe's coldness towards her and his disappearance to work that morning had left her with a funk that she was finding hard to shift, and sitting alone with her own brooding thoughts was doing nothing to pacify it.

But seeing the photo on Olivia's phone had only made things worse.

'How fucking dare he?' spat Mew. 'I knew he was up to something. We've only been here a short while and already he's lost interest in me. And with that floozy that Leland Franklin's been fooling around with.'

'It seems both Giuseppe and Missy are players, doesn't it? There's always been a very thin line between lovers and liars,' said Olivia.

'And I've been played like an accordion,' snapped Mew. 'Or whatever the Italian equivalent is. Why does it always happen to me? All men are like fish, they start to stink after three days, it seems.'

Olivia leant in to hug Mew. 'You deserve better. You always have done. And I am sure you will find it. Maybe just not with some gigolo in the Côte d'Azur. I'm thinking that this isn't really the right place to find the person of your dreams.'

Mew couldn't resist and gave Olivia a wry smile. 'Really? You surprise me. You seemed to be totally wrapped up with your dinner date last night at the restaurant, and seeing as you're still in the same clothes, I'm assuming that your night went very well indeed.'

'Er… yes, well, we'll see. I did have a quite wonderful evening, I must say,' fumbled Olivia. 'The food and the company were surprisingly good.'

Mew let her smile broaden. 'We couldn't help but notice. Well I'm pleased for you. I'm not the only one who deserves to find someone special, am I? So do you. And you're proof that happiness does not have to come in the shape of a man. Maybe I should take a leaf out of your book. That would certainly be one worth publishing, don't you think?' Mew stood up to leave. 'Now, if you'll excuse me, I have something I need to do. And thanks.'

'What for?' asked Olivia.

'Caring.'

Olivia felt her cheeks flush a little more.

As Mew went to leave, Christophe the waiter approached them. 'Can I fetch either of you a drink?'

Mew spoke. 'You sure can. Fetch this fabulous woman a My Fair Lady. Gin, orange, lemon, strawberry syrup and a dash of egg white.'

'No, really, I'm fine,' protested Olivia, thinking it was far too early in the day to contemplate a gin.

'Not a word,' said Mew, silencing Olivia with a point of her finger. 'You deserve it. For being somebody's Fair Lady and being my total knight in shining armour.'

Olivia felt her chest automatically puff with pride.

'And can you make a Quick Fuck as well, please.'

Olivia's cheeks were now nearly crimson. The quizzical look on Christophe's face showed that he didn't know the drink.

'It's a shooter. Look it up. One part Midori, one part coffee liqueur and one part Baileys. And you're to serve it to Giuseppe the pilot, the one who's been latched onto me for the last few days, when he turns up here. You tell him what it's called, that that's all he ever was to me and that he can crawl back into his helicopter and fly to Sodom and Gomorrah for all I care. Oh, and he's not welcome back in my suite again. You got it? '

Christophe didn't need asking twice and scuttled away to prepare the drinks.

It was a few minutes later, as he handed a still blushing Olivia her My Fair Lady, that their attention was caught by the sound of Mew shouting down to the beach from the balcony of her suite.

'Olivia!' she shouted. 'Talk about girl power… Check this out!'

Olivia watched as Mew held aloft a holdall – she recognised it as the one that Giuseppe had brought with him from the helicopter the day they had landed in St Tropez – and launched it with a celebratory cheer into the air. It arced through the sky, cleared the beach and landed with a considerable splash into the waters of the Mediterranean, sinking below the surface and out of sight.

Mew let out another holler of delight, gave a thumbs up to Olivia and Christophe and disappeared back inside her suite.

'What was that about?' asked a bemused Christophe.

'That, my friend, is exactly what she needed to do,' smiled Olivia. 'And cheers to her.'

Olivia sampled the delights of her My Fair Lady. It tasted good. But then she felt good. She and Mew had somehow bonded more than ever before, the slimy Giuseppe had been kicked into touch and she was counting every second until her next encounter with Fabienne.

CHAPTER 36

DC was seated outside a pizzeria at the harbour front. A red and white checked tablecloth covered the small table, with a demi carafe of wine upon it. A newspaper sat on the edge of the table. The demi carafe was nearly empty and DC was already contemplating a second. It wasn't like he had to do any work today, after all. There was nothing of importance until the opening night of Trésor the next day. He was pleased to be away from the group. They were irking him. Too many egos for his liking. Which was why he had decided to dine on his own. Away from the hotel, away from the drama and any melancholic thoughts. Plus, there was always a chance that he might bump into the muscular Henri again down by the harbour. DC would have given anything for another sampling of his beautiful, fleshy glories.

As yet, there was sadly no sign of him. But at least he was away from the others.

'You're wolfing that with some gusto, DC,' remarked a voice not exactly drenched in enthusiasm.

He'd spoken too soon. The words had come from Holly Lydon, who was walking along the harbour. The look on her face matched the tone of her voice.

'You sound cheery, deary. St Tropez a little too rich for your blood?'

'Not all of it, no.' Holly was still smarting about her meeting with Dexter. 'But some parts of it are definitely wedged up its own ass. Mind if I join you?'

Without waiting for an answer, Holly pulled back the chair on the other side of the table and plonked herself down opposite the critic. She glanced at the newspaper resting on the table. A large advertisement for Disney's *Beauty and the Beast* filled one corner of the front page. A photo of actress Emma Watson stared out above it.

'I was asked to audition for the stage production of that once, you know. Playing Belle on Broadway. It was in the early days of Crazy Sour. Just a six-week run between tours and the recording studio.'

'You never bagged it though, I presume,' offered a disgruntled DC as he watched Holly pick up the demi carafe and signal to a passing waiter for another glass. He was still sneering as the glass arrived and she helped herself to his remaining wine.

'Not a chance. I think they gave it to some ex-*Disney Club* Barbie who used to hang out with Christina Aguilera and Britney Spears. Can't remember her name. I think I was only there to make up the numbers.'

'I'm sure,' smirked DC, knowing full well who the part had gone to. He'd seen the production countless times and the leading lady was, in his opinion, somebody with more talent in their little finger than the likes of Holly owned in their entire bodies. 'I know a few people who auditioned for that,' he continued. 'I think Rosita did, for one.'

'Really? She's too sultry and, well, too Brazilian for Belle, don't you think? Belle needs to be all innocent and sickly sweet, which is why I didn't bag it, I'm sure, but Rosita is too over the top. Have you ever met a woman who thinks she is so beyond one hundred per cent fabulous? She treats every hallway or corridor at the hotel like a runway. If it wasn't for Leland would anybody actually know who the fuck she is?'

'Yes, she wasn't right for that part. Neither was Cher Le Visage. She went for it too, as I recall. Another one without the right image for the virginal Belle. A little too risqué, I would say. She could hardly burlesque around the ballroom, could she?'

Holly didn't reply. It was the mention of Cher's name that had silenced her. It was at the audition for *Beauty* that the two women had first met. Where their mutual friendship had first begun...

*

New York City, six years earlier...

'So do you enjoy the fame of Crazy Sour?' asked Cher Le Visage, running her hands down her William Tempest dress as she eased herself into the leather seats of the diner just off Times Square. She'd spent a small fortune on it for her audition and the last thing she wanted was for any excess creases to spoil the look. Even though the audition was already done and dusted.

'Fame isn't everything it's cracked up to be,' said Holly, sliding into the seat opposite her, her attire much more street and less designer – a tight pair of Levi's and a Hello Kitty candyfloss-pink T-shirt. 'And besides, surely a showgirl like you doesn't have any interest in pop puppets like me and the Crazy Sour girls?'

'You'd be surprised,' said Cher, placing a serviette into the collar of her dress. Greasy burger stains and fizzy-drink marks were other things her designer garb could do without. 'I've followed you girls for a while. Pop music may not be my thing but I like to keep abreast of what's popular and you girls are huge.'

'I would much rather strut my stuff around like you any day of the week,' said Holly. 'I've seen you perform online and you're incredible. I tried to show your stuff to both Mew and Leonie backstage once, to try and incorporate some of your moves into our act, but they didn't seem fussed. They just didn't get it.'

Cher shrugged. 'I'm fully aware that I am not to everybody's taste.'

Their food arrived and as the young women tucked into their plates, the conversation turned back to the audition they had just undertaken. They had met in the waiting area and immediately hit it off.

'So do you think you'll be offered the part?' asked Holly. 'I'm sure I won't be. I don't think I'm the perfect Belle. To be honest, I don't really want it. I only came to please my management. I think fluffing my lines in the audition was the final nail in my coffin anyway. Not that I meant to, of course.' Holly winked, suggesting that maybe the truth was otherwise.

'Not a hope in hell. I think I was only asked because a few other girls on my agent's books are up for it too. I think I just made up the numbers.'

'Well, I'm glad you did, because it meant that we were able to meet each other and that, as far as I am concerned, has been the highlight of the day.'

'You're easily pleased,' scoffed Cher, pulling a slice of gherkin from her burger with her teeth.

'You have no idea. When you're surrounded by two of the most stuck-up, prim and proper little bitches that ever walked the earth, meeting somebody with a bit of… well, sexiness about them is just awe-inspiring.'

'Thank you. And for what it's worth, the feeling's mutual,' said Cher, winking back at Holly. 'And I'm sure the other two aren't that bad, really. They're just doing what they need to do.'

The girls talked for hours, discussing everything from their shared love of *The Office* and *Breaking Bad* through to the finer points of whether Jennifer Aniston and Justin Theroux were in it for the long term. For the two young UK women, a little dose of girlie gossip in the Big Apple was the most fun thing either of them had done for ages.

Holly loved that her new friend made her forget about any pressures she'd been feeling about life in Crazy Sour, and when Cher suggested that they leave the diner and take themselves off to a bar and then on clubbing, Holly jumped at the chance. Cher was to be her new party girl. Her energy was like the sun to Holly and the pop star was happy to bathe in its rays for as long as possible.

Holly checked her watch as she moved her body around the dance floor at one of New York's trendier nightclubs. It was just after 3 a.m. The DJ, a young man by the name of Blair Lonergan, had kept the girls entertained with his beats ever since they'd entered the club just after midnight, fuelled by a multitude of cocktails and girlie excitement. Holly, aware that people had been staring at her in the series of bars they had visited throughout their evening together headed straight to the ladies to tie her giveaway curls back behind her head and slip on a baseball cap she had bought from a sports shop on the street near Times Square. It worked, as hardly anybody seemed to recognise her as a member of one the most successful pop bands in the world – and that was just what Holly wanted. Anonymity was hers. And that filled her with confidence as she and Cher sashayed together on the dance floor.

'What time is it?' said Cher, moving her body closer to Holly's so that she could make herself heard over a dub version of Grace Jones's 'Pull Up To The Bumper'.

'Gone three,' said Holly, aware that she could smell the alcohol on Cher's breath. They were that close. Holly swivelled the baseball cap on her head so that the brim of the cap was facing backwards. The look was pure ghetto but both women seemed aware that the action meant that nothing could impede their wish to be as close to each other as possible.

'We should leave,' suggested Cher. It didn't necessarily sound like a request to end the night.

'Really? But I'm having such a good time.' It was clear, though, that Holly wasn't saying no to leaving the club.

Before Holly could say another word, Cher leant forward and placed her lips on Holly's. The softness felt good, different to what Holly was used to, and without any thought she permitted her own lips to respond, opening to allow the kiss to deepen. As the two women let their new-found friendship flow into flirtatious experimentation, nothing else in the club seemed to matter. The music faded, the people around them blurred and any thought of the consequences of what they were doing was lost in the heat of the moment. It was only when they finally let their lips separate that suddenly the rest of club came back into clarity. For two women who spent a lifetime being watched by audiences, it appeared that right there on the dance floor nobody was even slightly interested in looking at what they were doing. They were both swimming in a sea of endless new possibilities.

Cher smiled and took Holly by the hand. There was a closeness in their actions that wasn't just sexual.

'Let's go. I fancy grabbing a bite to eat on the way home, and then we can go back to mine.' Holly willingly gave her hand. As they left the dance floor a reworked version of Cyndi Lauper's 'Girls Just Want to Have Fun' filled the air. It couldn't have been more apt.

*

'Would you like something to eat, Mademoiselle?' asked the waiter at the pizzeria, bringing Holly back from her thoughts of Cher. For a second or two, Holly said nothing, unable to concentrate on her surroundings.

'You've polished off my wine. You're not getting your lips around my pizza, love, so I suggest you order your own,' said DC.

'I'll have a margherita,' said Holly. And some more of that, please.' She pointed at the demi carafe. 'Make it a large one.'

She needed to drink. They had both eaten pizza on the way back to Cher's that first night. The first of many. The night they had first spent together.

Holly felt a wave of sorrow pass over her, as it always did when she thought of Cher. After everything that had happened. After all that they had been through. At the terrible thought of how it had all ended. The loss of the closest thing to a sister and a true friend that she had ever had. Why had it gone so wrong?

CHAPTER 37

'So your first marriage was not exactly a success, Rosita. Do you think you and Leland will tie the knot in the near future? You're not getting any younger.'

Rosita, despite being grateful for any press interest in her life, especially if it was outside Brazil, was becoming more than a little bored with reporter Shaun O'Keefe's line of questioning. She smiled as genuinely as her annoyance would allow across the table they were sharing in the Arlequin piano bar. Shaun was famed for being one of the rudest and most direct hacks in the entertainment world. But since he was interviewing her for South America's number-one film magazine's website, which she was fully aware was read by a huge number of people in various Latino territories around the globe, then she would have to put up with his questions. A Shaun O'Keefe byline carried kudos, even if she did find the man and his investigative ways onerous.

Rosita painted on her smile. The interview had been arranged at the last minute by her agent, after Shaun had read that the actress was in St Tropez as a prelude to Cannes. He was already in Europe, lining up interviews with Naomi Campbell, Zac Efron and Daniel Radcliffe, and even though Rosita was not even on the same radar as those three A-listers when it came to column inches, he knew that an exclusive with her for her home nation would pay big. Especially if he could get her to dish some dirt. So far he was fighting a losing battle.

Rosita had been married for eighteen months when she was seventeen, to a film producer nearly three times her age. He had promised her the earth then left her high and dry for another actress exactly eighteen months younger than her. Not a huge difference, but to the young and ambitious Rosita, it seemed like she and the new version were generations apart. The failure of the marriage had been well documented and was old ground that she was tired of talking about.

She gave her stock answer. 'I have always said that marriage is one of those things that maybe a woman should get over as swiftly as she can and at a very young age. A bit like chicken pox. Once you've had it once, you have no real desire to go through it again, Shaun.'

Shaun sighed and scratched his pen through the question on his pad. He'd heard that answer a million times in Rosita Velázquez's interviews and he had no intention of running such a tired old quote under his byline. He needed to find something a little juicier if he was to live up to his own dangerous reputation as a reporter who could lasso a celebrity into submission from a hundred yards away.

If Rosita wasn't up for talking about her first marriage then perhaps he could wrong-foot her into a meaty quote or two about Leland and his brother. That was why Rosita was in St Tropez, after all. Shaun started with Leland.

'Do you think Leland would marry you given that he's more than a little *friendly* with other women? Missy Terranova, for example.'

Rosita could feel her teeth clench as she tried to work out how to answer the question. Luckily for her, she didn't need to, as at that moment none other than Missy herself wandered into the piano bar. Alongside her was a smug-looking Giuseppe. Even though the two of them weren't linking arms, or even touching each other, there was definitely a spark between them that Rosita would have been blind not to have seen.

She pointed at Missy and Giuseppe. 'It appears Missy has moved onto pastures new, Shaun, wouldn't you say? Not that Leland ever was with her. She's not his type. He likes his women with an air of dignity and class. I would have thought that was clear.'

Shaun O'Keefe smiled and stared across at Missy and her companion. He'd interviewed her back in the States and found her as stupid as she was infamous. The article he had written about her painted a picture of someone who would make a room of vacuous pageant girls look like Pulitzer Prize winners. Missy's agent had tried to sue him for defamation of character but something about Shaun's copy made him as non-stick as the finest kitchenware.

Shaun was about to wave to try and catch Missy's attention. He would be more than happy to rub salt into the wounds he had already inflicted. But he didn't get the chance, as Christophe walked over to Giuseppe and handed him the drink that Mew had ordered for him earlier. He'd had it ready since she had asked.

'What's this?' asked the pilot with a smile, going to take the glass. 'I need a drink but I didn't order this.'

For a moment all conversation between Rosita and Shaun came to a halt as they both curiously listened in to what was happening.

'It's a drink from Miss Mew Stanton, sir. It's called a Quick Fuck. And she said…' Christophe went on to recount word for word what Mew had asked him to do. Including the fact that he was no longer welcome in her suite. As the smiles spread across both the faces of Rosita and Shaun, the one on Giuseppe's face quickly disappeared. Missy too felt a grimace work its way across her features.

'*Puttana*,' swore Giuseppe, knocking the drink furiously from Christophe's grasp. The glass bounced off the bar and smashed to the floor, spilling a streak of browny-green liquid across the tiles.

Christophe bent down to pick up the fragments of glass. By the time he stood back up both an angry Giuseppe and a somewhat confused Missy were already leaving the bar. Just as they were going out of sight, Shaun O'Keefe called out.

'Hi there, Missy, nice to see you.' Missy turned, her features contorting with rage as she recognised the journalist. Unable to stop herself, she marched over to where Shaun and Rosita were sitting and slapped him forcibly across the face. Shaun said nothing and merely signalled to Christophe, who was still standing by the bar. Within seconds security had been called and two burly French men were escorting a protesting Missy from the hotel. Giuseppe, no longer able to return to Mew's suite and having been informed that his belongings were 'at the bottom of the Mediterranean' was made to leave too, both of them being told that insulting guests and staff members would not be tolerated and that if they didn't leave then the police would be informed.

It was only when Missy and Giuseppe had been evicted that Shaun and Rosita began to speak again.

'*Puttana*. The Italian for whore, I believe,' sniggered the actress, enjoying the fact that Leland's latest bit of fluff had just been thrown out of the hotel. 'Nicely handled, Shaun, I must say.'

Rosita was pleased that the questioning about Leland and Missy had seemingly been forced into passing. She was keen to bring the interview to an end. It was clear that Shaun O'Keefe didn't have the slightest interest in her latest movie or what she was hoping to achieve at Cannes. 'I think it's time for me to leave, dear man. I have a massage booked for this evening.'

'Just another quick question before we end.'

Rosita painted on her smile again.

'How did Dexter react to finding you in bed with his brother Leland? That was what happened, after all, wasn't it?'

Now it was Rosita's smile that vanished. It appeared that not even the mightiest of slaps could knock the bloodhound out of Shaun O'Keefe. How was she to answer that one?

*

The Cape of Good Hope, South Africa, eighteen months earlier...

Rosita flicked off her iPhone, filled with the warm glow of romance. How could a row of heart and party popper emojis not cause a ripple of happiness to surge into her heart, especially when it was followed by the words '*Ten months ago today we met. Ten months ago I fell in love. Thank you for making me a happy man. Enjoy the shoot. Love Dexter xx*'.

Rosita sat in her make-up chair in the sizable tent on Dias Beach, near to South Africa's Cape of Good Hope, and grinned happily.

'Somebody's in a good mood,' remarked Tinks McVeigh, giving Rosita's face the final once over to make sure it looked as flawless as it needed to be.

'Why wouldn't I be? I have the most amazing man in my life and this ad campaign is paying me more than the last three crappy movies I've made put together. Life is sweet, my dear.'

Rosita had been picked by US soap star Montana Phoenix to film the commercial for her new aftershave for men, Hope Male. Montana had been a long-time fan of Rosita's work in her home country and thought that her exotic look would be perfect for the ad. It needed to be 'sexy, adventurous and dramatic' and Rosita fitted the brief to a tee. Montana's fragrances were some of the most successful celebrity brands in the world and to be part of her next launch was a major boost for spreading the word of Rosita Velázquez far and wide. Rosita had been flown from Brazil to South Africa's Cape of Good Hope to film the advert. It was the perfect setting with its jagged rocks, rugged coastline and unpredictable surf. And the name was an added bonus too.

'And you're able to look gorgeous and sexy leaning against some hunk of male model all day as you earn your seven-figure sum. There are times when I would literally kill puppies to have your life, Rosita.'

'I know, I'm a lucky bitch, aren't I?'

'So have you seen the man in question yet?' enquired Tinks.

She hadn't. The first choice for the advertisement had been actor Jeremy Pinewood, a Hollywood A-lister who was supposedly a real prima donna. He'd demanded too much money and was sidelined, much to Rosita's joy, as she had no doubt that he would have outshone her with any press opportunities.

'Not yet, but apparently he's been drafted in last minute. Here's hoping for a David Gandy or a Nyle DiMarco. I would be more than delighted to stand on a rock, the wind and surf blowing through my hair, with one of those two half naked alongside me.'

'Well, I will have to do.' The voice came from the door of the tent, where a man stood wearing nothing but a pair of board shorts and deck shoes. His body was chiselled to perfection, two sexy lines forming a V from the side of his six-pack down into the hidden treasures of his shorts. His chest was trimmed, but a short crop of golden chest hair was still visible and shone in the daylight. The thick blond hair on his head was styled into a tousled designer mess that sat perfectly and highlighted his hypnotic, deep blue eyes. His appearance caused gasps from both women.

It was Tinks who spoke first. 'Er... hi... It's Leland, isn't it?' She recognised him from his TV shows.

'Sure is.' His smile was toothpaste-advert bright. 'I'm Leland. Pleased to meet you.' He held out his hand for both Tinks and Rosita to shake. Rosita remained silent but the look on her face was one of deep appreciation fused with a smattering of confusion. She knew exactly who he was, and the man was a vision. If she was going to stand on a rock all day looking beautifully windswept and being paid handsomely for it then aesthetically she couldn't think of a better looking specimen to be pressed up against. Even if the connection between them was more than a little awkward.

The next few hours were spent with both Rosita and Leland perched on various rocks along the coastline in front of the camera crew. The advert would be aired in sepia, with both Leland and Rosita looking as if their bodies were dappled in moisture from the surf. The crashing of the waves behind them would signify the intensity of the love for each other that they were supposed to portray in the advert. Thankfully the day was a warm one and the South African sun heated their skin as they were sprayed with water to replicate the action of the waves.

The pair of them remained silent during filming, giving their intense down-the-barrel-shots with brooding excellence. They were also required to kiss, an urgency in their action as Leland was called upon to run his fingers through Rosita's long hair and pull her eagerly towards him. The coupling was dynamite and the crew applauded them as they took a break, Rosita hugged Leland and headed back to Tinks for a touch-up to her make-up for the next scene.

'Can you believe you're kissing your man's brother? It's all a bit incestuous and *Jerry Springer*, isn't it?' laughed Tinks, powdering Rosita's forehead.

'Say what?' asked Rosita. 'Dexter's brother? The adventurer?'

Tinks knew Rosita well enough to see straight through her. 'You are fucking kidding me,' she said. 'Excuse my language, but are you telling me that you have no idea who Leland Franklin is? Isn't the surname a dead giveaway? You're having me on.'

Rosita's cheeks coloured. 'Not really, no,' she bluffed. 'Dexter doesn't talk about his family. He's virtually watertight about our relationship, preferring to keep it away from the press as much as possible. I may have googled his brother and I may be fully aware of who he is, darling, but what can I do? I didn't know he was going to be the one employed for this campaign with me, did I? And seeing as he is, I think it's best not to rock the boat, don't you?'

'Why does Dexter keep you such a secret? If I was going out with you I would shout it from the rooftops. You're gorgeous.'

'Dexter is a private man when it comes to family and personal matters. I know he and Leland don't really get on but I'm not sure why. There's some history, no doubt. He probably doesn't even know that Dexter and I are together.'

That was the first complete truth that Rosita had offered. She wasn't sure, but it was the last thing she wanted to drop into conversation when seven figures were on the table. Who needed any kind of awkwardness? Rosita stared across at Leland, who was chatting to the director of the shoot, still wearing nothing but the board shorts, his outfit for the first part of the advert, and the most mesmerising of smiles. Rosita couldn't help herself as a flush of warm appreciation rushed through her. He was beautiful, yet the total opposite to Dexter. Two perfect men from one very varied gene pool.

'He looks nothing like his brother. Or at least his colouring is different,' continued Rosita. Mind you, there was a similarity in the cut of the jawline and the intensity of the eyes. Anybody could see that.

'I can't understand how you've not seen him on TV before. His programme is one of the most syndicated in the world now. He's famous in territories that you can only dream of,' said Tinks.

Rosita knew it. And it was those words that were still ringing in her ears when she met up with the rest of the crew later that evening, back at their five-star hotel in Camps Bay. She was wearing an ivory floral Stella McCartney dress that just skimmed past her underwear, spotlighting her deeply toned legs, and was cinched in underneath her breasts and the dress's deep-V neckline. The look was pure resort chic and drew whistles from Leland, Tinks and three members of the crew as she entered the bar they were meeting in.

'Wow, you look just as good in clothes as you do virtually out of them,' laughed Leland as Rosita approached. The second half of the shoot had seen both of them wearing nothing more than modesty cups, rolling around on the water's edge and making out, all as a result of the allure Hope Male. It was pure *From Here To Eternity*, but with fewer clothes and sexed up for the twenty-first century. Rosita hadn't found it the right time to mention her connection to Dexter and seeing as Leland hadn't said anything to her she decided that being half naked with your lover's brother, faking the height of sexual attraction, was not the perfect moment. There were moments, though, when she wasn't sure she was faking it.

The elephant in the room remained unacknowledged.

'Why, thank you, Leland. I do try to dress to impress.' Flirtation. If it was, then Rosita couldn't stop herself.

'So you and I will be staring down from billboards across the globe in a couple of months then.'

'And airing on every TV network on earth, I suspect,' beamed Rosita.

'It was a hot shoot. Both the temperature...' He left a moment's pause before adding, 'and otherwise.'

'I think Montana Phoenix and her people will be more than happy, don't you?' purred Rosita.

'And what a small world,' said Tinks, a hint of sarcasm in her voice.

Rosita shot her make-up artist a look that could stun a springbok at a hundred paces. Tinks took the hint and changed the subject. 'Shall I fetch some drinks?'

'I think that would be wise, Tinks, don't you? I'll have a champagne, please, darling. The best they have.'

'Make that two,' said Leland as Tinks headed to the bar. 'I do love a woman with expensive taste.'

For a moment there was silence between the two of them as they simply stared at each other. The attraction between them was palpable and was only interrupted when the director of the shoot chinked the edge of his champagne glass and made an announcement. As he began to speak, Tinks returned to the group and gave Leland and Rosita their bubbles.

'Right, everybody, I think we can all agree that the shoot today was nothing short of incredible. I have sent the rushes to Montana in America and she is delighted with what she has seen, as are the company funding the aftershave. She was particularly pleased with the chemistry between our talent, so will you all raise your glasses and salute our stars of the show, Leland and Rosita.'

As a flurry of 'Leland and Rosita' sounded around the bar, the director approached the pair and shook Leland's hand, followed by an adoring kiss on each of Rosita's cheeks. 'You guys rocked it today. Thank God Jeremy Pinewood was a no-go, because you two were the perfect team. I have to admit that I've never seen your show, Leland, and I actually had no idea who you were, but you were a complete natural in front of that camera and a joy to direct. So thank you. Now, if you will excuse me, I have a little something I need to organise.' The director left the group and disappeared out of the bar.

'So we make a great team, you and I,' remarked Leland. 'I'll drink to that.' Leland raised his glass and tapped it against Rosita's.

'It would seem so,' answered Rosita. For a second she contemplated bringing her relationship with Dexter into the conversation. But something stopped her, not wanting to venture into the awkward waters that the admission may bring. Out of sight, out of mind seemed to be the easiest, if not exactly the most careful, line to tread. And she was enjoying the danger a little more than she cared to admit.

The moment for confession passed and for the next hour or so the drink flowed and Rosita felt herself relax completely into the bubbles. As light-headedness took her she flitted between the crew members, professional to a fault, making sure that every one of them was personally thanked. As she did so, she kept casting furtive glances back towards Leland across the bar. He returned the favour throughout, smiling, no words spoken yet everything being said.

Tinks retired to bed, as did some of the crew. Rosita, by now more than a little giddy from the champagne, swerved her way to a piano on the far side of the bar. If there were still people to entertain then her role was to do so. Who said cameras were needed to turn on the razzle-dazzle?

As she approached the piano, a sudden wave of wooziness took her. Maybe she had drunk a little more champagne than she realised. She went to steady herself by sitting on the vacant piano stool. But as she lowered herself she missed the stool by several inches and landed hard on the floor. Leland appeared, standing above her, offering her a hand up.

'Woah there, sexy. Somebody seems to have lost their inner sat nav. I think maybe you've had a glass or two too many?'

'Nonsense,' slurred Rosita. 'I was going to sing a song for you. A Brazilian tango. A maxixe. We dance to it back home. You would love it.' Rosita linked her arms around her co-star, enjoying the feeling. Champagne blanked out any thoughts of Dexter.

'I am sure I would,' laughed Leland, also enjoying her close proximity. 'A Brazilian tango, eh? And there was me thinking that they first originated in the brothels of Buenos Aires. I'm sure I heard that when I filmed a show in Argentina.'

'Clever man. Now, how's about another drink?' Rosita raised her face towards Leland's and without thinking allowed her lips to find his.

'I think not. Let's take you to your room.' Leland looked around at the others in the bar. The crew were all deep in conversation and hadn't seen Rosita's tumble. Without letting them know, he escorted Rosita out of the bar, asked for her room number and key card at reception and, with his arms still wrapped around her, took her up to her hotel suite.

Shutting the door behind them, Rosita looked up into Leland's face once more. 'You called me sexy...' Any sense of loyalty to Dexter had now deserted her. She allowed her lips to find his once again. Leland didn't need to decide whether to reciprocate or not. The decision was made. It had been ever since he'd found out that he was working with her. His brother's girlfriend. The perfect quarry. His cock twitched into life in his trousers. His pushed his lips angrily against hers, swooped her up into his arms and carried her to the bed. Her own kisses were equally responsive, somehow the intensity of the situation seeming to alleviate her giddiness.

Leland let his hand travel down her body and move under the hemline of her dress. Her underwear was already damp with excitement. With a swift tug he yanked it down and allowed his fingers to explore. Rosita let out a sharp exhalation of breath as the fever of his touch took her.

'Take me now!' she cried.

Leland had never been a man to need asking more than once. Within seconds her Stella McCartney was removed, as were Leland's clothes, and he slid his member into her.

As they rocked into each other, the noise of a key card sounded at the door. Voices followed.

'Rosita will be so shocked that you've decided to surprise her for your anniversary. Ten months. It's not even a real anniversary, is it, but what a sweet thing to do, flying in specially. She'll be elated, no doubt. I didn't even know you guys were together.' The voice belonged to the director from the shoot.

'We've kept it on the low-down,' said the other voice. Dexter Franklin. 'I don't want the glare of fame ruining anything. Been there, done that. Thank you so much for keeping my arrival a secret, by the way. I'll just spread these roses on the bed and then head down to the bar to surprise her.'

The surprise was all Dexter's as he walked into the suite, a large bouquet of long-stemmed roses in his hand. They fell to the floor as he saw his own brother ploughing into his girlfriend. 'What the fuck?'

Leland looked up from the bed. He didn't even remove himself from Rosita. She looked on, a look of sheer panic crossing her olive skin. Was she imagining Dexter in front of her? Hallucinating? She feared not.

'Sorry, bro… Couldn't resist.' His response was pure arrogance.

'That's my girlfriend.' Dexter's voice, normally so deep and strong, descended into a miserable whisper. 'How could you, Rosita?'

'Yeah, I know. Sorry, bruv. Happy fucking anniversary by the way. Not that ten months really is.' Leland's smirk was fathoms deep. He'd been fully aware who Rosita was from the moment he'd laid eyes on her hours earlier. She was beautiful. She was sexy. But that didn't matter. She was Dexter's. And that meant he wanted her. He wanted to take her away from his brother. To ruin her. Like one of his toys when he and Dexter were children. The rivalry between them, for Leland, burned as viciously as ever. A streak of pure evil had run under his skin from the moment he had first caught Rosita's eye. From the moment he knew that she'd be powerless to resist. Pure good fortune had brought him and Rosita together, and it had allowed Leland to smash Dexter and Rosita apart.

As Dexter entered the bedroom, Rosita herself sobered up very quickly and was frozen in horror, suddenly aware of how stupid she had been.

*

Rosita stared back at Shaun O'Keefe across the piano bar table. 'I have no comment about that, Shaun, and I think the interview is finished, don't you?'

As the reporter begrudgingly packed up his things, realising that the actress had said all that she intended to say, Rosita made her excuses and left the hotel bar to return to her suite. That day in South Africa had been one of the worst of her life. Her drunken behaviour and foolish silliness had cost her dearly. She had lost Dexter and ruined what could have been. She had tried but failed to win him back. The bond between them was broken. Her life was now with Leland. Their union brought opportunities, but it also brought with it a whole host of hurtful complexities that she had never factored in. Her ambition had ruled over her heart and that was something that she had to live with every day.

When the Hope Male billboards went up around the globe, the image that was used featured Leland centre stage. Rosita, wrapped around the adventurer with her hair draped seductively across her face, was almost unrecognisable. She was also cropped out of nearly every shot in the TV campaign, Montana telling her that the brand 'wanted to concentrate on the masculine in the end'. The seven-figure pay cheque had proved to be incredibly profitable but the choice of shots meant that her star was both overshadowed and prevented from shooting into new time zones. And global fame was something that Rosita still deemed to be priceless.

CHAPTER 38

No family is ever perfect. That would be too much for any person to ask for. They argue, they fight, they even cease talking to each other at times, but in the end, family is family and the love will always be there…

Holly picked up her phone and dialled the number. She knew it off by heart.

She checked her watch. It was 1 a.m. in St Tropez. It would be late afternoon back in the States. The perfect time. Her delivery should have arrived and Mum, not that she would know it, would be able to gaze at one of her favourite things in Holly's absence.

A jovial female voice answered the call. 'The Mar Vista Care Centre, Quinn speaking. How can I help you?'

Holly had spoken to Quinn on many occasions. 'Hi, Quinn, it's Holly Lydon. I'm just phoning to see if my mother's parcel arrived. I'm in France and can't be there to bring it myself so I just wanted to make sure she's received it.'

'Her favourite hibiscus is sitting in front of her right now. I can see her in the lounge. She's looking straight at it. I swear Shirley smiles when it comes.'

Both Holly and Quinn knew that this was beyond unlikely and into the realms of impossible, but the thought still gave Holly some kind of hope that maybe a tiny flicker of light within her mother was still able to function, despite the severity of her stroke.

'How is she?' asked Holly. It was the same question she asked every time. The answer, especially coming from one of the care centre workers like Quinn, was always identical too. Upbeat without being forced. The truth too horrid to contemplate, so a sugarcoated version of it given instead.

'You know what, Holly, I reckon Shirley is sharper than any of us really know. There's still a glint in those eyes of hers that will outshine the rest of us for years to come. You mark my words.'

Holly took the words on board, her heart eternally grateful for the soft-soaping. 'Is she eating well?'

'Like a beast,' laughed Quinn. 'Although she won't be eating the frog's legs and snails like you over there in France, I dare say. We don't have anything that fancy here, Holly. We make do with good old dishes like mac 'n' cheese and home fries.'

'I've given the snails a wide berth, Quinn. A little too slimy for me. I prefer my snails in the garden or slowly climbing up a brick wall as opposed to in my mouth.'

'I hear you, Holly. I saw one being prepared on a cookery programme once, it looked like a big heap of booger.' Quinn began to laugh. One of those laughs that starts deep in the pit of your belly and ricochets its way out.

'Will you tell her I love her and that I'll be home soon? I'll bring her something traditional from France. And you too, if you're lucky. Anything you fancy?'

Quinn roared into life again. 'How about some handsome Frenchman to whisk me away to paradise! That would do me nicely. All fancy accent and chest hair. That would suit me.'

Holly had to move the receiver away from her own ear at the volume of Quinn's laughter.

'I'll see what I can do. So you'll tell mum that I rang and that I love her, okay?'

'Of course I will, my lovely.'

'Thanks for that, I'll see you soon.'

'Bye, precious girl. Speak soon.'

Quinn hung up just as one of the managers at the home walked into reception. 'Was that Holly Lydon?' he asked, his manner brusque and clipped.

'Sure was, she's in France,' replied Quinn.

'Well, next time you speak to her, tell her that she's due to pay for her mother's care. She's behind with her latest payment and if she can't cough up then I'm afraid we can't look after her mother anymore.'

Quinn didn't reply and merely muttered under her breath as the manager hurried off, clipboard in hand. She was still muttering when she reached Shirley. Her head was stooped and hung down. The hibiscus sat in front of her on the table. Her eyes were definitely not on it, despite what Quinn had told Holly.

'Your daughter sends her love, Shirley. She's coming to see you soon.' She looked back over her shoulder before continuing in a whisper. 'And hopefully she will be paying up so that we can keep you here, despite what Mr Scrooge out there says about it. It would be such a shame to lose you. Now let me clean you up.'

Quinn bent down and wiped away a long line of dribble that was hanging down from Shirley's mouth.

Back in St Tropez, Holly's face was streaked with a long line of tears as she lay down to try and sleep. She knew she was behind with the payments for her mother's care. There were some things that could never be soft-soaped. She knew she wouldn't sleep much tonight.

*

The opening night at Trésor was less than twenty-four hours away. Dexter slipped his arm around Toni's waist and pulled her close to him as he surveyed the finishing touches they had put into place in the restaurant. She had done a great job. She'd managed to do a great job ever since he'd first poached her from the other bar. She worked hard and she played hard. He liked that.

Toni seemed as determined as him to make sure that every last detail of Trésor was as magnificent as it could possibly be. Flourishes of colourful sequins and confetti were spread across each and every table. All loose threads had been snipped from the chairs and scatter cushions strewn around the restaurant. There were no uneven folds in the billowing masses of material that cascaded down from ceiling to floor. Even Dexter's choice of background music for the evening, carefully picked by the chef and his planning team for the event, had been critically gone over by Toni, her suggestions given and changes made if Dexter deemed fit. The event team had vacated the restaurant hours ago, clipboards in one hand and mobiles in the other. They did a great job. They were on the payroll. They had to. But the petite blonde waitress was earning nowhere near as much as the specialists he'd brought in, but it was her that was still here at the restaurant, making the final few touches as the time approached one in the morning. She'd been quite a find. In all areas of his life. He pressed his lips against hers and savoured the softness of her mouth.

'You're amazing, you know that? You never stop working,' said Dexter. 'This place is as ready as it will ever be and you have made it look incredible, Toni.'

'Me and your team of planners, yes,' replied the waitress with a knowing smirk. 'They like to think they know what they're doing, don't they? They are pretty… What is the best word… *animated*?'

Dexter knew exactly what she meant. The team that had been employed to turn the space into Dexter's vision of a Moroccan-themed delight on the Côte d'Azur were supposedly one of the best money could buy and were listed as one of the top three event planners in London, but Dexter had to admit there was definitely a touch of the *Absolutely Fabulous* about them. They seemed to spend more time drinking wine down on the harbour front, shouting on the phone to try and persuade some on-trend, stick-like model to turn up for the opening, than actually helping with the sheer graft of bringing the restaurant together. Dexter would have kicked off big time had it not been for the fact that their organisational powwows away from Trésor meant that he had more time to spend with Toni. He liked her. She was attentive, had a good eye for detail and was deeply ambitious.

'I like to work as much as possible. It's the way I was brought up. You are given an opportunity, you work hard and you make sure that a job is done to the best of your capabilities. You never know when the money will run out and so you make the most of it while it's there.' It was why she had been so keen to earn some much-needed cash from the photos of Holly answering a call of nature behind the bus a few days before. 'When opportunity presents itself, you greet it with open arms.'

'Well, I'm incredibly grateful that you have made this place look nothing short of a million dollars. Or several million euros.'

The waitress moved onto her tiptoes and kissed Dexter, showing her appreciation of his praise.

A voice interrupted their embrace. 'Sorry, have I walked in on something? I was just seeing if there were any last-minute things that needed sorting?'

Dexter turned to face the man who'd spoken and grinned.

'Doesn't anybody in your family ever stop working?' he asked, his question aimed at both the man and the waitress.

'Christophe is like me,' said Toni. 'He works as much as he can and seizes opportunities when he sees them.'

'My sister's right,' smiled Christophe, running his hands through his golden locks. 'Our parents taught us well.'

'Well, I am very grateful for your hard work, Christophe. Setting those bugging devices up for me at the hotel was very useful. Very useful indeed. And I trust you're still on for working tomorrow at the opening?'

'Of course, I can't wait.' *Especially when you're paying me so well*, he thought.

Dexter was indeed paying over the odds for Christophe, but he'd already proven himself to be a useful person to have on Team Dexter.

'Have you just finished a shift at the hotel?' asked Toni.

'A double,' smiled Christophe, rubbing his thumb and forefinger together to indicate that the money would come in useful.

'Well, let's get out of here, get some shut eye and then we'll all be fresh for tomorrow,' said Dexter. 'It's going to be quite a night.'

'I'll grab my bag,' said Toni, her heels clipping across the floor as she went to find it.

'How did you get in here, by the way?' Dexter asked Christophe.

'The door was not locked.'

'That'll be the bloody events team leaving it open when they left earlier.' Dexter was annoyed, but not really enough to care.

'I saw them in Sénéquier on the way here. They're fairly merry, shall we say.'

'*Quelle surprise*,' said Toni, returning with her bag.

The three of them made their way to the door.

As they ventured out into the night air, Christophe turned to his sister as Dexter locked the door.

'Are you coming back to the apartment tonight?'

She glanced at Dexter. His look said that she definitely wasn't returning to the small backstreet apartment she shared with Christophe.

'*Non.* I'll be staying… *elsewhere.*' She leant forward and hugged Christophe, kissing him once on each cheek. 'See you tomorrow. *Je t'aime.*'

Christophe headed off in the opposite direction to Dexter and the waitress, his silhouette vanishing into the night.

'You're so lucky to have a brother that you love,' Dexter mused, letting his hand naturally slip into hers as they walked.

'Christophe is adorable. We always look out for each other. I love him.'

Dexter knew that he could never say the same about Leland. Brotherly love was a definite non-starter in the Franklin household. As tomorrow would prove.

*

Mew couldn't sleep. She looked at the clock on her bedside table. It read just before three in the morning. She'd been awake for the best part of two hours now, tossing from side to side under the soft cotton sheets. She'd been exhausted when she had crawled into bed, having spent most of the night fending off irate phone calls from Giuseppe demanding to know why his belongings – especially his national identity card and his beloved Jabra Coach headphones – were now both ruined thanks to a medal-winning dive into the Mediterranean Sea. He had left at least six messages, containing a mixture of English and Italian swear words, before Mew had decided to silence her phone and head for bed. The man wasn't worth any more brain-strain on her part and Missy was welcome to him.

Mew pushed back the sheet and got out of bed. She wandered to the bar on the far side of her suite and poured herself a shot of brandy. The heat of it felt good against her throat as she took a swig. Maybe it would help her sleep. Maybe not.

Picking up her purse, Mew moved out onto the balcony. The night air had cooled but was still warm enough for her to sit outside wearing just a T-shirt and a pair of pants. The moon rested high in the sky, almost at full capacity, illuminating the panorama she could see from her balcony, from the twinkle of lights as boats bobbed slightly up and down on the calm waters of the Med to the dim glow of small villages spaced out on the hills in the distance. It was a beautiful scene and for a moment she reflected on how far she had come. The life she now led was so far removed from the one she'd experienced growing up. All those hopes and dreams had come to fruition. But at what cost?

She opened her purse and pulled the photo she always returned to from the back of it. She gazed at it in the moonlight and smiled. A bittersweet smile. She turned it over and looked at the handwriting on the back. Almost faded but still just legible. '*If I forget myself, will you remember me?*' A tear rolled down her cheek, before she'd even had time to think about it. Happy times. One team, one dream. But it hadn't lasted.

A sound came from the balcony located a couple along from hers. She looked up at the noise. It was the sound of a chair being pulled across the tiles of the balcony floor. She spotted Holly, also with a drink in her hand, sitting down, just as she was, and staring at the peaceful scene in front of them. As if aware that she was being watched, Holly turned to face Mew and raised her glass. It was hard to tell from a distance but as the light caught Holly's face as she glanced across, Mew thought she spotted tears on her cheeks too. Another woman who obviously wasn't able to sleep. Another woman with her own woes. A woman with whom she had shared so much.

Mew raised her glass back at Holly and smiled. That was something they hadn't shared with each other for the longest time. The simplicity and the beauty of a smile. It housed no agenda. And for the first time in ages Mew actually felt something other than utter dislike for her former bandmate.

CHAPTER 39

Opening night

The normally dimly lit backstreet of St Tropez where Trésor was located was ablaze with colour and action. A stretch of red carpet had been unfurled and ran almost the whole length of the street, from the impressive tile-framed arched wooden doors that Dexter had insisted on having purpose-built for the restaurant, nearly all the way down to the famed Côte d'Azur harbour at the end of the street. It was wide enough for guests to walk along and was flanked by an army of paparazzi photographers, ready to snap the perfect shot of any celebrity they deemed fit to fill the column inches of their chosen outlets. A few reporters, those deemed not important enough to have personal invitations to the festivities within, stood alongside the photographers, their questions at the ready.

Members of the events team busied themselves with clipboards and headsets, talking their own language of PR psychobabble to anyone who cared to listen. The hypnotic sound of singing, the seductive beats of drums and the taut, shrill plucking of pear-shaped ouds filled the street from a group of musicians playing an enticing mix of Moroccan music to welcome the guests. The scents of cinnamon and clove kissed the air, fusing to give an intoxicating aroma to the proceedings. A belly dancer swayed her body, pendulum-like, to the rhythm of the beats, wisps of fabric undulating around her as she flicked her body to the notes. Outside the main doors themselves, Christophe and one of his fellow waiters stood to greet guests with glasses of Mahia fig spirit to evoke the taste of Morocco or glasses of Veuve Clicquot to emphasise the decadence of the evening.

The early evening air was already warm, but the heat was added to by a young male fire dancer who stood, a tray of burning drinks on his head, moving his muscular body up and down, careful not to spin his flammable beverages anywhere near the reporters and photographers gathered. His body, a granite slab of pecs and abs, was wrapped in nothing more than the wispiest of amethyst-coloured waistcoat, bedecked with an array of coloured jewels, and a pair of silk harem pants.

Unsurprisingly, the man's lack of clothing and mass of muscles was the first thing that DC Riding spotted as he manoeuvred himself out of his cab and walked into the street leading to Trésor's main entrance. When there was food to be tasted he was normally the first to arrive. Tonight was no exception.

Ignored by the reporters and paps gathered, always a source of constant annoyance to DC, he attempted to wiggle his own rather ample proportions to the sounds of the Moroccan band as he sidled up against the man with the burning drinks on his head.

'Well, aren't you hot stuff?' cooed DC, revelling in both the music and the vision of flesh in front of him. As there was no one else to impress as yet, the dancer, seemingly oblivious or ignorant to what the critic was saying, gave a glacial white grin and continued swaying his solid flesh. DC placed his hands in the air and attempted to do the same. The moves may have been similar but that was where any resemblance ended. As the reporters and paps erupted into action behind them, the dancer sashayed off down the red carpet, leaving DC both alone and a little deflated. He harrumphed and moved inside the restaurant entrance, grabbing a Mahia from Christophe as he did so.

'Evening, Monsieur,' said the waiter as DC blew past.

'Good God. Do you work in every bloody place in this town?' asked DC, not stopping for an answer and descending the steps into the main body of the restaurant.

The cause of the commotion behind DC from the reporters and paps was the arrival of Leland Franklin and Rosita Velázquez. They were trailed by Tinks McVeigh, her make-up bag ready to go should Rosita insist on touching up on the red carpet.

Not that Rosita should have been in need of any extra *maquillage*, seeing as Tinks had spent the best part of four hours putting together Rosita's 'look' for the opening.

Rosita was wearing a baby blue, floaty, kaftan-style dress with a plunging neckline slashed virtually all the way down to her navel. It was only her ample breasts and some well positioned tit-tape that managed to keep the couture creation in shape. Her hair was tied back into a thick waterfall of ponytail and three strings of pearls decorated her coiffure, meeting in the middle of her forehead where they were joined by a large silver and gold brooch covered in pearls. The look was sheer exotic sensuality. The brooch was large enough to be spotted from afar but not too large that it overshadowed the masterpiece of make-up that Tinks had performed on her face. Dark purple smoky eyeshadow under perfectly shaped brows and around deeply black-lined eyes were a winning combination, especially when teamed with a virtually nude lipstick. Her arrival in St Tropez may have been straying deeply into the realms of trashy, but tonight Rosita was working Moroccan magic with a class of her own. And that class was magnificent. Well, she was on the arm of one of the most famous men on TV after all. And she'd be lying if she said she didn't hope that his brother would notice how beautiful she was too, especially as she still had designs on Dexter perhaps being her escort to Cannes if Leland declined. It was always wise to prepare for every eye-catching opportunity. Rosita smiled as the photographers' flashes popped in her direction, though she suspected that they weren't totally for her. That she was merely the 'arm candy'.

Leland was in head-to-toe white, wearing a lightweight jacket and crisp cotton shirt, open at the neck with a cravat of baby blue to match Rosita – her idea – and linen trousers. His face was far from happy and indeed he could barely crack a smile as the cameras exploded along the red carpet. His stony expression worsened as a reporter from the crowd shouted out 'Where's Missy?' Rosita clenched her jaw and ignored the comment, whereas Leland stepped forward, his fist raised. He was in no mood for cheap digs and swipes about his love life. He had heard that Missy had gone off with Giuseppe, and even though he knew that Missy was no more than a casual shag, it still made him feel second best to another man – and that was not something Leland ever liked to be. And waiting hours for Rosita to get ready for the opening night had vexed him further. To be honest, the fact that she was here at all was now beginning to irk him.

'Cool it, Leland,' hissed Rosita through gritted teeth, determined that he wouldn't cause a scene. He gripped her by the arm quite harshly and attempted to move her towards the restaurant entrance.

'Is there any competition between you and your brother, Leland?' It was another question the press had fired at him a million times. He was in no mood to answer.

'Fuck this,' he spat from between pursed lips. 'I'm going inside. The sooner this is over the better. Are you coming?' He pulled Rosita's arm to make her follow him, his grip some-what painful. But the actress wasn't ready to move just yet. As far as she was concerned there were photo opportunities with the fire dancer, belly dancer and Moroccan band to be considered. She'd spotted them already. What was the point of dressing up authentically if she didn't grasp every authentic opportunity?

'Ow, Leland, you're hurting my arm.'

Leland moved off and disappeared inside the restaurant, snatching a glass of champagne as he did so. He had already drunk it and procured another by the time he reached the bottom of the steps leading into Trésor.

Rosita smiled as picture-perfectly as she could, but was more than aware that as soon as Leland left her side virtually every camera stopped popping. His star was bigger and brighter in the backstreets of St Tropez than hers, that was for sure. After a few seconds of silent awkwardness, Tinks linked her arm into Rosita's and marched her client into the restaurant. She could see the upset that Leland was causing her. She'd seen it before. It was at moments like this that Tinks realised that she actually considered Rosita to be more of a friend than simply somebody she earned good money from.

Grabbing two Mahias, Tinks passed one to Rosita. She could see tears beginning to form in Rosita's eyes. Rejection often had that effect.

'Don't you dare cry, Rosita!' snapped Tinks, sharply but without malice. 'Nobody is worth your tears and just remember that after Cannes every photographer out there will be wanting to take your photo for every magazine in the world.'

'Bless you, Tinks, but I hardly think that shitty mummy movie I've just finished is going to turn me into the next Julia Roberts, do you?' Rosita said bleakly.

'Maybe. Maybe not. But more to the point, if you start crying I will have to reapply that eye liner and that's a work of art that Michelangelo would be proud of.'

'Then I promise I won't.'

'Thank you,' said Tinks. 'Now, talking of Michelangelo, did you see the abs on that fire dancer outside? He was built like one of the Ninja Turtles. He can heat me up between the sheets any day he likes.'

Rosita and Tinks were both considering his rock-hard abs as they descended into Trésor.

Mew had intended to walk the red carpet into Trésor with Giuseppe by her side. A hot anonymous mystery man was always a great way to gain news coverage, but doubtless the pilot would be currently showing Missy Terranova the delights of his *cockpit* in Monte Carlo or Juan-les-Pins.

Mew decided that if she was to make an entrance then maybe she should try a different tack. Which is why she had asked Olivia Rhodes to accompany her. What would look better to reporters than a jilted girlfriend turning up to her ex's restaurant opening, especially one who she had publicly slagged off quite ferociously, than with a female on her arm? Actually, one thing would. Two females on her arm. So when Olivia said that she would be going to the opening with Fabienne Delacroix, Mew had invited them both to walk the red carpet with her. Olivia was delighted. Fabienne less so. She was going there to work, not hobnob with vapid celebrities. But when Olivia told her how excited she was about the idea, the reporter had decided that for once it might be best to park her principles and do something nice for the woman that she was becoming increasingly fond of. Fabienne was never someone to let her emotions dupe her, but she knew already that Olivia was something rather special.

Mew had spent the afternoon giving the two women a make-over into what she thought would make the best lesbian-chic splash for the paparazzi. She managed to tear Tinks away from Rosita for a short while to give both women an expert lesson in lipstick, powder and paint. And then, under the guise of wanting to thank Olivia for her hard work and help in making her see the light about Giuseppe, she took them both shopping to some of the finest designer stores in Tropez.

As they hit the red carpet, Mew was wearing her hair off her face, open blouse, no bra, a mass of flowing Free Soul jewellery and a tight pair of trousers. The look screamed feminine with a strong masculine edge. On Tinks's recommendation she had gone heavier with the make-up to give her added drama. She had kitted Olivia out in one of Diane von Furstenberg's iconic wrap dresses and teamed it with Gas Bijoux accessories. The look was completely alien to Olivia, but with Tinks's feature-softening make-up expertise and Mew's fashion flair, the end result was nothing short of incredible. Olivia had never looked better and with Fabienne by her side she wasn't sure that she had ever felt better either.

Fabienne was harder to please and had only agreed to the suggestion of a makeover when she saw the excitement in Olivia's eyes at the notion. Mew had finally plumped for a rockier look for Fabienne from a boutique store called Trinity. The dress she chose was black, loose fitting and stylish and cinched in at the waist with a heavy metallic belt. Not that she was keen to admit it, but Fabienne actually thought that the end look suited her immensely and could hardly believe that she was looking at herself as she stared in the mirror before leaving for Trésor. Olivia's look of approval only confirmed to her that she had made the right choice in submitting to Mew's instructions. As the three women posed for photos on the red carpet, Fabienne felt an unusual sense of fashionista-fabulous running through her. As a one-off, in-the-spotlight moment, maybe the life of a celebrity wasn't all that bad after all. Perhaps she wouldn't feel as out of place in St Tropez's VIP Room as she had once imagined.

Mew held the two women close to her on either side as the flashes illuminated the backstreet. She was very much used to posing for the cameras and would be lying if she said that she didn't enjoy the attention. As she stared around at both Olivia and Fabienne, their wide-eyed smiles told her that they were rather enjoying it too. It was a full five minutes before the trio of women, having excitedly posed with the belly dancer too for exotic effect, made their way towards Trésor's entrance.

Holly stepped out of her taxi with a heavy heart. Thoughts of her mum were laying heavy on her mind. What would happen if she couldn't persuade Dexter to dish up the money for the compromising photos? Holly's stream of income was becoming narrower by the second. She needed the cash, even if her heart told her it was dirty money. But it was what she needed to do to keep caring for her mother.

She was nervous about walking the red carpet too. It was something that she hadn't done in a good while. Would people still want to take her photo? A glamorous one and not just one of her relieving herself behind public transport? There were some pages of *Heat* magazine you wanted to be on and some that you didn't.

Holly stepped onto the red carpet and posed, waiting to see the reaction. Fire dancer to one side of her, belly dancer to the other. Music filled the air. Her outfit, a strapless tube dress she'd bought on eBay for twenty dollars but was hoping she could pass off as a wannabe Victoria Beckham, looked good on her and clung to her curves in all the right places. She had tied her hair back, hiding her trademark red curls behind her head. She had done it for coolness and comfort, but as the photographers' flashes failed to materialise she suddenly thought that maybe it had ventured into the realms of camouflage. Perhaps it hadn't been such a wise decision.

Holly stood motionless for what seemed like the longest time. She could feel the voice of a timid little girl crying inside her. This wasn't the brash Holly Lydon working the red carpet, fresh from another sell-out Crazy Sour world tour. This was the Holly Lydon who just wanted to put things right with the world and wasn't quite sure how to do it.

Suddenly a hand slipped into hers and gripped it firmly. Holly looked around to see who it was. Mew. She had been watching Holly's arrival from the entrance to Trésor and felt a piece of her heart breaking as she watched the once dynamic Holly struggling on the red carpet. Leaving Olivia and Fabienne to make their way inside, Mew made a decision to help the girl who had shared so much with her. Both good and bad.

Holly smiled as she looked at Mew. Something had passed between them the night before on the balcony. No words had been spoken, yet a million bridges were somehow... perhaps not rebuilt, but constructed for the first time.

'Time for a Crazy Sour reunion, don't you think?' Mew's words were for the benefit of those gathered. She moved her hand up to Holly's hair and tapped it gently. Holly understood her meaning and pulled at the clip holding her curls in place, allowing them to tumble free around her face.

As if it were Bastille Day fireworks, lightning seemed to fill the air as every photographer gathered started to click away at their cameras, their flashes detonating. Murmurs of '*C'est* Holly Lydon' and 'Crazy Sour' rang out as the mental cashpoints in every photographer's mind calculated that a pic of two of the three former members of the one-time biggest girl band in the world, together on the red carpet, was sure to convert to considerable cash.

The two young women posed together, automatically falling with ease into their classic poses. For a moment it was as if they had stepped back in time, making a classic headline-grabbing pose as they headed to the Brits, the Grammys, the Teen Choice Awards – they'd worked them all. All that was missing was their third Crazy Sour member, Leonie, but at that moment in St Tropez, it didn't matter. Posing *a deux* was *parfait*.

'Remember rule number one,' said Holly, turning to Mew. 'Leave them wanting more.'

'I hear you,' winked Mew, contemplating the fact that for the first time in the longest age she was actually enjoying her memories of time in the band with Holly.

Still holding each other's hands, the two of them walked the rest of the red carpet and disappeared inside Trésor. Christophe held out his tray of drinks as they arrived and both women took a Mahia. Holly swigged hers back, relieved that the potential disaster on the red carpet had been averted.

'I'll take another of those, thank you very much, Christophe,' she smiled, popping her empty glass back on the tray before taking another. 'And Mew, I just want to say…' She turned to face her former bandmate, but Mew was already heading down the stairs into the restaurant.

'…thanks.' As she said it, Mew, halfway down the stairs, turned back to Holly and winked. The look between them was reminiscent of the one they had shared on the balcony the night before. No words. But a mass of understanding.

*

The tables were laid, the champagne and Mahia flowed and the scented air was filled with the excited murmurings of the night ahead. Dexter Franklin stared out at those gathered in the main body of his restaurant through the door of his kitchen. His staff were already working up a sweat preparing his new slant on a fusion of French meets Moroccan. The food would be delicious, he had no doubt. As he scanned the celebrities and names who had flown in for the event, the organisers still manic with clipboards, he knew that the night would be his. Just as planned. He picked out the people that he needed to be there, ticking them off in his brain one by one. Brother Leland, diva Rosita, call girl Holly, ex Mew and critic DC. His lips curled into a knowing smile as he considered what was about to be served to his illustrious guests. Revenge, regrets and explosive revelations.

Dinner was about to be served...

'Let the banquet begin,' he said softly as he closed the door and went back into the kitchen.

CHAPTER 40

'How long till I seek out the chosen few?' asked Toni. 'Are you sure that you want Christophe and me to do the waiting in that room?'

'Absolutely,' said Dexter. There was no hint of doubt in his voice. 'You know the plan, you know the seating order. You know what to do. Christophe can serve the food. You deal with everything else.'

'So when do you want them?' she asked.

'Let them mingle for a bit. There's enough celebrities here for them to spout nonsense to for a while. Let them have a few drinks and then the payback can begin.'

'You are so devious,' said Toni, her smile showing that she liked the idea.

'Let's just say I intend to make sure that it's not just the Mediterranean sun that will be making that lot hot under the collar.'

'Why are you doing this?' the waitress asked idly.

'Why?' remarked Dexter. 'Oh, that's easy.'

He didn't elaborate, but in his head there was only one name. Cher Le Visage.

*

Iguazu Falls, Brazil, five years earlier...

The forest floor was littered with falling leaves as Dexter and Cher walked along the narrow pathway arched with trees in the Brazilian forest. The sound of gushing water echoed in the background from the many falls that flowed where Brazil met Argentina, and the air was moist with droplets.

'This place is incredible,' said Dexter, attempting to hold Cher's hand. 'Did you know that the surface water flowing over the main Iguazu Falls is actually twice the amount that goes over Niagara? That is some mass of water.'

Cher couldn't give a stuff. All she knew was that the constant moisture in the air and insane humidity was making her hair frizzy, and with her performance, albeit it bottom of the bill, less than twenty-four hours away, the last thing she needed was a troublesome do. She had enough on her plate as it was.

'I'm so pleased we could be here together,' said Dexter. 'This is a major gig for me, catering for such a huge charity event, and to think that I had no idea you were going to be here too. Why didn't you tell me? How come you are?'

Cher didn't bother to mention that she'd managed to wangle her way onto the bill through someone she had once sucked off in the name of ambition. Dexter may have been her on/off lover for a few months now, but the last thing he needed to know was just how desperate her career prospects had become. Her attitude towards him at the moment was the less he knew the better.

'Do you know the myth behind Iguazu Falls? It's one of the new wonders of the world and is steeped in legend. You must have read the signs at the hotel,' said Dexter, his excitement about the place almost schoolboy-like.

'No, I can read them later,' said Cher.

'I can tell you. It's an incredible story and really romantic.'

Romance. That was the last thing she needed to be hearing about from Dexter. Romance and Dexter were two words that she needed to try and keep as separate as possible right now. At least in her opinion, if not in his.

'Do you want to hear?' asked Dexter.

Cher knew she had no choice.

'Well, apparently years ago there was a huge serpent called Boi who lived in the falls. Once a year the local tribes would pick a young woman and sacrifice her to the serpent as a way of keeping the serpent happy. They would have a massive sacrificial ceremony. One year a man called Taroba became the leader of one of the tribes and the woman who was picked to be sacrificed was a beautiful female called Naipi. Taroba was in love with Naipi and the last thing he wanted was for her to be killed, so the night before the ceremony he kidnapped her, placed her in a canoe and tried to escape up the river.'

Even though Cher's mind was elsewhere she had to admit that the story Dexter was telling did interest her. 'So what happened? Did they escape?'

Dexter continued, happy to know that Cher was potentially captivated.

'No, they didn't, because apparently Boi was angry about them trying to avoid the sacrifice and decided to vent his anger on them both. It is said that he split the river, creating the Iguazu Falls from the long beautiful hair of Naipi, and that he turned Taroba into trees as a warning to any others who thought about disobeying him. How mean is that? I won't kidnap you and take you off in a canoe, I promise.' Dexter let out a laugh and went to wrap his arms around Cher. Not sure how to stop him, she let his arms rest there as they walked. She winced a little as his arm connected with her shoulder.

'I think my hair would make more of a whirlpool right now. This place is giving it a bendy kink that I'll have to iron out before tomorrow's show,' remarked Cher. Her words were far from jolly. Even surrounded by the beauty of the Iguazu Falls, she was finding it hard to hide her feelings. It was something that Dexter, despite trying to be as upbeat as possible, was well aware of. Unable to spin any more bonhomie, he removed his arm from around her, bit the bullet and asked, 'Are we okay?'

Cher knew that they weren't. For her, they hadn't been for a while.

Where had it all gone wrong? Cher cast her mind back over the last six months.

Cher Le Visage had met Dexter Franklin in Soho. She had been performing at part of Burlexe at the Shadow Lounge, an evening that promised 'showgirl inspiration to make you feel frickin' fabulous'. Her near bottom-of-the-bill listing hadn't made her feel that way, but at least the celebrity crowd gathered seemed to enjoy her act. Amid a flurry of *Big Brother* boneheads and *Love Island* lotharios, Cher had spotted Dexter straight away. His dark hair, brooding eyes and comic-book-hero jawline had caught her attention before she had even begun to gyrate her first tassel. And from what she could see, he was there on his own. This fact was proven when he offered to buy her a drink at the Shadow Lounge bar as one of the other acts on the line-up did their thing.

Two bottles of champagne later it was clear that bubbles weren't the only thing the chef was ready to dish up. As they slalomed down Wardour Street at two in the morning, the effect of the fizz taking hold, Dexter flirtatiously pushed Cher into a dark sandwich shop doorway and let his fingers do the walking. Cher, a highly-sexed woman always happy to find the next carnal high, was more than receptive. Within thirty minutes they were back at his Chelsea home, having taken a cab.

For the first few months, life with Dexter was good. His star in the gastronomic world was rising and his name was being mentioned worldwide alongside the likes of Nigella, James Martin and Gordon Ramsay. And that meant more money coming in from all over the globe. But Cher's light was fading and more time at home in the Chelsea flat she was now sharing with Dexter due to lack of gigs meant that boredom and temptation kicked in. Especially if she was on her own. When Cher had a sexual itch to scratch and Dexter's fingers weren't around to scratch it then somebody else would have to do it for her. And they did.

The sex between Cher and Dexter, when it could happen, was fast, furious, kinky and very satisfying – but it was quality, not quantity, and Cher's libido needed both. To Cher, nothing was off-limits in the bedroom. Vanilla she was not. And even though Dexter obviously shared most of her major kinks, their time apart began to force her mind and body into straying. Before she knew it, Dexter's kinks and desires were no longer top of her priority list.

Two months before securing the gig in Iguazu, her first in a while, she answered the phone in Dexter's flat to the man who would become her latest conquest. A voice she knew but had never spoken to. A voice that immediately flirted with her and, despite her connection to Dexter, made it clear that perhaps they should meet while Dexter was away on business. A man whose voice was laced with exciting danger. A man acting as a spark to light her emotions. A man who obviously didn't give a shit if he was treading on his brother's turf. Leland Franklin. And that two-fingered attitude lit up Cher's interest and desires like a bushfire. Their affair began. Wild, hard sex. To Cher, Leland's appetite was equal to her own. It was powerful, all consuming, dirty, dangerous. And rougher than she had ever known, the thin line between pleasure and pain often not just passed but completely destroyed.

It was Leland who was on her mind as she began to talk to Dexter in the forests of Iguazu. She had taken the gig there not just for the money. She knew Leland would be there and she needed to speak to him. What she hadn't planned on was Dexter being there too. Especially as she needed face time with Leland. Things had become out of control, even for Cher's wild ways. But now that Dexter was by her side she needed to tell him the truth. Having them both in such close proximity had brought it to a head. Dexter deserved the truth. Or at least as much of it as she wanted to share. She owed him that. They still lived together. Dexter assumed they were happy together. Were they in love? She wasn't sure. He may have still been, but she wasn't anymore.

'We need to talk,' said Cher.

'That sounds ominous.'

'I don't think this – us – is working.'

She'd been expecting him to explode. But somehow he didn't. He was icily polite.

'May I ask why?'

'We're away from each other so much.'

'And?'

'I find it hard being at home alone.'

'You're happy to be living in an SW3 postcode rent free, that's for sure.'

Cher had known that the subject of money would raise its ugly head. It always did with her lately. Not having any spare cash would always be an issue. The injustice of it all was beginning to irk her constantly.

'Then I need to move out.' She knew it was the right thing to do, even if the thought of trying to find the cash for somewhere else, especially in such a trendy area, would require the mystical and conjuring skills of Criss Angel. But she did have a trick or two planned.

'And if I don't want you to?' Dexter said, trying to remain calm about Cher's wobble about their relationship. He could see where she was coming from, even if he didn't agree. Work was taking him away more than it used to.

'I've made up my mind.' Cher knew what she needed to do. Both now and in the future.

'Let's talk when we get back home,' said Dexter, determined not to hear her decision. 'Get this show out of the way first and then we can decide what to do. Both of us. Together.'

'This show. Sure, it's going to be fucking fabulous, isn't it?' snapped Cher, her patience vanishing. 'Surrounded by stupid little pop acts and a bunch of fucking divas. Have you not seen the line-up?'

'No,' replied Dexter. 'I do the catering, not the cast list. Except for you, of course.'

Cher's anger grew at Dexter's almost flippant manner. 'I have made my mind up. You can't make me stay. I find it lonely in the flat.'

Dexter felt the hairs on the back of his neck stand on end. 'So there's someone else then?'

Cher felt her blood begin to boil. But not enough to let it erupt.

'No.'

Dexter could feel in his gut that she was lying. He'd ask her again when they returned to the UK.

The chance would never come.

*

'Okay, boss. The room is ready,' said Toni.

'All places arranged?' asked Dexter.

'Yes, absolutely.'

'Then tell the chefs to start serving the others in the main room. I need the others busy while I entertain the chosen guests. And once they're in there, make sure they realise how lucky they all are to be given special treatment. They're cut off from the rest and that's how I want it. They're in for a night they will never forget. Never.'

Toni hurried off to follow her orders.

CHAPTER 41

Toni made a beeline for Holly. Firstly because of her love of Crazy Sour back in the day and secondly because she was rather keen to see the ex-singer's tube dress close up. It was chartreuse in colour and contained diamond-shaped slashes that revealed tantalising stretches of skin down her back. It was the perfect colour to complement Holly's vivid hair – the clash between the two working with designer style. The slashes revealed that there was no way that Holly could risk wearing any kind of underwear and also showed, in the bottom diamond, the small tattooed heart at the base of her spine, similar in style to the hibiscus on Holly's foot. The waitress was adoring the overall look and for a brief second felt guilty about sending photos of the faded star to the papers. The stylish female in front of her was a million miles away from the one crouching behind the bus with her knickers pulled down.

The waitress knew that the time would come when she and Holly were face to face and this was it. She wasn't sure if Holly would recognise her. Unfortunately for her, she did. Straight away.

'Well, fuckity doo, look who it is.'

Toni could feel a flush of colour to her cheeks as she realised she'd been caught out.

'It's the skank from the bus who obviously gets her kicks from taking photos of people when they're…' Holly wasn't sure how to say what she needed and plumped for 'going about their business.'

'Look, I'm sorry about that—'

Holly cut her short. 'Too right, how would you like it if you had shots of you plastered all over the internet while you're squatting down on a dirt track?'

'I didn't think,' lied the waitress.

Holly could feel her anger mounting. Being in the public eye was one thing, but it didn't give anybody the right to try and ridicule her for their own financial gain. Take a selfie or ask for an autograph, sure, but don't sneak a shot when someone's taking a much-needed wee stop.

'I hope you were well paid for your photos. Obviously being a waitress doesn't pay as much as being a pop star did.'

Toni felt her own annoyance rise. 'Pop star? You told me you worked in a toothpaste factory, remember?'

'And you didn't tell me that you were going to take photos of me having a piss,' snapped Holly. 'So I guess neither of us are that honest, eh?'

'Well, I'm sorry. But I needed the money. And for what it's worth, you went for a good price.'

For a millisecond, that fact pleased Holly. At least she did still have some kind of star quality – even if it had faded considerably since her Crazy Sour days.

'So tell me…' Holly scanned down to look at the waitress's name badge. 'Toni. What time are we being fed in this place?'

Toni went into professional mode, glad that her grilling was, for the moment, over. 'Mr Franklin has sent me personally to collect you as you are one of his special invitees to dine in our top-class private room next door. If you would like to follow me, there will be an exclusive menu just for you and those gathered.'

Holly liked the sound of that – as did DC, who had sidled up alongside her. 'Did I hear mention of *an exclusive menu*? I trust that I will be privy to that as well.'

Toni recognised him from the pictures Dexter had shown her of those people she was to approach. How could she not recognise him? DC Riding was certainly unforgettable.

'Indeed you are, sir,' answered the waitress. 'If you'd like to follow me too.'

'I do love a touch of VIP, don't you, darling?' cooed DC, linking arms with Holly and grabbing another drink from a nearby waiter as they passed a duo of the free-standing filigree Moroccan lamps that were dotted all over the restaurant. They were almost as large as DC, each with a flame burning inside. DC's thoughts automatically returned to the solid mass of muscle that was the fire dancer outside. Now why couldn't he be taking DC off to a private room, instead of some dainty little filly of a waitress? That would be much more pleasing.

*

Having deposited Holly and DC in the room, Toni headed to the far side of the restaurant where Rosita and Leland were engaged in a conversation with Shaun O'Keefe, the needling journalist who had interviewed the actress the day before. He was the last person Rosita wanted to see, but when he'd cornered her and Leland underneath a minaret-shaped alcove decorated with jewel-coloured cushions, she had no choice but to emboss the most rapturous smile upon her face and engage in idle chit-chat. Leland was not so press-needy or press-friendly and merely ordered the nearest waiter to 'keep his glass filled'.

Rosita was pleased of the interruption when Toni arrived.

'Welcome to Trésor, Ms Velázquez and Mr Franklin. Dexter has requested that you both accompany me to a special dining area where you will both be treated to exclusive delicacies he has prepared for you.'

'Just us?' barked Leland, draining his glass. He hoped not, seeing as the restaurant was already filling up with women he would much rather be spending time with than his actress girl-friend. Sadly no Missy, but there were a few who had definitely caught his attention already.

'No, there will be a select few joining you.'

'Oh, we're the elite, how fabulous,' cooed Rosita. 'It's always rather lovely to be put on a pedestal, don't you agree, Shaun?'

Rosita turned to the journalist and smiled, fully aware that the waitress hadn't mentioned his name.

'Indeed. That does include me, I hope?' he suggested.

'I'm afraid not. You'll be dining in here with the other guests,' replied Toni as politely as possible.

Rosita couldn't hide her glee at Shaun's downgrade.

'If you'd like to come this way.' Toni motioned towards a door on the far side of the restaurant.

'Of course. Our pleasure. Sorry to cut things short, Shaun, but I am sure my lovely make-up artist will keep you com-pany,' she said, motioning to Tinks, who was just joining the group. 'She's powdered virtually every cheek in Hollywood so I'm sure you'll have lots to discuss. Ciao for now, darling. Oh, the joy of being an A-lister. If I were you, I would want to be me too.' As a smug Rosita followed Toni through the throng of people in the room, an already swaying Leland moved behind her, trying to make eye contact with as many females as pos-sible while he still had the chance. A semi-seething Shaun was left with a bemused Tinks, standing underneath the Moroccan arch.

'Where are they off to?' she asked.

Shaun didn't bother replying.

*

Having deposited Rosita and Leland in the room with Holly
and DC, Toni made her final trek to search out the remainder
of the people that Dexter required. As she did so, she bumped
into Christophe, who had finished serving drinks at the doorway and was now heading to the private room as Dexter had
instructed.

'How's it going?' he asked his sister.

'So far, so good.'

'So what is this special room all about? Why are we being cut
off from all of this?' he asked, scanning the room.

'I have no idea,' replied Toni. 'But Dexter has plans, and
what he wants, I am more than happy to give him.'

'I saw that last night,' smirked Christophe. 'You like him,
don't you?'

'Let's just say I'll be sad to see him leave St Tropez when he
heads off to open his next restaurant.'

Christophe smiled. 'Well then, you'll have to entice him to stay,
won't you? Or maybe to take you with him. He's a good payer.'

'It's all about the perks, not the pay.' Toni winked, her meaning clear. 'Now get yourself in that room and start serving more
drinks and nibbles. I have two more people to collect.'

Toni moved off in search of Mew, who was talking to Olivia
and Fabienne, nibbling on a minty pitta chip. She was enjoying it much more than she cared to admit. Having maliciously
slagged off Dexter's food in the past with such public gusto, she
was kind of hoping that Trésor's gastronomic treats would be far
from first rate. It would give her historic public spat with him so
much more credibility.

'*Bonjour*, ladies,' chirped Toni. 'Mr Franklin has requested
that Ms Stanton and Ms Delacroix accompany me to a private

function room where they will be treated to a special meal for the evening.'

'Oh.' The voice of dejection came from Olivia Rhodes.

Fabienne came to her rescue. 'You can tell Mr Franklin that I will be dining with my companion for the night, Olivia. No offence to you, Ms Stanton, but I would like to spend time with Olivia while she is here.'

'None taken,' offered Mew, pleased to note Olivia's widening smile. 'And Olivia is Dexter's publisher, so it hardly seems fair to leave her out in the cold.'

Toni knew that this was not an option.

'Would you just wait a few seconds?' Toni rushed off to the kitchen to speak to her boss. She returned almost immediately. 'Do excuse me, an oversight on my behalf. Ms Rhodes is of course invited too. I didn't realise.' A complete lie, but Dexter had been more than happy for Olivia to join the private party. Especially if it kept Fabienne happy. He wanted Fabienne there.

'Then lead the way,' said Mew.

*

Nine people stood in the private room off the main dining area at Trésor. Two of them, Christophe and Toni, were employed to be there, threading between the small crowd and offering Moroccan delights and drinks. One reporter, Fabienne Delacroix, made polite conversation with everyone there, not afraid to introduce herself to Rosita and a clearly under the influence Leland as the journalist behind the story about them in *La Riviera News*. Actress Rosita clenched her jaw as Fabienne revealed her identity. Adventurer Leland merely spat 'fucking hack' and carried on drinking. Fabienne tried to make as much eye contact as she could with Olivia, who was also circulating the room and wondering what lay ahead. Olivia was still buzzing from

Fabienne naming her as her 'companion'. She would have preferred 'date', or totally swooned at the mention of 'girlfriend', but Rome wasn't built and all that.

Ex-Crazy Sour members Mew and Holly stood in a huddle together, the two women seemingly more at ease with each other than they had been in years. Both were uneasy about the evening ahead for different reasons, but were enjoying the sense of unexpected camaraderie between them. Critic DC scanned the swathes of brightly hued material draped down the wall of the room and fingered his way around the large oval table that dominated the room. Five dinner settings were laid out around the table. Another smaller table, rectangular in shape, sat in the corner of the room, two places set upon it. One had been added to it since DC had first found himself in the room. He grabbed a briouate of goat's cheese, coriander and sundried tomato from a tray in Christophe's hands and popped it in his mouth. As he noisily chewed, he asked, 'So what happens now?'

He didn't have to wait for the answer.

It was Toni who announced, 'Ladies and gentlemen, please welcome your host, Dexter Franklin.'

The doors opened.

Nine people. And then there were ten.

CHAPTER 42

A round of applause would have been customary as Dexter entered the room. He was the host who had paid for nearly all of those gathered to be there, after all, but the silence was deafening as the chef took two steps into the room and closed the door behind him. It was only brought to an end by a forced clap from Olivia and the words 'Great to see you, Dexter, this place looks amazing.'

Dexter, his dark hair slicked back off his face and wearing the whitest of chef whites, nodded gratefully to Olivia and looked around at the people in front of him. Rosita regarded him with an air of regret; for what she had done to him, for what she had lost. For what could have been. She had to admit he looked magnificent, and given their surroundings she was immediately transported back to their initial meeting in the backstreets of Morocco's blue village many years earlier. Leland arrogantly raised his glass in his brother's direction and placed his hand around Rosita's waist. It was the first physical contact he'd attempted with her all evening. Mew also looked on and considered, like Rosita, how good Dexter looked. She pushed aside any thought of attraction by immediately thinking of the dismissive text he had sent her to end their relationship. Holly felt her temperature rise nervously as she looked at the chef again, knowing that he was the man who potentially held the major card as to how her future would pan out – and more importantly that of her mother, Shirley. She just didn't know yet whether that card was an ace or a joker. DC felt a ripple of anticipation.

Dexter smiled at them all, their reactions just as he had expected. He acknowledged Fabienne and motioned for Toni to seat his guests where he had planned. 'Welcome to Trésor, everybody. If you would like to take your seats. The food will be arriving shortly.'

Toni walked around the outside of the large oval table. The far end was free of a setting. There were two on either long end of the table and one at the opposite short end. Moving clockwise around the table from the non-set end, Toni gave her orders. 'Ms Stanton, if you would like to sit here,' she said, reaching the first setting. 'Mr Franklin, you're here,' she said to Leland, reaching the second. 'Next will be Mr Riding, then Ms Velázquez and then finally Ms Lydon.'

'And what about us?' enquired Fabienne, beginning to wonder just why she was there. It was wonderful to be with Olivia, but apart from her new-found semi-bonding with Mew, she had no interest in any of the other people in the room.

Dexter spoke. 'You and Olivia will be here.' He gestured to the rectangular table in the corner of the room. The two settings were alongside each other and both faced the large oval table in the middle. It was an odd arrangement but it gave them both full sight of everyone else in the room.

It was only when everyone had taken their seats that Dexter spoke again. 'Now enjoy your food. I shall see you later.' He left the room.

The door opened again and a team of about half a dozen men dressed in traditional Moroccan robes stepped into the room. The music of the band that had been playing outside on the red carpet filled the air as speakers in the room burst into life. Each of them carried trays of Moroccan delights, given an added twist of French *savoir faire* by Dexter and his kitchen team. Each of the men, all young and buff and obviously picked because of their good looks, wore a brightly coloured robe. Together they were a deluxe palate of gemstone colours, befitting the dazzling shades of the rest of Trésor – a rich ruby red, a dazzling blue sapphire, a vibrant citrine yellow, a deep purple tanzanite, a zesty peridot green and a blazing orange garnet. The overall look was hypnotic and intoxicating. The fire dancer and the belly dancer from the red carpet followed the men into the room, flexing their bodies to the faraway magic of the music. They continued to do so, much to the appreciation of most of those gathered, as the food was served across the tables.

'So is that all we see of Dexter?' asked Mew, now loud enough for Leland, sitting to her left, to answer.

'I gave up trying to understand my brother when we used to play Blind Man's Buff together, and that was a whole other lifetime. At least the food looks half decent,' slurred Leland, who had been drinking steadily without pause.

Within seconds both tables were full of food and the guests tucked into the feasts on offer as the dancers shimmied around them. Chargrilled quail with pomegranate molasses, sautéed fresh calamari with smoked paprika and cumin mayonnaise, a duo of lamb with dukkah crust, grilled red mullet with black olive tapenade and zaalouk, and a rosewater and raspberry frozen chiboust with fresh figs. The food was rich, amazing, steeped in flavour and to the satisfaction of everybody in the room. The atmosphere may have been a little uptight to begin with, but thanks to a constant flow of drink from Toni and Christophe, the ambience soon seemed to thaw.

It must have been nearly an hour later when the men in robes returned to the room. DC rubbed his belly in appreciation as they came in. There would always be room to critique and suggest improvements, of course, but he had to say that Dexter had managed to pull off a totally taste bud-delighting menu.

As the men cleared the table, aided by Christophe and his sister, it was Rosita who asked the question that many of them had been thinking over the course of their meal. She aimed it at Toni as she removed a plate from in front of the actress.

'So why have we been put in this room, away from the main area of the restaurant? It's a beautiful room, but if we are to gain a real feel for the restaurant itself then surely we should be back in there.' She pointed to the door behind her that led back to the main dining area.'

'Mr Franklin wanted to make tonight special for those gathered in this room, Ms Velázquez, that is all I know. You can ask him when he returns. He will be with you once the plates are cleared, I am sure.'

'Well, I suppose it is rather a beautiful room,' replied Rosita. 'It reminds me of where I first met Dexter. A gorgeous little blue village in Morocco called Chefchaouen. I was there for Brazilian *Vogue* and he was there…'

'To buy things for the cookbook he was writing and for future ventures. Typically Moroccan things. It was where he went after the show we worked on together finished.' It was Mew, sitting diagonally across the table, who had scissored into Rosita's sentence mid-flow. 'I remember I was jealous about him going there. I really wanted to visit as I'd read about it *Wanderlust* magazine. But he said that it was to be a purely business trip and that he would be concentrating on his work.'

Rosita let out a laugh, unable to contain it. 'How bizarre.'

'Sorry?' replied Mew, her hackles suddenly raised.

'I just find it bizarre that he should say that it was a business trip seeing as it became such a pleasurable one for him. Well, for both of us.' There was a gloating note in Rosita's voice, fully aware that Mew had been the casualty of her romance with Dexter. Their affair had been much publicised.

'It was there that he dumped me,' said Mew, remembering the cold text she had received from the chef. 'His loss.'

'And my gain, darling. My gain.'

'You mean?'

As ever, Rosita couldn't help but show off. 'Dexter has always been the most private of people with his affairs, but yes, we were together for a while. Before I, er, met Leland...' Her words trailed off as she stared over at her boyfriend, who was now engaged in conversation with an awkward-looking Holly.

'Yes, and after he dumped me. You're telling me that your skanky Brazilian ass is the reason I was binned.' Mew knew that Dexter was a private man when it came to affairs of the heart, but she couldn't quite believe that her constant googling after she'd been dumped hadn't turned up the merest whiff that Rosita Velázquez had been the woman that she was canned for. Given her lack of fame beyond the Brazilian borders, maybe it wasn't that dynamic a pairing. Certainly not one with the sizzle that she and Dexter had given to the press. It was a fact she was keen to share. 'I guess nobody was interested in somebody that wasn't really that famous outside the slums of Brazil.'

'*Puta,*' snapped Rosita, leaping to her feet and grabbing her glass, smarting from the insult. She emptied it across the table, in the direction of Mew. The liquid landed on the table and splashed onto Mew's outfit. It was now Mew's turn to leap to her feet.

'You bitch!' She was about to grab her own glass to retaliate when a voice interrupted, loud enough to silence everyone in the room.

'Ladies, ladies. No need to waste some of the finest champagne in the world. I paid a small fortune for that. Just calm down.' It was Dexter who spoke, having returned to the room. He shut the doors behind him; his workforce, all apart from Christophe and Toni, had left the room.

Olivia once again clapped her hands at his arrival. 'The food was simply divine, Dexter, just…' Her words disappeared, her praise fruitless, as Mew leapt in again.

'You never told me that you dumped me for her,' she barked, jabbing her finger towards Rosita.

'Why would I, Mew? It was nobody's business. Why should I want to share who I fall for? I may be portrayed as a playboy and somebody who has a woman on the go all the time, but when have you ever heard me kiss and tell or seen me splashed all over the pages of *Hello* with my latest squeeze? My fling with you was only publicised like crazy because somebody on the show must have thought it was a good idea. I hated the fact that it was all over the papers. Makes it all a bit cheap and tawdry.'

'Which I imagine it was,' offered Rosita, staring directly at Mew.

Mew was lightning-quick to respond. 'You can just go screw yourself, woman, and fuck off back to Rio.'

'I rest my case. She speaks like a sewer rat from Crackland, the drug slums of Rio. Why you were ever with *her* is beyond me, Dexter. You must have been out of your mind.' Rosita jabbed her own finger against her temple to highlight her opinion.

'Oh, shut the fuck up, the pair of you. Fighting like a pair of fucking fishwives over my sodding brother. You ended up with the better one, Rosita, so count your fucking blessings. And you…' Leland, his patience at hearing the two women argue obviously threadbare, pointed at Mew. 'If you fancy a go at the bigger and better brother, then you know where I am.'

Mew curled her lip in disgust. A horrified Rosita chose to ignore the drunken words. They were not a surprise to her. She had heard similar from Leland before.

'Suit yourself,' slurred Leland. 'Seeing as you're one of the few women in this room I haven't banged. Apart from the Ellen Fan Club over there of course.' He waved his arm in the direction of Olivia and Fabienne. Both women raised their eyebrows and Fabienne whispered something in French that was evidently very insulting.

'I think that's enough, don't you, dear brother? Now sit down.' Dexter's words were sharp 'Pour him another drink.' He ordered Christophe to fill Leland's glass, and watched as Leland, and indeed all of the others, returned to their seats. Despite the anarchy within the room, it was clear that Dexter was there for a reason.

It was Mew who attempted to have the final word, muttering as loudly as she could, 'I just think it's a strange coincidence and a bit sodding bizarre that you invite both me and the woman you dumped me for to travel here to sit in the same room.'

'I'll actually agree with that,' remarked Rosita. 'It's hardly comfortable.'

Dexter walked round to the head of the table and stared at his guests. Toni approached him and handed him a small silver device. As he turned his back on those gathered and faced the wall behind him, he pointed the device, a remote control, and pressed a button. A large screen descended from the ceiling of the room and virtually covered the entirety of the wall.

Dexter turned back to face his audience. He looked over at Fabienne and Olivia at the back of the room. 'Miss Delacroix, you might want to start making some notes.'

Fabienne nodded and reached into her bag for her recording device. Dexter had told her to bring it when they'd met at Sénéquier, but she had no idea why.

For a moment there was silence. An air of worried expectancy hung in the air. Dexter looked at Mew and broke the hush.

'Me inviting you and Rosita here was not a coincidence. The same as inviting DC and Holly and Leland isn't a coincidence either. It's all been calculated. All the way along. I wanted you here. Sure, a few things have cropped up unexpectedly – you bringing along that pilot, Olivia deciding to come along too, Rosita's ridiculous arrival on the yacht, Leland bringing another bird along – but apart from that you have all done exactly what I thought you would do.' Dexter turned to look at his brother. 'I assumed you'd bring somebody other than your girlfriend, by the way, which is why I sent you and Rosita separate invitations. A leopard – or should I say a cheetah – never changes his ways. And I guessed it would spice things up between you two. Make you realise the error of your ways.' The last barbed comment was aimed at Rosita. 'I've been watching you all ever since you arrived. Even in the piano bar at the hotel that evening you were all *supposed* to meet me.'

All eyes were upon Dexter. Just as he'd hoped.

'You were there?' asked DC.

'No, but thanks to a few well-placed cameras from Christophe here I was able to see and hear everything.'

The waiter nodded to Dexter but made sure that he didn't make eye contact with any of the others, apart from Holly. Even though he'd been well paid for the spying job it still felt like he was betraying them all. But Holly was the only one he really cared about. He mouthed the word 'sorry' in her direction.

'You spied on us,' said DC. 'How very Mata Hari.'

'Who?' said Holly.

'A famous spy from World War One, Holly,' answered Dexter. 'She was an exotic dancer and high-class prostitute too. I'm very surprised you, of all people, don't know of her.' Holly felt her cheeks stain red.

'And that's another real coincidence – that you should mention a famous exotic dancer, DC. Because that's the reason I invited you all here.'

'I thought it was for the food,' said DC, confused.

'And I look forward to your glowing review,' said Dexter. 'But the real reason we're here is to talk about this lady.' Dexter pressed the remote control and a photo of Cher Le Visage popped up on the screen. A rumble of disgruntlement flowed around the room.

'Cher Le Visage,' said Dexter. 'A woman I was lucky enough to share my life with for a while.'

'You and she were together?' shouted Mew. 'Is there anyone you've not been with?'

'We were living together. Right up until the day she died. That horrible day in Iguazu, Brazil.' He pressed the button again and a newspaper clipping appeared on the screen: '*SHOWGIRL FOUND STRANGLED AT BRAZILIAN CHARITY EVENT*'.

'How ghastly,' said Olivia.

'Oh, it was,' replied Dexter. 'One of the worst days of my life. I was questioned along with everyone else. I found her body. The story disappeared fairly quickly. The death of a showgirl who had become bottom of the bill was hardly world news. But she was my all. I never publicised that we were together. I never do. Plus my name wasn't as big back then as it is now.'

'What has this got to do with us?' asked Leland. 'That was years ago.'

'It was five years, brother, almost to the day, that I saw her dead eyes, opened in terror, and the scratch marks on her neck where she had struggled. I can still see it now. That vision will never die.'

'I'll ask again. What has it got to do with us?' Leland was clearly exasperated.

'We were all there, weren't we?' He circled his fingers at the people sitting at the main table. 'Mew, Leland, DC, Rosita, Holly. All of you were there and all of you knew her. Not that I knew it at the time. But I do now.'

'So?' replied Leland.

'So?' repeated Dexter. 'So? So her murderer was never found and I believe it might be one of you.'

CHAPTER 43

'You must be out of your tiny mind,' said Mew, standing up. 'I really don't need to hear any of your stupid ramblings about my…' She trailed off, not sure of what she was about to say.

'I think the word you're looking for is *sister*,' said Dexter. 'That is what Cher was to you, was she not? Your elder sister. Not that Cher was her real name, of course. Nobody would ever think that Cher Le Visage was the big sister of wholesome little pop star Mew Stanton. But if they looked at her passport, like I had to when I sorted through her belongings after her death, then maybe they'd have made the connection. Cher was born Lydia Stanton and had dreams just like her sister, didn't she?'

A photo of Mew and Lydia together as children flashed up on the screen. Two sisters, hairbrushes in hands, pretending to be pop stars. Mew must have been about five or six, Lydia about to become a teenager. Rosy red circles of powdery make-up were smeared across both their cheeks and an attempt at grown-up lipstick was clear as the girls pouted into the camera. It was a photograph of pure, unadulterated joy and happiness.

As everyone in the room turned to stare at Mew, she could feel the tears welling in her eyes. That had been such a happy day. One of many. She and Lydia pretending to be Madonna or Billie Piper, or singing Lydia's favourite song of all, 'Believe' by Cher. That was why Lydia had chosen that name when she managed to move into showbusiness a few years later as a showgirl. Cher. She'd loved the glamour of the name. It sounded so Hollywood to her.

Mew felt the tears spring forth as she gazed at the image. For a moment she was totally lost in days gone by. A time before any issues arose. A time when family was all. The main priority in life.

More images appeared on the screen of Mew and Lydia together in the past, including the one of the two girls with their mum that she still hid at the back of her purse.

Dexter spoke. 'I found loads like this. All hidden away. And her diary. It wasn't hard to work out that you two were sisters. The photos say it all – you haven't really changed, Mew. And Lydia's diary documents all of the happy times you used to have together. Until you disowned her.'

'I didn't disown her. I was told to. It wasn't my choice,' spat Mew.

'You put ambition before your own family. The only family you had left.'

Mew tried to stare at the screen through her tears. An image of her and Lydia together sitting on the beach on a day out. Two young women, Mew about seventeen. A snap she hadn't seen for years. Somewhere along the UK south coast. Brighton, if she remembered correctly. It had just been the three of them. As it always had been. Lydia, Mew and their mum, Emma. Mum had taken the photo. One of the last she ever took. Things were so unspoilt then. Mew lost herself in the photo and began to explain.

*

Brighton, twelve years earlier...

'Fish'n'chips for tea back at the caravan?' asked Emma Stanton.

Mew loved the idea. What seventeen-year-old wouldn't, especially when on holiday? 'Lashings of salt and vinegar, brown sauce and a pickled onion included?' asked Mew, running her hands through the pebbles of the beach they were sitting on; the same spot they'd pretty much sat on during the whole of their week-long holiday at the coast. She was sad they only had one more night to go. She loved it here. The piers, the kooky shops, the melting pot of people. Brighton was a place she adored.

'Of course,' answered Emma.

'Then I'm in,' shrieked Mew.

'I'll prepare my own dinner, thanks,' said Lydia, or as she was now professionally known, Cher Le Visage. 'If I am to keep this waist of mine trim and not go piling on the pounds then sadly fish'n'chips is off the menu for me. Even if it does sound divine.'

'Why do you have to have such a tiny waist?' asked Emma. 'It's not natural for a girl in her early twenties to be so skinny. You need some curves.'

'I have curves, Mum, lots of them. I just need to make sure they don't wobble in places where they're not supposed to wobble. Dita Von Teese has a twenty-two inch waist and swears by parsley smoothies to keep in shape. And she's the ultimate burlesque star, so I can hardly go pigging out and think I'm going to be as good as her when I hit the stage.'

Lydia, aka Cher, had been 'hitting the stage' for a few months now and was finally achieving what she had dreamt about doing ever since she had first discovered showgirl Dita on TV. The feathers, sequins and moves of a showgirl were the sexiest thing Lydia had ever seen and she had been determined to follow in her idol's high-heeled diamante footsteps. She may not have been twirling in the big time yet, but a few gigs in London's West End and a spot on a touring burlesque production were certainly gaining her a solid fan base and an ever-growing mass of feathers and sparkle. But nights on stage wearing a minimal amount of coverage meant days of abstinence when it came to calories.

Mew couldn't have been more proud of her sister, adoring the fact that she was living her dream. She too had aspirations to move into the spotlight her sister was now tasting, but she knew it would be her vocals that would find her fame and not her curves – something she was more than confident about as she belted out Natalie Imbruglia's 'Torn' in the confines of their holiday caravan later that evening.

'Orders, please,' interrupted her mother, coming in from outside.

'Fish'n'chips for me, please,' said Mew. 'And make it a large portion of chips. I'm starving.'

'I'm good, ta,' said Lydia.

As their mother left the caravan to walk to the local chip shop, Mew looked across at Lydia, who was practising some of her onstage moves in front of the full-length mirror at one end of the caravan. As she peacocked her arms out and swiveled her hips, Mew marveled at how skilled her big sister was becoming, making every move a flourish. It was a fact she was keen to share.

'You're getting much better, you know.'

Lydia didn't stop her practice but smiled at Mew's reflection in the mirror. 'Thank you. Sure I can't tempt you to try a few moves with a feather and a flounce?'

'There is no way I could do what you do. All of that flesh on show would not be good for me. And if it means that decent food is off the menu then it's a no.'

'Your voice will see you filling Wembley Stadium before you know it. That's some set of lungs you've got on you.'

'Could you imagine? That would be such a dream come true.'

'Reach for the stars, little sis.'

'Now there's a tune,' smiled Mew, and burst into song.

Mew was still singing when a knock came on the caravan door. At first neither she or Lydia heard it, but as it became louder and more urgent they realised that they had better answer.

They were greeted by a police officer and the manager of the campsite they were staying at. The looks on their faces made it instantly clear that something was very wrong.

'Girls, I think you had better come with me. I'm afraid there's been an accident,' said the manager.

The next five minutes were the worst the two sisters had ever encountered. Even worse than knowing that their own dad had walked out on them, never to be seen again, only three months after Mew had been born. Emma had been crossing the road outside the caravan park to walk to the fish and chip shop. She should have used the crossing but for some never-to-be-known reason she hadn't, and when a motorbike had come flying around the corner she hadn't stood a chance. Even though he was under the speed limit, the force of the impact and the subsequent knock on her head she'd sustained from falling back onto the pavement had killed Emma instantly.

The perfect family holiday had ended in tragedy. Two sisters brutally orphaned.

Lydia did her best over the years that followed to act as both big sister and mother to Mew, but time away from home with her profession and trying to earn a crust to keep a roof over their heads meant that she couldn't be the 'mother' she needed to be. Mew, although grateful for her big sister, couldn't help but feel alone and sometimes resentful about the cards that life had dealt her. No dad, no mum and what felt at times like an AWOL sister.

Things changed when the opportunity to be part of Crazy Sour came her way. But even though the singing stardom she had always craved seemed to be around the next spotlit corner, she, Holly and Leonie soon found out that being part of a wholesome new pop band was not always as glittery as they may have believed. Especially when it came to protecting the image of the band.

Mew could still recount the one-on-one meeting she was called to with the Svengali behind the band before she was allowed to sign on the dotted line.

'So, you don't have boyfriends, you certainly don't have sex or blow fans backstage and you don't get seen in public doing anything that could bring the band into disrepute. That includes drink, drugs and any skeletons in the closet.'

'Okay.' All Mew could picture in her head was a front row of adoring, screaming fans chanting her name.

'Have you ever been pregnant?'

'No.'

'Arrested?'

'No.'

'You gay?'

'No.'

'Have your parents ever done anything that I need to know about – been Nazis, kiddie-fiddled, been in the Ku Klux Klan, any shit like that?'

'No, my mum died and my father, well… I haven't ever known him.'

'Any chance he could resurface?'

'He doesn't know what I look like, so it's unlikely.'

'What about brothers and sisters?'

'I have one sister, Lydia – or Cher Le Visage, as she is known now,' said Mew proudly.

As soon as she said it, Mew could tell that maybe it hadn't been the right thing to do.

'She sounds like a hooker.'

'She's a showgirl. A burlesque star.'

'And if you want to sign on the dotted line, she doesn't exist. No cutesy girl group member of mine is going to have a sister who twirls tassels off her titties, you hear me?'

'But she's my sister, she's looked after me, more or less, since my mum died.'

'And that's all well and good, but let me ask you a question or two, sweetheart. Who is LeToya Luckett? Who is Michelle Stephenson? Who are the girls who never made the grade with The Pussycat Dolls?'

'I don't know.'

'And neither does the rest of the world. LeToya was one of Destiny's Child before they hit the big time, Michelle was one of the original Spice Girls before they climbed to the top, and I couldn't name a Pussycat Doll that wasn't Nicole Scherzinger if my life depended upon it. I dare say they were the ones who didn't get on with the management. Beyoncé and Co. always played the A-game. So if you want to add your name to that list of unknowns then feel free – run back home to your flesh-flashing sister. If you want to be in a band like Crazy Sour then you play by my rules, because they are the only ones I play by. You get it?'

Mew knew that she had no choice. Not if she wanted to be Beyoncé. She still needed to ask the question though. 'So what does that mean? I can't talk to her or what?'

'Talk to her all you like, but if the press ask, you're an only child. If they get wind that you have some kinda stripper as a sister then you'll be replaced in the group quicker than you can say "download". That clear?'

'Yes. I guess.'

'It'll be in your contract. I'll make the changes and if you want to stay with me then you sign it. Up to you, but at least we know where we stand.'

Mew knew exactly where she stood. Up to her earrings in confusion and worry. Having to choose between her chance at fame and her relationship with her sister. Whether to choose pop glory over gene pool?

She spoke to Lydia about it. At first she was supportive, saying that this was Mew's 'big chance' and that nothing or no one should spoil it, she should do as the management said.

Cold ambition had won. Mew signed along the dotted line. It was the dotted line that would eventually ruin the relationship with Lydia that she had once treasured.

*

Her sister's life had ended violently, backstage in Brazil. As Mew wiped the tears from her cheeks in the room at Trésor, she looked at the others staring at her. Their eyes hurt her skin, made her feel dirty. But wasn't that what she had done to 'Cher' the moment she signed that contract? Turned her into a dirty little secret for the sake of her job. Her fame.

'I had no choice. Holly, you know that? Didn't you have to hide things too to stay in the band?'

Holly also looked like she was tearing up.

'I understand, Mew. I never knew you'd lost your mum so tragically. And I certainly never knew that Cher was your sister. Fucking hell. You kept that quiet.'

'And you know why better than anyone. It was my only option. If I wanted to stay in the band then that was the price I had to pay, and once the cash came rolling in then I suppose it was easier to count that than count regrets.'

'Did Cher mind?' It was Holly who asked.

'Not at first. But then things changed. And they changed forever.' Mew's voice cracked as she thought back to her last encounter with her sister.

*

Iguazu Falls, Brazil, five years earlier...

'Oh, you're acknowledging me now, then?'

Cher had snapped at Mew from the moment she walked into her dressing room. 'And stop looking at this place like it's some kind of hovel. We can't all be in the super-duper massive dressing room, can we? Not all of us are top billing.'

'That's not my fault, is it?' Mew was in no mood to argue with her sister, although she had to admit that Cher's backstage area would have fitted into one of the toilets in Crazy Sour's dressing rooms.

'I thought you were cool with me having to keep you a secret. It's not my choice.'

'I was at first. You wanted to be in this poxy little band and I certainly wasn't going to stop you living your dream. I'm not that much of an ogre.'

'You never have been. I don't like not talking about you.'

'Then change it. Talk about me. Sing about me from the rooftops on *This Morning*. Jump up and down on the sofa on *Oprah*. Imagine the interviews I could secure off the back of that news.'

'You know I can't.'

'All I know is that you *won't*.'

'The band is bigger than ever now and I can't let anything ruin it for me.'

'Then pay me for my silence. I need cash and you have shit-loads of it.'

'You know I can't. I'm not earning as much as you think. Management take most of it, we don't write our singles, a lot of it is tied up in stuff and all the endorsements we do for products don't pay as much as you'd imagine and…' Mew became annoyed at having to justify herself and reality checked. 'Why the fuck should I answer to blackmail? You earn what you earn for the work you do and so do I.'

'And surely blood is thicker than any amount of no-calorie shitty drink you agree to splash your face across? I need the money. What would Mum say if she knew that you were leaving me high and dry? Disowning me like this. She'd be turning in her grave.'

Mew gritted her teeth in anger. 'Don't you bring Mum into this. She was always the first to show us that hard work paid off. She would never have resorted to blackmail and cheap threats.'

'It's not a threat, it's a promise. You give me the cash I need or I'll tell the world who I really am to you. How I'm the sister that fame forgot. Or rather, that you chose to forget about.'

'And then I'll be out of the band and we'll both have no money, will we?'

'Welcome to my fucking world, Mew.'

Mew didn't know what to say. The person she was talking to was someone that she no longer seemed to recognise. What happened to the big sis who used to sing into her hairbrush with her?

Cher continued. 'Do you remember what we used to say to each other all the time after Mum died? When we were first trying to deal with it all. How if we had to be away from each other, or life kept us part for whatever reason, then we just had to remember that phrase.'

'Of course I do.'

'Well?'

'Well what?'

'Say it,' said Cher.

'*If I forget myself will you remember me?*'

'Exactly.'

'You wrote it on the back of the photo I keep in my purse.'

'Hidden away from prying eyes, no doubt. Never sees the light of day.'

Mew could feel discomfort begin to mingle with the anger she was feeling. Cher was right, she did hide the photo away.

'Well, it seems that pop life has made you forget all about me, and I think it's time you remembered, don't you? Or else I'm telling the world. Cher Le Visage, born Lydia Stanton, is your boob-swinging big sister.' She jiggled her breasts for effect. 'Do you think mums across the world and their little teenage daughters will be loving that?'

'You know they won't. Why would you do that?'

'Because I don't have a lot of choices, and I kinda figured that the family bond between us would count for something.'

'So why blackmail me?'

'Because you leave me no option. That band of yours is far from wholesome, believe you me. I'll bring it down if I have to, one way or another.'

Mew felt as if needles were being dragged across her skin. She could feel her heart beating faster as she thought about what she had to lose. How something that had taken years to build could crumble with one headline. She couldn't let that happen. She wouldn't.

Feeling a panicking rage brewing inside her, she looked around the dressing room, searching for an answer...

*

Mew was pulled back from her thoughts of Brazil by Holly tapping her on the shoulder. 'Mew, are you okay? You zoned out.'

'Of course she's not,' said Dexter. 'She's reliving the fact that she never even went to her own sister's funeral. How she has literally erased her from her life since she first became one of the girls in your little pop band. And how she will never be able to say sorry to poor Cher. Oh sorry… Lydia.'

'You evil bastard,' said Mew, tears flowing again.

She sat herself back down at the table.

'Now,' said Dexter, rather enjoying himself. 'Who's next?'

CHAPTER 44

'Oh my God, Cher Le Visage was your sister. Now that is an image-killer, isn't it?' piped up Rosita, running her hand through her mass of hair and staring at the photo of Mew and Lydia on the screen. 'Who'd have thought it? You managed to keep that secret for such a long time. As did she. She never mentioned it to me once when I worked with her.'

'Well, why would she, Rosita? You and she were hardly bosom buddies, were you?' said Dexter. 'You never shared cosy chats on the telephone and girly nights out, did you? Let's be honest, you couldn't stand her.'

Rosita could feel the metaphorical spotlight in the room swing from Mew onto her. She shifted uncomfortably in her seat as she felt all eyes fall on her. Fabienne Delacroix could be heard feverishly scribbling in the corner of the room, keen to take in every juicy morsel. The evening was looking like it would be celebrity carnage and she was lapping it up

Rosita coughed a little with nerves. 'Cher and I were fellow artists – except, of course, I am a much huger star and obviously my expertise is in a totally different field. My skill is not merely swinging some tassels to the latest Shakira song.'

'Oh, the irony, Rosita,' said Dexter.

'Sorry? What irony?'

'You criticising Cher for her work. How rich is that, coming from the woman who would happily trade her grandmother to a passing salesman if she thought it could make her star shine a little brighter.'

DC let out a minor guffaw at Dexter's words as the room watched Rosita's olive cheeks flush red with embarrassment.

'You know you would,' sniped Leland, his speech now very slurred. 'I've never met your grandmother, so I'm hoping you gained a good price.' He smiled and raised his glass in his girlfriend's direction. Rosita's response was to mouth the words 'drop dead' back at him across the table.

'So I am ambitious, what of it?' asked Rosita. 'You have always known that.'

'Your ambition is brutal, Rosita. I knew that when we were together. It was pretty obvious to me that you would do anything to further your career when our relationship ended.'

Dexter shot a deadly look at his brother, remembering the moment he had found Rosita in bed with Leland. The image was still raw and painfully fresh in his mind. As Rosita tilted her head downwards, still shamed by her actions, Leland merely raised his glass again in mock salute.

'You don't care who you hurt to further Brand Velázquez,' continued Dexter. 'Me included. And you were certainly happy to make sure that Cher never managed to shine, weren't you? Playing understudy and second fiddle to her was never a role that was going to sit pretty with an inflated ego like yours.'

'I don't know what you mean.' The actress was indignant.

'Maybe we should ask DC,' ventured Dexter. '*Muse Magnificent* was supposed to be the show to turn Cher into a major international star, and it probably could have done – had it not been for you, Rosita. You were understudy on that show, after all.'

'And I lost out too when DC pulled the show. It could have finally made me a star in America. Working on an off-Broadway production would have been great kudos for me.'

'It's true, Rosita ended up out of work too,' offered DC, his interest piqued now that mention of his dream production had been thrown into the evening's proceedings.

'But that's what she wanted, wasn't it, DC?' said Dexter, pacing across the room in front of the screen. 'If she couldn't be the leading lady then she decided that nobody else could. Even if *Muse Magnificent* had been a huge success, who would remember the understudy from their one or two performances?'

'But it wasn't,' stated DC. 'It tanked with box office ticket sales and I decided to pull it.'

'On whose recommendation?' asked Dexter.

'My own. And the investors of course.'

'And a certain disgruntled understudy who didn't want to be part of a doomed production, especially after being tagged as second choice to a leading lady who was obviously turning your dream into a nightmare.'

'Cher was difficult, shall we say,' conceded DC.

'She was a bitch and you know it. You must have known that when you were with her, Dexter,' snapped Rosita, finally boiling over. 'And why didn't you ever bother to mention that you and she were such great lovers?'

'Because it had fuck all to do with you. I keep my relationships secret, if I can. It's how I roll. We're not all about advertising ourselves to such a brash level as you, Rosita. Not everything needs to be measured in column inches.'

'She was a cow and *Muse Magnificent* was never going to work with her in the lead role. It should have been mine. I could have shone in it and seen my name in neon lights on Broadway. Another string to my fabulous bow. She was a cabaret star, not a true one. Not like me.'

'Still the understudy though,' whispered Olivia to Fabienne, a little louder than planned, so that Rosita and the rest of the table were able to hear it. A snigger rose from both Holly and Leland, who seemed to be enjoying the destruction of his girlfriend a little more than he should.

Dexter continued, 'It was Rosita who persuaded you to pull the show, DC, and you know it. It was Rosita who couldn't bear to see Cher being given a chance to shine. It was Rosita who provided the venom to take away any chance that Cher had of making the show work. And it was Rosita who suggested that you push the blame onto Cher for the show failing before it even made it to opening night.'

DC merely pulled a face, contorting his features into a frown at Dexter's words, but his reaction appeared to confirm what Dexter was saying.

A fact that Rosita was keen to dispute.

'Prove it? If I was such a nasty bitch to your ex-girlfriend then why did you stay with me? Why were you with me in the first place?'

'Because I didn't know until I saw *this* just how nasty and ruthless you could be.'

'Saw what?' questioned Rosita, her voice cracking with nerves.

'This…' Dexter pointed to the screen where a screenshot of an email appeared. 'Written from you, Rosita, to DC, to persuade him that the show had to be pulled. And that Cher was the reason that it would be a catastrophe.'

'What the fuck?' barked DC. 'How the hell have you got hold of that? How did you know about it in the first place?'

'You told me about it, DC? Don't you remember?' said Dexter.

As Rosita shot a penetrating bolt of toxic anger in the critic's direction, Dexter smiled and said, 'Let me remind you…'

*

New York, just under two years earlier...

DC Riding's entrance into the stark yet stylish interior of New York's latest restaurant was as flamboyant as ever. In complete contrast to the metallic surfaces and chrome domes that dominated the entirety of Dexter Franklin's NYC Vibe restaurant, a place the chef hoped was to become the heartbeat of New York's trendy Meatpacking District, DC had decided that his outfit for the night should be full-on, eye-burningly bright, opting for a dazzling two-piece suit in a Keith Haring print. His brightness on the outside was in complete contrast to his feelings on the inside. He felt rough. Rougher than rough. DC was smothered with the flu.

DC had been feeling under the weather ever since he'd flown to New York from his London home two days earlier. He should have cancelled, really. New York was a place he loved but it always held bad memories after the failure of his dream production, *Muse Magnificent*, and he needed to be in top form to even contemplate facing his shattered dreams in the Big Apple. In his wildest dreams, his name would have been inducted into a Tony Awards Hall Of Fame by now, with the likes of Stephen Sondheim, but a failure before opening night was not even going to light one bulb in the smallest off-Broadway theatre, let alone bring him the accolades he craved. Which was why he had flown to NYC to show his face at the opening of Dexter Franklin's latest restaurant. Work was work, cash was cash, and even if he felt like death, he'd rather be there than at home, nursing his ever-running nostrils.

Having made his way into the main dining area, the first person he saw was Rosita Velázquez. It was hard to miss her as she too seemed to have dressed from the same eye-popping colour palette that he had. Her dress, clam-shell tight, was a micro-beaded creation in colours ranging from candy-floss pink to bright fuchsia.

'Evening, dear. There's hardly room for any of your internal organs inside that dress, let alone the food on offer tonight. One nibble and those beads will be pinging like popcorn.' His voice was layered with congestion, a fact Rosita noted straight away.

'At least I look better than you sound, you poor man. Where have you come from? The local morgue?'

'Very funny,' smirked DC. 'I feel like crapola, but how could I miss sampling your new boyfriend's latest restaurant and seeing you again, dear Rosita. It's always such a pleasure, after all. Besides, I have a deadline for some of the world's biggest publications.'

'Dexter has worked his ass off for this,' smiled Rosita. 'Even I have had to take a back seat. Luckily the film offers have been flowing in to keep me busy, darling.' A total lie. Apart from regular work in her homeland of Brazil, Rosita's professional diary had numerous blank pages where she might as well have written 'Plus one to Dexter's needs.'

'Still waiting for that big break to turn you Jolie massive? No change there then.'

'I had a lot to claw back after the mess that was *Muse Magnificent*, thanks to you, DC.' Her tone was light but the suggestion was that she still blamed the critic for the entire sorry *Muse* mess.

'But you were the one who told me that canning it was for the best—' The critic's words were cut short as Rosita raised a perfectly manicured hand in the air and waved at someone across the far side of the room. 'Must fly, darling. Dexter insisted that I work the room. I may not be on the menu but I am just as delicious, no?' She started to move away, but not before using her other hand to point at DC's face. 'And wipe your nose, for God's sake. You're like a leaky tap. This is supposed to be a designer restaurant, not a doctor's waiting room.' And with that, Rosita was gone.

DC sniffed again and checked out his reflection in one of NYC Vibe's many mirrored surfaces. Despite his colourful attire, his face was ashen and Rosita was indeed right, his nose appeared to be trying to vacate itself of anything that festered inside.

'Good Lord, I need drugs, and not of the sort that this lot in here are going to be chopping up on the toilet cistern all night,' mused DC to himself. He reached into his pocket for the tablets he had brought with him, the strongest he could find, given the night ahead, and downed them with a glass of champagne grabbed from the nearest accommodating waiter. Fizz and flu tablets. It would be his combination of choice for the hours ahead. His head felt immediately fuzzy with the champagne. He beckoned over another waiter carrying a tray of tasters and took a couple. Two little squares of toast with a creamy mix of pink piled high upon them. He ate them both. They tasted like cardboard and he pulled a face of dislike. He was used to it. Over the last forty-eight hours everything he had eaten had the texture of something you would buy from a hardware store. Everything was bland, and for someone who loved their food and was expected to critique it accordingly, that was the kiss of death. He grabbed another champagne to wash it down. At least that was a little more palatable and of the finest quality – even if it was somewhat wasted on the current state of his taste buds.

The evening passed with DC finding himself seated between Nikki Rivers, a socialite, and an attractive Brit actor, Aaron Rose, who had made it big in the States on a cable TV show. The conversation was stilted, DC in no mood to socialise, and the three courses may as well have been made from balsa wood as far as the critic was concerned. Flavours and textures all merged into one. Regular tablets to try and aid his flowing nose and a continually full glass of bubbles were the only things keeping the false smile painted on his rounded face.

After the food had been served and consumed and a speech given by Dexter, DC rose to his feet to mingle a little more. The combination of medication and Moët hit him and he staggered away from the table – straight into the path of Dexter, who attempted to grab the critic and keep him steady on his feet.

'Easy, tiger. You seem to be enjoying the drink, that's for sure. I trust you found the food equally as good? I hear you're doing a write-up for some big names. What did you think?'

'Very nice, dear boy.' It was a lie, but now was not the time to be brutally frank. Not when you're face to face with the man behind the meals.

'Then I trust you'll say good things. It's always imperative we please you guys. Critics can be sharper and more dangerous than the most razor-edged of fish knives. I'm so pleased you've flown over.' Dexter was in professional gushing overload.

'It was an excuse to catch up with your dear lady,' slurred DC.

'Yes, I hear you and Rosita go back a bit. She was involved in a production of yours wasn't she? *Muse Magnificent*. Bit of a non-starter sadly.'

'Biggest bloody disaster since the *Spider Man* musical. Not even a webbed wonder could save that flopperoo of a turkey. At least Rosita was right in persuading me to bail before *Muse* joined the ranks of the biggest Broadway bombs.'

'I thought it was you who pulled the plug?' said Dexter.

'Darling man, show me a gay man who would willingly pull the plug on a camp theatrical extravaganza all by himself. Even if I did know it made sense. No, it was Rosita's email that finally convinced me that a man has to do what a man has to do.'

'Her email? I thought it was down to low ticket sales.'

'Of course. Sadly Cher Le Visage was not putting bums on seats, but I would have let it run to opening night at least. It was my dream. But Rosita spelt it out for me loud and clear. She has quite a venomous tongue on her, hasn't she?'

Dexter angled a glance over to Rosita who was on the far side of the restaurant, deep in conversation with Aaron Rose, doubtless scouting for work. 'She has her moments, yes. So what did she say?'

'Well, she hated Cher – that was clear. The two of them never really got along and Rosita being understudy was never going to work, was it? That lady of yours will always want to be number one. I think she was adamant that nobody was going to shine if she couldn't. She wanted me to fire Cher on countless occasions and put her in the lead, but I couldn't. Rosita may be adorable but in New York, darling, she's nobody. She's only shining tonight because she's with you. Fame by association.'

DC was becoming more and more loose-lipped as the drink and medication took further hold.

'You're one of the few people who knows that we're actually together, and I do think Rosita is a star in her own right.'

'Back in Rio maybe, but in this city she's hardly Cameron Diaz, is she?'

Dexter chose to ignore the fact that an obviously away-with-the-fairies DC was throwing shade at his girlfriend. He was much keener to bring the conversation back to the subject of Rosita's email and her hatred of his ex-squeeze, Cher.

'So, what was written in this email? I can guess it was acidic.'

'Darling man, you have no idea. The deadliest of snakes could be taught a thing or two by Rosita when it comes to venom.'

'So tell me…'

*

'And you did,' smiled Dexter, pointing back to the screen at Trésor. 'There are some tasty little nuggets there that I am sure your fans, Rosita, would hate to see in print should this email ever gain more notoriety.' It was a veiled threat, but a threat nevertheless, and one that Rosita immediately cringed at. She knew what was coming.

Staring around the room, Dexter started to quote from the email filling the screen.

> *Your production was doomed from the minute you gave the leading role to that useless, hateful piece of talent. How I can be considered second-best to someone like that, who merely dances for a living, is beyond me, and how a man of your kudos could be fooled into thinking that she would be a worthy leading lady is nothing short of a joke. Fire her sorry, talentless ass or pull the production before it's too late.*

> *I will not go down with the ship, DC. You know what you need to do to make this better. That bitch will never make the production what it needs to be. Only I can make it a success.*

> *Keep a skank like Cher in the leading role and you will become a laughing stock – not just in New York, but around the world. I know it.*

'Pretty nasty words, Rosita. So how come you hated Cher so much?' Dexter asked.

Tears stinging her eyes, Rosita stared directly into Dexter's face. She knew in that moment that their love for each other was lost for good. Never to return.

'I didn't hate her. I just hated the fact that I was her understudy. It was demeaning for me.'

Dexter wasn't convinced.

'Rubbish. It was more than that. If you couldn't shine then nobody could. That's it in a nutshell, isn't it?' stated Dexter. 'Blind ambition leading you to trample on others yet again. Cher was heartbroken about *Muse* being pulled. We'll never know whether it could have worked but your email to DC made sure that she never got the chance.'

'I was thinking about my own reputation too.' Rosita's words came across as pitiful and weak.

'You always do. I know that better than anyone.'

'But I'm no killer. I would never...'

'We'll see...' He left the words hanging like a noose.

As a sense of accusation seemed to flow in Rosita's direction from around the room, DC rose to his feet and marched towards Dexter. As he spoke, a fine spray of spittle flew from his lips.

'Listen here, you pompous twat, where on earth did you get this email from? That's private communication between me and Rosita. Did you hack my computer? Because if you did, I shall inform the authorities.'

'Wind your neck in, DC. You'll only be explaining how you let the thief into your own house.' Dexter spoke with a smug sense of complacency.

'What do you mean?'

Dexter nodded to Toni, who walked to the door of the room and opened it. On the other side, waiting patiently, stood a muscled man, six foot three in height with a skinhead, wearing a pair of shorts, a vest top and flip-flops. DC recognised him immediately as Henri, the rent boy he had enjoyed some time with a few days earlier. Toni shut the door behind him.

Dexter spoke. 'Meet Henri, everybody. I know one of you has met him before. Maybe with not so many clothes on though, eh, DC?'

Crimson splashed through DC's fat cheeks.

'*Bonjour*,' said Henri, his accent as thick and French as Notre Dame.

'Or should I say *Henry*,' added Dexter.

'Alright, mate,' nodded Henry in DC's direction again. This time his accent was broad cockney. 'Have you got over your beating yet? Nice to see you again. Third time now.' He winked at a disbelieving DC.

DC remained silent for a minute, all eyes on him, before eventually saying, 'What do you mean third time? I have only met you the once.'

It was left for Dexter to explain. 'It's only the second time you have met *Henri*, DC, but you've actually met Henry before. Maybe this will jog your memory.' Dexter flicked his remote control at the screen and Rosita's email was replaced by a photo of a blond-haired man with a full ginger beard.

At first the connection was opaque, but then slowly everyone in the room began to recognise the man in the photo as the same one who stood before them. The wide eyes, the full lips…

'Oh my God, it's you…' said Holly.

'It's amazing what a shave and a skinhead can do for a person. Plus a put-on foreign accent, of course,' said Dexter. 'Meet Henry Woodingdean, rent boy and part-time actor. I found him in the gay press. Recognise him now, DC? You last saw him with full beard and hair about a year or so ago. At your flat in London. You picked him up in a gay bar in London's Old Compton Street and he gave you a night to remember.'

DC was floored. 'Yes, but what...' His words petered out.

'What has that got to do with me?' asked Dexter. 'Well, after you told me all about Rosita's email when we were in New York, I started thinking. I needed to see it for myself. To see just how full of vitriol she could be and how spineless you were for letting her bully you into binning Cher's show. You told me that night at Vibe, when you were whacked out on medication and booze, that you'd kept everything from the show in the vague hope of resurrecting it one day. Quite the organised man, aren't you. Positively anal, in fact. You even told me that all the digital communication was stored in a Hotmail folder, and that all of the physical stuff – like the production brochures that never saw light of day, the letters from top industry people saying how excited they were to be working on your show, photos of you and Cher together – they were all stashed away in a, what did you call it, your "box of dreams", ready to be resurrected should you ever manage to get the show off the ground again. I could barely shut you up but it was all bloody useful information. All I needed was to get someone into your house to work their way into your computer and maybe have a root through your *box of dreams* to see if there was anything else about poor Cher there.'

'But you couldn't have known that I would invite this young man back to mine...'

'The whole world knows you can't resist a pair of guns and a night of bedroom action. You've been vocal enough about paying for it on several occasions. I've heard you at launches. I don't think there is a waiter in my employment that you haven't offered to spank, wank and show a good time to.'

Olivia let out a small embarrassed giggle at Dexter's coarse words.

'I had you watched. I knew where you live. Most chefs do. Found out the bars you frequented and when you went. You're a man of routine, DC. Most Sunday afternoons, if you're not working, will find you at the Admiral Duncan in London, isn't that right?'

DC remained silent. There was no point in disputing it. It was his favourite gay pub.

'I found Henry and made him an offer he couldn't refuse: to conveniently be in the right bar at the right time, flex his pecs in your direction and suggest going back to yours. Like you, Henry shares a pretty wild streak in the bedroom, so it was very easy for him to tie you up, get you all worked up with sexual anticipation and then make his excuses to freshen up while he searched your house for the box and to see if he could find the email on your computer. It didn't take too long – luckily you'd left your Hotmail open. Henry told me he didn't even have to get you drunk or drugged up in the hope that you would tell him your password. When Henry forwarded me the email, I then asked him to change his appearance, become Henri and join us here in St Tropez. I sent him to your hotel and the rest you know.'

'But why? You already had the email.'

'You could have killed Cher. She wanted to sue your ass, I know that.'

'But I didn't kill her.'

'How do I know? Cher suing you for every penny you have would have crippled you.'

DC, becoming more flustered by the moment, floundered at Dexter's interrogation and ignored the motive. Just as with Rosita moments earlier, he could now feel the eyes of suspicion landing on him.

'But why let me enjoy another, er, interlude with Henri or Henry here or whatever his bloody name is?' snapped the critic.

'Simple. Because I want to make sure that you never ever write a bad word about any of my ventures again. Thanks to the shit you wrote about my restaurant in New York my entire career nearly went tits-up. Just because you couldn't taste anything because of your fucking flu doesn't give you the right to say things like...' Dexter flicked the screen again.

'*Dishes that were as unattractive and unappetising as roadkill... New York, maybe. Old pork, definitely. I've chewed better pencils.*'

'I am always honest with my words,' challenged DC. 'The food was dreadful and I had been commissioned by some big names in the publishing world to tell the truth. It's what we critics do.'

'And because you couldn't taste anything and had deadlines looming you decided to slag my food off. Well, that was the last time.'

A sudden sense of bravado washed over DC. 'Dear boy, no chef will ever dictate what an esteemed critic such as me will write about a restaurant. I'm already beginning to think that some of tonight's offerings may be making me feel a little sick. Maybe I should spread the word.'

'Hence why I asked "Henri" to pay you a visit. If you write so much as one unsavoury word about Trésor then these will be uploaded onto every social media outlet out there in a flash. And I apologise in advance to anybody in the room easily shocked.'

A series of photographs appeared on the screen, all taken by 'Henri' in DC's St Tropez hotel room. They were beyond explicit and showed DC in various naked poses on the bed, tied up, obviously drugged into oblivion and making use of the various sexual toys brought to the room by the rent boy.

DC was mortified.

'You wouldn't dare,' he hissed.

'Just try me,' replied Dexter. 'Now sit down, shut up and start thinking about some fabulous adjectives to use about to-night's food.'

As a horrified DC returned to his seat, Henry left the room with a flourish of his arms and the words '*au revoir*'. His accent was comedy thick.

'So if you reckon DC didn't kill Cher, then who did?' slurred Leland.

'Well, Leland, it could have been you,' said Dexter.

CHAPTER 45

'I've been called a ladykiller on many occasions, bro. When you look like this you tend to,' said Leland arrogantly. 'But I think you're barking up the wrong tree on this one, don't you? Why would I want to kill some two-bit showgirl, especially one who was shacked up with my brother? She really wasn't that important to me.' There was a distinct sneer in Leland's voice as he attempted to trivialise his cross-examination.

'To stop *this* from becoming public.'

For once it was Leland who remained silent as an image of Cher appeared on the screen. It was a selfie headshot, obviously taken by Cher on her mobile phone. Despite how beautiful she was, no one in the room focused on that. Instead, all eyes were drawn to a large lozenge-shaped bruise across one of Cher's eyes. As Leland remained silent, a gasp of horror and disapproval burst from those gathered, especially Mew and Holly. Rosita turned her head away from the screen and looked directly at Leland. For a brief second he looked back at her, his face blank, and then turned his head back to the screen.

'So she has a black eye. Did she fall off her cheap heels or something? What does that have to do with me?' Leland blustered.

Dexter clicked the remote control and a series of images of Cher appeared on the screen. All of them had been taken by herself and showed various bruises, ranging in size across her body. The majority of them were on her face, either around her eyes or across her cheeks, but some were visible on her arms, legs and across her breasts. Dexter stayed quiet for a few seconds longer to allow the room to take in the full horror of the images, and also to compose himself as he stared at the discoloured flesh of the woman that he had loved for a period of his life. Even though Cher was no longer a physical presence in his life, the emotions he had once carried for her still burned strong. To see her as she was on the screen – so raw, exposed and vulnerable – still cut deep into his heart.

'Poor Lydia. Did you do this to her?' Mew hissed, her hands trembling with rage.

'Get real,' Leland sneered, but his voice lacked conviction.

'What kind of man would do that?' asked Fabienne, still taking notes of everything that was happening.

'A bastard,' stated Holly, not really sure as yet whether to believe that Leland was to blame.

'Why would I want to use Cher as a punchbag?' asked Leland, his words devoid of remorse and almost of any emotion.

'A power trip. Control. Call it what you will,' said Dexter. 'It's what you do. You can't help yourself. It's always been that way.'

'Says who? You can't fucking prove that I did that.' He pointed at the screen, his voice trembling slightly through the slurring.

Dexter signaled to Toni, who handed him a small notebook, an image of a 1950s pin-up splashed across the front of it. Dexter held it up for the room to see.

'This says so, Leland. Cher's diary. Another thing I found when I had to sort out Cher's affairs after she died. I didn't open it for ages. Reading a woman's diary is not part of my nature. There's a privacy that should be respected even after death, don't you think? So I placed it in a box with some of her other things and stored it away. For ages I didn't go back to it. But eventually I did and when I found the diary again I chose to look inside and read what was there. It may not have been the right thing to do, but it certainly gave me a much clearer picture of what Cher was going through in the run-up to her death. Sleeping with my brother, for one.'

'So… It's not the first time we've shared a woman, is it?' volleyed back Leland. 'If she wasn't getting what she needed from you then far be it for me to refuse her wants.'

'I don't think what she needed was to be knocked about and bullied and frightened by you. Cher and I were very much together, but we were relaxed with each other when it came to our sex life. I don't need to say any more, but the fact that she was sleeping with another person isn't something I really mind. Some might understand that, some might not. I'll be honest, I don't care. I'd have preferred it to be anyone but my lowlife brother though. Cher's diary revealed something that I will never forgive. It was the moment I realised that I hated you. The moment when you stopped being a brother to me. I should have known what you were like from the way you treated me when we were kids. You were always pretty free with your fists back then as well.'

'Do you really think I care?'

'No, you never have. It's what you have always done. Sibling rivalry. It's always been that way. Seeing what was mine and trying to make it yours. Taking it through any means possible, including violence if need be. I lost count of the times you tried to intimidate and bully me when we were young. You were always hell-bent on destroying anything that was precious to me. And it didn't stop in adulthood. You did it with Rosita, determined to take her from me. Sadly her ambition made it easy for you. She was weak. As was Cher. And when she found out what a bully you were, she was powerless to stop. It's all documented in the diary, along with the photos that we've all seen here. You've always been a bully. You can't help yourself.'

'So she liked it rough.' Leland shrugged dismissively.

'If you read her diary you'll see that she didn't. At first you were an excitement, a distraction for her when I was not there. A titillation. But the affair between you was a rough one that spilled from the realms of bedroom domination and sex games into a place where she was afraid to say no to you, scared of what you would do. Verbal abuse, physical abuse, violence. She wrote it all down. It's horrible reading.'

'Cut the fucking drama. What kind of man are you to not even notice when your girlfriend is rocking up with bruises all over her?'

'She lied to me. Said she'd walked into a cupboard door, banged her arm against something. She made excuses and gave explanations if I ever questioned her. I didn't know about the bruises she was suffering on the inside until I read the diary, detailing all the ways you bullied and abused her. You did the same to me when we were kids. I hated you, was scared of you, but I couldn't do anything about it...'

Dexter could feel the rage bubbling under his skin as he spoke, and for a moment he sensed that he was losing his composure. A panic enveloped him that threatened to ruin what he needed to say. He wouldn't let his brother make him feel as he had night after night during their youth. He took a deep breath before continuing. 'Anything that was mine you would try to break and ruin. My bike, my toys, my clothes. Looking back, it's all clear. Classic bully behaviour. How many times did we fight? You picked on me for no reason. When we were at school, when we were at home, as I lay in bed at night. Anywhere you could, but always when nobody else was there to see. Nobody to tell you how wrong it was. You had such arrogance. An inability to control your own aggression. But a toy can be replaced, a bike rebought – when you bully a person, beat a person, the mental scarring is irreparable.'

'But that doesn't make me a killer, does it?'

'How easy would it be for your aggression to stray from a thump or a slap or a pressured grip into a strangulation? For you to take your aggression to a deadly level? Only you know that. Once a bully, always a bully.'

'You can't prove a thing. Investigations were made into Cher's death and there was no evidence to suggest it was me. These are just the words of a jealous, pathetic, spineless, insecure brother who is green with envy about what I've achieved. Hung up on his own failings in life. So unless you can prove something, I suggest you shut the fuck up and quit with your wild and unfounded accusations about me being a murderer.'

Rosita was unable to contain her silence anymore. 'Dexter may not be able to prove you killed Cher, but you are a bully, Leland. I can testify to that.'

'Shut it, woman,' fired back Leland.

'No. Why should I? I've been quiet long enough. How many times have I had to cover up bruises from you? Just ask Tinks about the number of occasions on which I have had to ask her to add an extra layer of powder to disguise a dirty reminder of you from the night before as I go on set or walk onto the red carpet. And the verbal abuse. It's always been there.'

'So why have you put up with it?' interjected Mew, unable to remove the images of her sister she had seen on the screen from her mind.

'Isn't it obvious? Stupid ambition. I thought being with him would make me a bigger star.' She indicated Leland. 'Plus the fear of what might happen if I walk away.'

'You need me. You love me. So you have delicate skin, it's not my fucking fault, is it?' barked Leland.

'I don't need you anymore. I don't love you anymore. And after seeing what you did to Cher, no woman will ever love you again. I'll make sure of that.'

'It will be nothing more than the ramblings of two stupid women. One dead showgirl and one pumped-up diva searching for publicity on the back of her much more successful boyfriend. Actually, yeah, make that ex – we're through. I was bored of you anyway. Talentless cow.'

'Bullying to the last. You really are a touch of class, aren't you?' said Holly, who had been silently brewing with anger about the revelations about Leland. Seeing tears forming in Rosita's eyes at Leland's insults was the straw that broke the back of her silence.

'Another ex-shag piping up,' snapped Leland. 'What the fuck do you want?'

Holly could feel the rage spreading through her veins. Cher had become a good friend to her, an equal who matched Holly perfectly when they could find time to be together, and allowed her to live life to the max when they were able to party. They had experimented and been intimate together, but their relationship was not a sexual one, it was about a playful understanding and a mutual desire to be a free spirit. To momentarily escape from life and the pressures that it contained. To see her friend in such a state of victimisation, and to hear Leland being so verbally brutal with Rosita, had made her question everything that she had experienced with the adventurer. He was hypnotic, enticing and dangerous. That was clear. But she was beginning to wonder if she hadn't fully realised the severity of the danger. Looking at him now, he was mad, bad and dangerous to know.

Brutality against women. Something no female should ever have to endure. Flashes of her fear when she was a young girl, smelling the hot, tobacco-tinged breath of Uncle Warren and feeling his hands moving across her flesh, filled her mind – and for a moment she became that helpless victim once again. Maybe Cher had felt the same. Maybe even Rosita. Holly was looking at them in a new light. Memories of her lovemaking with Leland back in Brazil and at The Abbey filled her brain. Lovemaking? Who was she trying to kid? It had always been sex. Hard sex. Brutal sex. Sex where Leland had always been in control. Had always manoeuvered her, sometimes with force, now that she thought about it, into what he wanted her to do. All in order to please him. In order to stay metaphorically on top. To feed his ego and fuel his power trip.

Holly felt she needed to explain herself. 'I started an affair with Leland in Iguazu, at the place where Cher was murdered. Like most women, I imagine, I found him alluring and captivating. He was what I needed at the time – a release, an escape, a distraction. We were very alike. Leland worked for me on many levels. Our affair ruined Crazy Sour. It broke up the band. I threw away pretty much everything that had been built up so successfully around me. I'm sorry about that. I really am.' Holly looked over at Mew, who merely nodded, affirming her understanding and appearing to accept the apology. 'But I was in a bad place, my mind was pretty much fucked with the madness of the group and Leland seemed like the perfect find. He seemed cool. Even if he was wearing the shittiest shirt I'd ever seen – swordfish and hibiscus designs all over it – what the fuck was that about? So not cool at all.' Holly let her mind wander briefly before bringing it back to the point at hand. It was strange, the things that popped into your mind at the most random of times. What she needed to think about now was being there for Rosita and more so for Cher. 'You were rough with me too, Leland. Not to the extent of poor Cher but enough for me to now realise what a bully you are. What a poor excuse of a man. I'd happily tell the world what a pathetic specimen you are.'

'Just as Cher was going to. Isn't that right, Leland?' said Dexter, ready to deliver his final blow. 'It's all in the diary too. How she wanted to expose you as a bully. To tell the world about the violence that the so-called people's action man was capable of. She needed the money and wanted to make you suffer. That's what she threatened you with, wasn't it? That she'd share the contents of this diary with the press. She was at rock bottom, and turning the tables on you was her only way out. She needed to do it for herself. It wasn't ever going to be easy or pretty, but she felt it was what she needed to do. Poor Cher had no other option. She tried to blackmail you in Iguazu, didn't she?'

'Believe what you want,' Leland hissed, slamming his glass onto the table. 'I've had enough of this shit.'

Leland pushed his chair away from the table, stood up and moved as quickly as his drunkeness would allow towards the exit. Pushing Christophe out of the way, he opened the door and disappeared out of sight.

'Go after him! Don't let him get away with murder!' shouted Mew, looking at Dexter.

Dexter remained motionless.

'What are you waiting for?' said Mew. 'He killed my sister.'

'But that's just it,' said Dexter. 'I don't know whether he did. You all had motives to want her dead. Maybe even you, Holly. That was in the diary too.' He tapped the cover of the book. 'But perhaps that doesn't matter now.'

For a moment Holly looked perplexed. What did Dexter know? She was the only person he hadn't zoned in on yet. But as he said, maybe that didn't matter right now. It wasn't the time.

'Leland Franklin killed my sister,' repeated Mew as the others in the room began to stand up. 'Dexter, you need to call the police now. Finally justice can be served.'

'But it can't be,' said Dexter. 'Because even though I think that he probably did, I have no evidence whatsoever to say that my brother killed poor Cher.'

CHAPTER 46

Despite what Dexter had just said, Mew was in no mood to listen to excuses. As far as she was concerned, Leland Franklin was the person behind her sister's death and she needed to face off with him. She needed to discover the truth, for her sister's sake. She may not have been honest with Cher when she was alive, but she owed it to her now, to her happy memories of Lydia, to do everything she could to make things right. She ran from the room into the crowd still gathered in the main room of Trésor, up the stairs and out into the warm late-evening air of St Tropez.

The backstreet where the restaurant was situated was now a vision of relative calm, all signs of fire dancers and Moroccan musicians gone. Mew looked around, hoping to spot Leland, but he was nowhere to be seen. The sound of music from inside the restaurant hung in the atmosphere, a gentle rhythmic beat. It petered out to nothingness as Mew made her way down the backstreet, away from the restaurant and towards the lights of St Tropez's harbour. She had no idea whether Leland would have stumbled in that direction, but it seemed a more likely option than him disappearing into the virtual darkness of the town's hidden alleyways. Especially given his inebriated state.

Mew could feel her brain racing at a million miles an hour as she scanned the bars and restaurants along the portside, looking for Leland. He was one of the most famous TV stars in the world and doubtless his appearance in one of the Riviera hot spots would cause a reaction. But he was nowhere to be seen. She ran past Sénéquier, her eyes flitting across the red tables and chairs placed outside the bar. A sea of overly made-up faces and sun-tanned complexions stared back at her, but the blond hair and blue eyes of Leland Franklin were not among them. The superyachts on the water bobbed up and down, the water lapping gently at their bows. Partiers enjoying their cocktails stood on deck, swaying to the beats of their on-board music as they looked down on those not exclusive enough to be invited on board. Leland was again not among them.

For what seemed an eternity, Mew paced up and down the portside, unsure where to look. She sat down on one of the rectangular stone bollards at the far end of the harbour, near where a smaller vessel, doubtless still worth millions, had moored itself for the night. The boat was in darkness and the only lights were the far-off ones coming from the St Tropez bars. Mew took a deep breath as a wash of emotion flooded through her. She thought of Lydia and her aspirations of becoming Cher Le Visage. How she had gone so far, but how she herself had never publicly acknowledged her own sister's talent. Since that horrid day in Iguazu five years earlier, when Cher's last breath had been taken so cruelly from her, Mew had never been able to do so. She reached down into her purse and pulled out the photo of herself, her sister and her mum. It wasn't easy to see in the evening light, but she knew every millimeter of the dog-eared photo so well that she didn't really need to see it with perfect clarity. She turned the photo over in her hands and read from the back. 'If I forget myself, will you remember me?' Her sister's handwriting. The tears sprung forth, Mew unable to stop them. Her sobs echoed through the air, loud and pitiful, finally released from the depths of her guilt and misery.

As the tears rolled down Mew's face and onto her trousers she felt an arm wrap around her shoulders. She looked up to see Holly.

'There you are, we've been looking everywhere for you. Did you find that son of a bitch?'

Mew wiped her face with the back of her hand and sniffed. She was still holding the photo.

'No, I haven't. And who's we?'

'Olivia and Fabienne headed off the other way to see if they could find him. Olivia was really worried about you. You know she has a soft spot for you, don't you?'

Mew let out an involuntary laugh. It felt good. 'You don't say! Yeah, I had noticed. That's why I'm pleased she's met this Fabienne woman. They seem pretty loved up.'

'And how are you?' asked Holly. 'Is that the photo you always used to sneak a look at when we were in the band, popping it back in your purse without me and Leonie spotting you? We weren't that stupid, you know.' Holly laughed, keen to try and keep Mew's misery quashed.

Mew offered up the photo to Holly. 'Yeah, it's me and Lydia – or Cher – and my mum. Now neither of them are around. It's so hard to think about how we were before… Life before Crazy Sour seems like a trillion years ago now.'

'You loved it, didn't you?' asked Holly.

'Yes. Didn't you?'

'I hated the fame. Believe it or not I'm quite a simple girl at heart. I have my wild side but playing the fame game wasn't really everything I thought it was going to be.'

'You loved the money and the perks, though.'

'But where did that get me? Complete dissatisfaction and a string of crappy fellas. Including Leland Franklin.'

'I know that he's the reason the band had to split. I blamed you but I know it was his fault really. You were just an easier person to focus all my anger on,' said Mew.

'I can understand that. But look at you now. Top chef, number-one author with your recipe book. I bought it, by the way.'

'Really?'

'Yep. I used to love cooking with my mum when I was younger. She was a great chef.'

'I'll send her a signed copy,' joked Mew, not picking up on Holly's use of the past tense.

'No, we don't cook anymore. She's not able to.'

'Sorry?'

Mew shifted herself across the wide stone bollard and patted the space for Holly to sit alongside her. As she did so, Holly handed her back the photograph.

'You're not the only one without a mum anymore.'

'Oh my God, I'm so sorry. I had no idea she'd died. She was so proud of you in Crazy Sour.'

'She's not dead.' Holly explained to Mew about her mum's illness and how she had ended up in the residential home in America. Mew's eyes widened in sympathy as Holly unfurled her story. She reached out and held her hand as she spoke. Without intending to, Holly let everything tumble from her lips, including how she could no longer pay for her mother's care and how she had come to St Tropez with the sole purpose of trying to blackmail Dexter with the incriminating photos she had of him. Tears streamed down her face as she spoke.

'What are you going to do?' asked Mew.

'To be honest, nothing. It's been sitting uneasily with me for a while. I think Dexter's suffered enough. Whoever killed Cher has made sure of that. I'm so sorry about her, you know. I liked her – a lot. I really never knew she was your sister, not even when…' Holly was unable to finish her sentence.

'When what?' Mew was curious, but there was no malice in her tone.

Holly made a decision. Suddenly opening up to Mew about everything seemed the right thing to do. They had shared so much and survived. Perhaps now was the time to put all of her cards on the table. Whatever the consequences.

'I was really good friends with your sister. She got me. I loved everything about her. What she did. What she said. Her personality on and off stage. She was dynamic and magnetic. There was an instant friendship. We met at an audition and we… well, we became really good mates. She allowed me to forget about all the crappy, grown-up things I'd had to deal with in life and just be me. We were pretty mad together at times. More of my wild side coming through, I guess.'

'That doesn't surprise me. You and my sister were a lot more similar than I would ever have admitted when we were in the band. I could see a lot of her in you.'

'I really did care for her. She was a good soul.'

'So why did Dexter say you had reason to kill her too?'

For a second, Holly was stunned. 'First off, let me tell you honestly that I didn't kill her. But there's a reason I've been feeling uneasy about Dexter's photos. All this talk of Cher has reminded me of some of the things we did together, and I know there are some photos of me that Cher took when we were, er, experimenting, shall we say. We were both wild, and we'd get drunk and things would spill into the realms of… well, I'll spare you the details but they're not for family viewing, put it that way. Cher hinted that she would show the photos to the world and suggested that I pay her money to keep them hidden. She cornered me in Brazil at the charity event to tell me as much.

She was in a bad place, I don't blame her. It's exactly what I would do. It's exactly what I am doing with Dexter.'

Holly paused, contemplating exactly how alike she and Cher actually were. 'It seems like she was firing off at everybody and anybody that day. Including those she cared about. I'm not ashamed of the photos, but they were of private moments and if I'm ever to have a chance of getting myself back on my feet again then photos like that need to stay buried. How can I really try to blackmail Dexter when I felt so horrid about somebody trying to do it to me? It doesn't sit easy. Even for a cow like me.'

'You're not a cow. You never were. I just think you and I misunderstood each other.'

'But I was the one who fucked up.'

'We all did. Including my sister. Look at the facts. We've just been sitting in a room full of people who pretty much all had reason to want rid of her. That's pretty tragic.'

'But she was suffering,' replied Holly, determined to defend Cher. 'We all doubt ourselves, and she was just doing what she thought she had to do to survive. But sadly it was that fire to try and succeed that killed her. Nobody should have to go through abuse like that. Those bruises left more than a mark on her skin, that's for sure. Believe me, I know.'

Mew could sense that there was something else that Holly wanted to say. 'How?'

Holly took a deep breath, and then decided to let it all out. She told Mew about her horrible abusive experiences with Uncle Warren. How frightened she had been whenever he was around. How she would freeze with fear as he ran his hands across her, cry herself to sleep and then wake up the next morning only to remember that she could never forget what had happened. 'It's a feeling that never goes away. The feeling of abuse is always there. No matter what degree it is, it's never something that can be justified.'

'At least that bastard is dead now,' said Mew. 'You never have to face him again. The right person died. I can't say the same about my sister. She was the victim. Despite every bad thing she may have attempted to do in life – as we all have – she didn't deserve to die.'

Holly still had her hand in Mew's, the two women bonding over their traumatic experiences. As Mew finished what she was saying, Holly squeezed her hand firmly. It wasn't just a gentle squeeze for comfort. It was for something much more immediate. Her eyes widened as she pointed past Mew towards the figure who had just come stumbling into view from around the corner of the harbour.

The blond hair hanging down over his forehead, the baby blue cravat he'd been wearing around his neck all night and the zigzagging of his drunken walk made him instantly recognisable.

It was Leland.

CHAPTER 47

The hairs on the back of both Mew's and Holly's necks stood immediately to attention and the noise from the bars of St Tropez faded to nothing as the hulking shape of Leland Franklin came towards them. The night was heavy with anticipation. Mew had wanted to find him ever since running out of Trésor but now that he was lumbering towards her and Holly, a wave of worry ran through her. She knew that she needed to make this moment work. It was pivotal. To her past, her present and her future.

Leland spied the two women in front of him. 'Might have guessed you two bitches would quit the party as soon as I left. Nothing worth checking out anymore?' Mew guessed he'd been drinking since leaving the restaurant, although why anyone would actually serve him was beyond her. Leland was hammered.

'Haven't you done enough damage to last an eternity with that foul mouth of yours?' snarled Holly. 'How many people do you want to slag off in a lifetime? Mind you, better that than using your fists, eh?'

Leland pointed at Holly as best he could, his finger waggling from side to side as he tried to hold himself steady. 'Don't you confuse me with some bloke who goes around punching women for fun. I don't, it's just sometimes during sex things can turn a bit brutal. You fucking loved it.'

'Actually, I didn't,' stated Holly. 'There were times when I told you to stop and you wouldn't. I was just lucky enough to not suffer like some of the others obviously have. Like Cher did.'

'She was virtually a stripper, for fuck's sake. You don't do that kind of thing unless you expect blokes to be hands-on. She may as well have been spreading her legs around a pole and inviting punters to slip fifties up her snatch.' Leland swayed again, his concentration on stringing a sentence together and his focus on remaining upright not exactly working hand in hand.

'That's my sister you're talking about, and she was a showgirl, not a stripper. There's a massive difference,' said Mew.

'Tell that to her fucking tits,' scoffed Leland, bringing his hands to his own chest and making the shape of a pair of breasts.

'You're so full of bullshit – about women loving it when you become brutal and how they're gagging for freaks like you to be "hands-on" with them to the point that they're bruised and sore. You fucking disgust me, man. And to think the world reckons you're such a great guy. The good-looking, macho explorer. I hope the only thing you explore is Hell.' Mew could feel her inner rage growing as she looked at Leland. How could someone so adored by the public for his looks and machismo charm be so ugly on the inside? She hated him.

'When I'm in Hell I'll give my regards to your sister, eh? She was hardly a fucking saint. No wonder she ended up dead.'

'You made sure of that, didn't you?' replied Mew. 'I know you did it.'

'You know fuck all. No one can pin that shit on me. The Brazilian police couldn't, so why would you two skanks be any different?'

Holly had no idea whether Leland was behind Cher's death or not, but if Mew was going down that line of accusation then she was certainly not going to let her do it alone. The two of

them had always made a good team, despite their many differences.

'But it was you, wasn't it? Even if no one could prove it. You
must be so fucking smug that you managed to get away with it.
And the drama of killing a stripper with their own feather boa.
That's doing it with style, isn't it?' said Holly. She looked across
at Mew as she used the word 'stripper' to let her know that
she had picked it deliberately to bait Leland and not as a diss
to Cher. Mew understood and decided to run with the baton
Holly was using.

'Yeah, Leland, it must have been such a buzz for a powerful
man like you to see the life fading from my sister. To see her eyes
bulging as her final breaths left her body. You with your strong,
masculine hands wrapped around her, strangling the life from her.'

Holly spoke again, not allowing Leland to intervene. 'To feel
number one, like you always tried to be with your brother, to
know that she couldn't get one over on you with her blackmail.
You couldn't allow a mere woman like Cher Le Visage to dent
your image and let anyone see that you are anything less than
the perfect adventurer we see on the TV.'

'Is that why you did it, Leland?' asked Mew.

'Is that why you did it?' repeated Holly. Their timing, just as
it had been in Crazy Sour, was perfect, the rhythmic synchroni-
sation between them bang on. Leland, still staggering, swung his
head from left to right as the two women spoke at him.

'You couldn't let her ruin you, could you, Leland?'

'You wouldn't let her ruin you, would you, Leland?'

'She had to die, didn't she, Leland?'

'She deserved it, didn't she, Leland?'

It was then that Leland snapped, his mind suddenly taken
back to the dressing room in Iguazu. To Cher greeting him at
the door, demanding money for her silence about the abuse he

had put her through. Her threats about the photos and the contents of her diary. Her wish to end their relationship, to not be a victim of his abusive ways any longer. And her want to ruin his image if he didn't agree. In a mad rage he had felt his hands reach for the feather boa and then wrap it around her throat, choking the last whisper of life from her. It was what she deserved. Nobody was going to ruin what he had gained. What he'd built up. Especially some two-bit stripper.

'She got what she fucking deserved and you bitches will never be able to prove that I did it. I had to kill her. There was no way some cheap ho in feathers and shit was going to try and kill off my success. I'm part of the biggest TV show on the planet. I take on Mother Nature and win. So there was no way that Cher Le fucking Visage was going to be my downfall. Shame she had to die though – she was a good shag while it lasted. But she got what she deserved. You bitches always do.'

Holly and Mew looked at each other. Their eyes locked and, without saying a word, they both knew what they needed to do. Totally in sync, they both raised their arms and pushed their palms against Leland. He was a powerhouse of a man, but the combined strength of the two women and the unsteadiness of Leland meant that he easily toppled towards the edge of the harbour.

'What the f—'

Leland never finished his sentence as he tumbled backwards and into mid-air. As he fell back, his head connected with the edge of the yacht that was moored on the bollard that Mew and Holly had been sitting on earlier. There was a dull thud as his skull hit the vessel and before the sound had even ended Leland's body fell out of sight into the dark waters of the St Tropez port. It made a soft splash as it landed, the noise somehow muffled by the boat and the hour of the night.

Mew and Holly looked at each other. Neither of them had regret in their eyes.

'Do you think he's dead?' asked Holly. Fear gripped her but somehow she didn't panic.

'I hope so,' said Mew, shivering at the thought.

'We've killed him. Holy shit.' Holly's voice began to wobble, the full realisation of what they had just done beginning to hit her.

'We did it for Cher,' reasoned Mew. The vibrato in her own voice suggested that she too believed that wasn't reason enough.

Attempting to keep a lid on any potential panic about their actions, Holly continued with their defense. 'Yes, we did. We did it for Cher. It's what Leland deserved. He killed her. He just said so. He admitted that he strangled her. We did this for your sister and my good friend and for every other woman that bastard man raised his hand to. And to prove to all of those abusive men out there that they don't always win,' said Holly, her mind spinning into overdrive. Her thoughts were suddenly full of the predatory Uncle Warren and her own teenage nightmare. Alongside the disgust she felt for him and what he had put her through, what she and Mew had just done to Leland seemed somehow justified and almost lightweight in comparison.

Both women, attempting to cage their panic, walked to the edge of the harbour and stared down at the spot where Leland's body had fallen into the water. The light was soft but they could see that he was face down on the surface. He was dead. Of that there was no doubt.

'How did you know he did it?' said Holly.

'I guessed. It was something you said earlier about the shit shirt he was wearing at Iguazu. I remembered seeing someone, from behind, wearing a shirt like that, going into my sister's dressing room. I'd forgotten it, Christ knows how given the vivid pattern, but when you mentioned it and after all of the revelations about Leland and Cher I kind of put two and two together and hoped it made four. As it happens, I was right.'

'Justice has been done.' Holly attempted to sound sure, despite the worries of what they had actually done pinballing through her brain. If she could be strong, then maybe Mew could too. They could survive this together. As a team. But if she let herself weaken, she suspected that both women would crumble Jenga-like with fear about their actions.

'You were incredible, by the way,' stated Mew.

Holly let out a nervous laugh. 'Yeah, I'm an awesome accomplice to a killing, eh? Maybe I should start dancing around like Uma Thurman in *Pulp Fiction*,' she grinned, her voice rich with a mixture of sarcasm and fear. 'We make a great team.'

'We do. I guess we always did.' There was still an unsteadiness in Mew's voice, and her gaze oscillated in many different directions as she spoke, attempting to stare into the darkness to see if they had been seen. Her own fear allowed to look everywhere yet nowhere at the same time.

'So now what? We should tell the police.'

Mew thought for a second, a collage of consequences crashing through her mind, none of them pleasurable: jail, a court case, the press, the branding of the women as killers. Murderers of the people's action man. She made a snap decision. 'Why?'

'A man is dead,' said Holly. 'And a famous one too. We should report it. We've just killed Leland Franklin. But the authorities would understand why we did it. We can say it was self-defense.'

'But nobody except us knows. He could have left the restaurant, drunkenly stumbled down here and then fallen in the water. It's really quiet at this part of the harbour, away from the main strip of bars and restaurants. We can say that you and I were looking elsewhere for him and we couldn't find him. I'm your alibi and you're mine. We can do this for each other. Think about the alternatives. I can't go to jail, and neither can you. Think of your mum. Hasn't she suffered enough? Haven't we all?'

For a moment, near silence fell, the gentle lapping of the harbour waters and the distant orchestra of the bars the only sounds that hung in the air. Holly thought of her mother and the potential that she could die while her daughter languished at Her Majesty's Pleasure. Even from beyond the grave, Leland would be able to ruin her life yet again. She knew what she had to do. 'That could work,' she said.

'Nobody saw what happened,' replied Mew. 'Nobody.'

'Except me. I saw everything,' said a voice from behind the two women. Holly and Mew swivelled round to face the figure standing there.

CHAPTER 48

'Fuck, you saw it all,' said Mew. Panic lassoed itself around her and a stab of barbed panic plunged into her soul once again. Suddenly there was another person to consider. Another human affected by their actions.

Standing in front of them both was Olivia Rhodes. She was shaking at what she had witnessed. Both girls noticed it and also the look of horror that was painted across Olivia's face. Tears started to prick at Mew's eyes at the thought that she and Holly had been caught out.

'Oh my God, Olivia, we didn't mean to do it,' lied Mew. 'Leland admitted that it was him who killed my sister. We panicked and he fell. We didn't mean for him to die. Honestly we didn't.' Mew could feel her tears about to fall as she confessed.

'Think about what he did to Cher, to others, to women like us,' said Holly, her own sense of dread and fear returning cloud-like to smother her. 'Surely you can understand that, Olivia. Nobody needs to know about this.' A ripple of pleading ran through Holly's words.

The picture of horror on Olivia's face softened and a semblance of a smile stretched across her face.

'I did see it all. I heard what you said, saw what you did. I saw him fall. I couldn't quite believe my eyes, but I don't blame you. I think Leland Franklin got everything he deserved, don't you?'

Mew and Holly tried to take in Olivia's words. 'You mean that you agree with us killing him?' Mew's voice cracked as she gazed into Olivia's eyes.

'Did you set out to kill him? Or premeditate all of this? No. Did Leland take poor Cher's life? Yes. I think perhaps his death was the only fitting outcome, don't you?'

'But this isn't from the pages of one of your authors' thrillers, Olivia,' said Mew, still unable to fully take on board that Olivia was on their side. 'This is real life. We killed him.' Her voice dipped to a whisper as she stated the last fact.

'I know it's real life. And so were the bruises on Cher's body and the venom that spewed from that devil's mouth.' Olivia pointed to the water where Leland's lifeless body still bobbed. 'But I thought you two handled it incredibly well. I couldn't have done it any better if I'd edited the story myself,' said the publisher. 'It would seem horribly unfair if you two took the blame now, wouldn't it? After all that he had done.'

'You mean…?' Mew didn't know how to finish the sentence.

'I'd have done exactly the same. He deserved what he got. He killed that poor woman… your poor sister, Mew.' Olivia's voice possessed more strength and authority than Mew had ever heard before. Something inside was burning bright and letting Olivia own the situation. A fact that both Holly and Mew were becoming increasingly grateful for.

Olivia continued to speak. 'Mew, I'm so sorry for your loss. Now here is what I suggest we do. Fabienne is still up at the other end of the port, looking for that scum. I'll text her and say that none of us can find him and suggest that maybe we head back to Trésor and finish the evening. We tell everyone that we couldn't find that dreadful bully and that doubtless he will turn up with a stinking hangover for his flight home. Does that sound like a plan?'

Mew sighed with relief and more than a dose of grateful disbelief too. 'You're not going to tell on us? Report us to the others? To the police?'

'Why would I do that?' replied Olivia. 'Who wins then? Nobody. Now, are we all agreed on this plan of action? I think we need to stick together on this one. Hurry up, there's not a moment to lose. Are we agreed?'

Mew spoke. 'I say that sounds like a plan, Olivia.' Both Holly and Mew could feel a sheet of worry and dread float off their shoulders and into the night air as they realised that Olivia was indeed on their side.

'A bloody good one,' added Holly. 'But are you sure you won't regret this, Olivia? We all have to live with this. We can't act all innocent with everyone else and then one day you change your mind and admit we all lied to their faces. Somebody has died here.'

'This is the only solution. And it's a perfect one,' said Olivia. 'I think any woman would have done the same as you two did, don't you? I don't blame you. The bastard deserved it. We just won't give anybody else the chance to blame you either.'

'Thank you.' Mew let a smile spread across her face. 'Thank you so much. If only every woman was just like you, Olivia.'

'And if every woman was just like you, dear girl, I really wouldn't know where to look,' remarked Olivia. 'It's a good job I'm hoping to be a one-woman kind of girl from now on.'

'Will you tell Fabienne?' asked Mew.

'You leave that to me, but I really don't think she needs to worry her head about that man, do you? Now, come on, the pair of you. I'll text Fabienne and tell her that we'll meet her outside Sénéquier and head back to Trésor together. Smiles on, ladies – *teeth and tits*, as you would say, Mew. And not a word about that dreadful bully and what's happened. We can do this.

Haven't you two performed all your lives? Well, it's time to do it again. We just need to work out our stories. And as a publisher, I don't think there is anybody more qualified, do you?'

Mew linked her arm into Olivia's and Holly did the same on the other side. Olivia felt like an almost maternal figure to the two young women as they joined together. Joined in mind, in spirit, in story and in deceit. She was looking after them. The three women walked away from where Leland's body was still floating face down in the water, a swirl of deep red blood looping away from the break in his skull where he had hit the yacht. He had performed his last adventure.

Justice had been served, even if it was in the most unconventional of manners.

CHAPTER 49

When the four women arrived back at Trésor, all of the guests from the special screening room that Dexter had set up were now back in the main body of the restaurant.

The numbers had thinned out somewhat, but a group of about twenty or so still mingled around, desperate for yet another freebie drink or a complimentary nibble. Those who hadn't been picked to head into the special room kept enquiring about what 'delights' had been served to the chosen few. Nobody cared to answer. The response 'Oh, we were all accused of possibly killing a showgirl in Brazil half a decade ago' didn't exactly seem like the perfect after-dinner banter.

As soon as the women returned, Fabienne and Olivia took themselves off to one of the minaret-shaped alcoves and parked themselves on the coloured cushions scattered there. Fabienne was buzzing about the night's 'floor show' and admitted to a surprisingly calm Olivia that the launch had been one of her most exciting ever. So much better than the usually vacuous celebrity affairs that she had to cover for her job at *La Riviera News*. There was something about privileged celebrities being put in their place and made to squirm that had metamorphosed the evening into a better one than Fabienne had enjoyed for the longest time. And spending it alongside Olivia had made it even more of a thrill. As one of the Trésor waiters offered glasses of champagne to the two women, Fabienne leant in and kissed

Olivia fully on the lips. For a moment the room and the colours around them vanished as they both lost themselves in the pleasure of the touch.

'*Merci,*' said Olivia as their lips parted.

'*Vous êtes les bienvenus,*' whispered Fabienne. Olivia melted at the accent, as ever.

They continued to stare into each other's eyes, oblivious to those around them. High on the wings of *amour.*

*

Dexter headed straight over to Holly and Mew as soon as he spied them. He'd kept one eye on the door ever since their departure. He noticed that they both seemed a little flushed and red of cheek when they reappeared.

He cut directly to the point. 'Did you find him then?'

It was Holly who replied, taking a deep breath before she did so, running over the story that she, Mew and Olivia had decided on. 'No. I think Leland is long gone. Unless he's propping up the bar at some backstreet St Tropez boozer, then we don't know where he is. Fabienne and Olivia were looking as well as us and they couldn't see him either. He'll turn up for his flight home no doubt, stinking of booze and arrogance.'

Rosita, her eyes still a little bloodshot from her earlier tears, approached the group too. She'd been chatting idly with fellow guests since the women had left in search of Leland, but wasn't able to concentrate on anything other than the evening's revelations about Cher. Even talking about herself and her latest movie didn't interest her. 'So, do you think my boyfriend killed Cher?'

'If you want my honest opinion, I think he did,' stated Mew calmly. Even though an unstoppable volcanic fire of worry bubbled away inside her, to those around she was an unruffled vision of composure. 'And I think he's done a runner. We might not ever see him again.'

'He'll turn up for his show. He'll be wanting to beat his chest Tarzan-style on some far-flung tropical island to impress some talentless female celebrity who wants to suck his cock. It's all he ever does behind my back anyway,' sniped Rosita.

'So I'm assuming the relationship is over,' remarked Dexter.

'Yes. I may be a great actress, Dexter, but not even I can play the role of happy girlfriend anymore. The man has always been a little heavy-handed with me too and I think I deserve better, don't you?'

'You had better,' declared Dexter. 'And you threw it away.'

'And I think you have rubbed enough salt into all of our wounds tonight to season every dish at the *churrascarias* of São Paulo. We all seem to have made many mistakes. Even you. But I can't quite wrap my head around the idea that perhaps Leland is a killer.'

'Any of you could be,' argued Dexter. 'It might not have been Leland. It could be any of you. It could be none of you. It could be something that I'll never find the answer to, but I needed to bring you here to make you remember Cher and face up to the things you did. She may not have always been the sweetest person in the world, but I loved her despite everything and nobody deserves to die like that. Strangled so cruelly.'

There was a strange silence as Mew, Holly and Rosita listened to Dexter talk about Cher. They had all been intimate with him too, and seeing his eyes mist over with romantic memories about the showgirl was awkward in the extreme. Especially given their individual connections with her.

It was Mew who broke the silence. 'So, I have to ask, Dexter. Did you know Cher was my sister when we dated?'

The potential prickly nature of the grouping became too much for Holly to bear and on hearing Mew's question she linked her arm into Rosita's and asked her to accompany her to 'the little girl's room'. A protesting Rosita was reluctantly pulled away. It was the first time Mew and Dexter had been alone since Mew's arrival in the Côte d'Azur.

She asked again. 'So did you know?'

'Yes, I did.'

'Is that why you dated me?'

'It's why I wanted you on *Someone's Cooking in the Kitchen*. I handpicked you for that. I needed to find out about the girl who disowned her sister, even if you had apparently been forced to. Cher never told me about it when she was alive. She kept you a secret from me, just as you kept it from your fans. I found the evidence after she was killed. It was the only piece of the diary I read at first. After finding Lydia's passport I needed to know more. I had to get close to you.'

'As close as you did?'

'That wasn't planned. You're a good looking woman, Mew. I just wanted to see how you reacted when I asked you about family and things like that. But I was happy to get closer to you. To find out more. I don't regret what we did together. You proved yourself a worthy winner.'

'Is that all I was to you? A winner on your show? The way you ended things was so wrong – saying I was a good "contestant". And by text. That was awful. I thought we had so much more together. I was falling for you. And then you chucked me for Rosita. It was so hurtful.'

Dexter knew he needed to be truthful. 'I was never in love with you, Mew. I'm sorry if that sounds cruel. Your sister was the woman I loved, and then Rosita after that – until she betrayed me – but I did enjoy our short time together. Even if it was a little too public for my liking. Despite being on TV, my love life is a very private thing to me. My relationships with

Cher and Rosita weren't splashed all over the papers. When we finished, and I admit that I didn't handle that very well, you went running to the papers and slagged off everything about me. That hurt. A lot.'

'Well then, it looks like we're even, doesn't it? We've both hurt each other,' said Mew.

'But we've moved on,' added Dexter. 'Maybe we can be friends again. Put everything behind us and let our memories of your sister heal our differences. Besides, it really is thanks to her that your amazing culinary career started. If she hadn't been your sister, then maybe you wouldn't have ended up on the show and you wouldn't have had this incredible new start in life, where your books are even outselling mine. Which I'd like to stop, by the way.' He smiled, his voice a fusion of sarcasm and respect, despite everything.

'I guess so. Maybe Lydia was looking after me even from beyond the grave. Once a big sister, always a big sister.'

'I guess so too,' agreed Dexter. 'I wonder what she would have made of your new chap, the Italian pilot.'

Mew couldn't help but smile, at both the thought of her sister as a guardian angel – doubtless a beautifully feathered and frilled one – and also at the mention of Giuseppe. She hadn't thought about him all night, which proved that he was indeed no more than a few-day dalliance.

'Oh, yeah, the pilot. Let's just say that it's Missy Terranova who's sampling that man's *chopper* now. I suspect that's why Leland was on such a mission to drink himself into oblivion all night. Missy and Giuseppe have disappeared together. Good riddance, I say.'

'There's someone out there for you, I know it,' said Dexter. 'And any man who hooks up with one of Leland's women is definitely not a keeper.'

'Talking of Leland's women, here comes Rosita,' whispered Mew, pointing across the room as the Brazilian actress and Holly returned from their trip to the bathroom. Rosita looked more fresh-faced, having obviously reapplied her make-up – or rather, demanding Tinks touch it up for her.

'Well, you two are smiling, which is a good sign,' remarked Holly, looking at Dexter and Mew. 'Especially given the dangerous waters that conversation was steering into. All sorted?'

'We've built a bridge or two,' said Mew.

'There's been a few built tonight,' replied Holly, looking directly at Mew. She understood exactly what her former bandmate meant.

'Whereas mine with Leland has been blown into a crater the size of a Brazilian Olympic stadium,' observed Rosita. The sentence was a fact and not a regret.

'Keep it that way.' Holly and Mew spoke as one.

DC, who had been sitting Buddha-like in an alcove being grilled by reporter Shaun O'Keefe for the last half an hour about what had been going on behind the closed doors of the special room, suddenly interrupted the group. He was still fanning himself, beads of sweat grouped at his hairline despite the late hour of the night.

'No sign of the bully, then?' he asked. 'Olivia just told me he's vanished. I was buggered if I was going to start roaming the streets looking for him. I've better things to do.' Though he had no idea what. 'So did he kill Cher? Looks like it, I guess. Always thought he was the cocksure type. All macho and heavy-handed. It's no surprise. But Rosita, darling, you're better off out of it. You don't need a bully like that in your life – even if he is one of the most famous faces on TV. Find somebody else. Be like Taylor Swift and start dating anyone who's vaguely famous, dear.' He paused, looking at Dexter. 'Oh, you already have.'

Rosita was not to be dissed. 'From what we have seen on screen tonight, DC, it's you who likes things a little on the "heavy-handed" side. A lady like me was shocked. Who knew you were such a dirty piggy?' Rosita pushed her finger into DC's belly and squealed, much to the hilarity of the group gathered. 'Where is your dear rent boy anyway?'

'Very funny,' deadpanned DC. 'Anyway, Leland Franklin isn't the only one who's disappeared into the night. Henry seems to have done so as well. I will never forgive you for setting me up, Dexter. Even if he was hung like a porn star.'

'TMI!' snapped Rosita.

'Henry's gone. He left with the fire dancer. He's his boyfriend. Another hiring of mine,' replied Dexter. 'And I don't want your forgiveness. I just want good reviews from now on. Honest ones. Because you know that my food is honestly good. Otherwise… boom!' The chef pressed an imaginary button as if he were posting the photos of DC online.

'Understood. Anyway I'm not here to talk about my sex life. Shaun O'Keefe wants some shots of me, Rosita and Mew together for his blog and website. I need to borrow you two.' He looked at Holly. 'Sorry, he didn't request you. No offence.'

'None taken,' smiled Holly as the others walked away, leaving her and Dexter alone.

'So why did I escape public humiliation on your screen of guilt tonight, then? Everyone else had their turn, so why not me? I've not exactly been the nicest person to you, have I, threatening you with the photos I took.' Fear rose in Holly's throat as she asked, afraid of what the answer may be. Perhaps her time was still to come.

'I think we've all seen enough incriminating photos don't you?' said Dexter. 'I found some of you that Cher had obviously taken. I recognised the tattoo on your back and the one on your ankle, even if your face wasn't always clear in a lot of them. Plus, you were mentioned in Cher's diary too. You were good friends, that was refreshingly clear. But I guessed that if I didn't show yours then perhaps you would agree to forget about mine. From what I hear, you've got enough going on in your life with your poor mother. I know that's why you need the money. You told Christophe about it and he told Toni, and, well, she told me.'

'Oh, Toni, the waitress who sold the photos of me taking a leak behind the coach on the way here. Looks like we've all been snap happy.'

'If you need the money to keep your mother cared for, I'll pay it. Regardless of the photos. You didn't kill Cher, I know that. You've not got it in you. I think you were more of a friend to her than most people in her life. You're actually pretty soft underneath that hard pop-star, call-girl exterior. And Cher obviously cared for you deeply. That was clear.'

'I cared for her a lot too. And thanks for the offer, but no. I'll sort this out myself. She's my mother and I'm the one who should look after her. I'll work something out. It's family. It's what we do.'

'Well, the offer is there if you want a hand. It's looking like my own family has been blown apart.'

'You think Leland did it?'

'I'm sure of it. He's always been my main suspect, even if I might never know for sure. I can't prove anything. But I've always known first-hand what a brute he can be. Ever since I was a boy.'

'And how does that make you feel?' asked Holly.

'Karma will catch up with him eventually and bite him on the backside. If he did it, then he's the one who'll have to live with the guilt for the rest of his life. But, as a brother, he's dead to me.'

For a split second, Holly considered admitting to Dexter that she knew that Leland was definitely the person who had ended Cher's life. But what would that gain? Nothing. If Dexter already felt that Leland was dead to him then maybe it should be left as it was. He didn't need to know. Families never needed to know everything. She just hoped that the look on her face didn't give away the fact that she knew he was already dead for sure.

EPILOGUE

The body of Leland Franklin was found the next morning by an early morning dog walker taking her poodle out along the St Tropez portside. It was Dexter who was called to identify the body by the French police. Examinations discovered that there was a huge amount of alcohol in his bloodstream and it was deemed that a drunken Leland, a man who had risked life and limb around the world on *Frankly Extreme*, had died by accidentally falling into the waters of St Tropez as drunk as a lord. A smudge of deep red on the bow of a yacht and the crack in his skull proved that he was probably dead or at least unconscious before he hit the water.

Dexter was unsure of how he felt. His mood swung like a metronome between believing that maybe karma had indeed caught up with Leland for killing Cher, if that was the case, much sooner than even he had contemplated, and feeling great sorrow as he realised his only brother was gone for good.

The death of the TV adventurer dominated the headlines worldwide and the opening of Trésor in St Tropez was mentioned in every article written. More press was gained than any publicity campaign could ever have achieved and the PR team behind Dexter's latest venture could have not have been more pleased, not that they admitted this to Dexter. In the same way that downloads and album sales seem to shoot through the roof after a star's death, the connection between the opening night and the mysterious death of the owner's famous brother seemed to have people worldwide flocking to Dexter's restaurants. Business in the months following Leland's death quadrupled and sales of Dexter's cookery books saw him back at the top of the book charts, a fact that pleased Olivia Rhodes greatly. Olivia accompanied him on a worldwide book tour, as did Dexter's new girlfriend, a certain French waitress called Toni. Their relationship, for once, was not kept secret, Dexter deciding that perhaps Toni was the one that he could share with the world. A young woman who had no link to the fame game and a rock who had been there for him in those moments when he had needed comforting, crying himself to sleep at night as he mourned his brother, remembering the few good times they had shared. Dexter's love for Rosita and Cher had been a flame that burned bright, but there was something about Toni that made him feel that her light would be ablaze for the longest time.

Mew Stanton was for once happy to take second place – in the cookbook charts, at least – and felt that despite the secret she, Holly and Olivia would have to take to their graves, going to St Tropez had been an experience from which she had gained greatly. She may have crashed and burned in the game of love – or mere lust, if she was honest – with gigolo Giuseppe, but she had won so much when it came to understanding some of the things that had happened in her life. She finally felt she had some closure about the death of her sister, and the fact that in some warped way her sibling was responsible for her new career post-Crazy Sour helped her to feel that maybe everything does indeed happen for a reason.

St Tropez had helped Mew reconnect with Holly too. Their discussions about their families, Holly's torment about her time in the band and her dealings with Uncle Warren as a teenager gave Mew a much greater respect for and understanding of the other woman. Without Holly knowing, Mew contacted the care home where Holly's mum, Shirley, was living, and paid for a year's worth of treatment and care. When Holly found out she burst into tears and vowed to pay the money back to Mew. Mew's response was that there was no need and that she was happy to help while Shirley was still able to benefit. Mew, of all people, knew how quickly and savagely a family member could be ripped away for good.

Six months after the drama of St Tropez, Holly and Mew reunited with their third Crazy Sour member, Leonie, and a set of four new tracks were recorded and added to a new *Best Of* CD collection. The release topped downloads and sales charts worldwide and the band embarked on a mini world tour, taking in fifteen major cities around the globe. Suddenly Crazy Sour were hot again and top DJs like Calvin Harris, David Guetta and Blair Lonergan included funk-fuelled remixes of the band in their club set lists and requested to work with them. The three women enjoyed the tour more than any other they had ever done and at the end of it, even though they went on hiatus, the possibility of a future Crazy Sour big reunion was on the cards. The money they earnt from the tour meant that Holly, who was now sharing her LA home with her new French boyfriend, Christophe, and had given up any work 'on her back', never had to worry about her payments for her mother's care again.

In a strange twist of fate, Rosita Velázquez also profited greatly from the death of her one-time boyfriend. As the 'widow' of Leland, her trip to the Cannes Film Festival, with Tinks everpresent to make sure she was always perfectly presented, garnered more press on an international scale than she could have ever dreamt of. Through morbid association, suddenly Rosita was finding that her kudos as a primetime guest around the world was stratospheric, as she was always happy to talk about her life with Leland – even if she did rose-tint it somewhat, avoiding any mention of the hardships she had encountered as being part of his brand. If the world was still happy to place Leland Franklin on a pedestal as an action hero who died before his time, then Rosita was happy to let her 'time' be now. She could never know for certain what her heart told her was the brutal truth – that Leland was a killer. Ambition, as ever, came first and when her movies suddenly found themselves rereleased to new audiences in every time zone then Rosita felt that maybe her relationship with Leland had not been completely one-sided and all in his favour after all.

About a year after his death, she was cast as the lead in a film adaptation of the best-selling novel *Tragedy of a Showgirl*, written by a French journalist called Fabienne Delacroix. The story was loosely based on the real-life murder of Cher Le Visage and was written at the wish of Dexter Franklin. He had chosen Fabienne to be there on the opening night of *Trésor* as he knew that she would want to write about the story behind the showgirl's demise. At first he had thought that as the only reporter behind closed doors that night, Fabienne would be able to reveal to the world the splintered and ruthless nature of celebrity ambition and announce the name of his ex-love's killer to the world. Finally a meaty story for the journalist to sink her teeth into. But without this revelation, names were changed to protect the innocent, and indeed the guilty, and Fabienne decided to give up her job on *La Riviera* to concentrate on writing her first work of semi-fiction. The novel caused a bidding war, with Olivia's publishers the victors – somehow apt seeing as the publisher was now splitting her life between her work in the UK and living with Fabienne and her cat, Gisele, at their new love nest in Paris. Wasn't it one of Olivia's favourite actresses, Audrey Hepburn, who had said that 'Paris is always a good idea'? For

Fabienne and Olivia it was perfection. The novel was dominated by strong female characters, and even though the main heroine met a tragic end, Fabienne was determined that it would be the men of the story who turned out to be the ultimate victims. Artistic license was utilised, and when the novel and the subsequent movie topped the charts, Fabienne gave away the majority of her profits as charitable donations to both feminist and anti-bullying causes. Rosita herself became a spokesperson against bullying and abuse through her work on the film, never once naming Leland as the man who had caused her to be able to talk from experience. So many secrets from the real-life demise of Cher Le Visage were kept hidden or adapted, but it seemed right that it should be that way. A bit-part on the movie was given to Missy Terranova, now engaged to the pompous son of a buffoon US presidential candidate and trying her hand at acting, much to Rosita's annoyance. By release date, Missy's two lines had been edited out and disposed of for eternity on the cutting-room floor.

DC Riding dined out for months on the fact that he was there behind 'the closed doors' of Trésor on the night of Leland's death. He never told of his own involvement in the tragedy of Cher's final hours but he couldn't help but namedrop to anyone who cared about how he was one of the chosen few, handpicked by Dexter, a chef he never ever wrote a bad review for again, on that evening in St Tropez. As his waistline expanded at restaurants in every continent, so did his embellishing of the tale of what had gone on. So what if his version was glamourised to the max, taken to soap-opera proportions? Nobody could call him out. They weren't there, were they? He chose not to see those others who had been involved. He didn't need to see them again. They had seen more than enough of him on the screen that night in St Tropez.

St Tropez itself continued as a glitterati paradise for the rich and famous, with Trésor becoming one of the new major attractions for the designer-clad tourists. The billion-dollar yachts still sailed into town and the bars along the portside still filled with people desperate to be seen. But as well as showy cries of 'Oh, my dear, look, isn't that the fabulous so and so?' and 'Oh, darling, I haven't seen you since the exquisite such and such, have I?' a new question was often on people's lips: 'Isn't that the spot where that poor man Leland Franklin drowned?'

St Tropez may forever be famous for the landmark film *And God Created Woman*, but one thing was for sure, it would always be infamous for creating drama too. But most of the fashionable in-crowd visiting the sleepy fishing town would never know just how much.

LETTER FROM NIGEL

Bonjour everybody! I really hope that you loved reading the spicy antics of my latest novel, *Revenge*.

Revenge has been an absolute delight to write as I was lucky enough to set most of the action in a place that I think is the epitome of the jet-set lifestyle – the fabulous St Tropez on France's Côte d'Azur. I don't think there is anywhere that typifies more the glamour and the decadence of a sun-soaked celebrity destination and I loved spending some time there to research places for my characters to party. And they do love to party! The action in *Revenge* also headed to the wonderful Iguazu Falls in Brazil, which is one of the most magical places I have ever been to and I hope that you enjoyed me taking you there. I couldn't resist taking the characters to fabulous locations like Morocco, Austria, Sweden, South Africa, Saudi Arabia and New York as well, so we have certainly been flying high across the globe to chase the drama. Plus I had to bring it a little closer to home by setting some scenes in my favourite place in the UK, Brighton.

Did you have an inkling as to who might be behind the brutal murder of international showgirl Cher Le Visage? There were certainly lots of suspects, and when celebrity chef Dexter Franklin decided to round up a few of them for the opening of his new designer restaurant you could guarantee that revenge and payback were going to be on the menu. Did you like Holly and Mew, the ex-girl group members who were certainly not up for a reunion, or Leland, the daring adventurer with an eye for the ladies? Or were acidic critic DC or flamboyant Latina actress Rosita your faves? I'd love you to let me know. I enjoyed creating them all.

If my latest blockbuster put a smile on your face I would be tickled pink if you could leave me a review. Reading what glamfans have to say about my novels means the world to me, as I really love writing them. If you want to find out more about my books, and receive all of the behind-the-scenes gossip too, then head to my website www.nigelmay.net where I will take you on an adventure with all six of my novels so far – *Trinity*, *Addicted*, *Scandalous Lies*, *Deadly Obsession*, *Lovers And Liars* and now *Revenge*! If you enjoyed my latest book, then maybe you'd like to read some more! Sign up to my mailing list today.

Let's hook up for a good chat too – I love to talk about all sorts of glamour-soaked spicy crime and my life in general on Twitter (find me at @Nigel_May), Facebook and Goodreads. And if you'd like to keep up to date with the latest tantalising news on my hot new releases, just sign up using the link below.

Thank you for enjoying *Revenge* – I hope you loved reading it as much as I did writing it. Until the next chapter, see you soon – and enjoy my sixth book. Who doesn't love a good sexy six-pack, right?

Lots of love, Nigel x

ACKNOWLEDGMENTS

I can't believe that finally I have my six-pack! Six glam fiction thrillers, that is. Dreams do come true and I am forever grateful. My thanks to everyone and anyone who has picked up one of my books – or indeed all six. *Revenge* has been a joy to write and as ever I have a list of people I would like to say '*merci*' to.

Thank you to each of the Bookouture authors who has supported me along the way. You guys are an amazing team and we will always be in each other's lives, of that I have no doubt. To those at Bookouture HQ, I thank you for living the glam and for twenty-four-carat advice. And to Julie Fergusson and Lauren Finger for killer edits on this particular novel. Major racy read respect to Emma and Lauren. And to drama-fan Wayne Brookes who made everything possible way back when – I adore you, mister! You are the Bea to my Franky.

I wrote *Revenge* in the midst of moving house (never again!) so a million seaside kisses from my new home to those who made life and the transition easier. To Mel B and Jade for their open arms, Ryan Davis for friendship, Mel T and Phil (2B or not 2B) for cakes and warmth and to the crazy sexy cool Russell Kedian for unorthodox and 'kinky' gym action. To Kylie Rowan for setting the ball in motion and to Deb and Keith for coming to our rescue. Plus to perfect neighbours Caroline and Neil for waving us off. To the invaluable and fabulous Loen Love for superb advice and Mistress Jo-Jo Foster for making work things happen super quick. To Sam Smith for a roof over my head and sharing the red wine and muscle love. Telly high-fives to the magic hands of Ollie (those guns), Paulo, Jimmy, the Georginas, Anna, Craigo, Nathan, Scotty, Jake, Nipper, Stephen, Neil, Laura, Dermy and Posh Matt.

To my Brighton family – Alan, Vicky, Paul and Elia – love aplenty. We finally did it!! I adore you all so much. And to 'la famille Mendo', who set my love affair with *Revenge*'s la belle France in motion many years ago I say 'gros bisous'. Plus a million shiny memories of love and affection to Fidel, may his beautiful soul rest in peace.

Glitterball gratitudes to Matthew and perfect party band Madhen for letting me include them in my delicious world of *Revenge*. And to Alain at Sénéquier and Bruno Luchet for helping me hear the true heartbeat of St Tropez.

To my Glamazons – the ladies (and honorary gents) of *more!* – you are so special to me and always will be. And you include my very own Mew and Holly. Never change. You rock!

International adoration to the wondrous Belinda Jones – top authoress, friend, talent and dog-lover. You are the reason I started this journey. Love eternal.

Finally thank you to every single person who loves a slice of glamour and intrigue in their lives. Mine started back in the days of Shirley Conran's iconic *Lace* and has been rolling ever since. To anyone who still smiles when they say the line 'which one of you bitches is my mother?', never stop believing. Viva glam forever! You are all sin-sational!

32694320R00217

Printed in Poland
by Amazon Fulfillment
Poland Sp. z o.o., Wrocław